LUNCH LADY

2-FOR-1 SPECIAL

The Second Helping
books 3 & 4

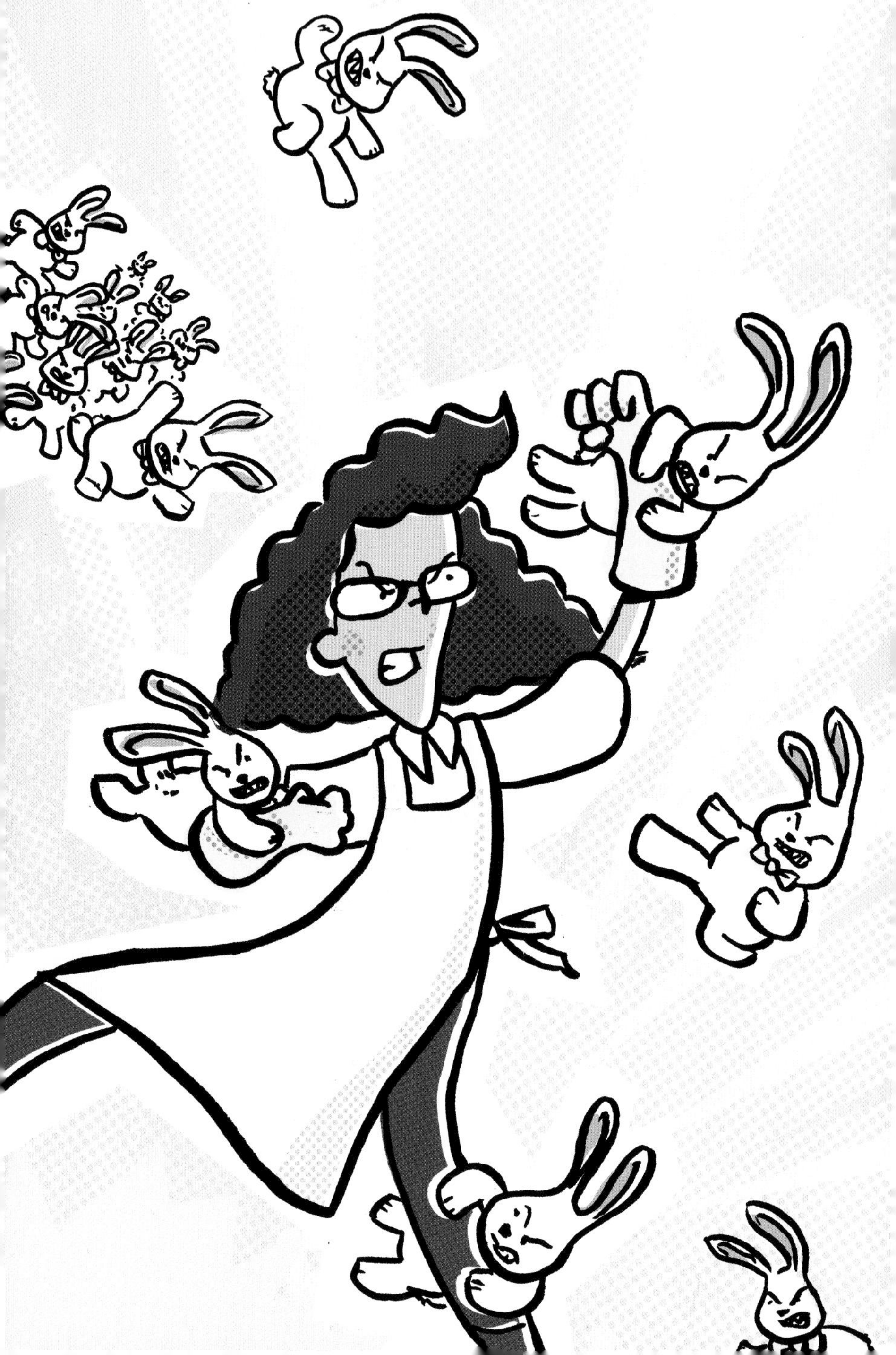

Jarrett J. Krosoczka

LUNCH LADY

2-FOR-1 SPECIAL

The Second Helping
books 3 & 4

colors by
Joey Weiser

Alfred A. Knopf New York

THIS IS A BORZOI BOOK PUBLISHED BY ALFRED A. KNOPF

The titles in this work were originally published separately and in paperback in the United States by Alfred A. Knopf, an imprint of Random House Children's Books, a division of Penguin Random House LLC, New York, in 2009 and 2010.

The Library of Congress has cataloged the individual books under the following Control Numbers: 2009014886 (The Author Visit Vendetta), 2009039783 (The Summer Camp Shakedown).

ISBN 978-0-593-37743-7 (trade)

The text of this book is written in 12-point CCHedgeBackwardsLower.
The illustrations in this book were created using ink on paper and digital coloring.

MANUFACTURED IN CHINA
November 2021
10 9 8 7 6 5 4 3 2 1

First Omnibus Edition

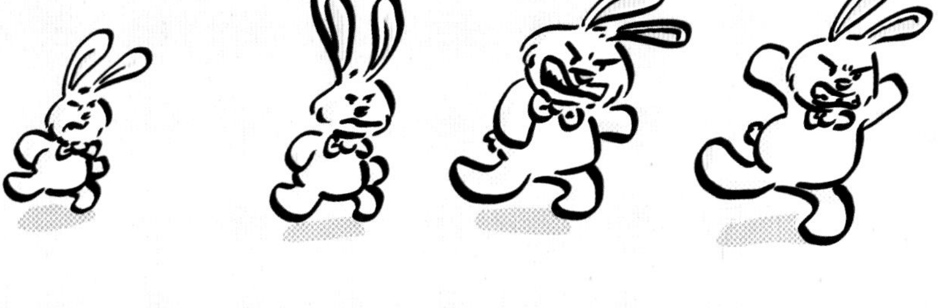

*FOR ALL OF MY FRIENDS FROM
THE HOLE IN THE WALL GANG CAMP
—J.J.K.*

CONTENTS

THE
AUTHOR VISIT
VENDETTA

PAGE 1

THE
SUMMER CAMP
SHAKEDOWN

PAGE 97

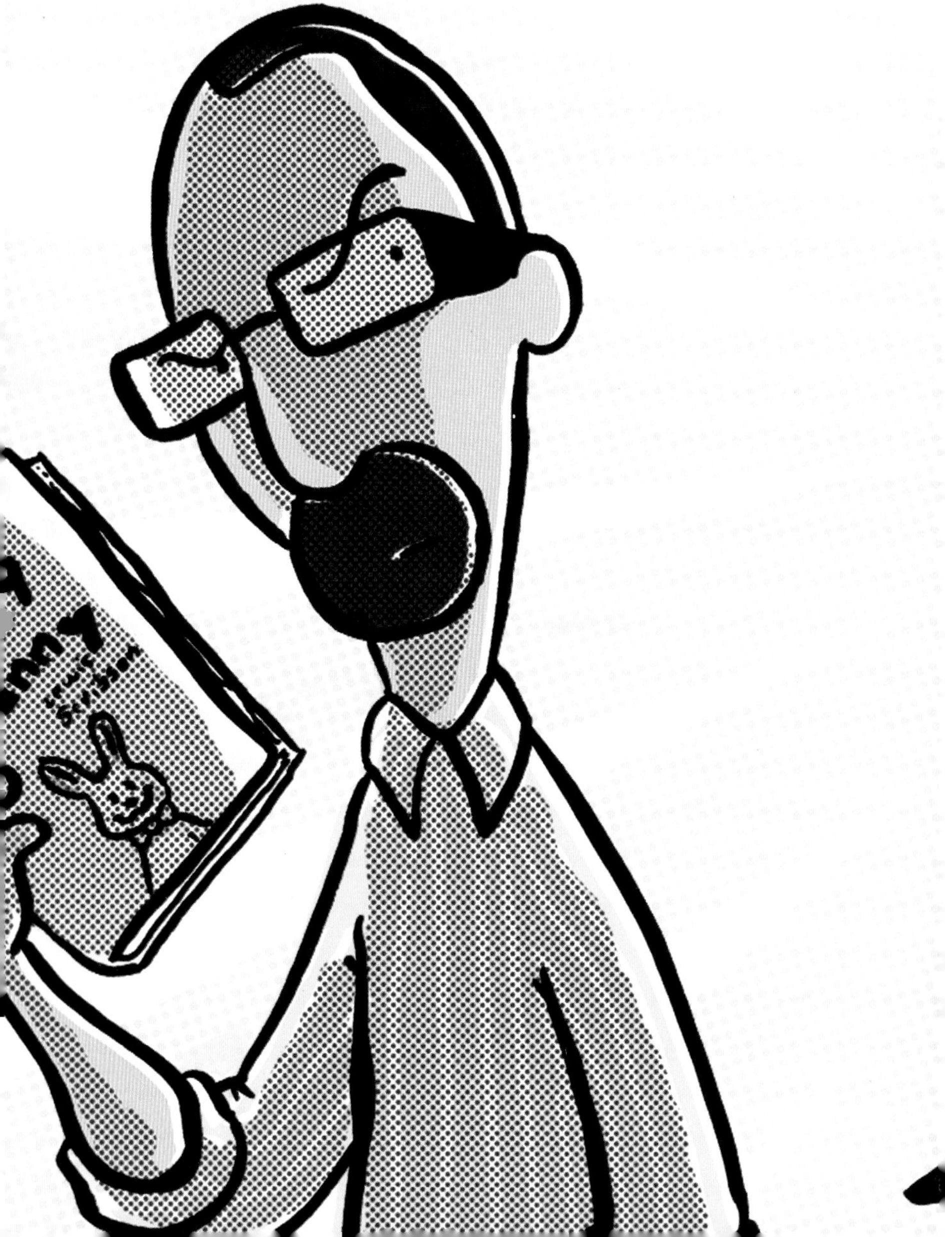

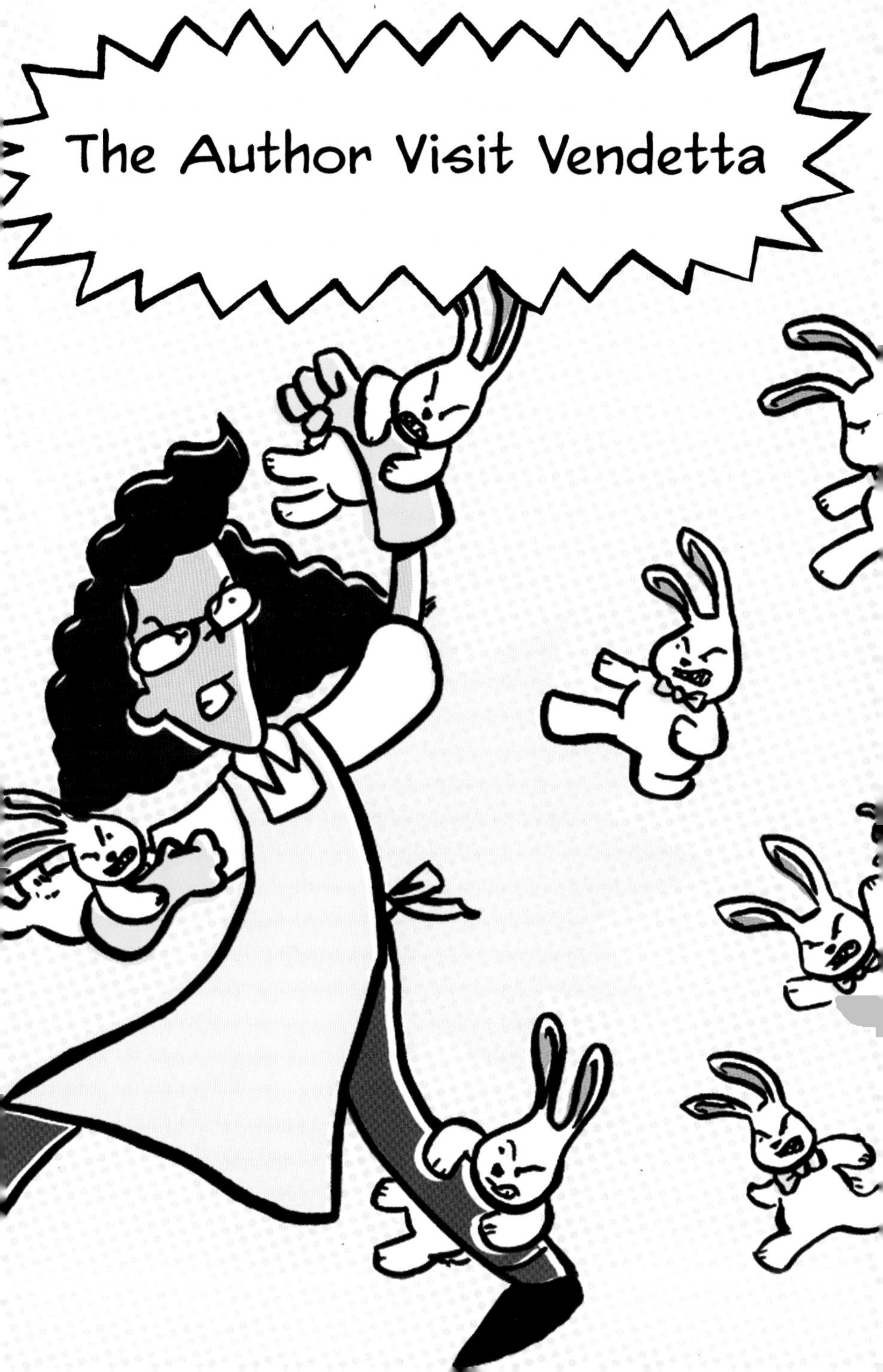
The Author Visit Vendetta

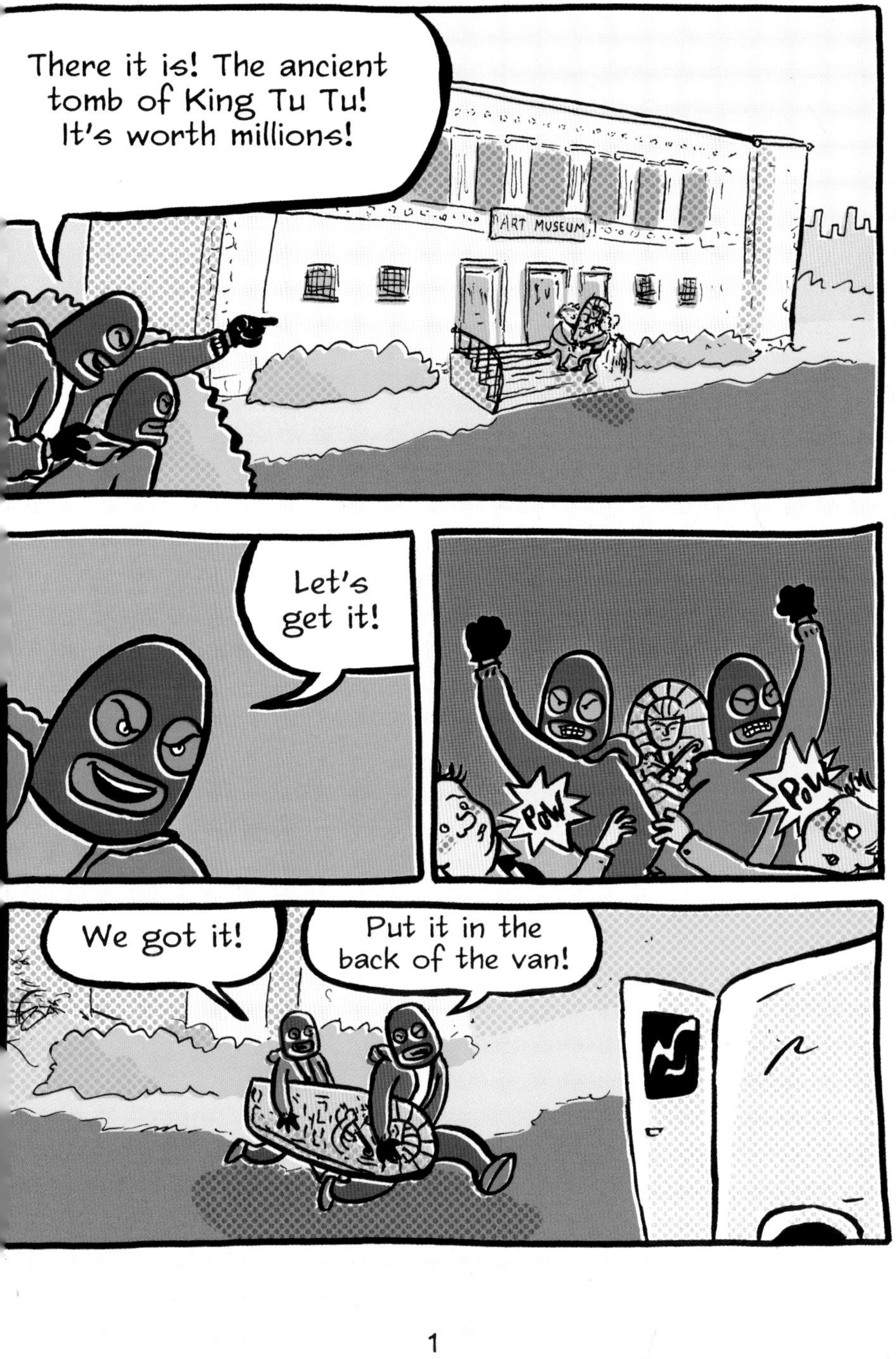
There it is! The ancient tomb of King Tu Tu! It's worth millions!
ART MUSEUM
Let's get it!
POW
POW
We got it!
Put it in the back of the van!

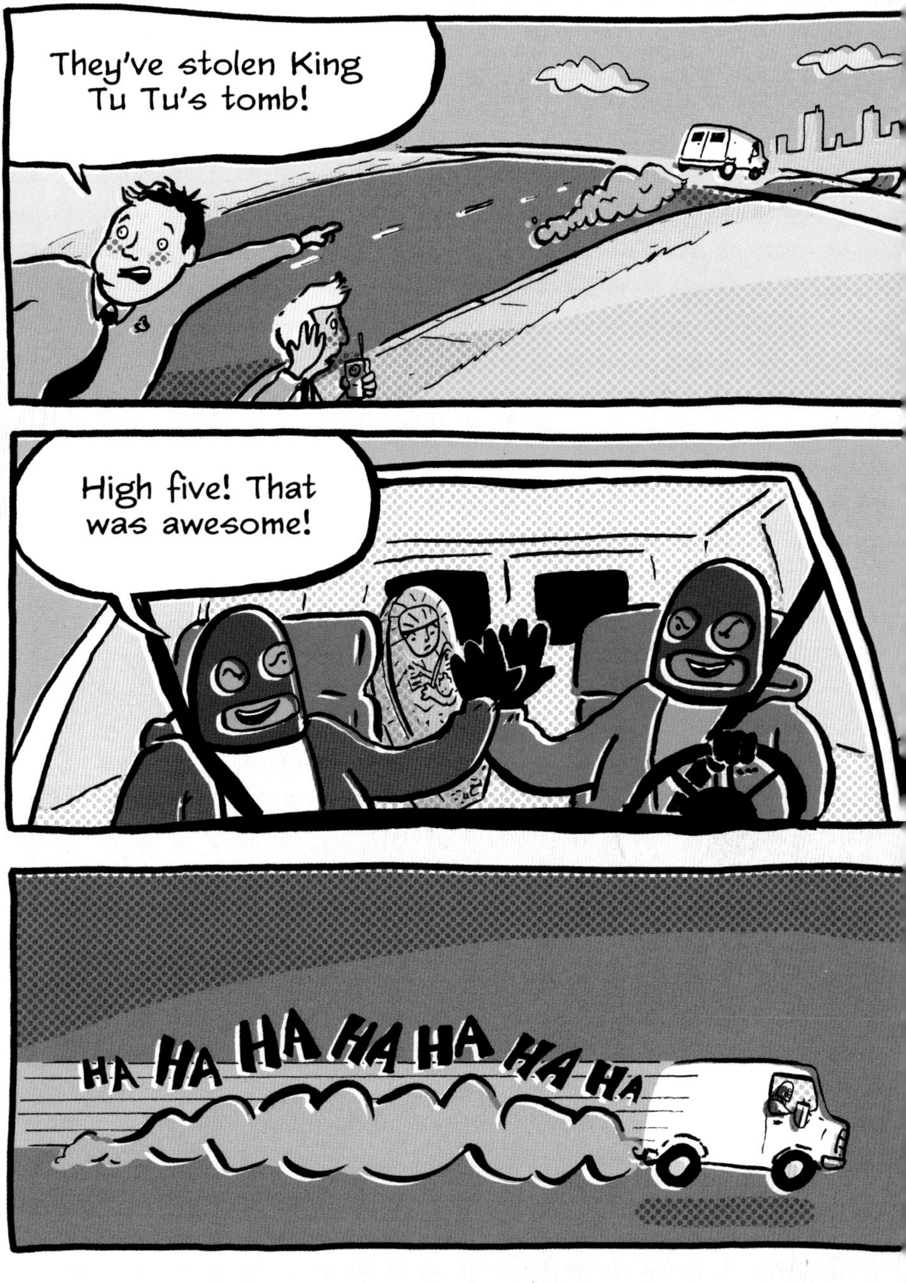
They've stolen King Tu Tu's tomb!
High five! That was awesome!
HA HA HA HA HA HA HA HA

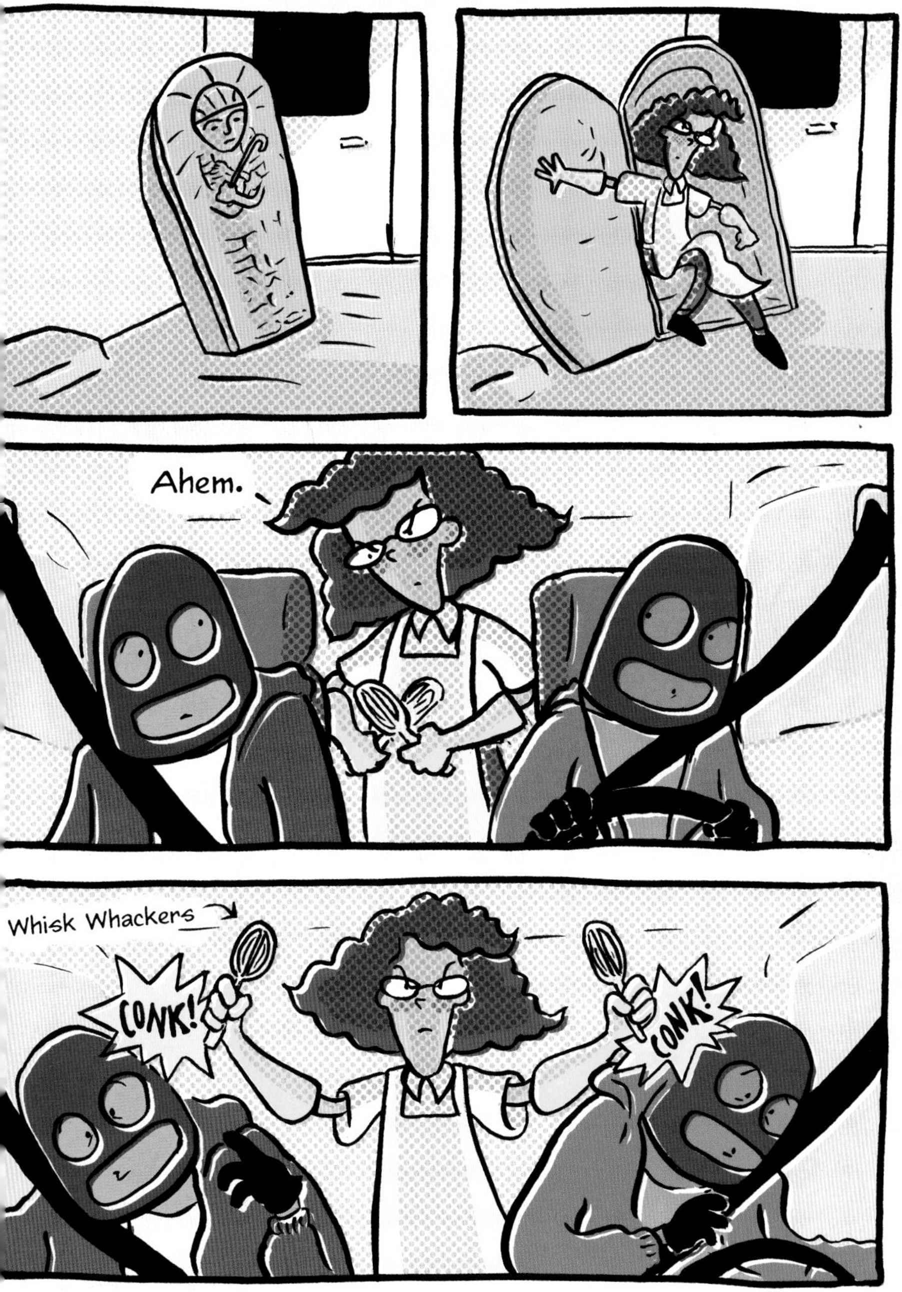
Ahem.
Whisk Whackers
CONK!
CONK!

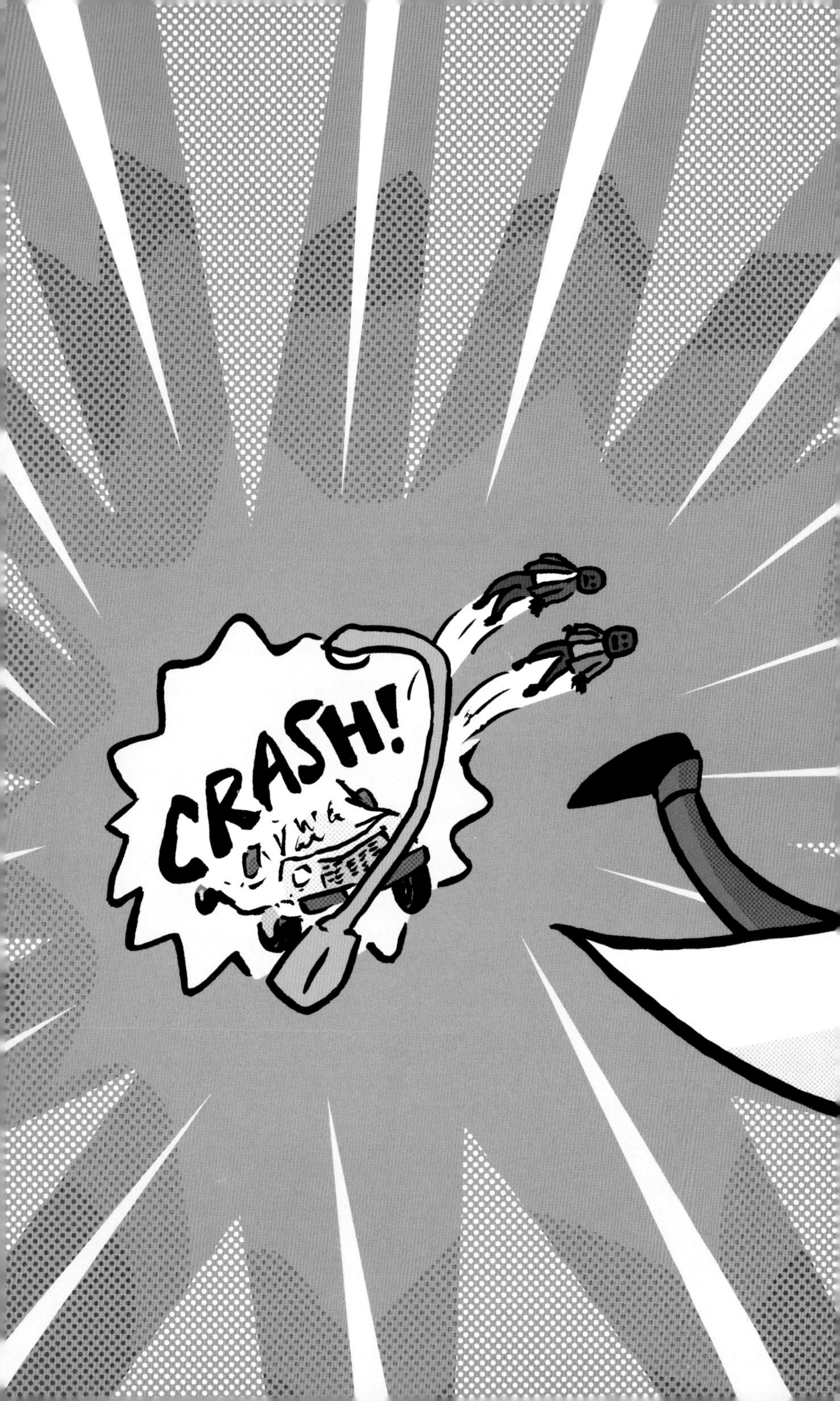
CRASH!

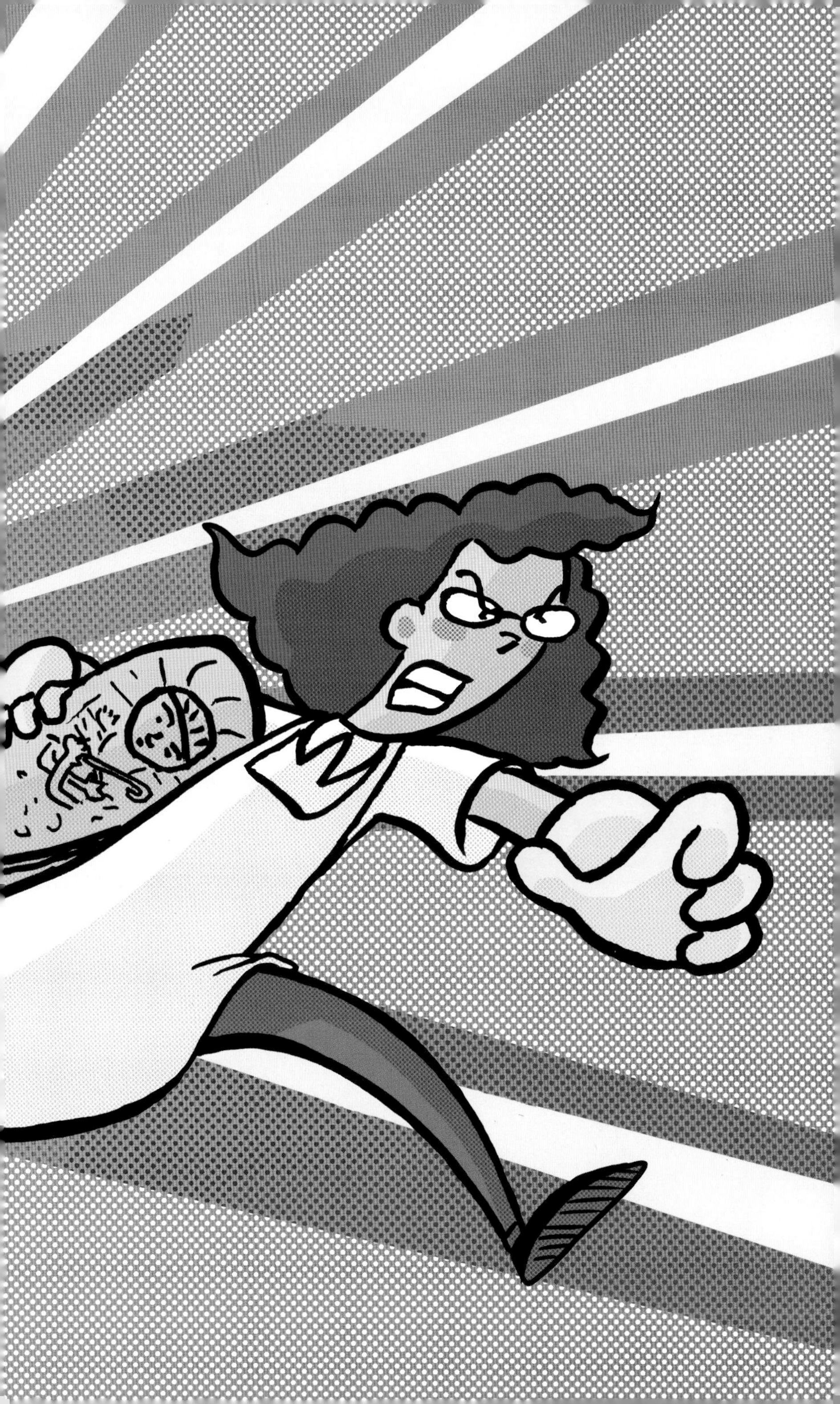

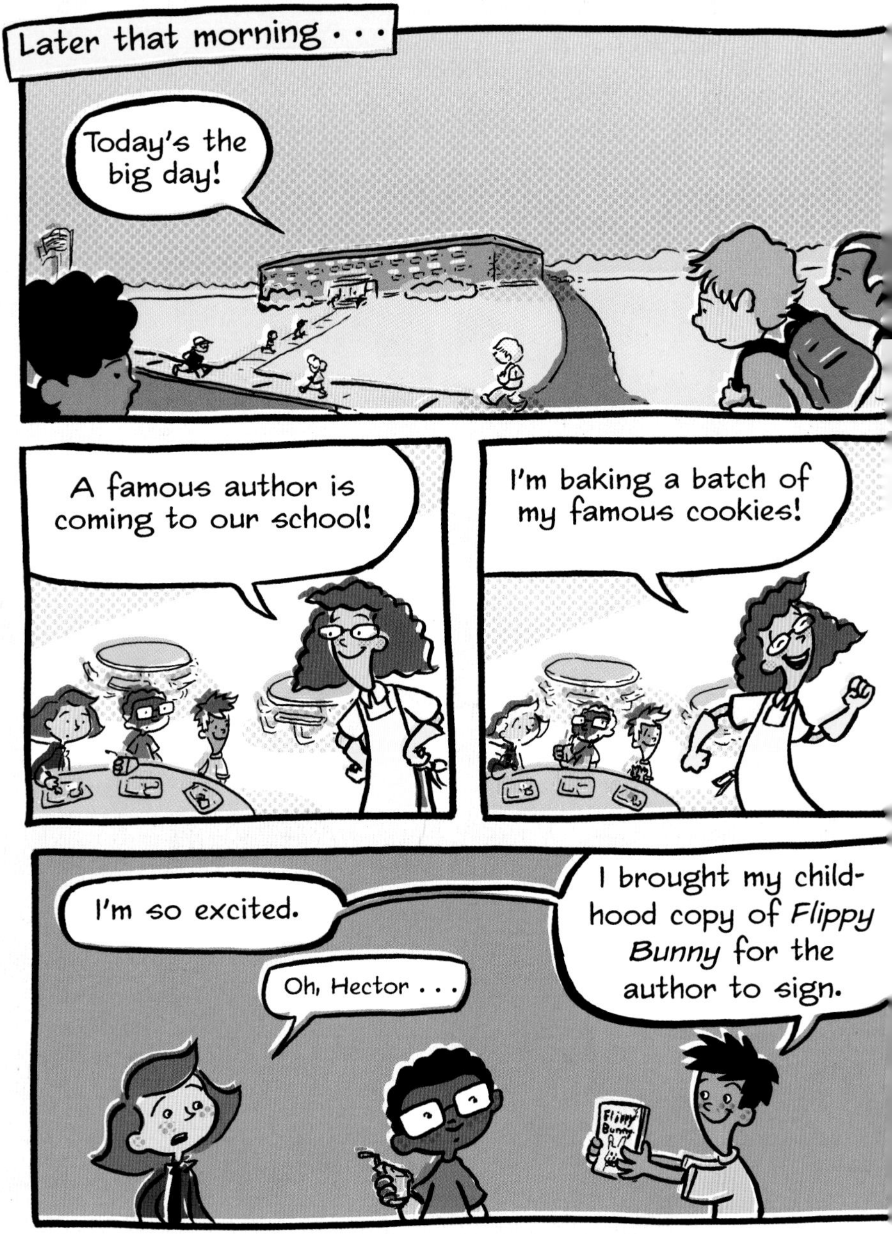

Later that morning . . .
Today's the big day!
A famous author is coming to our school!
I'm baking a batch of my famous cookies!
I'm so excited.
I brought my childhood copy of *Flippy Bunny* for the author to sign.
Oh, Hector . . .
Flippy Bunny

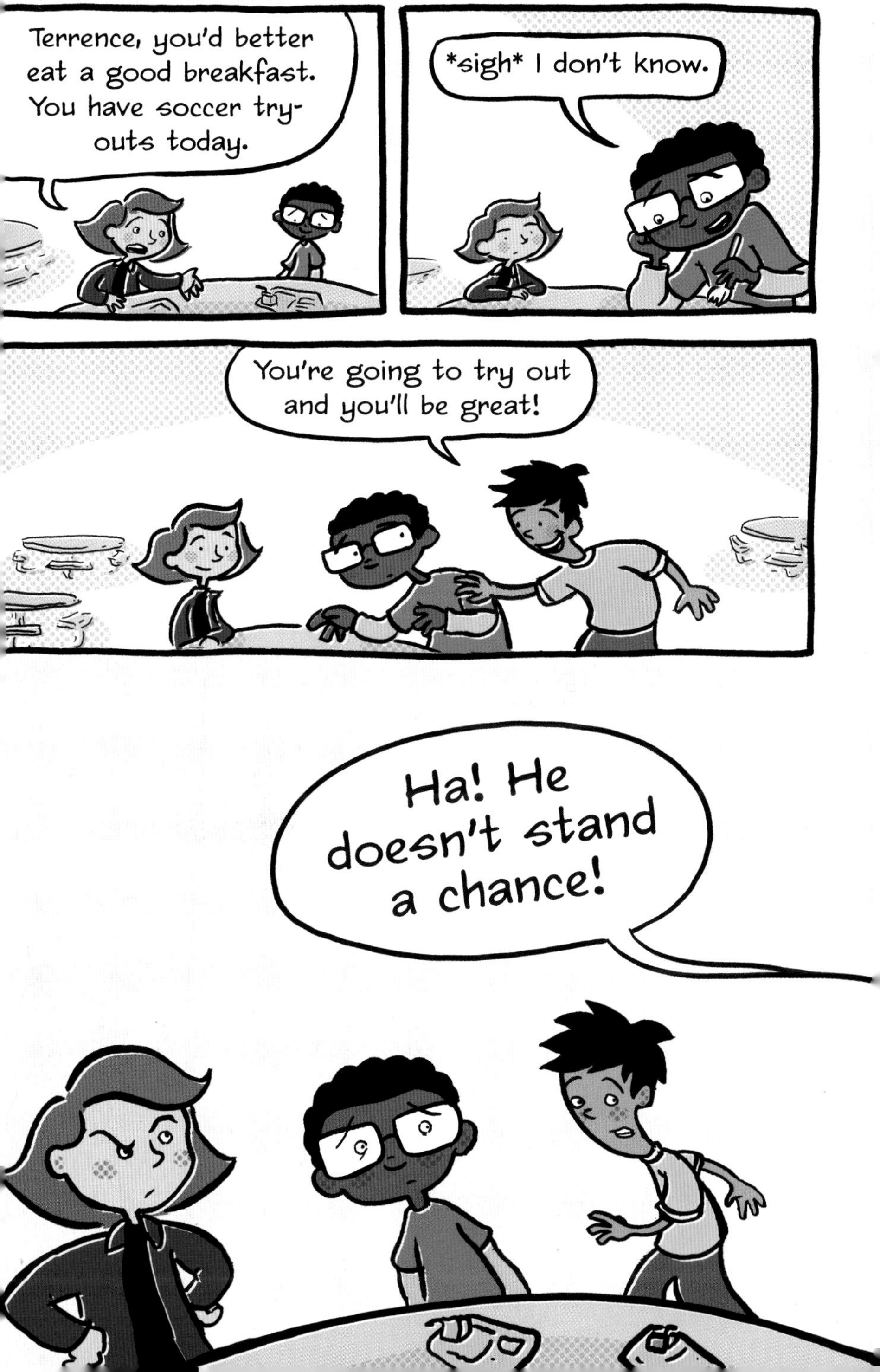
Terrence, you'd better eat a good breakfast. You have soccer try-outs today.
sigh I don't know.
You're going to try out and you'll be great!
Ha! He doesn't stand a chance!

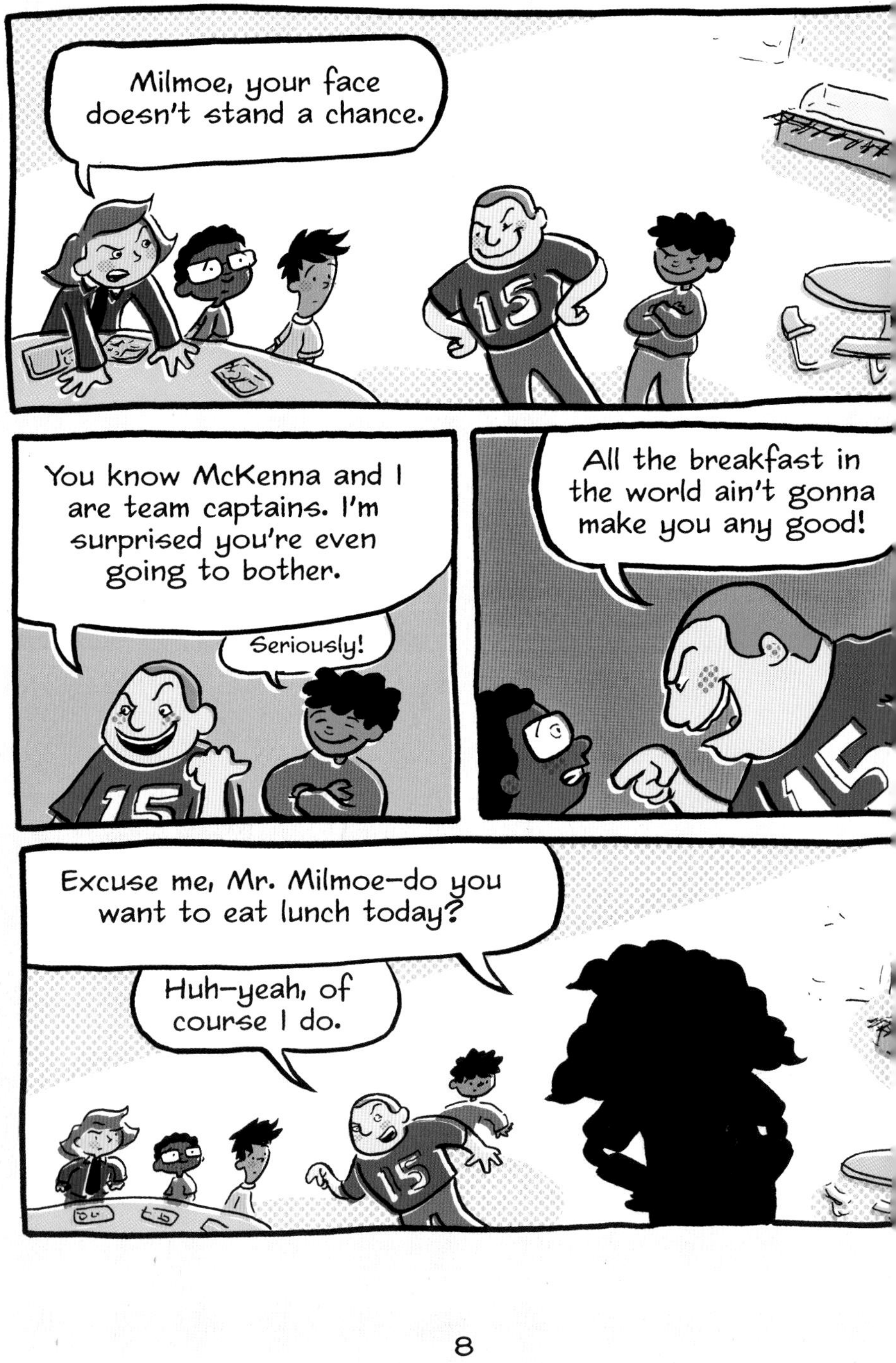
Milmoe, your face doesn't stand a chance.
You know McKenna and I are team captains. I'm surprised you're even going to bother.
Seriously!
All the breakfast in the world ain't gonna make you any good!
Excuse me, Mr. Milmoe–do you want to eat lunch today?
Huh–yeah, of course I do.

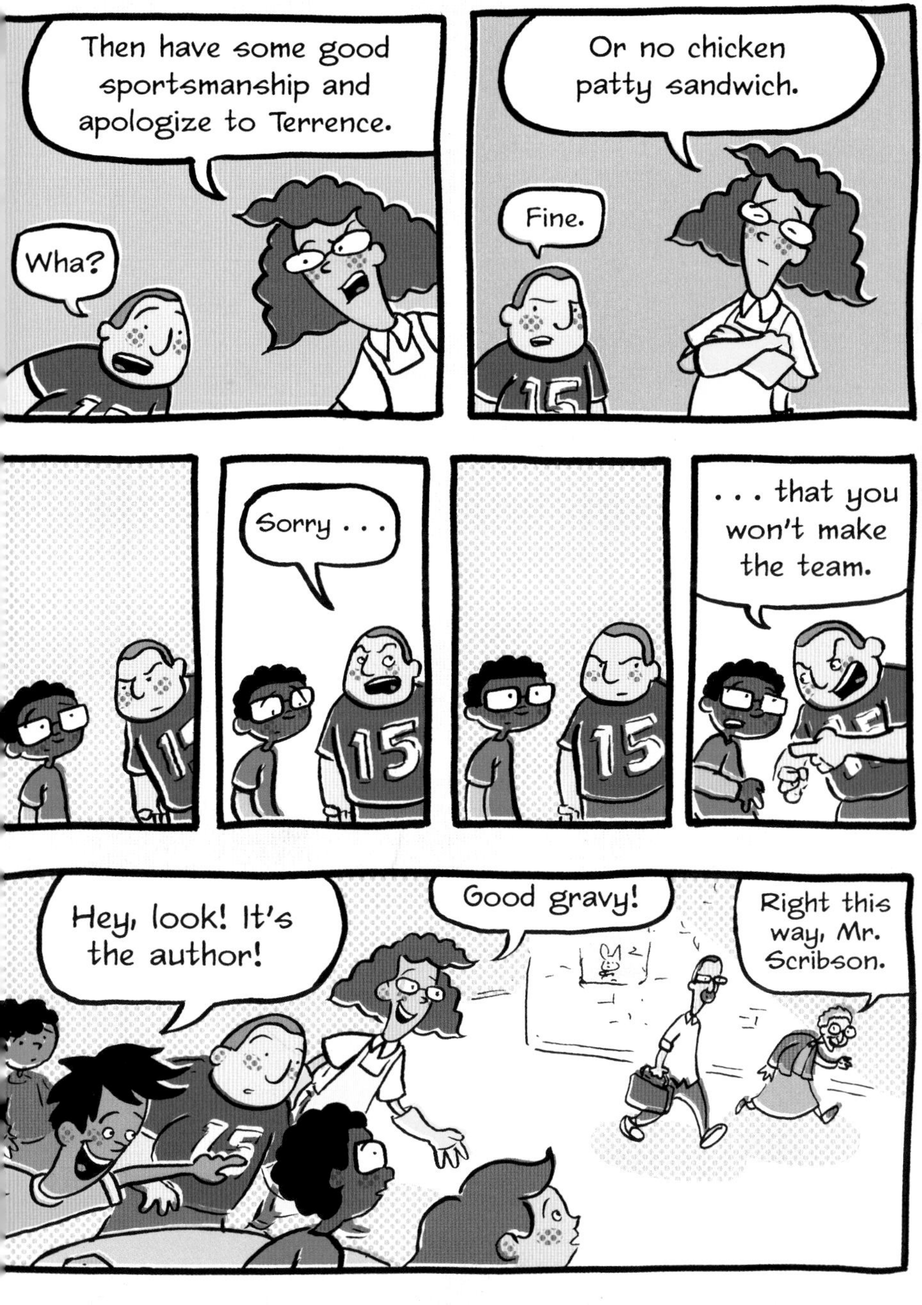
Then have some good sportsmanship and apologize to Terrence.
Wha?
Or no chicken patty sandwich.
Fine.
Sorry . . .
. . . that you won't make the team.
Hey, look! It's the author!
Good gravy!
Right this way, Mr. Scribson.

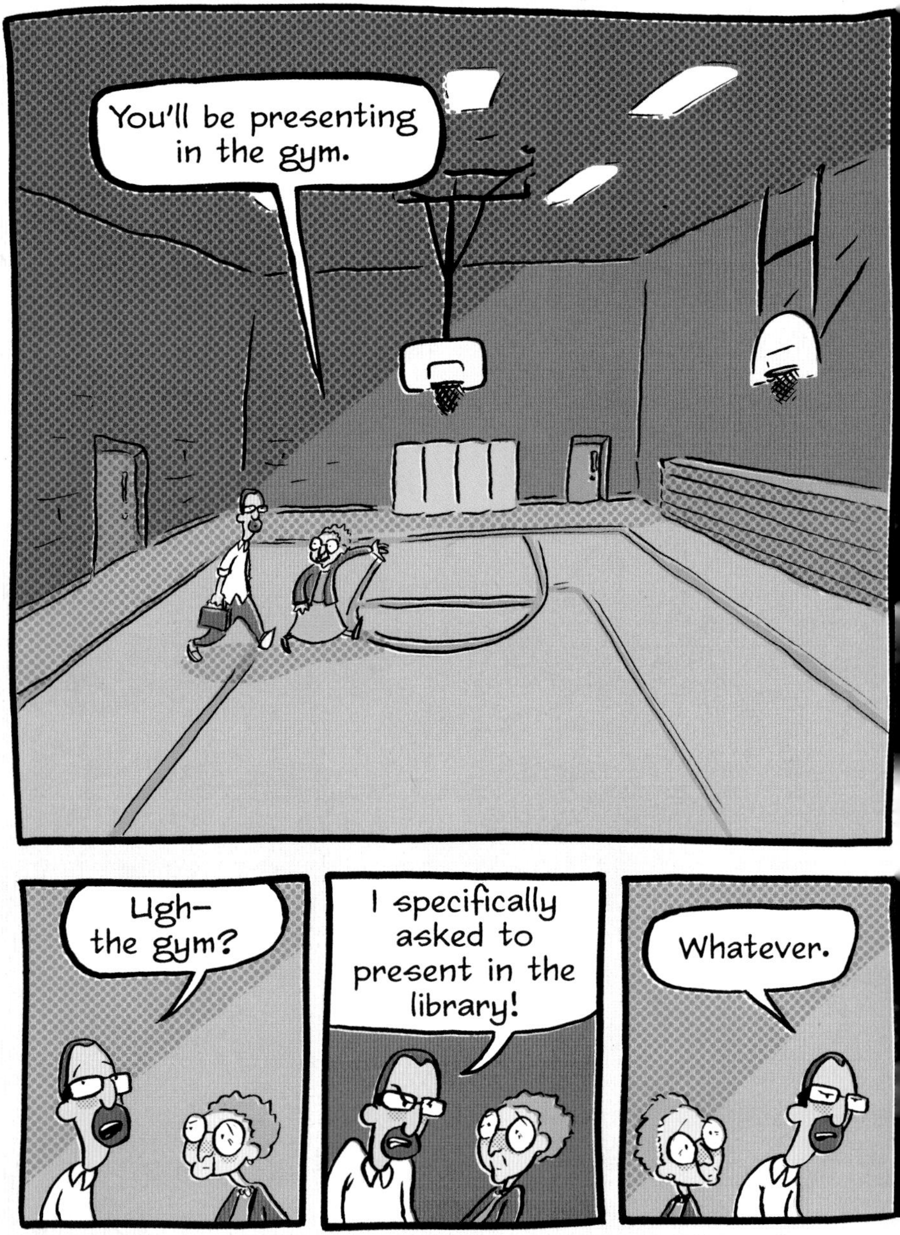
You'll be presenting in the gym.
Ugh— the gym?
I specifically asked to present in the library!
Whatever.

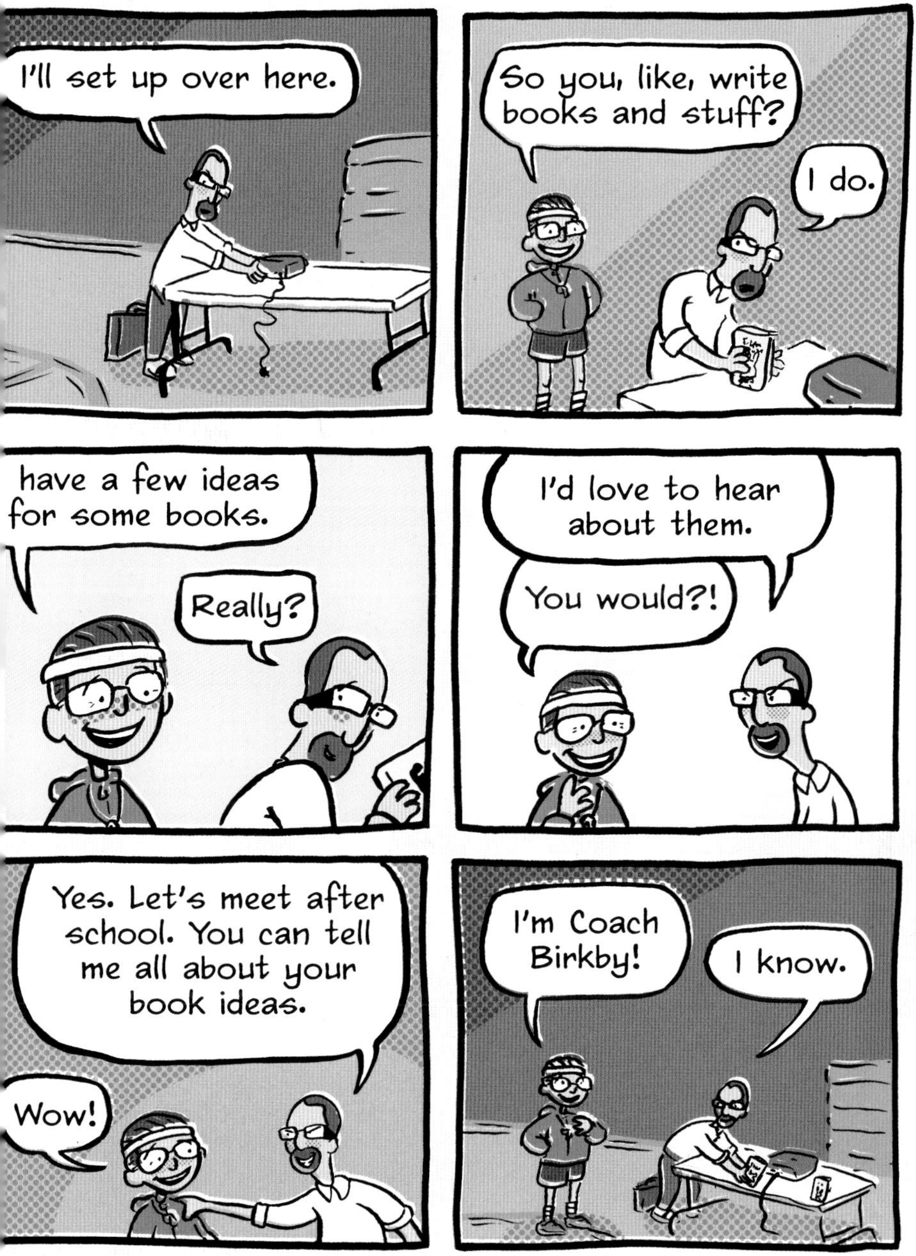
I'll set up over here.
So you, like, write books and stuff?
I do.
have a few ideas for some books.
Really?
I'd love to hear about them.
You would?!
Yes. Let's meet after school. You can tell me all about your book ideas.
Wow!
I'm Coach Birkby!
I know.

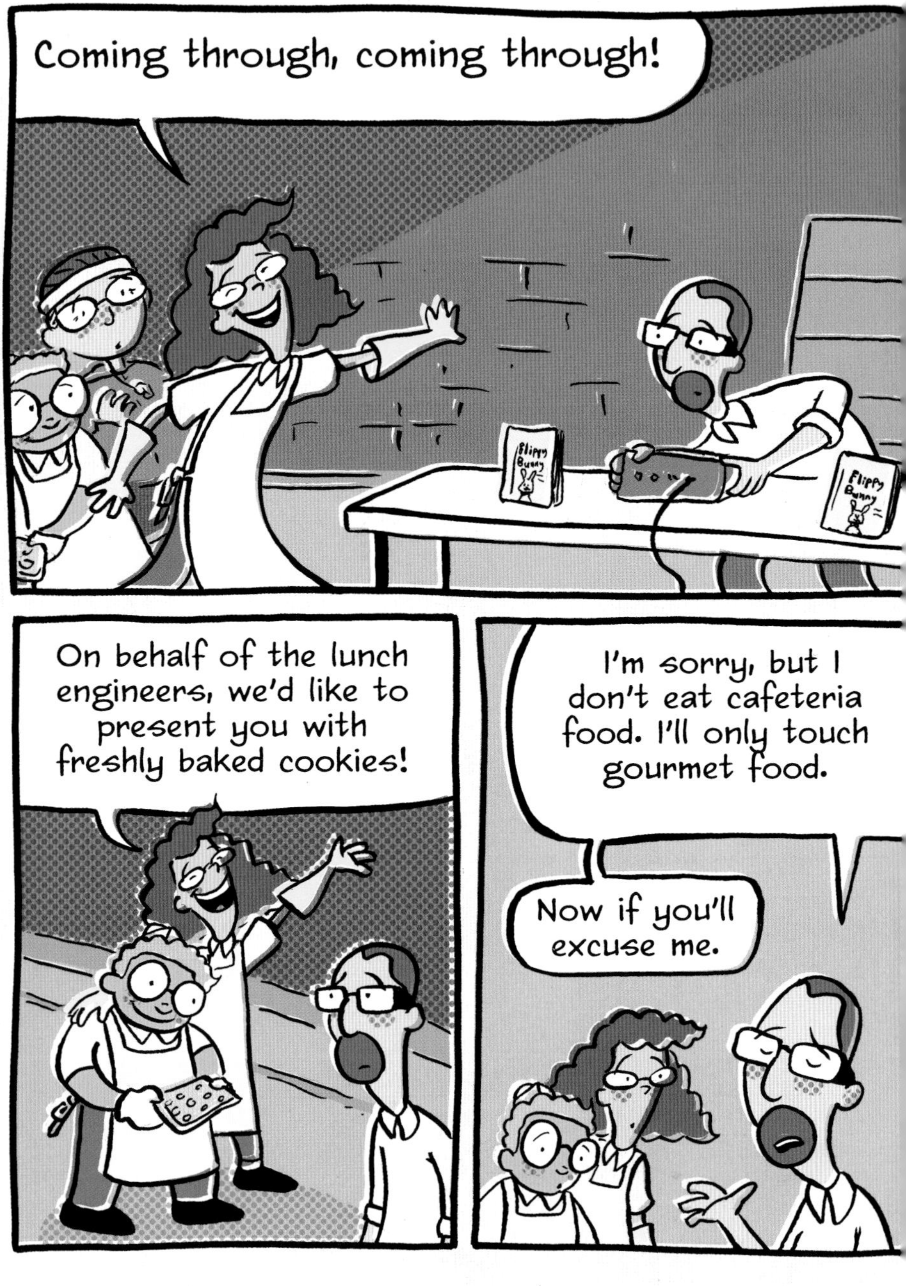
Coming through, coming through!
Flippy Bunny
Flippy Bunny
On behalf of the lunch engineers, we'd like to present you with freshly baked cookies!
I'm sorry, but I don't eat cafeteria food. I'll only touch gourmet food.
Now if you'll excuse me.

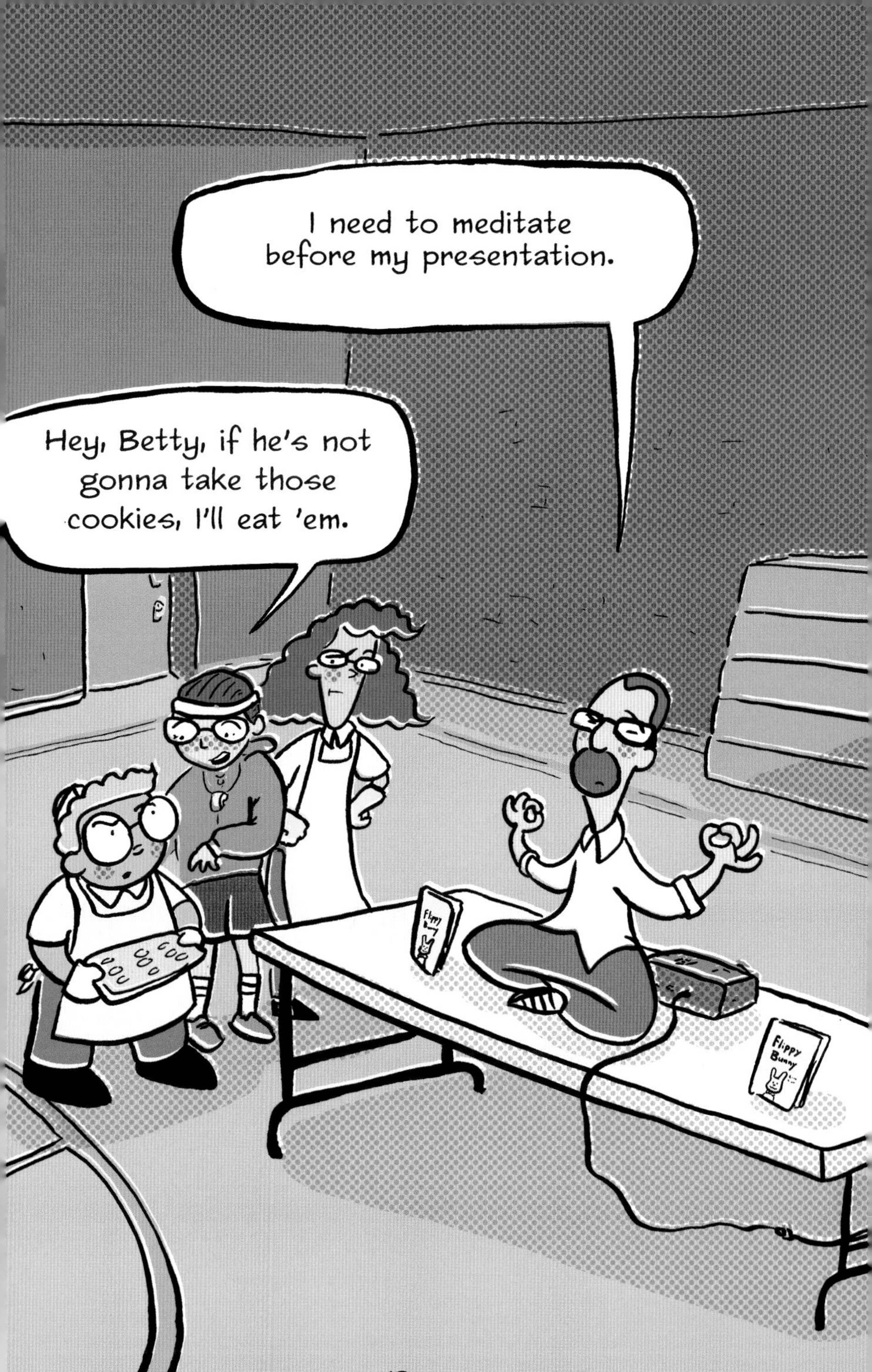
I need to meditate before my presentation.
Hey, Betty, if he's not gonna take those cookies, I'll eat 'em.
Flippy Bunny

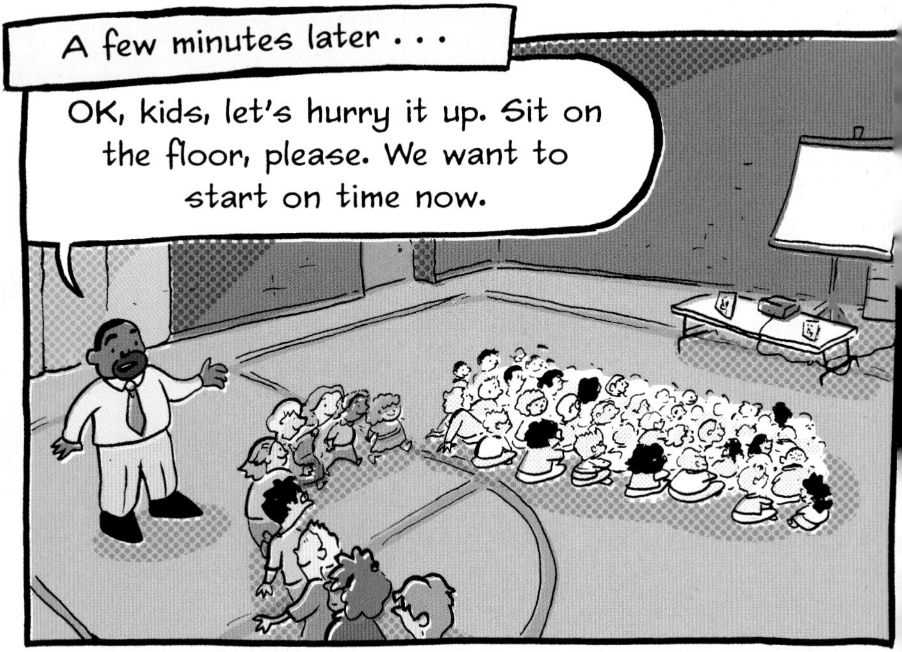
A few minutes later . . .
OK, kids, let's hurry it up. Sit on the floor, please. We want to start on time now.

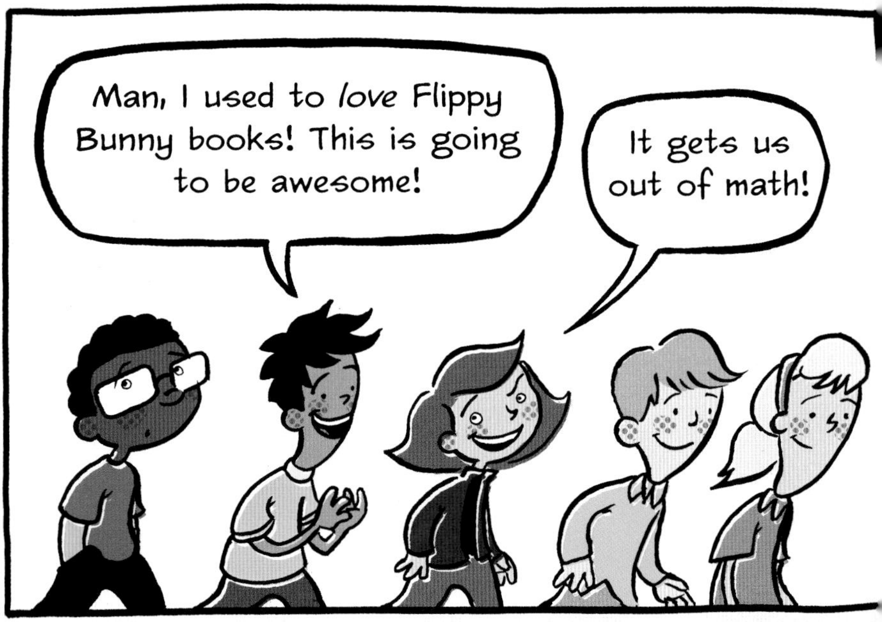
Man, I used to *love* Flippy Bunny books! This is going to be awesome!
It gets us out of math!

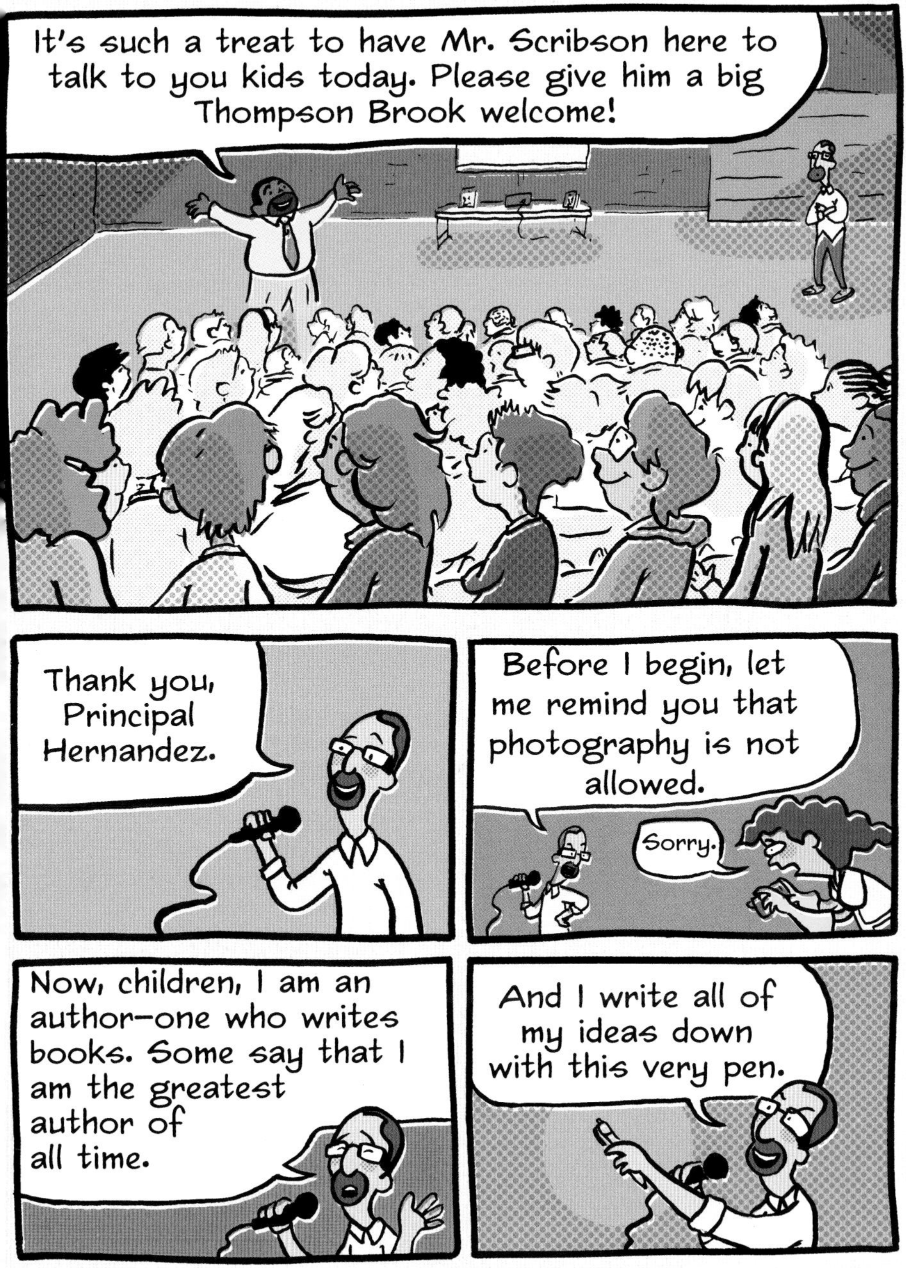
It's such a treat to have Mr. Scribson here to talk to you kids today. Please give him a big Thompson Brook welcome!
Thank you, Principal Hernandez.
Before I begin, let me remind you that photography is not allowed.
Sorry.
Now, children, I am an author—one who writes books. Some say that I am the greatest author of all time.
And I write all of my ideas down with this very pen.

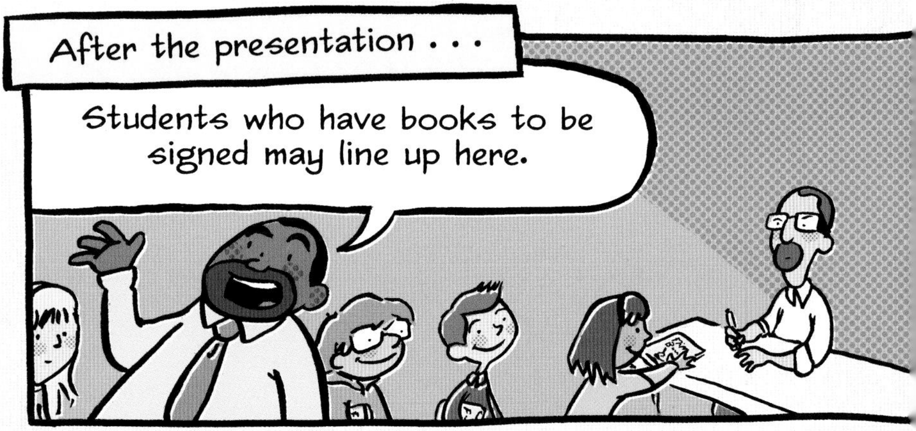
After the presentation . . .
Students who have books to be signed may line up here.

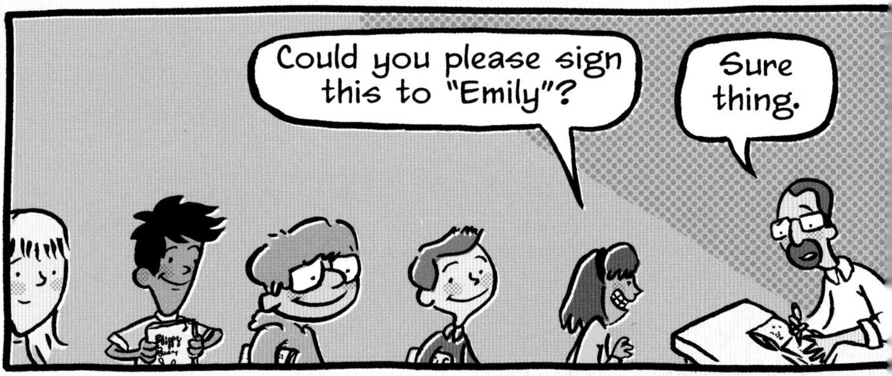
Could you please sign this to "Emily"?
Sure thing.

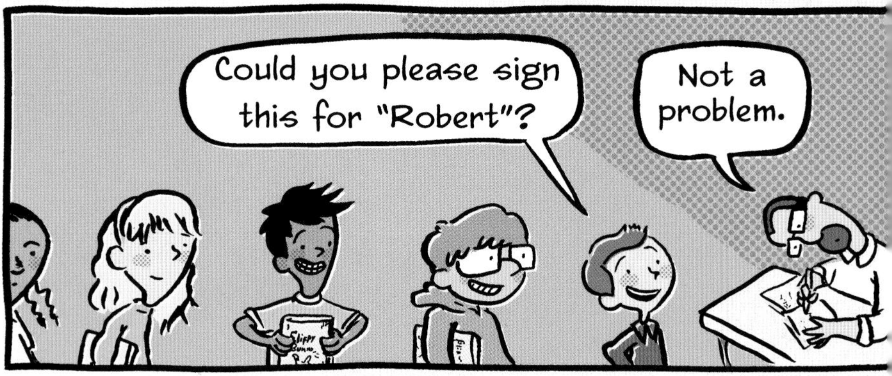
Could you please sign this for "Robert"?
Not a problem.

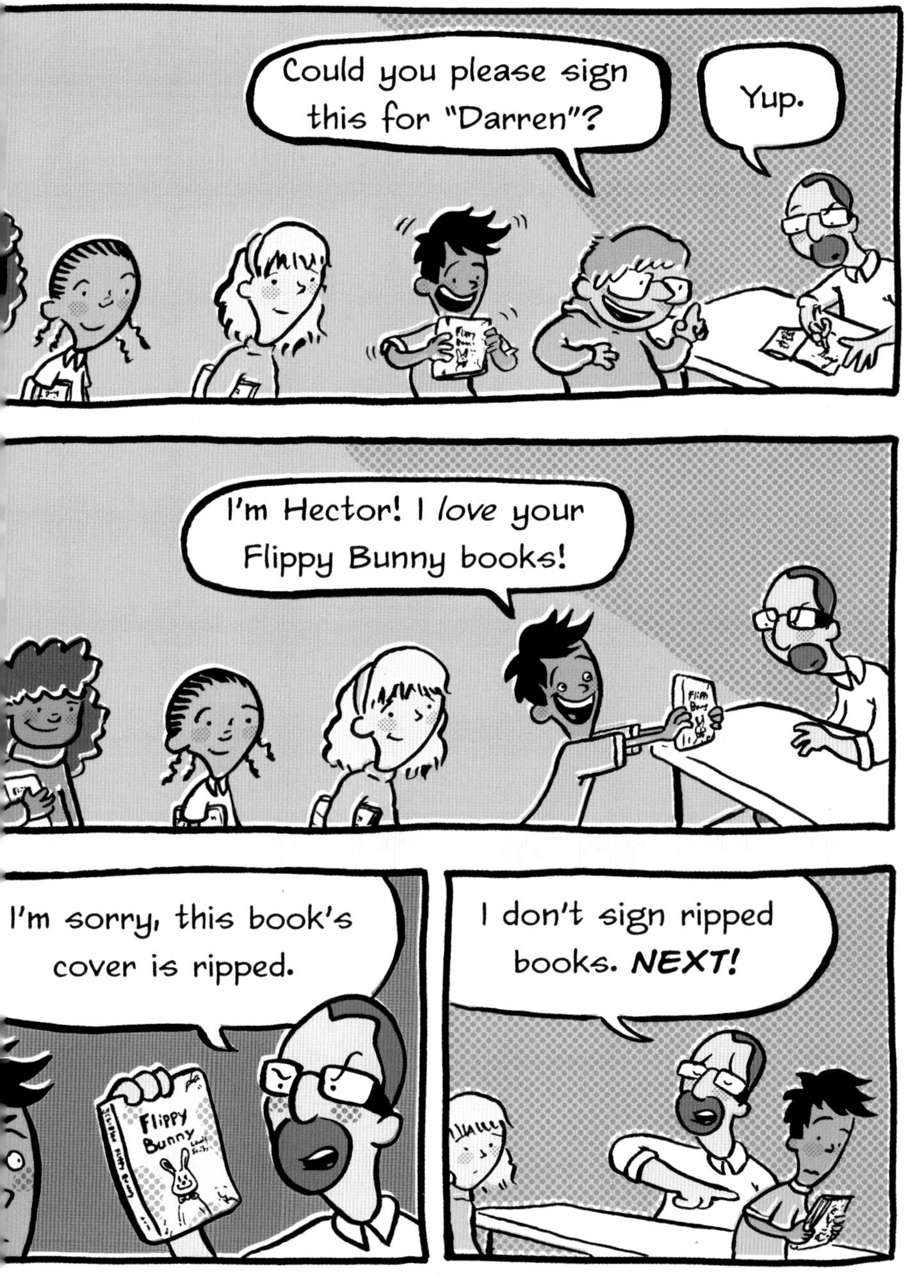
Could you please sign this for "Darren"?
Yup.
I'm Hector! I *love* your Flippy Bunny books!
I'm sorry, this book's cover is ripped.
Flippy Bunny
I don't sign ripped books. ***NEXT!***

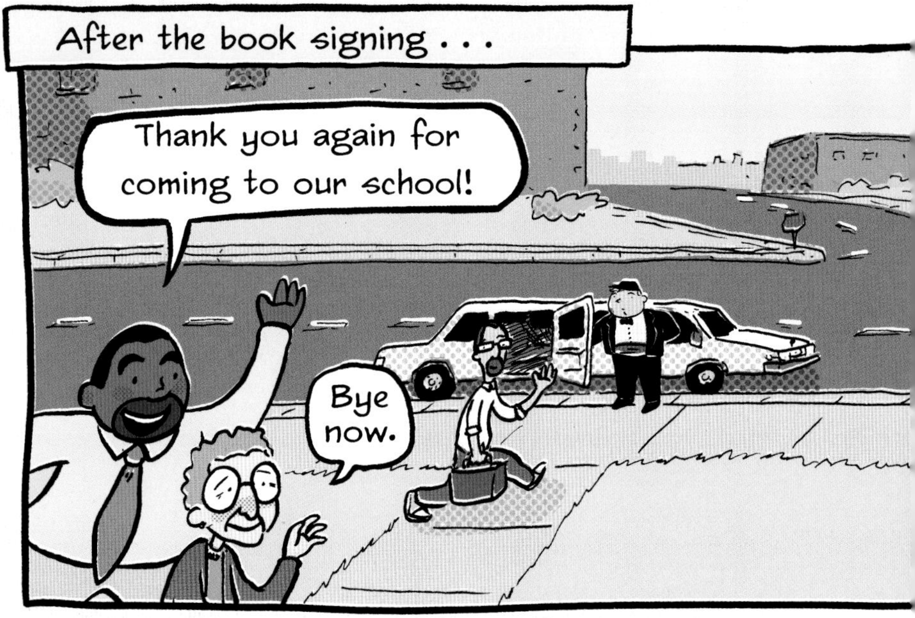
After the book signing . . .
Thank you again for coming to our school!
Bye now.

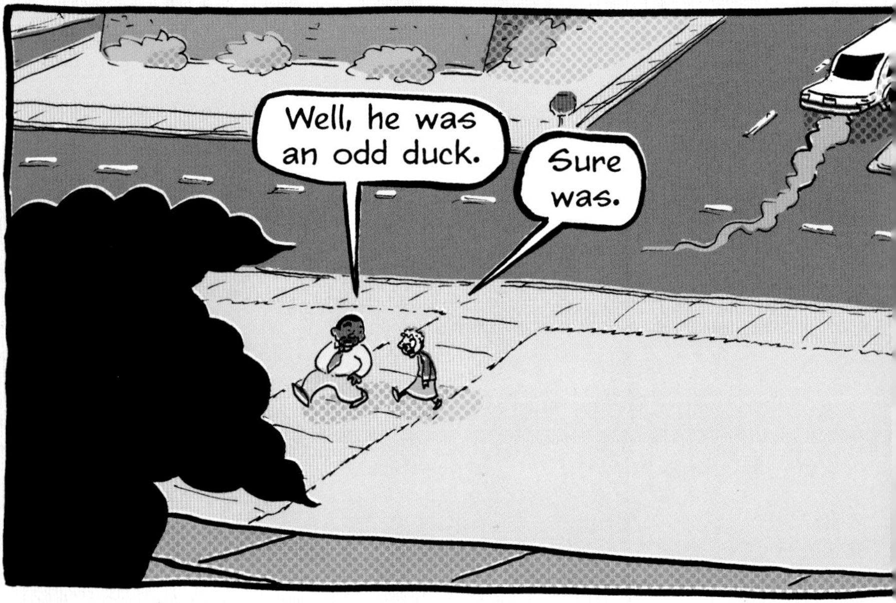
Well, he was an odd duck.
Sure was.

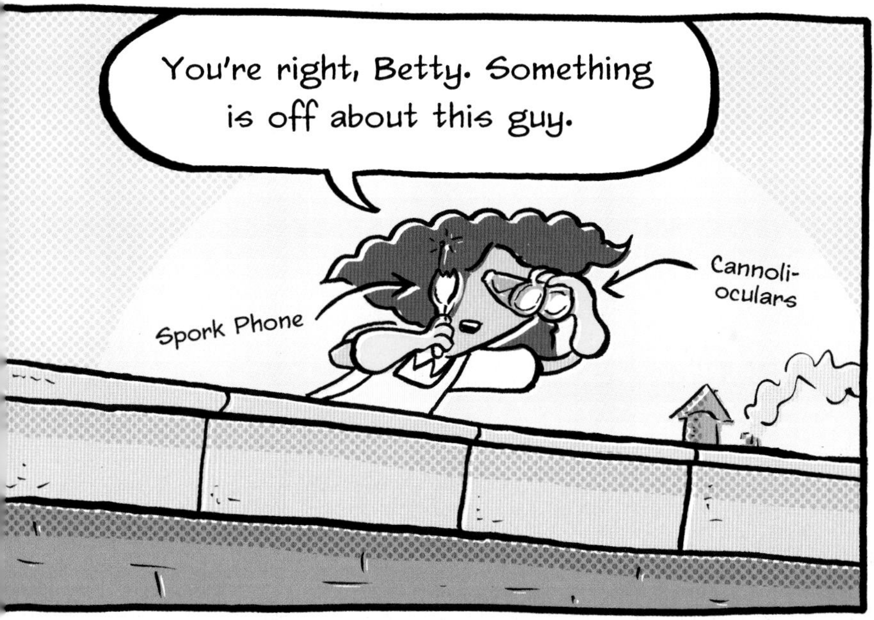
You're right, Betty. Something is off about this guy.
Cannoli-oculars
Spork Phone

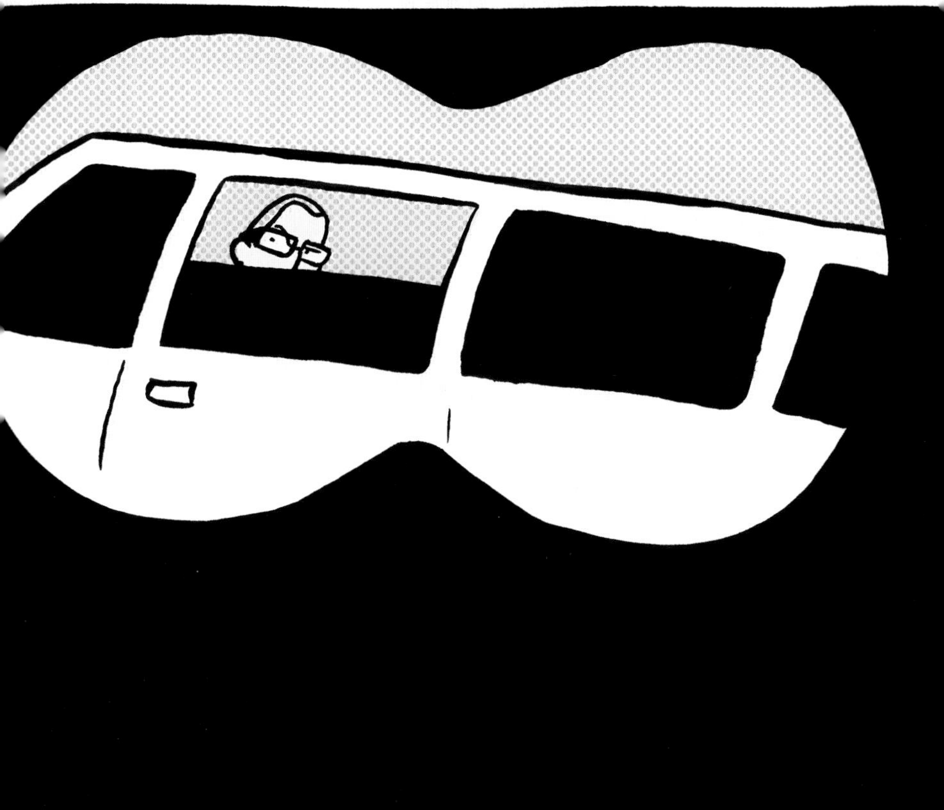

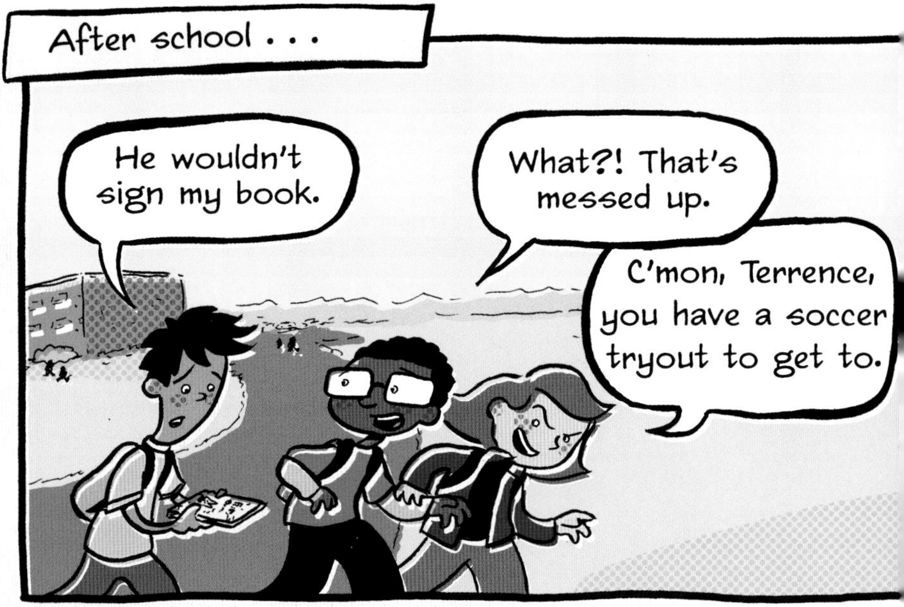
After school . . .
He wouldn't sign my book.
What?! That's messed up.
C'mon, Terrence, you have a soccer tryout to get to.

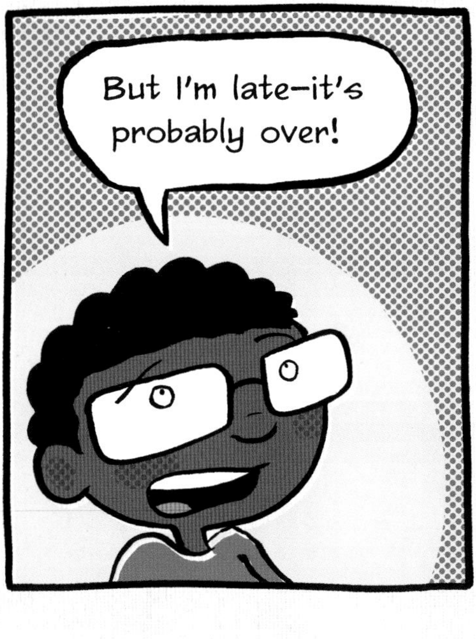
But I'm late–it's probably over!

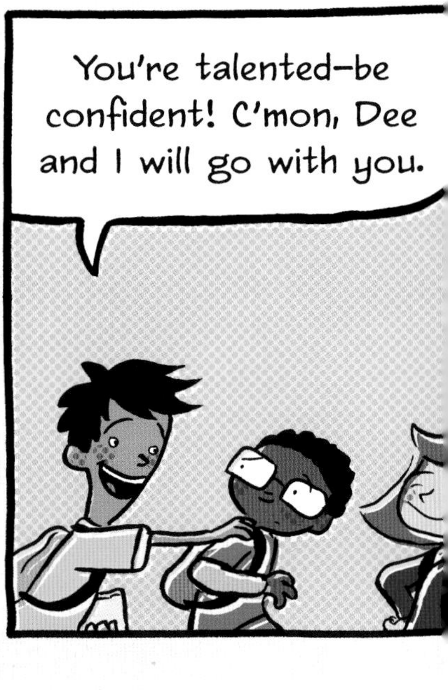
You're talented–be confident! C'mon, Dee and I will go with you.

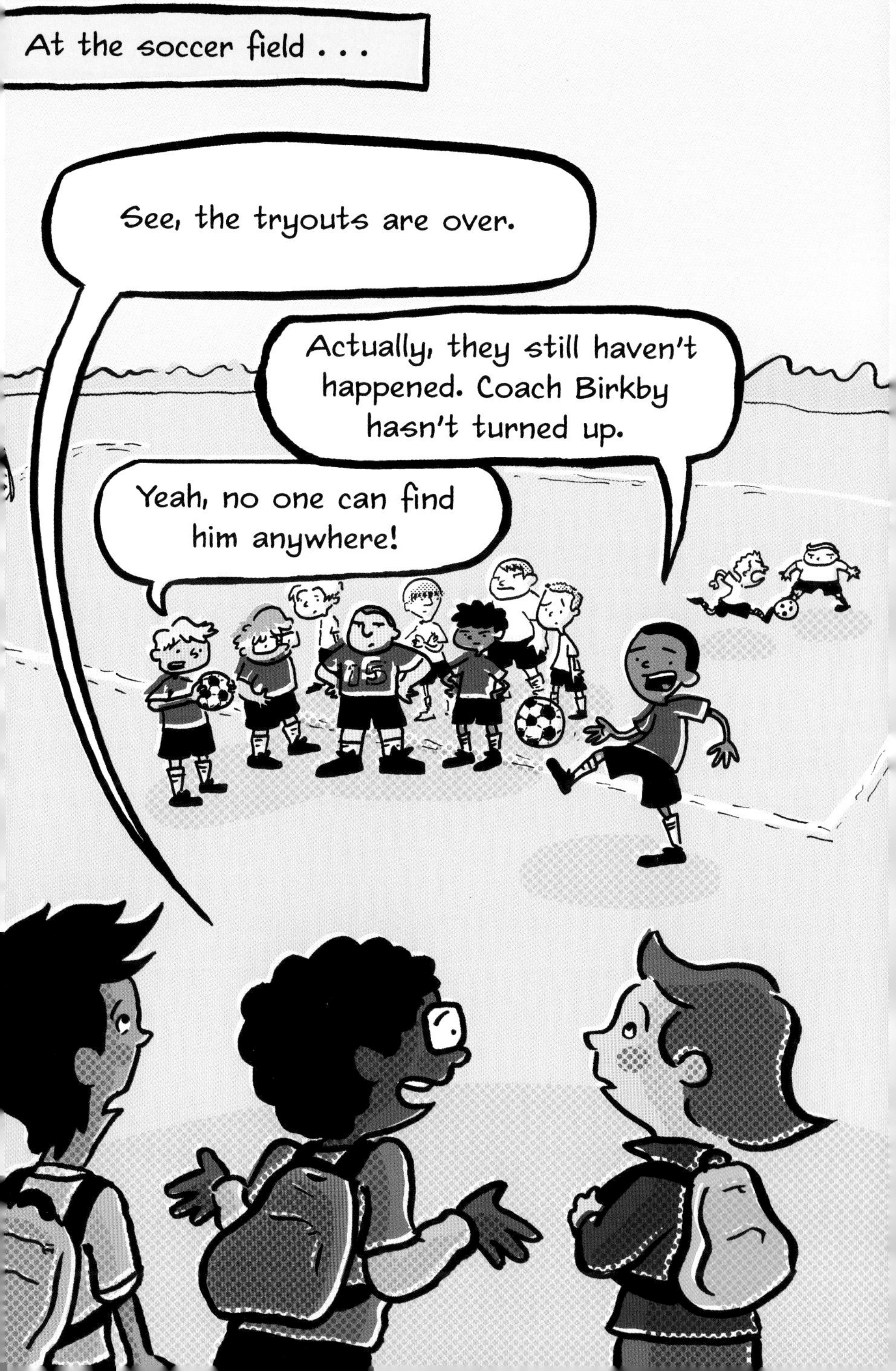
At the soccer field . . .
See, the tryouts are over.
Actually, they still haven't happened. Coach Birkby hasn't turned up.
Yeah, no one can find him anywhere!
15

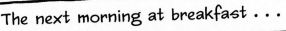

The next morning at breakfast . . .

. . . and he completely missed tryouts.

So they were canceled.

Weird.

Well, if you'll excuse me, I need to . . . um . . . get lunch ready.

Hector, why do you look so disappointed?

I'm still bummed that Mr. Scribson wouldn't sign my book.

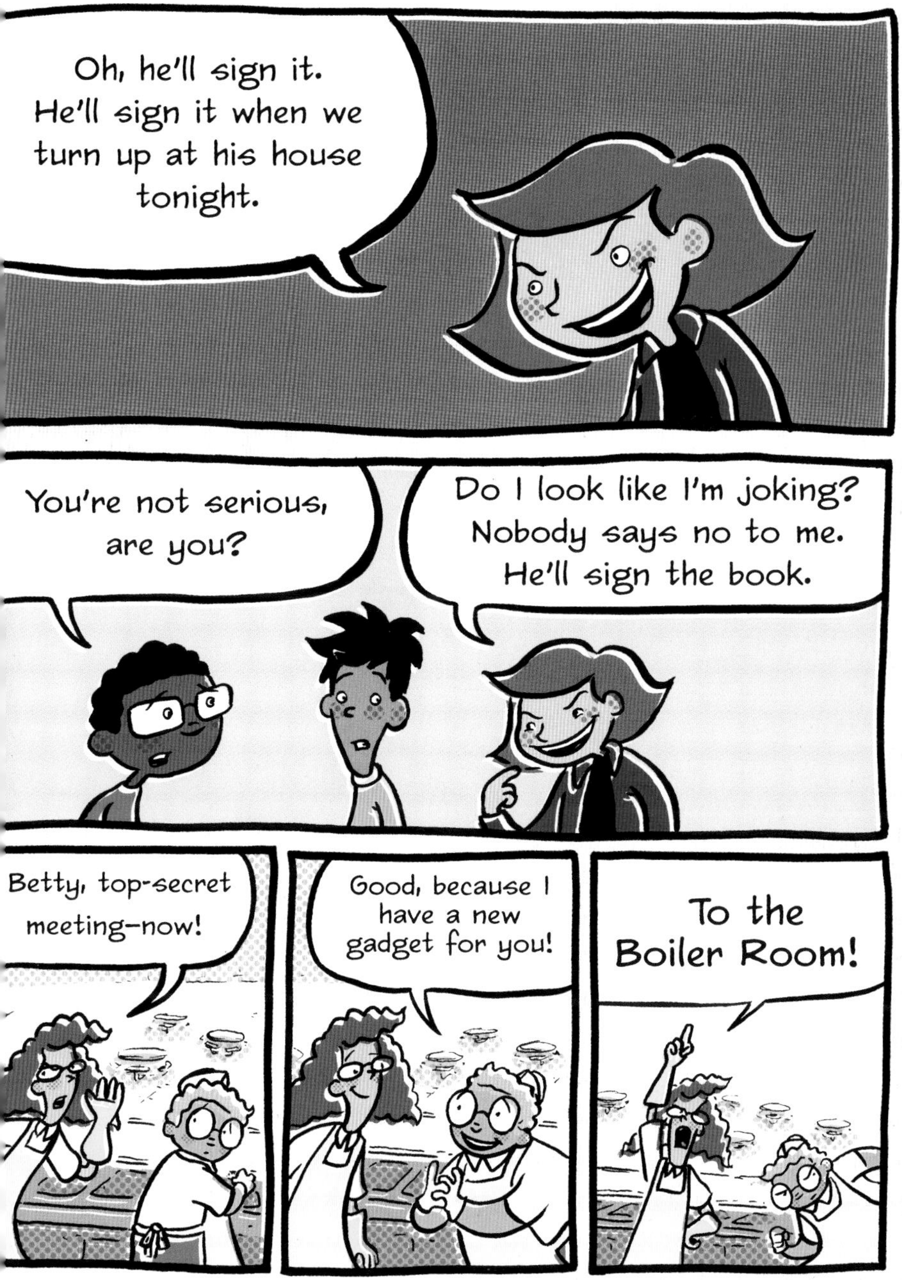

Oh, he'll sign it. He'll sign it when we turn up at his house tonight.
You're not serious, are you?
Do I look like I'm joking? Nobody says no to me. He'll sign the book.
Betty, top-secret meeting—now!
Good, because I have a new gadget for you!
To the Boiler Room!

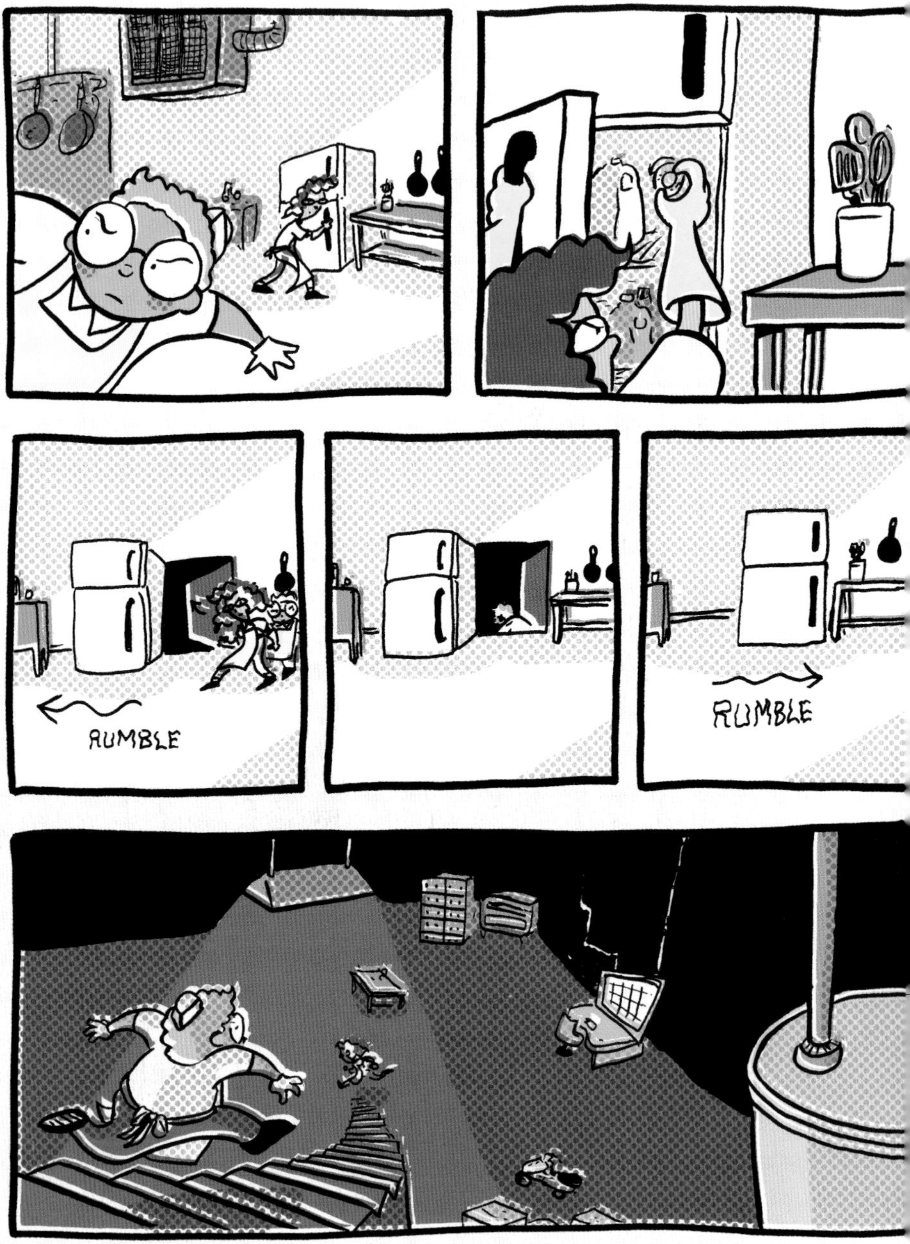
RUMBLE
RUMBLE

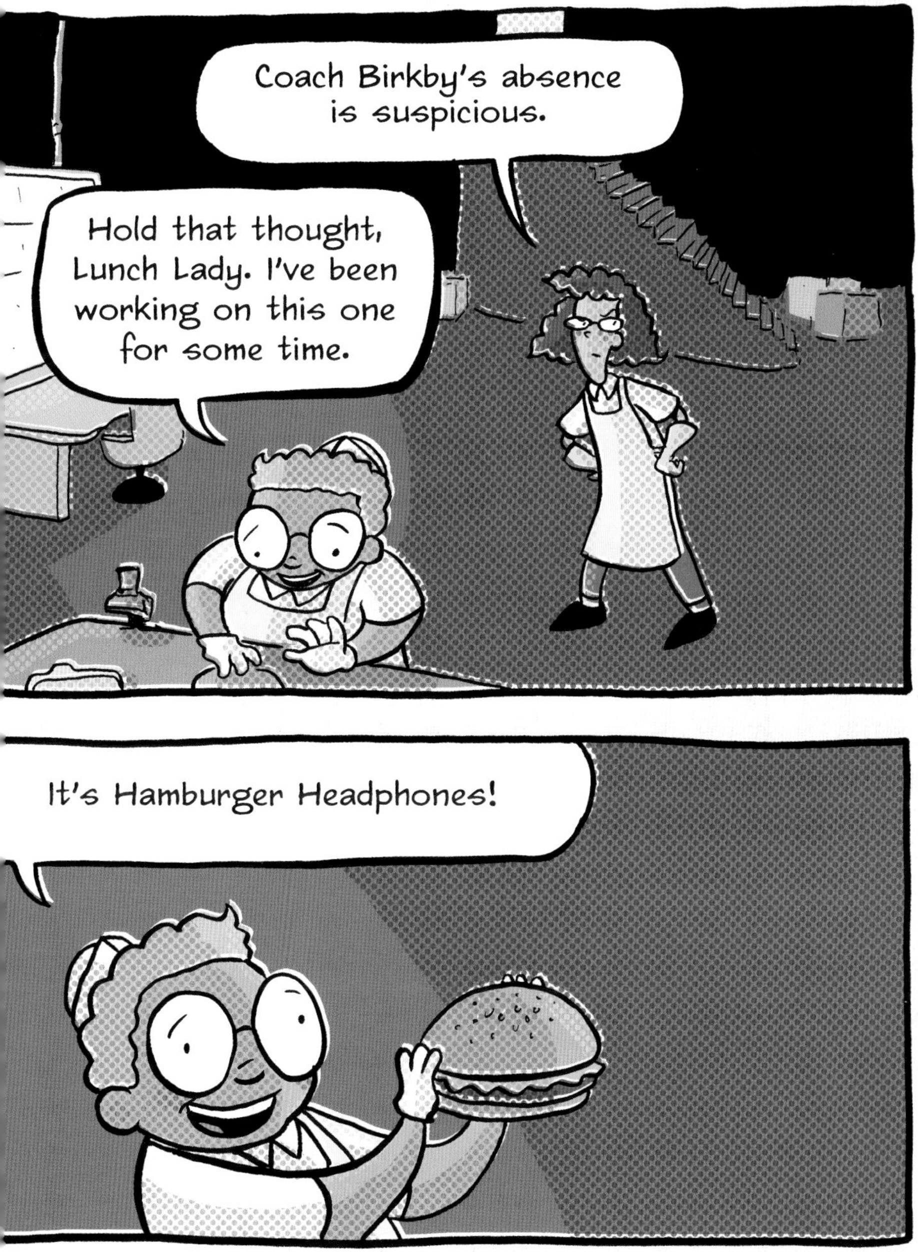
Coach Birkby's absence is suspicious.
Hold that thought, Lunch Lady. I've been working on this one for some time.
It's Hamburger Headphones!

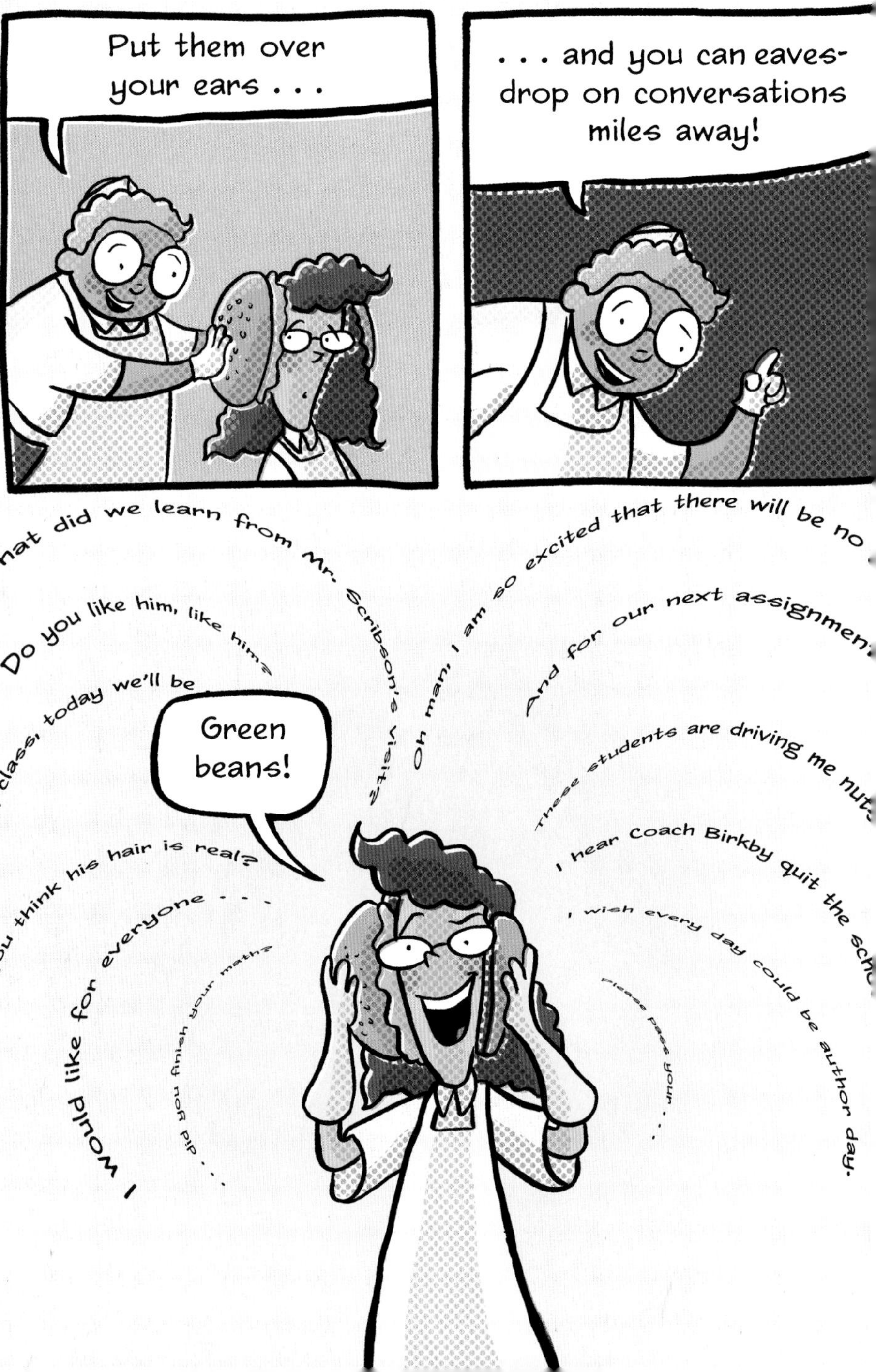

Put them over your ears . . .
. . . and you can eaves-drop on conversations miles away!
What did we learn from Mr. Scribson's visit?
Oh man, I am so excited that there will be no
Do you like him, like him?
And for our next
OK, class, today we'll be
Green beans!
These students are driving me
Do you think his hair is real?
I hear Coach Birkby quit the
I would like for everyone . . .
I wish every day could be author day.
. . . did you finish your math?
Please pass your . . .

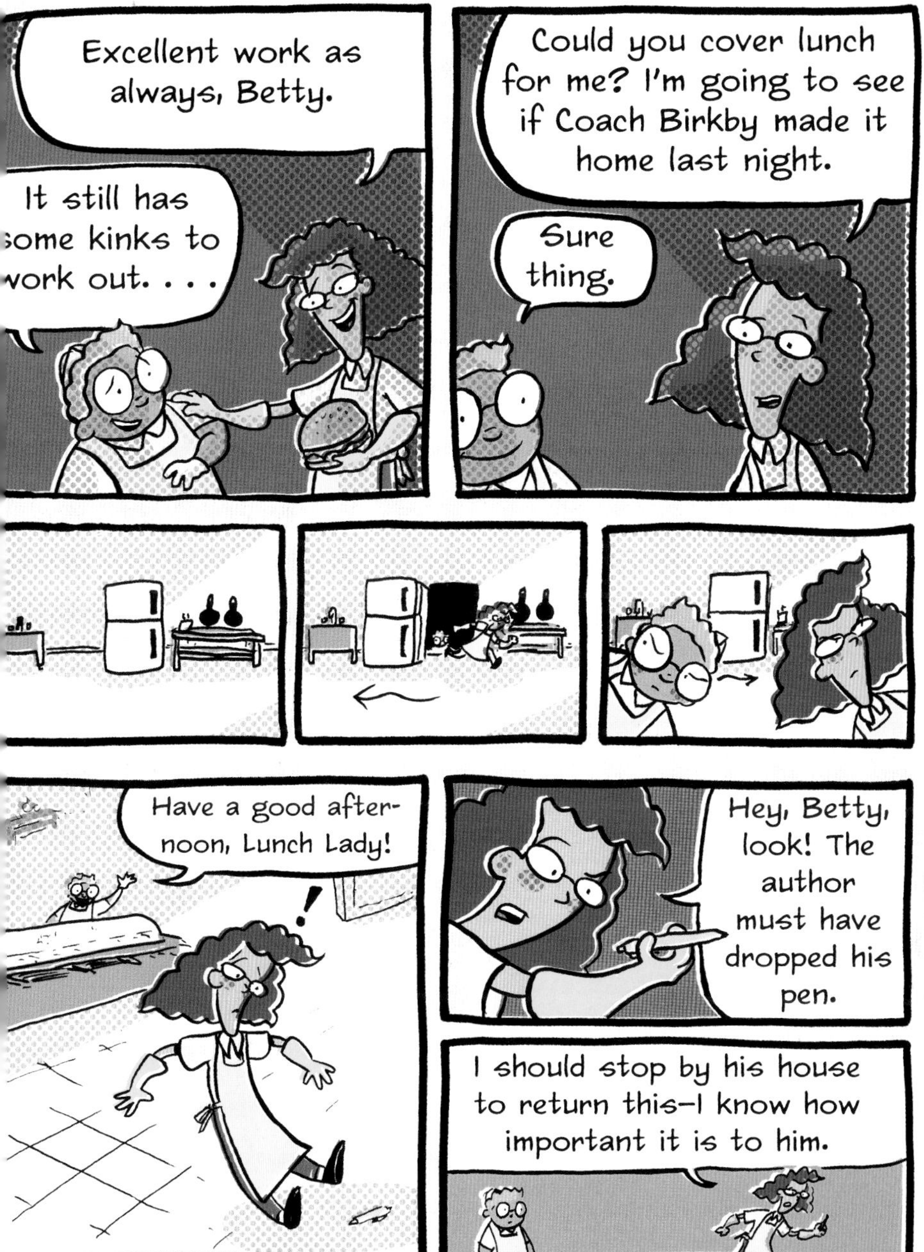
Excellent work as always, Betty.
It still has some kinks to work out. . . .
Could you cover lunch for me? I'm going to see if Coach Birkby made it home last night.
Sure thing.
Have a good after-noon, Lunch Lady!
!
Hey, Betty, look! The author must have dropped his pen.
I should stop by his house to return this—I know how important it is to him.

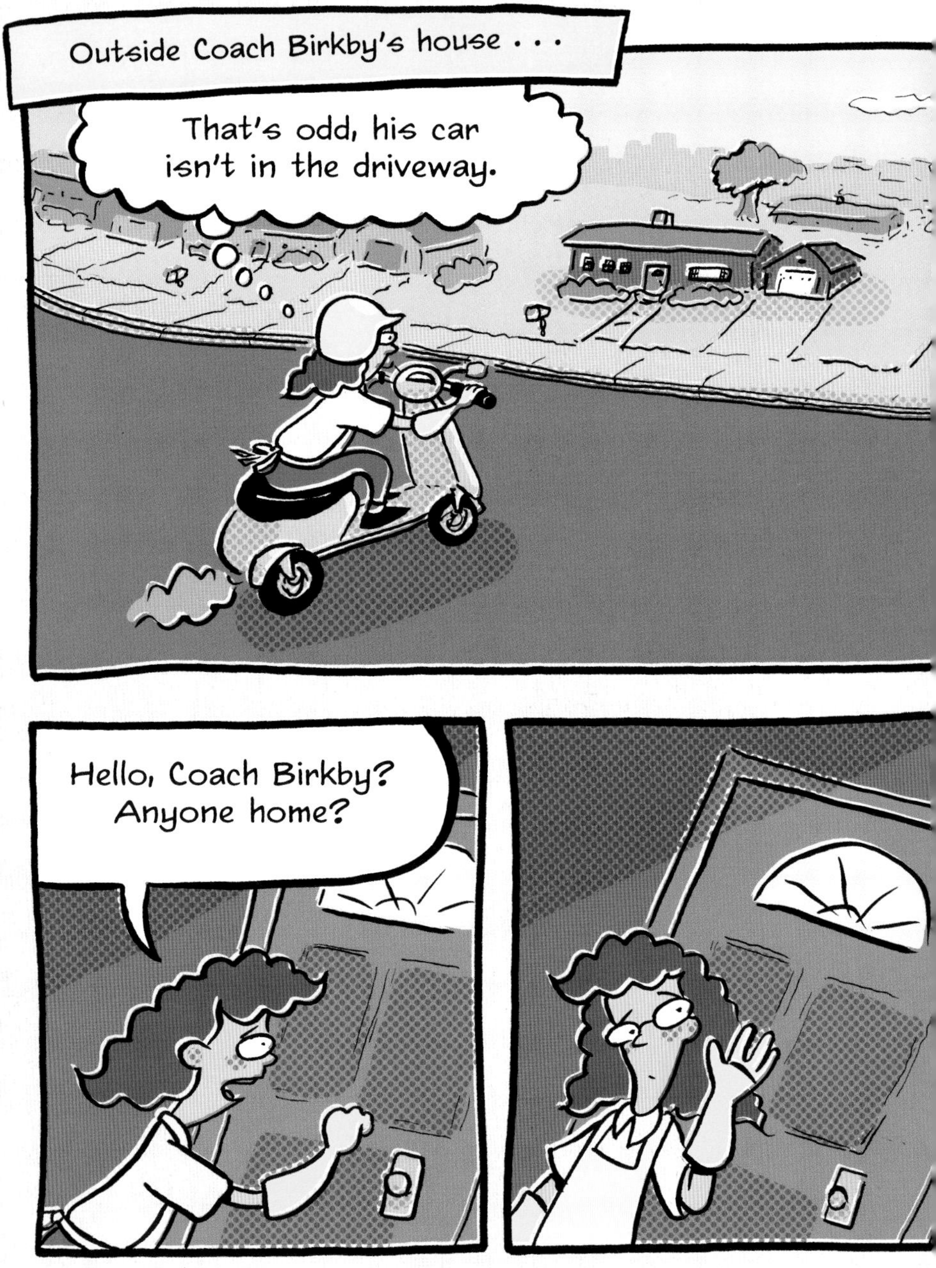
Outside Coach Birkby's house . . .
That's odd, his car isn't in the driveway.
Hello, Coach Birkby? Anyone home?

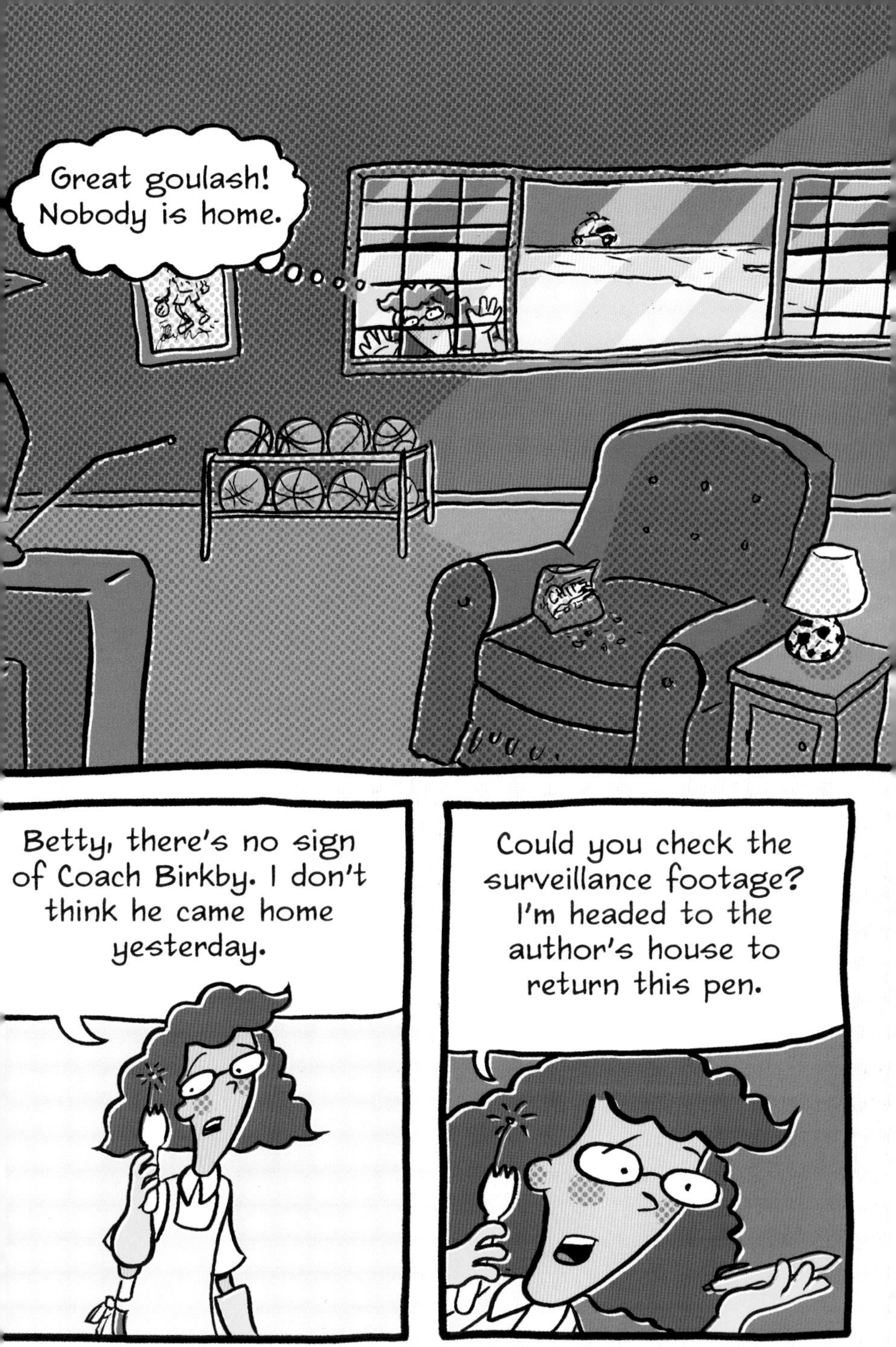
Great goulash! Nobody is home.
Betty, there's no sign of Coach Birkby. I don't think he came home yesterday.
Could you check the surveillance footage? I'm headed to the author's house to return this pen.

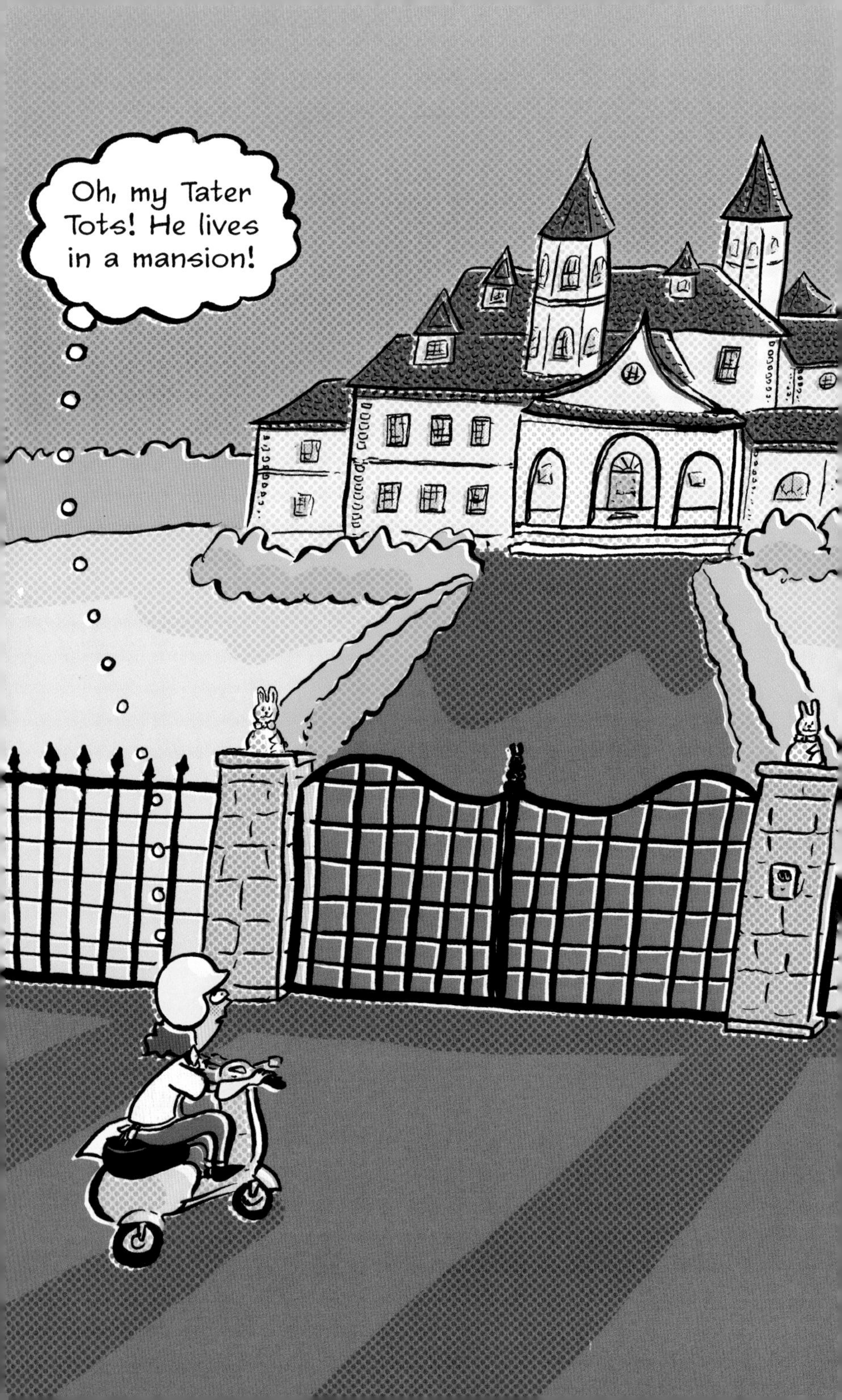
Oh, my Tater Tots! He lives in a mansion!

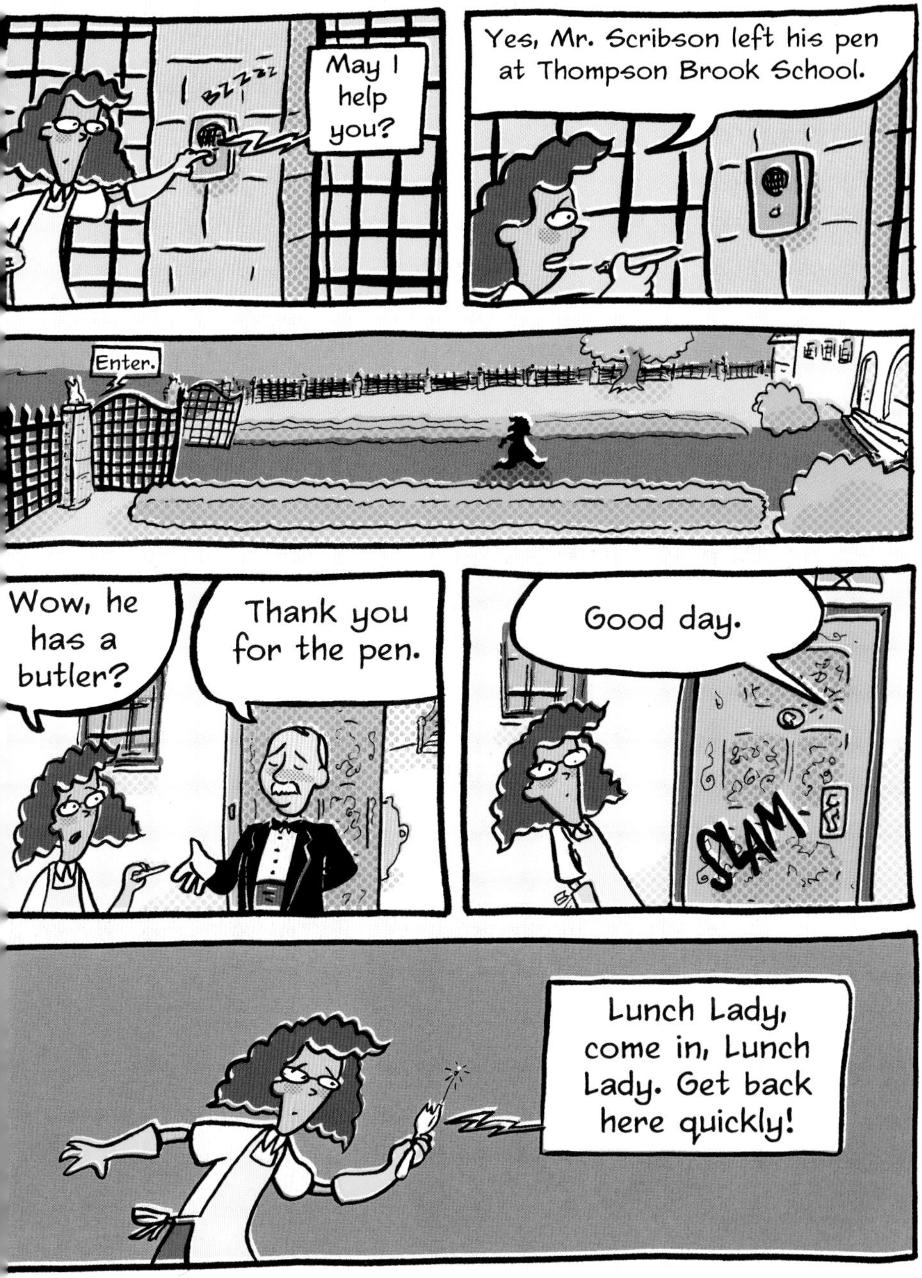
BZZZZZ
May I help you?
Yes, Mr. Scribson left his pen at Thompson Brook School.
Enter.
Wow, he has a butler?
Thank you for the pen.
Good day.
SLAM
Lunch Lady, come in, Lunch Lady. Get back here quickly!

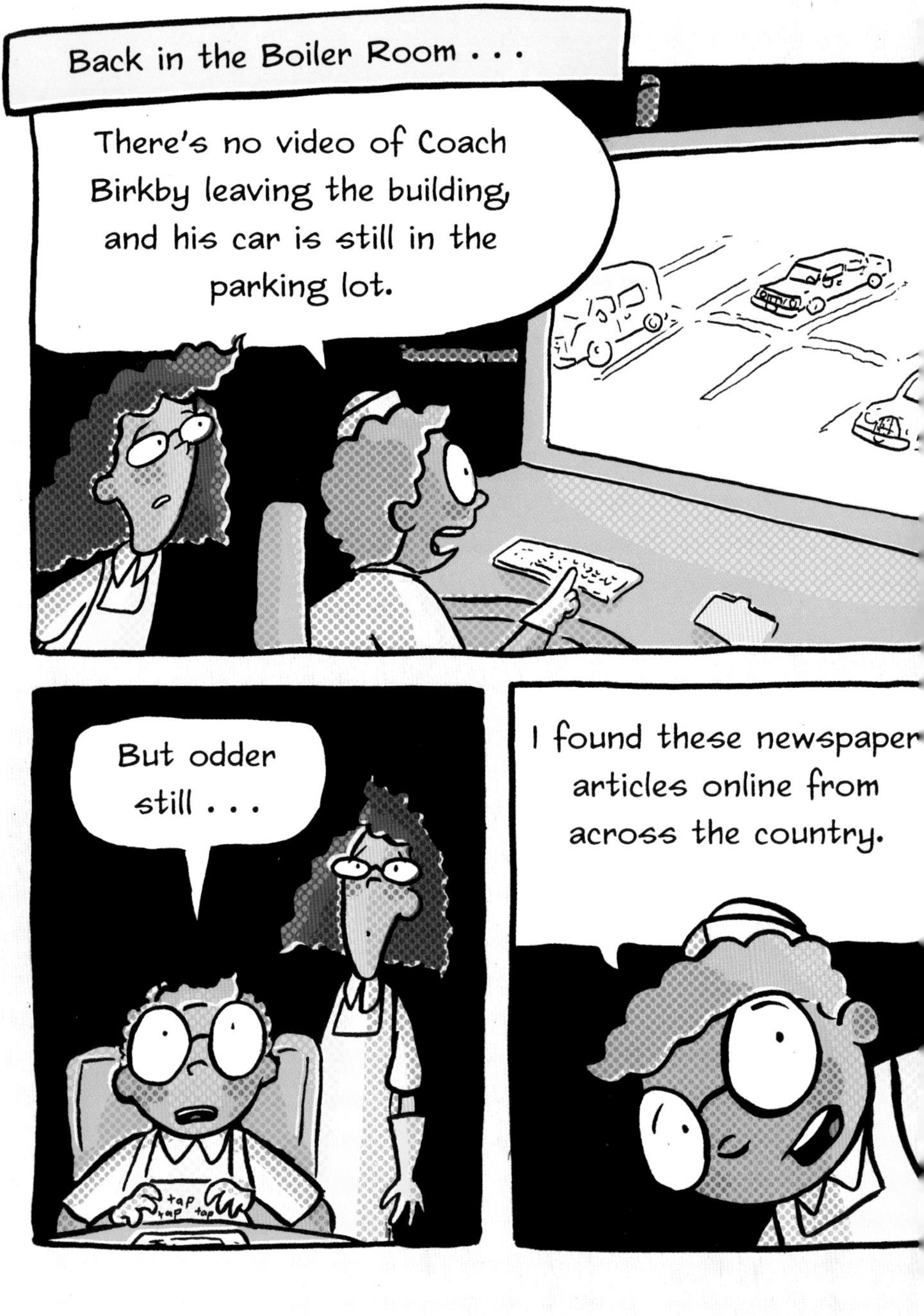
Back in the Boiler Room . . .
There's no video of Coach Birkby leaving the building, and his car is still in the parking lot.
But odder still . . .
tap tap tap
I found these newspaper articles online from across the country.

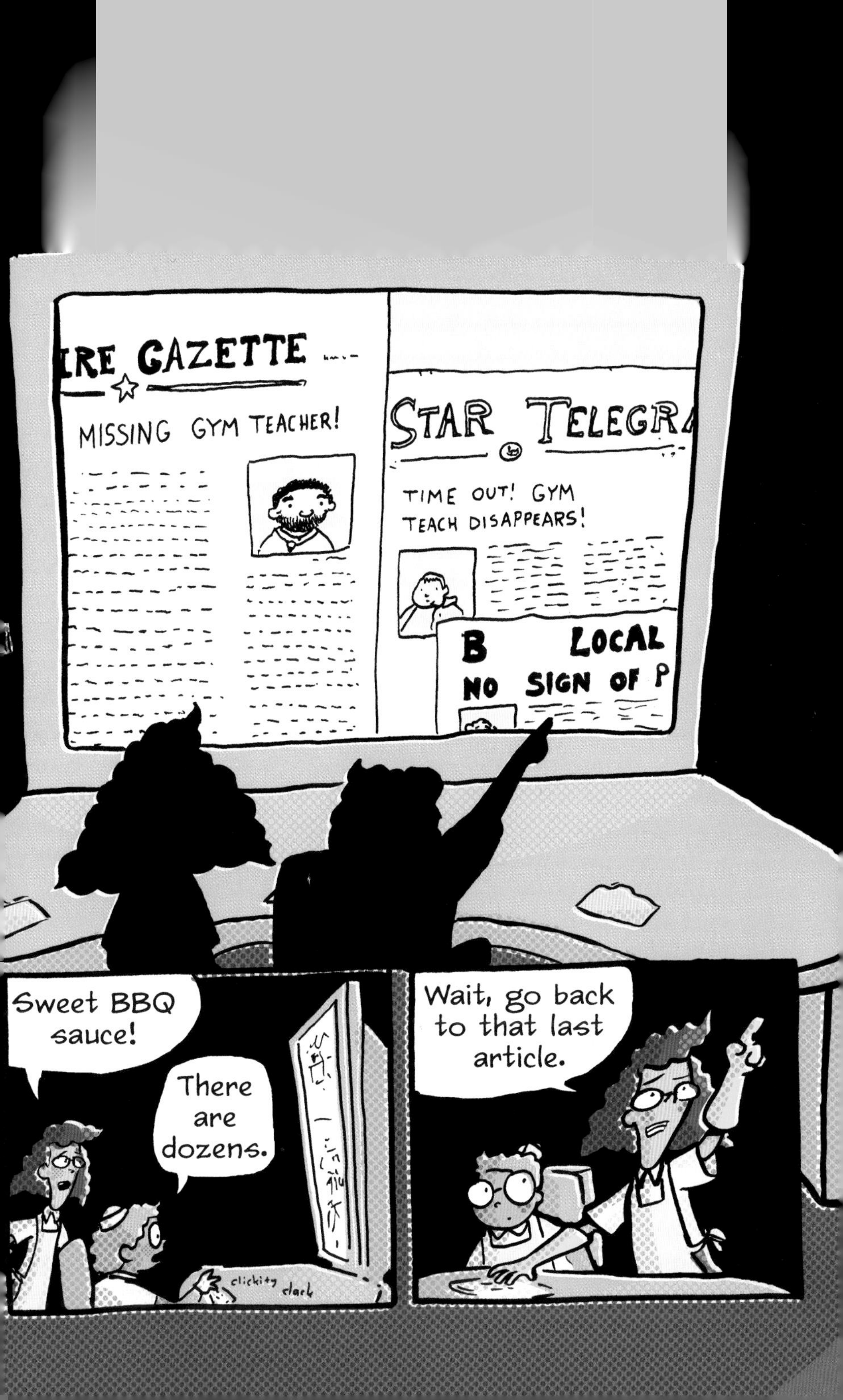

IRE GAZETTE
MISSING GYM TEACHER!
STAR TELEGR
TIME OUT! GYM TEACH DISAPPEARS!
B LOCAL
NO SIGN OF P
Sweet BBQ sauce!
There are dozens.
clickity clack
Wait, go back to that last article.

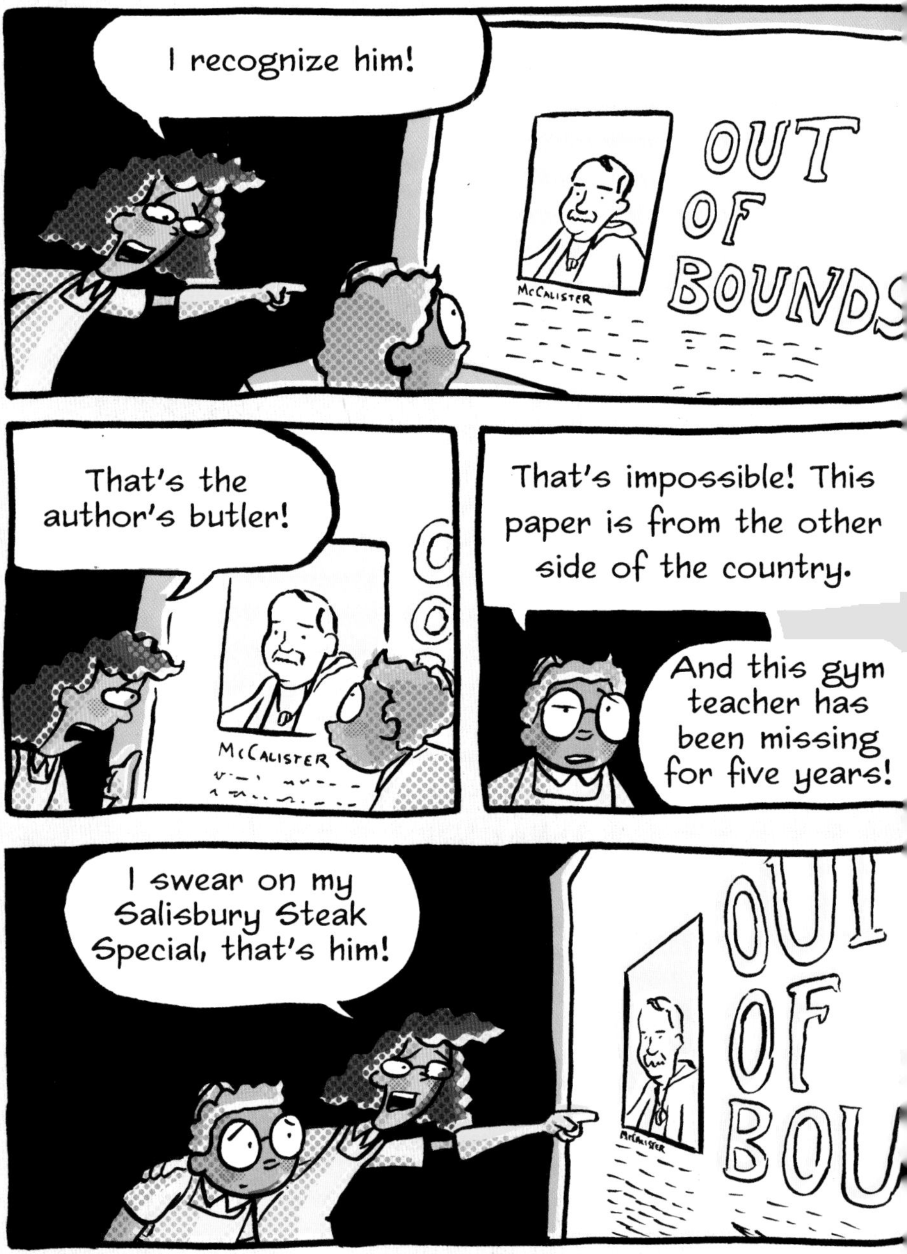
I recognize him!
OUT OF BOUNDS
McCALISTER
That's the author's butler!
McCALISTER
That's impossible! This paper is from the other side of the country.
And this gym teacher has been missing for five years!
I swear on my Salisbury Steak Special, that's him!

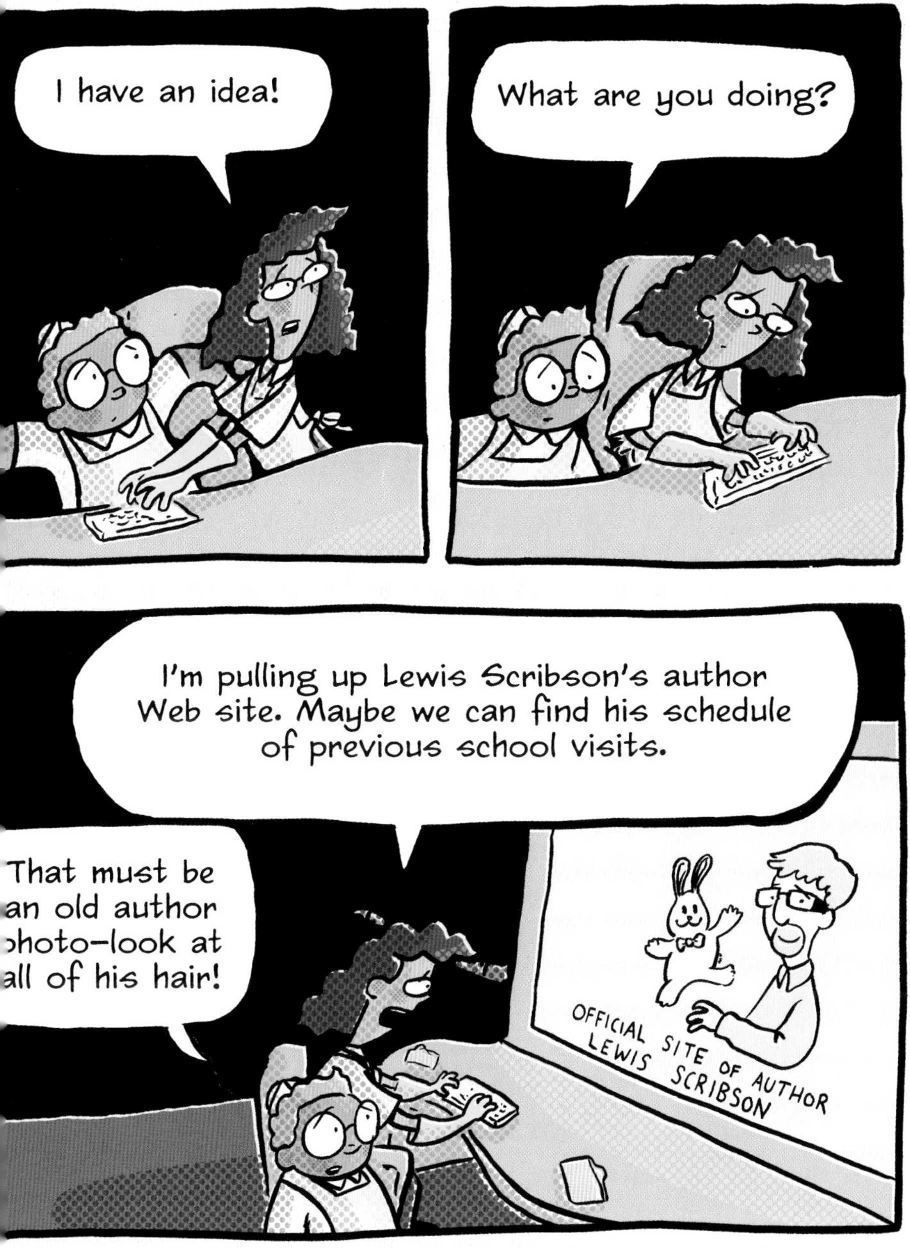
I have an idea!
What are you doing?
I'm pulling up Lewis Scribson's author Web site. Maybe we can find his schedule of previous school visits.
That must be an old author photo—look at all of his hair!
OFFICIAL SITE OF AUTHOR LEWIS SCRIBSON

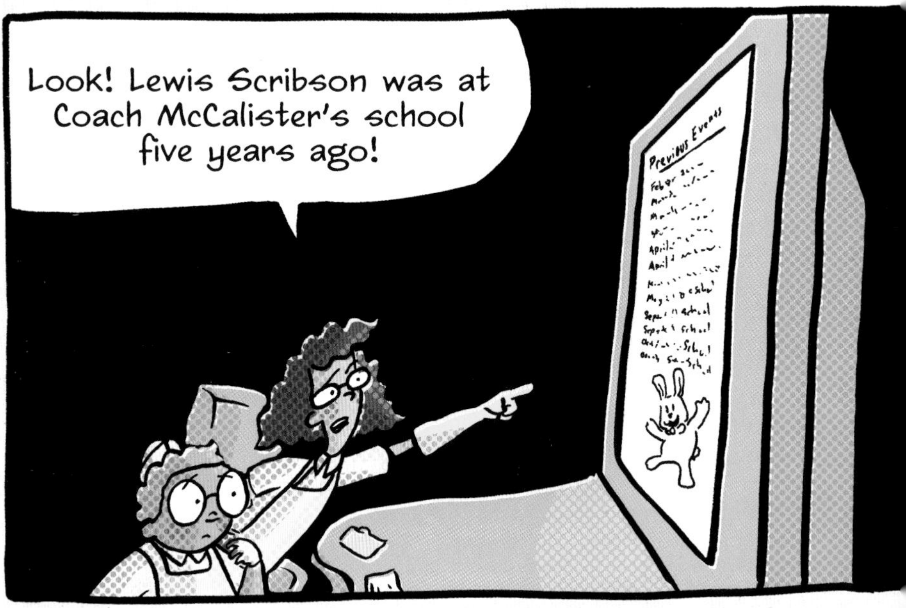
Look! Lewis Scribson was at Coach McCalister's school five years ago!
Previous Events

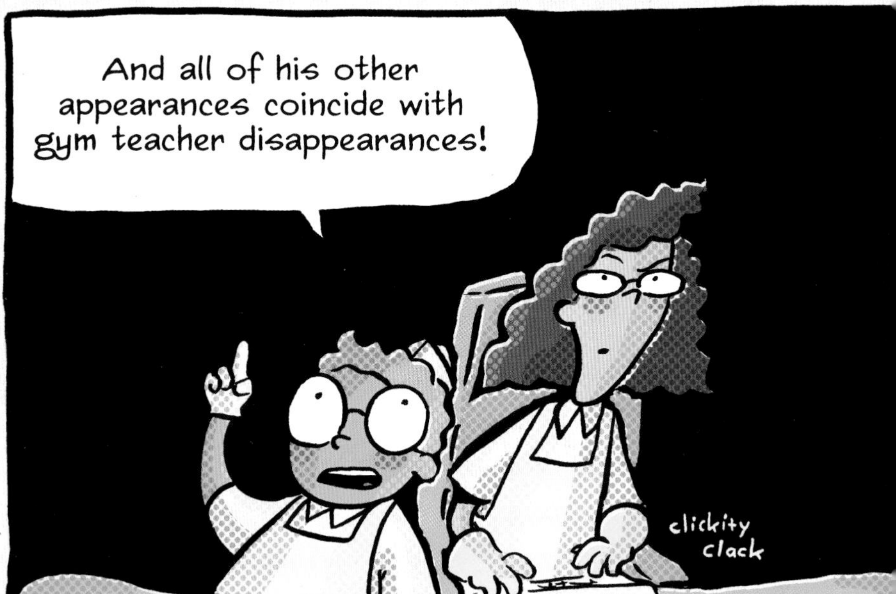
And all of his other appearances coincide with gym teacher disappearances!
clickity clack

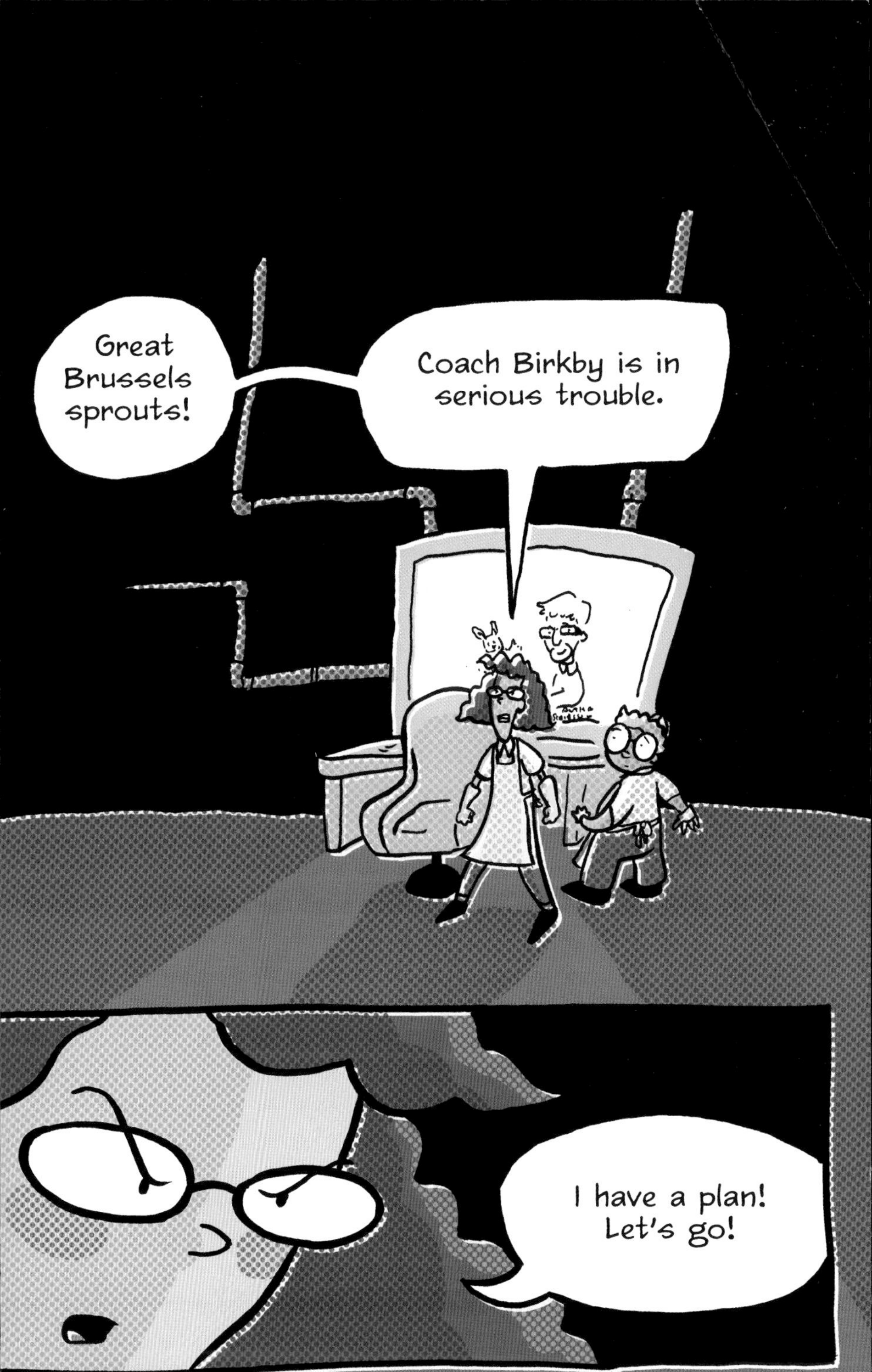
Great Brussels sprouts!
Coach Birkby is in serious trouble.
I have a plan! Let's go!

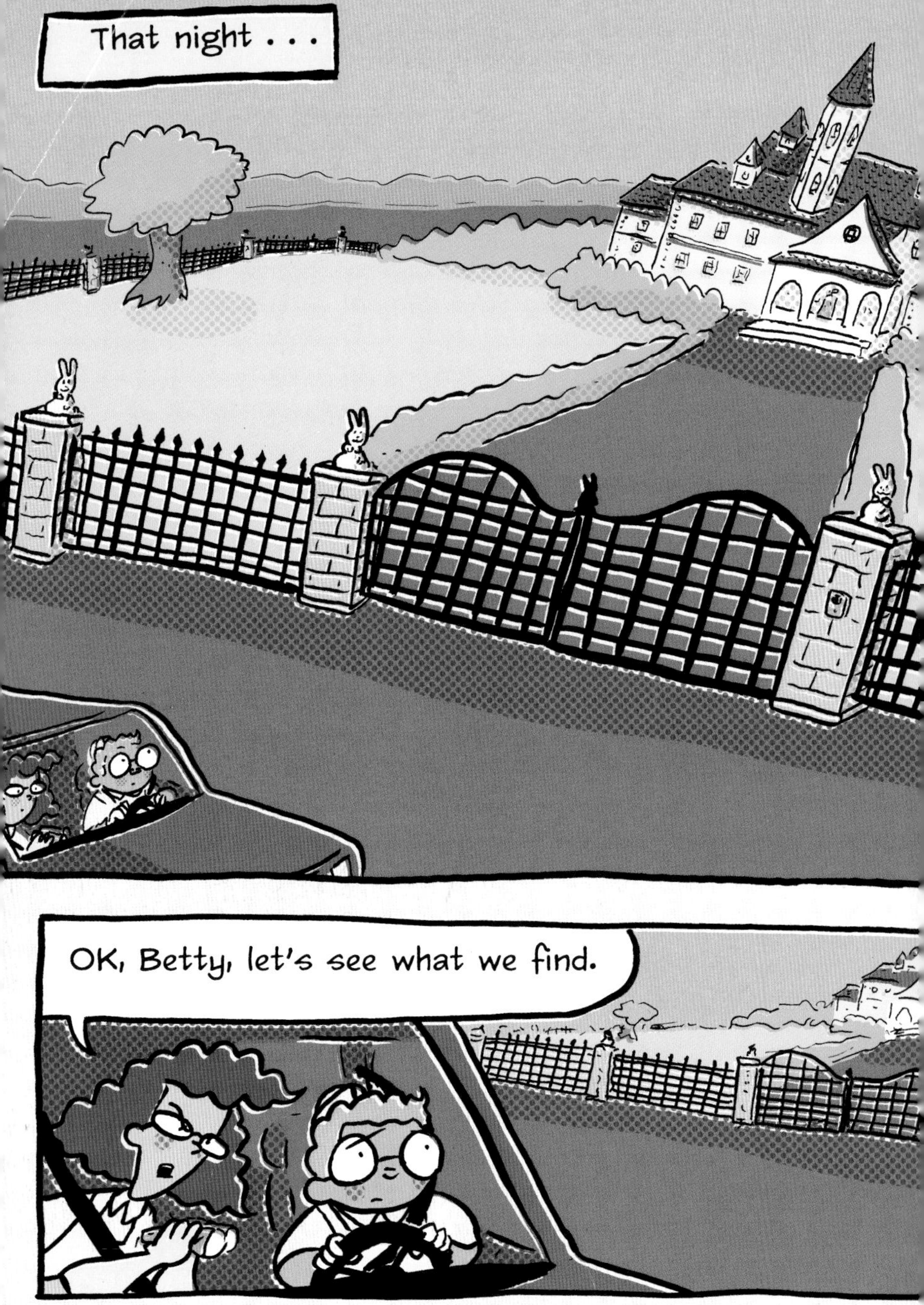
That night . . .
OK, Betty, let's see what we find.

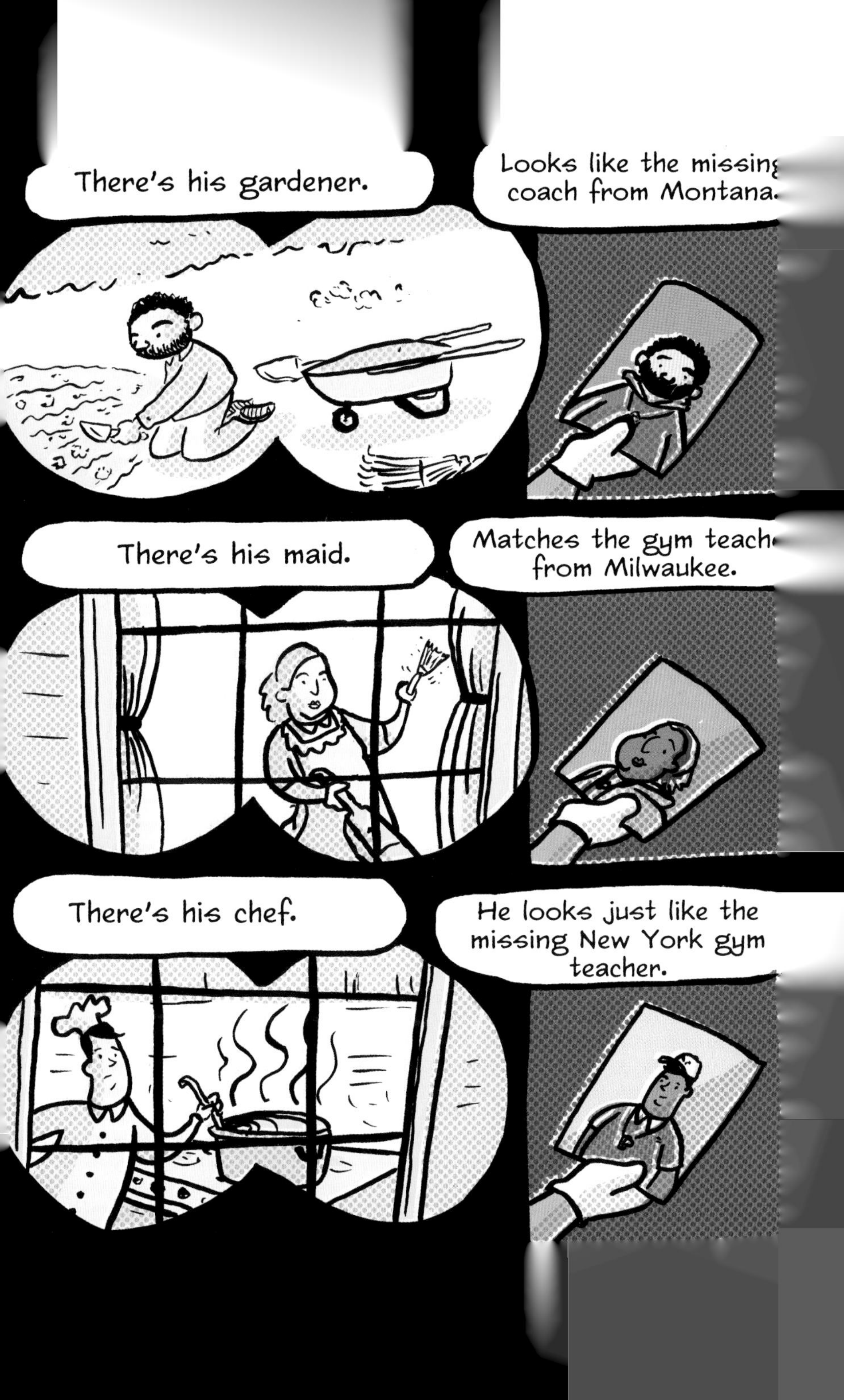

There's his gardener.
Looks like the missing coach from Montana.
There's his maid.
Matches the gym teach from Milwaukee.
There's his chef.
He looks just like the missing New York gym teacher.

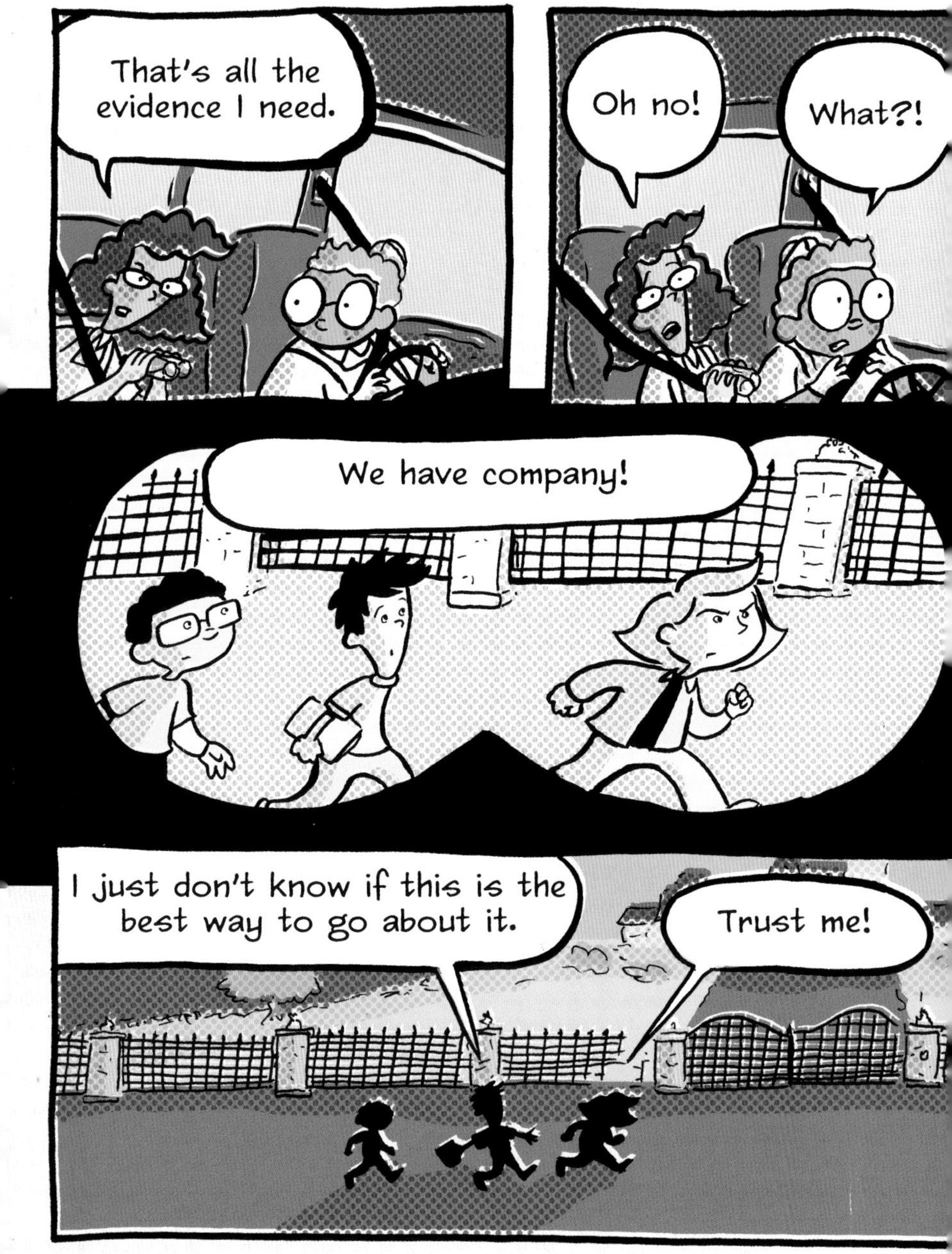
That's all the evidence I need.
Oh no!
What?!
We have company!
I just don't know if this is the best way to go about it.
Trust me!

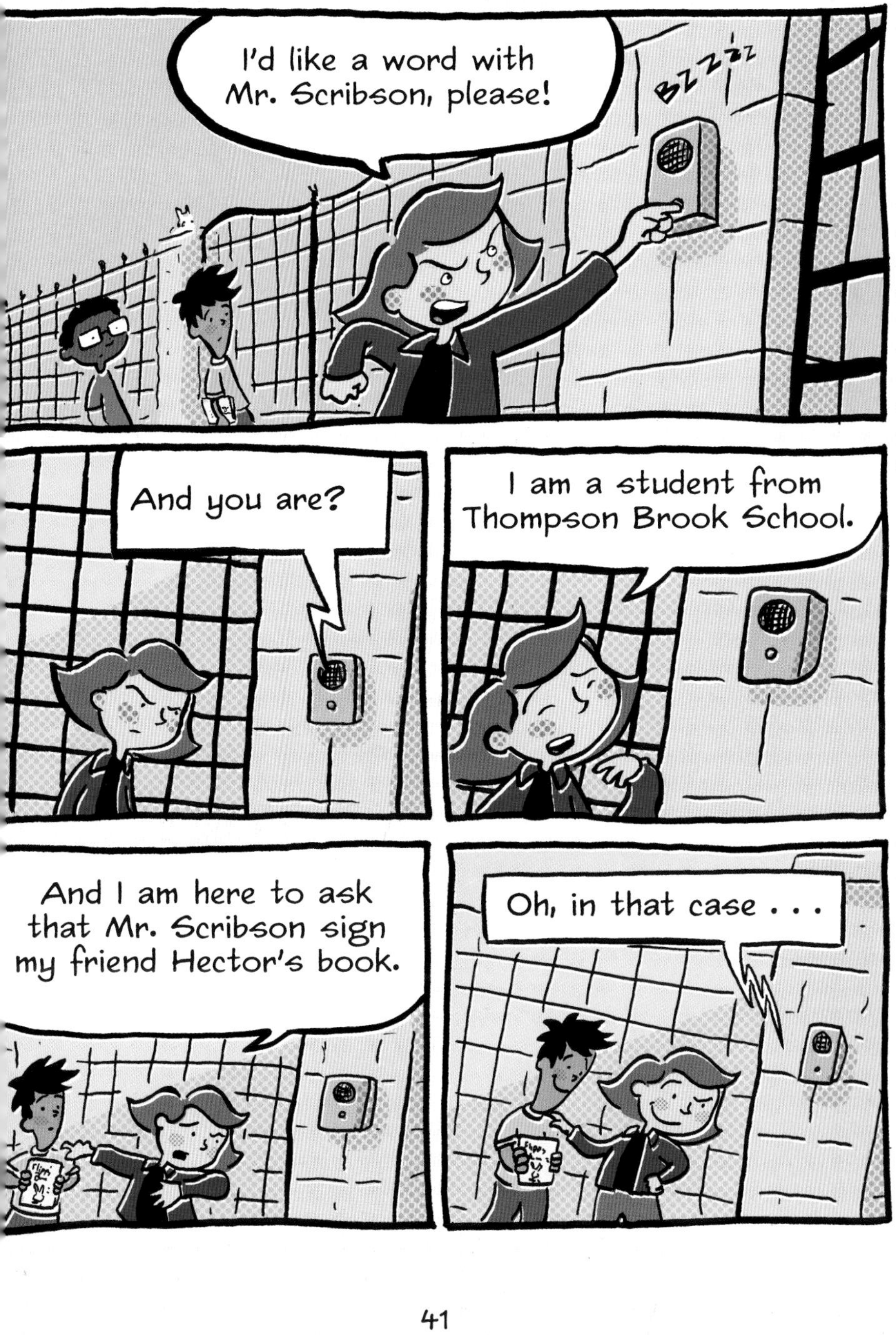
I'd like a word with Mr. Scribson, please!
BZZZZZ
And you are?
I am a student from Thompson Brook School.
And I am here to ask that Mr. Scribson sign my friend Hector's book.
Oh, in that case . . .

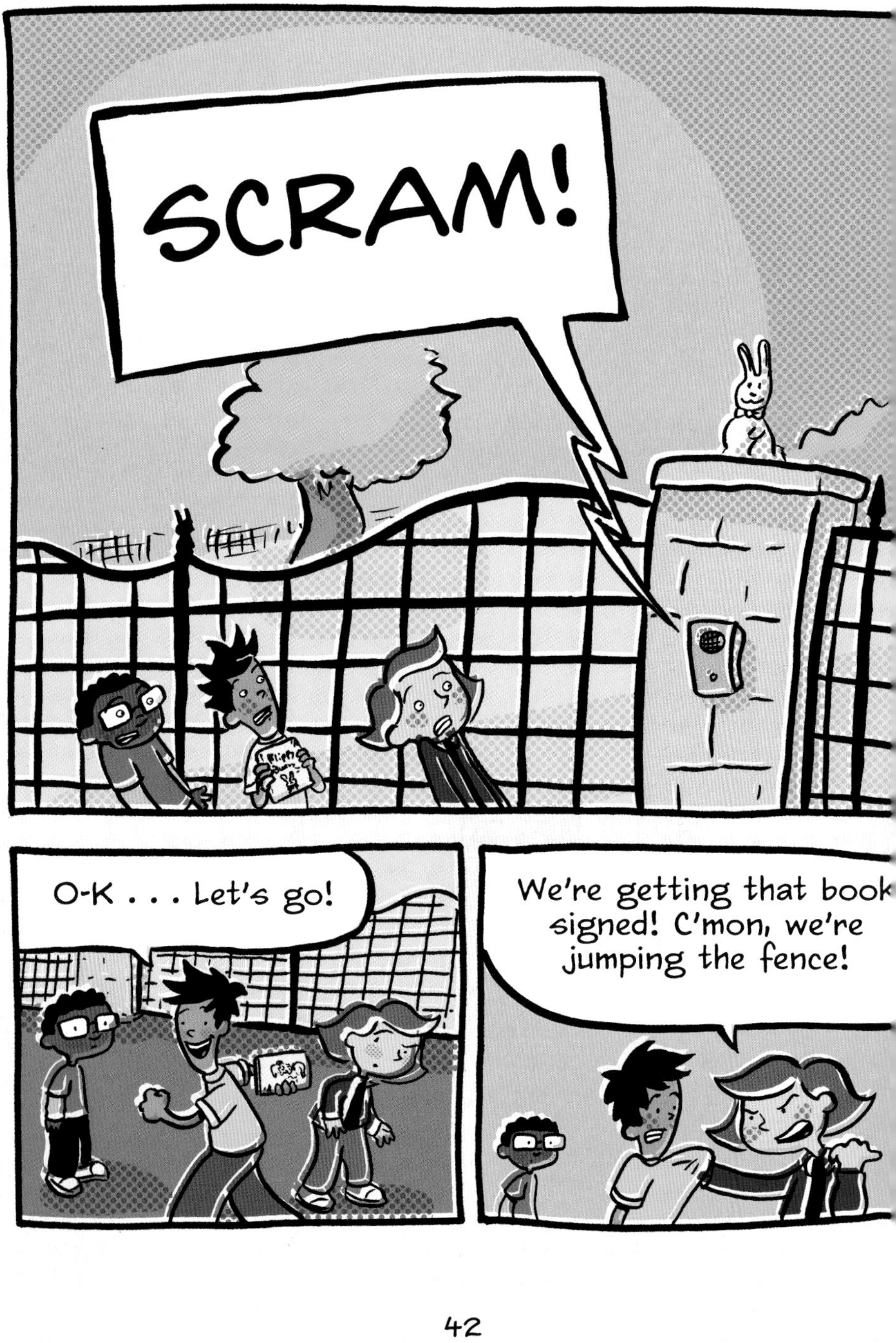
SCRAM!
O-K . . . Let's go!
We're getting that book signed! C'mon, we're jumping the fence!

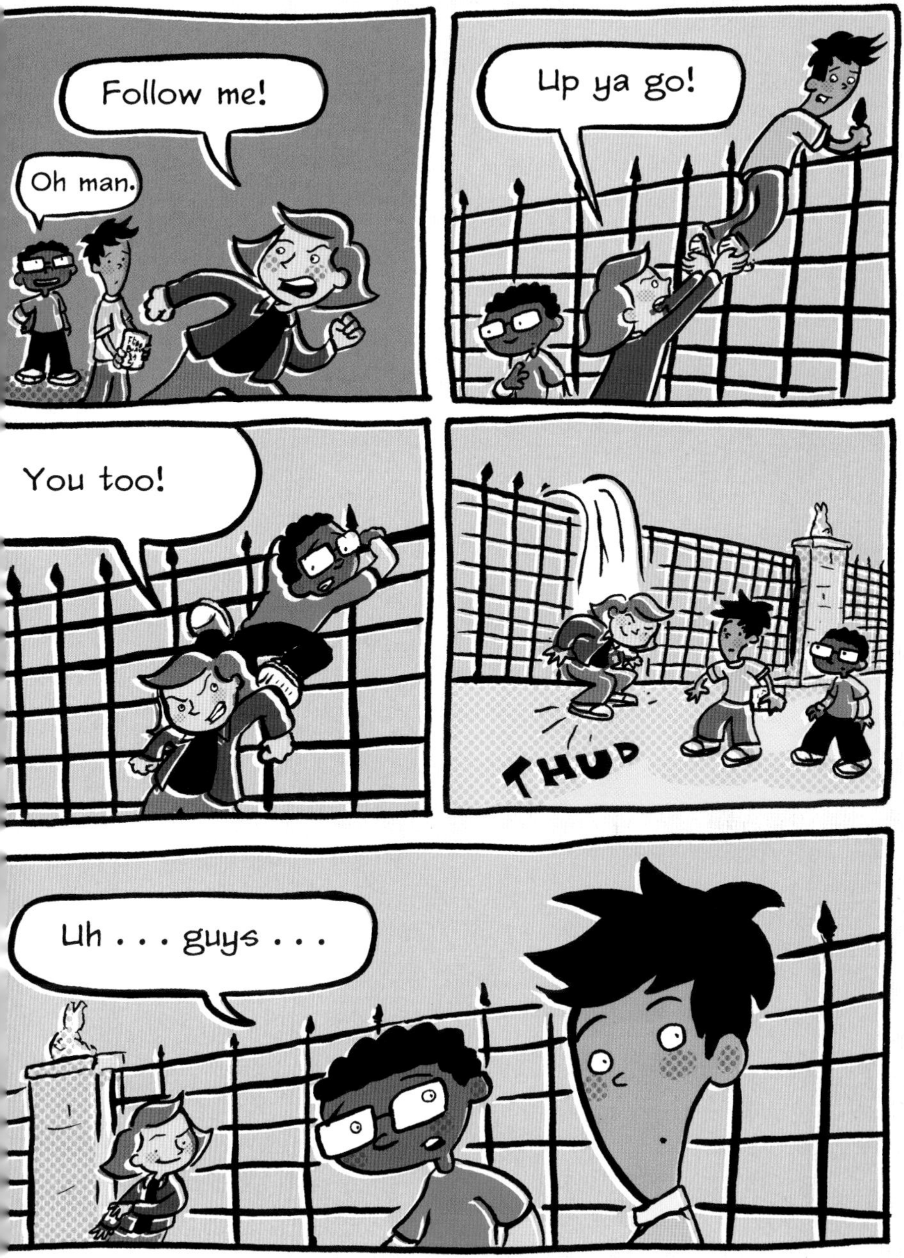
Follow me!
Oh man.
Up ya go!
You too!
THUD
Uh . . . guys . . .

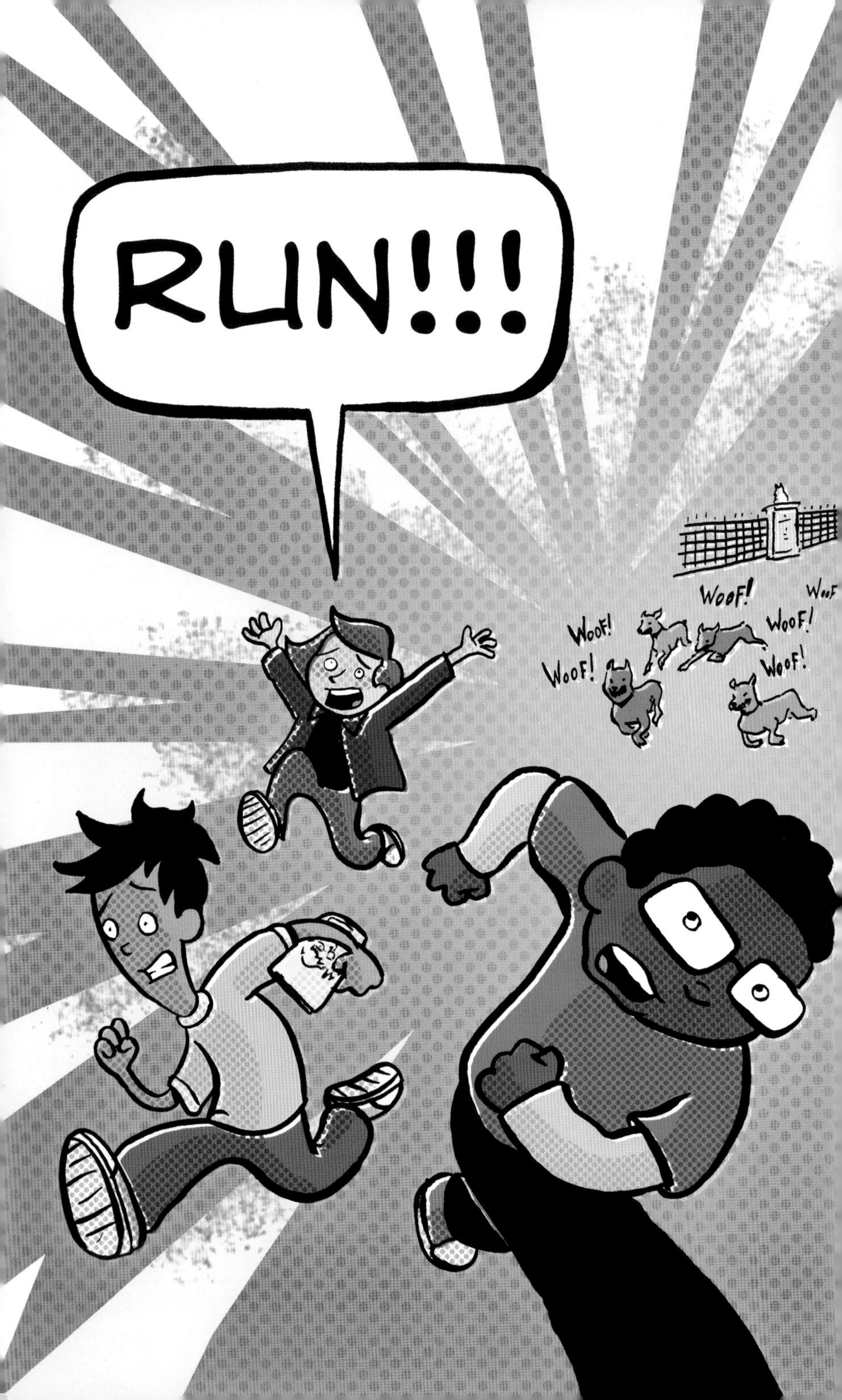

RUN!!!
WOOF!
WOOF!
WOOF!
WOOF!
WOOF!

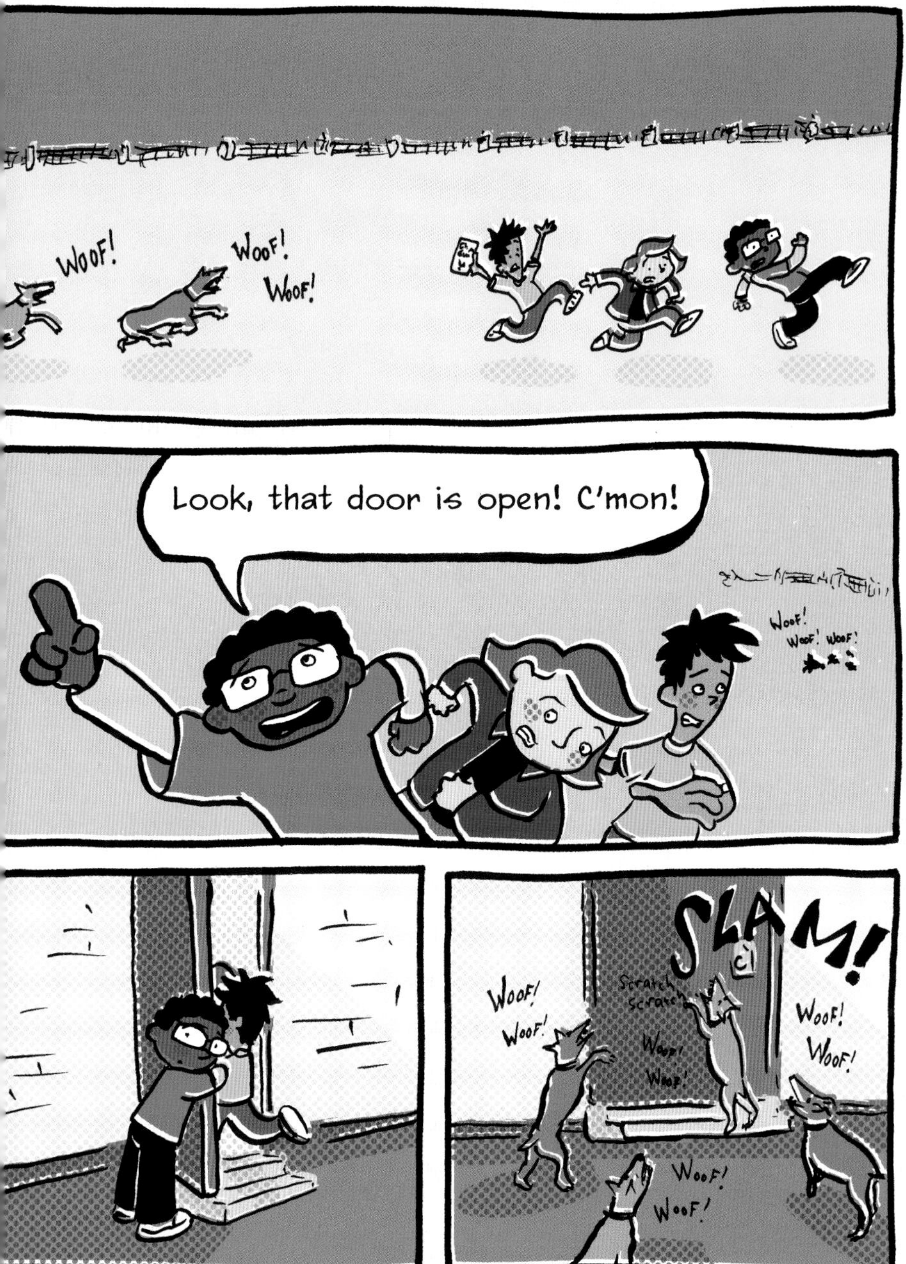
WOOF!
WOOF!
WOOF!
Look, that door is open! C'mon!
WOOF!
WOOF! WOOF!
SLAM!
WOOF!
WOOF!
Scratch
Scratch
WOOF!
WOOF!
WOOF!
WOOF!
WOOF!
WOOF!

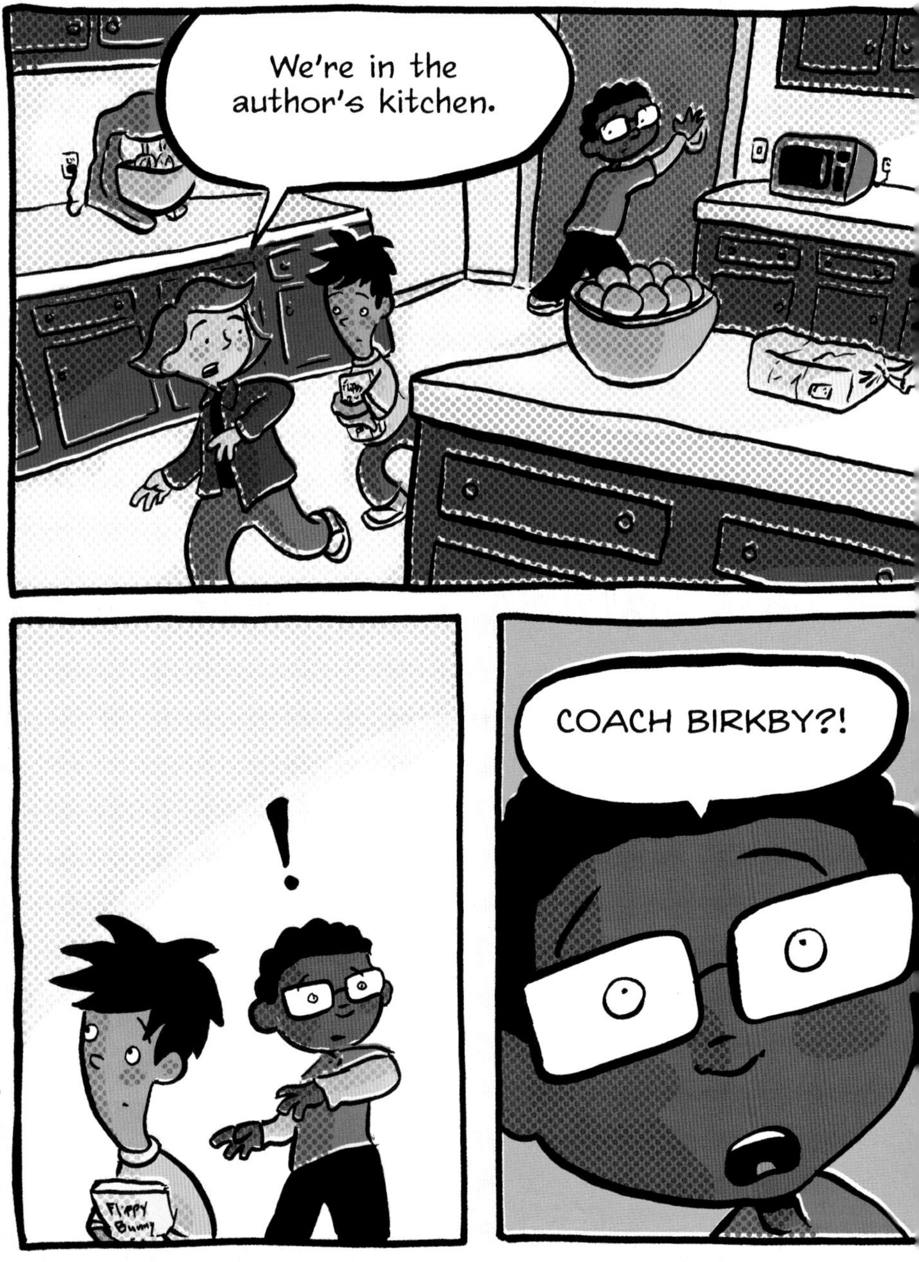
We're in the author's kitchen.
!
COACH BIRKBY?!
Flappy Bunny

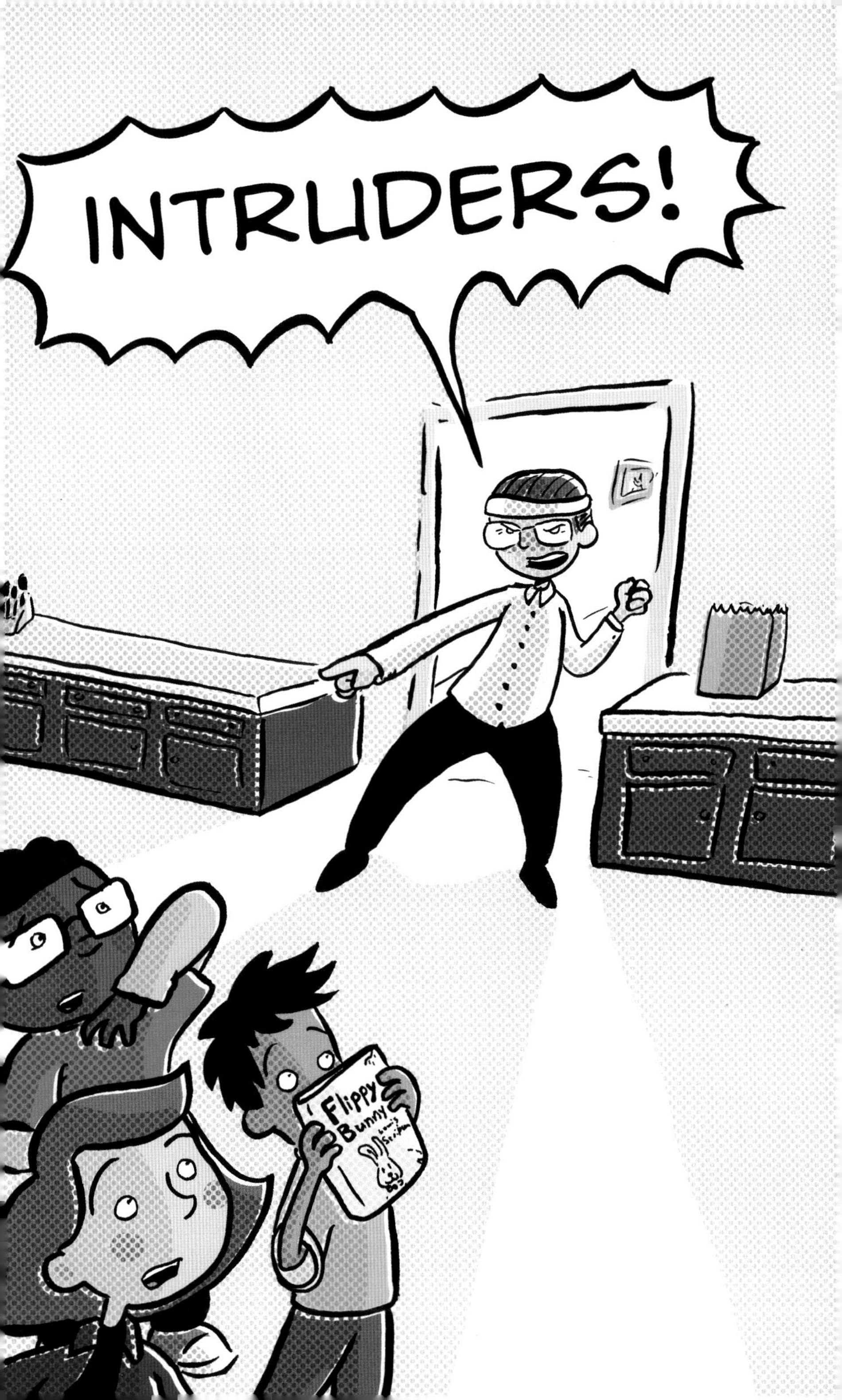
INTRUDERS!
Flippy
Bunny

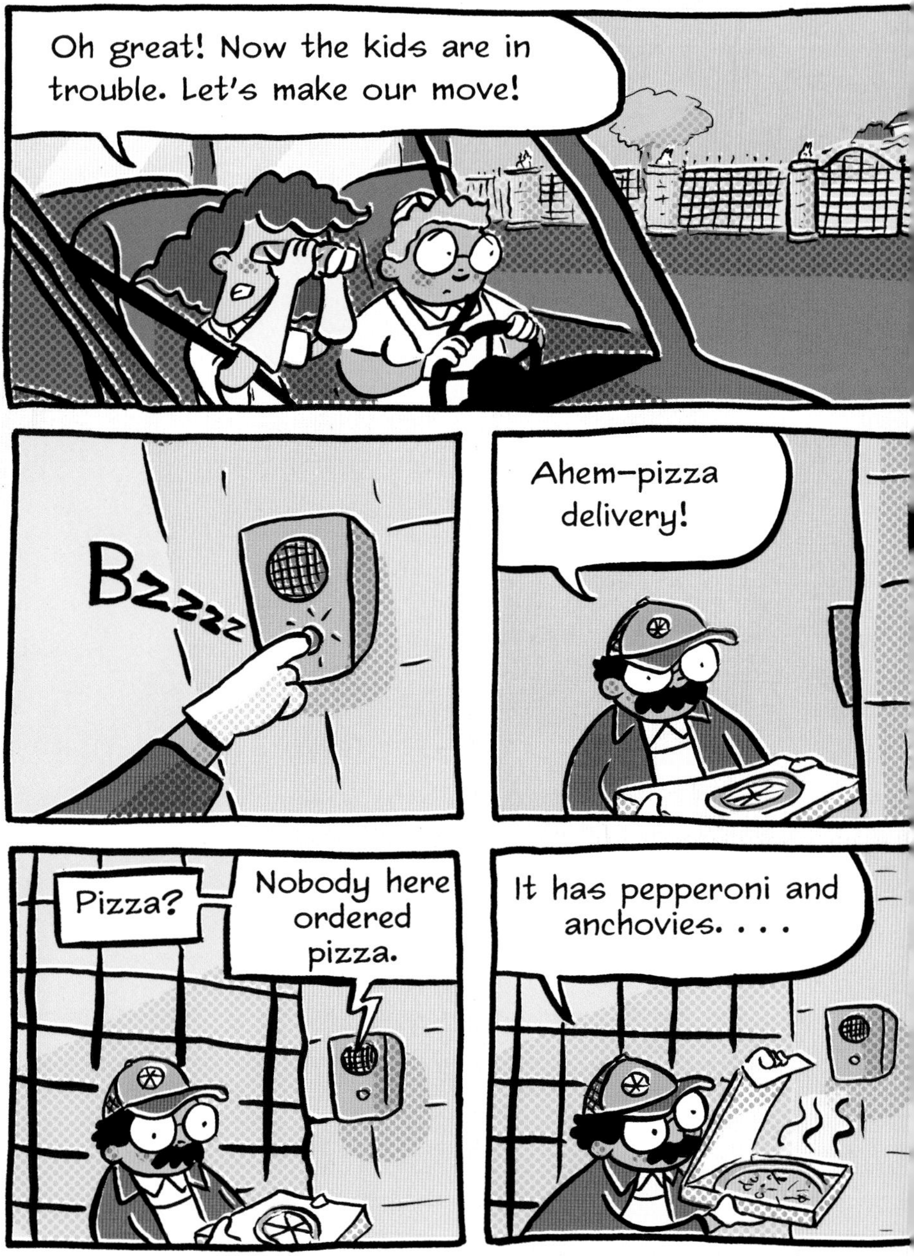
Oh great! Now the kids are in trouble. Let's make our move!
Bzzzzz
Ahem—pizza delivery!
Pizza?
Nobody here ordered pizza.
It has pepperoni and anchovies. . . .

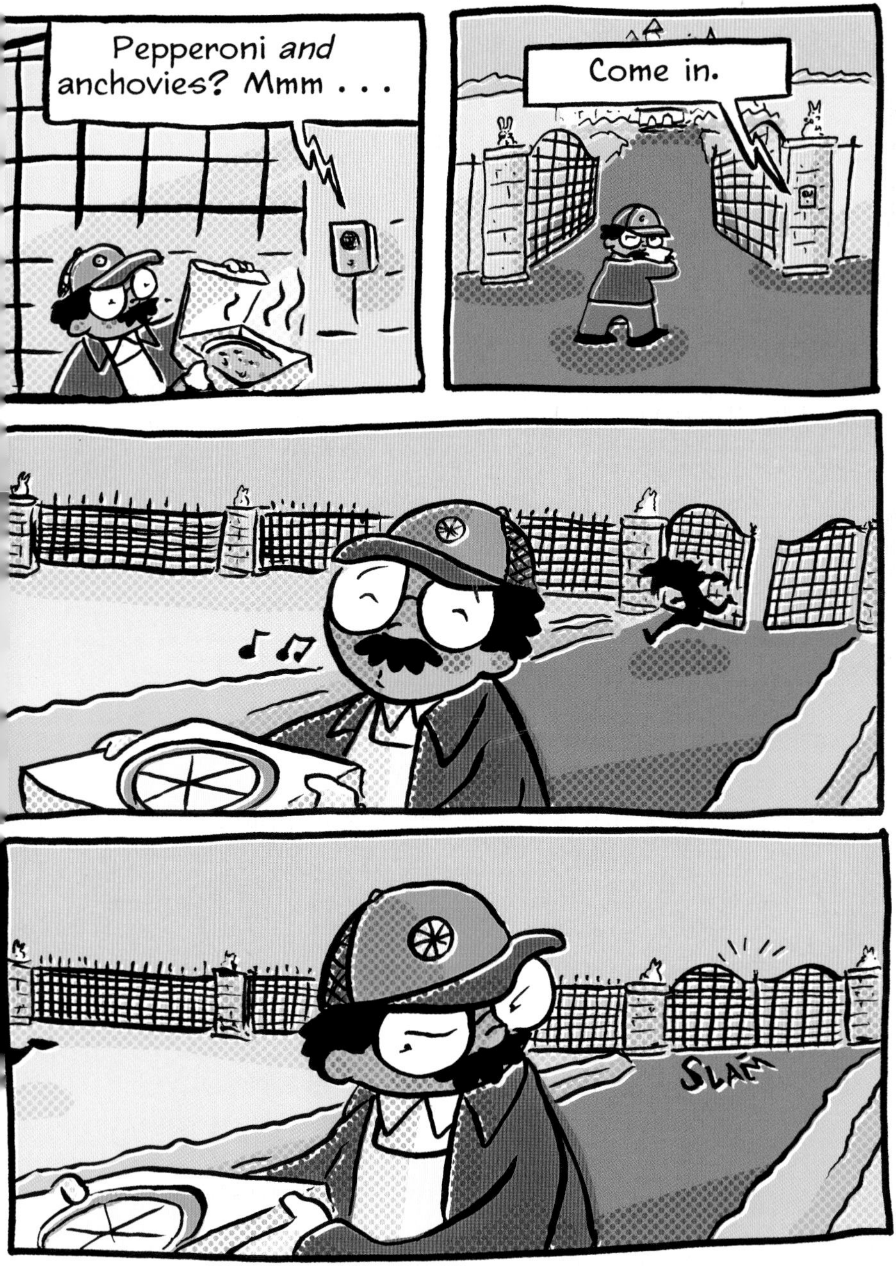
Pepperoni and anchovies? Mmm . . .
Come in.
SLAM

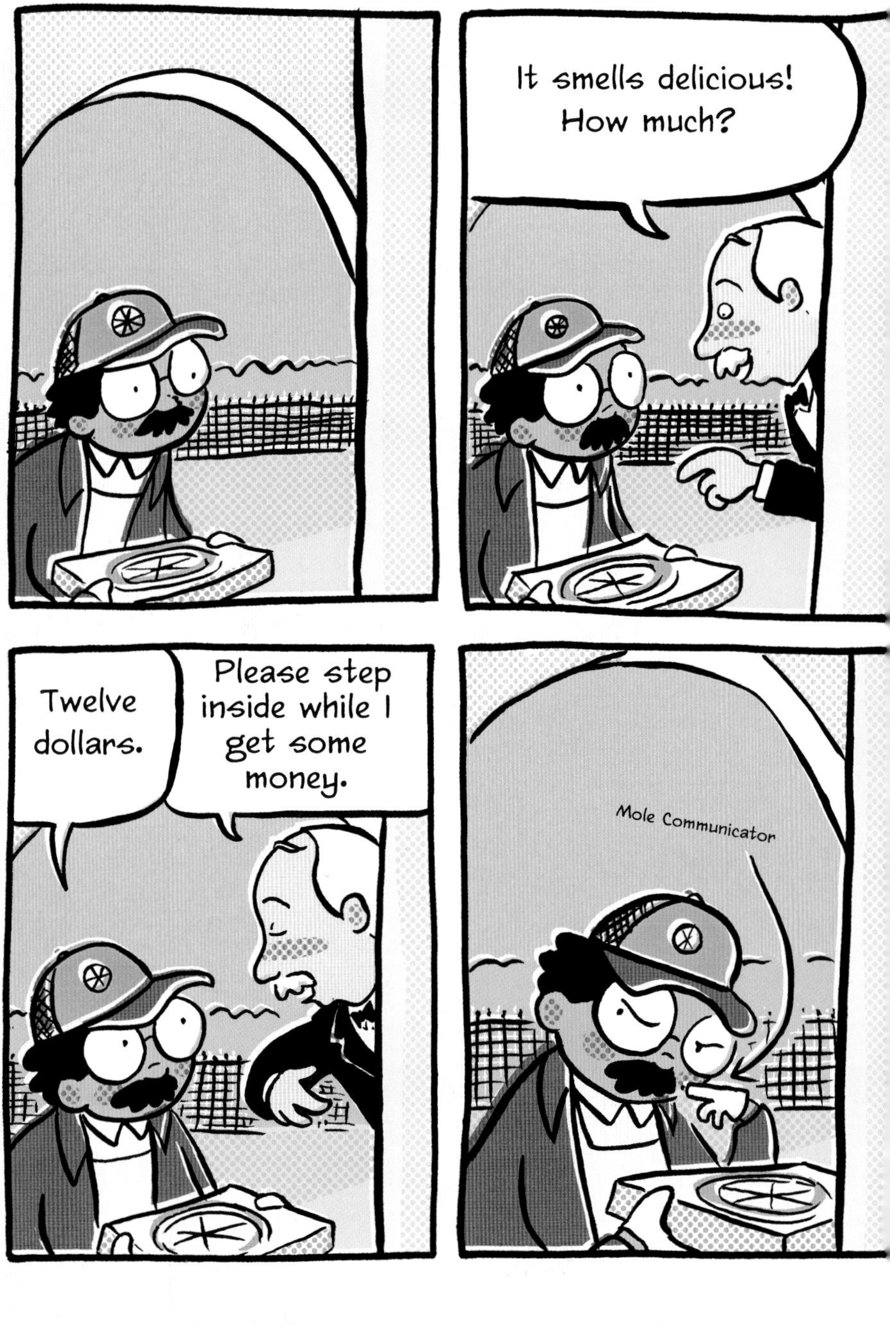
It smells delicious! How much?
Twelve dollars.
Please step inside while I get some money.
Mole Communicator

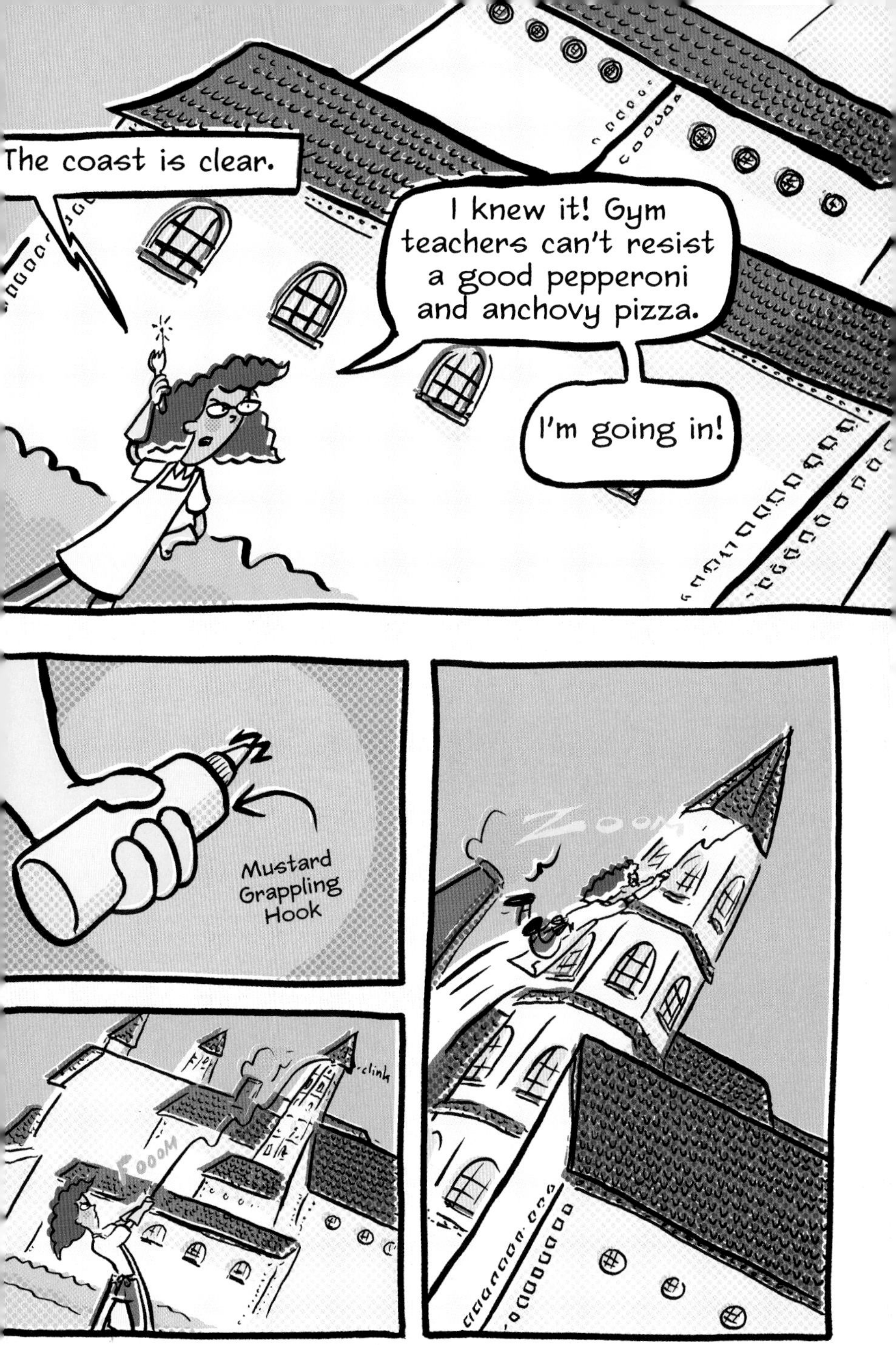
The coast is clear.
I knew it! Gym teachers can't resist a good pepperoni and anchovy pizza.
I'm going in!
Mustard Grappling Hook
FOOOM
clink
ZOOM

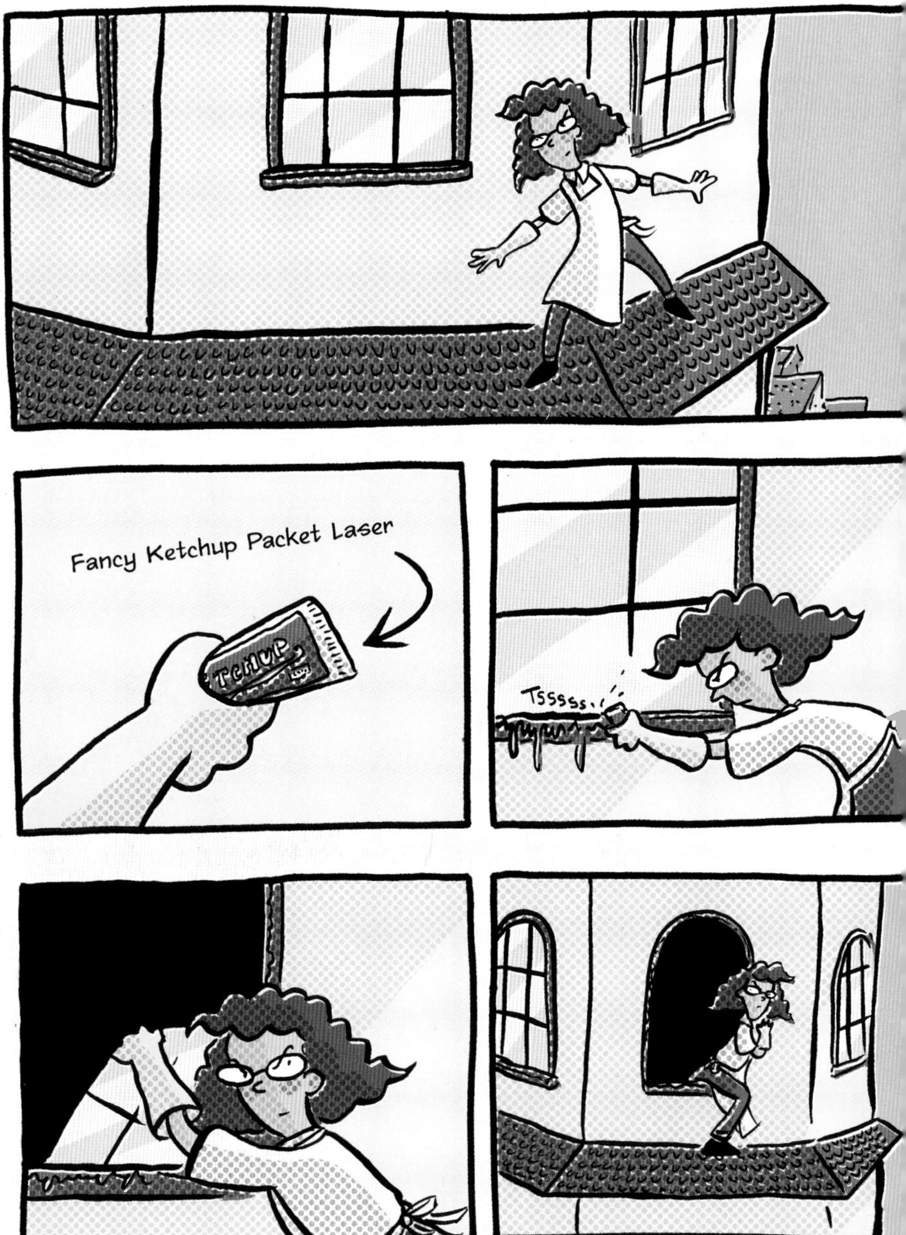
Fancy Ketchup Packet Laser
TCHUP
Tssssss

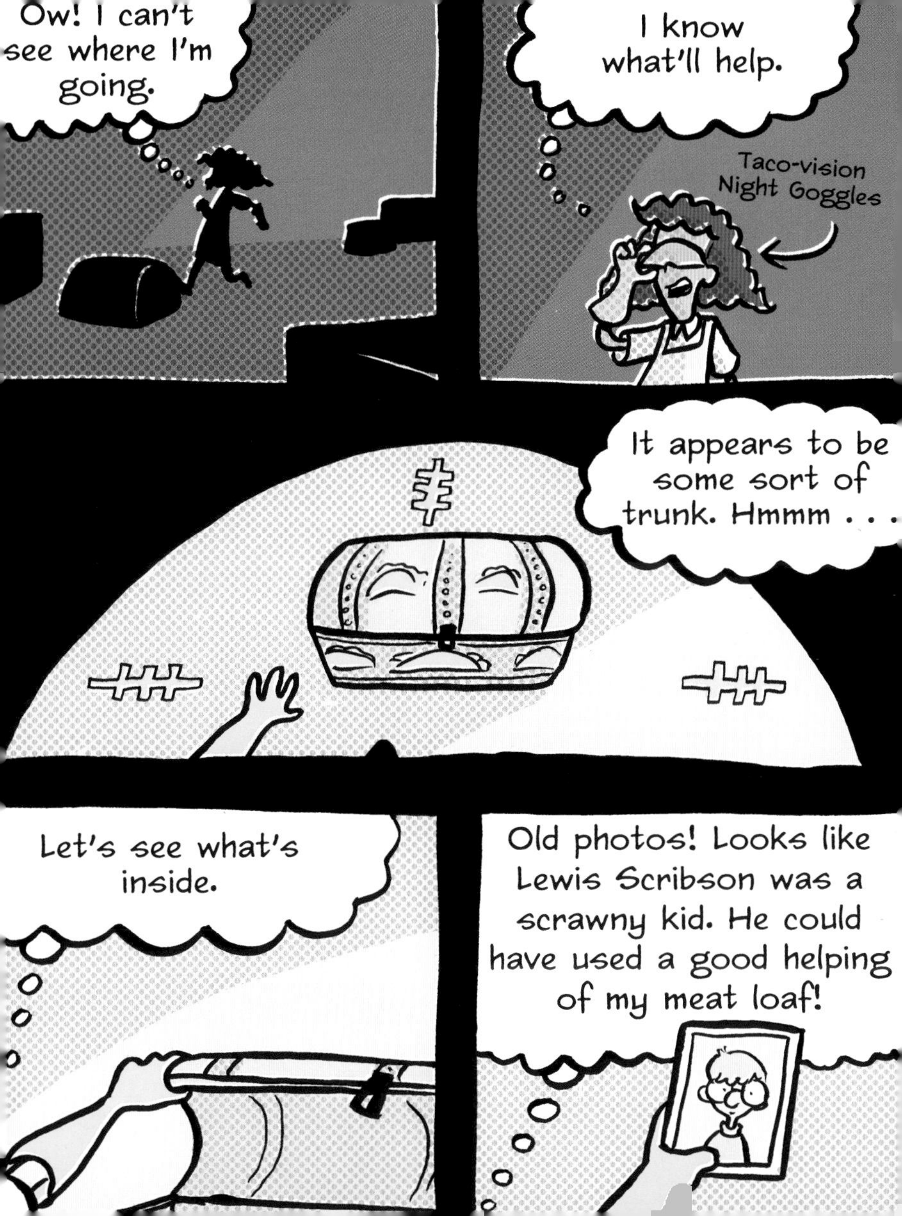
Ow! I can't see where I'm going.
I know what'll help.
Taco-vision Night Goggles
It appears to be some sort of trunk. Hmmm . . .
Let's see what's inside.
Old photos! Looks like Lewis Scribson was a scrawny kid. He could have used a good helping of my meat loaf!

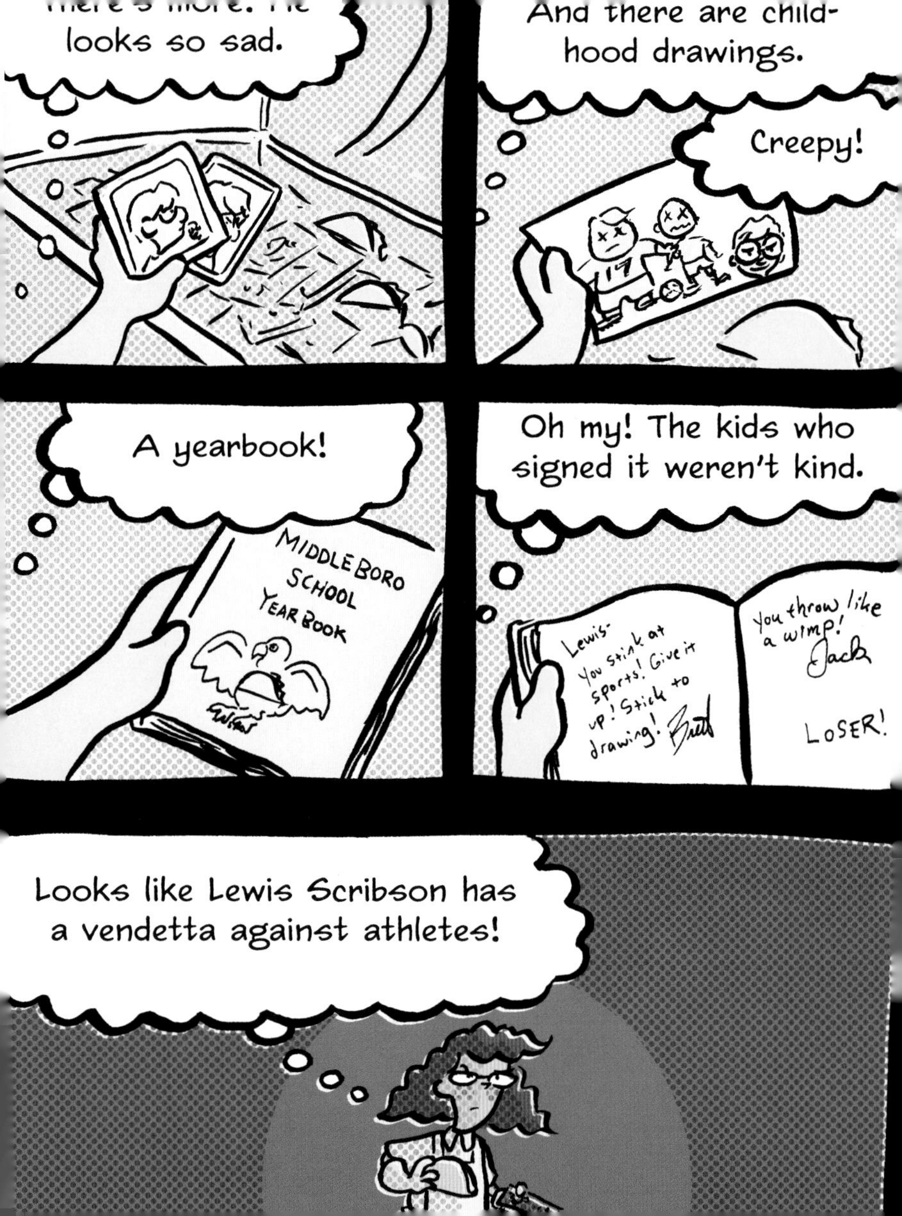
looks so sad.
And there are child-hood drawings.
Creepy!
A yearbook!
MIDDLE BORO SCHOOL YEAR BOOK
Oh my! The kids who signed it weren't kind.
Lewis- You stink at sports! Give it up! Stick to drawing!
You throw like a wimp! Jack
LOSER!
Looks like Lewis Scribson has a vendetta against athletes!

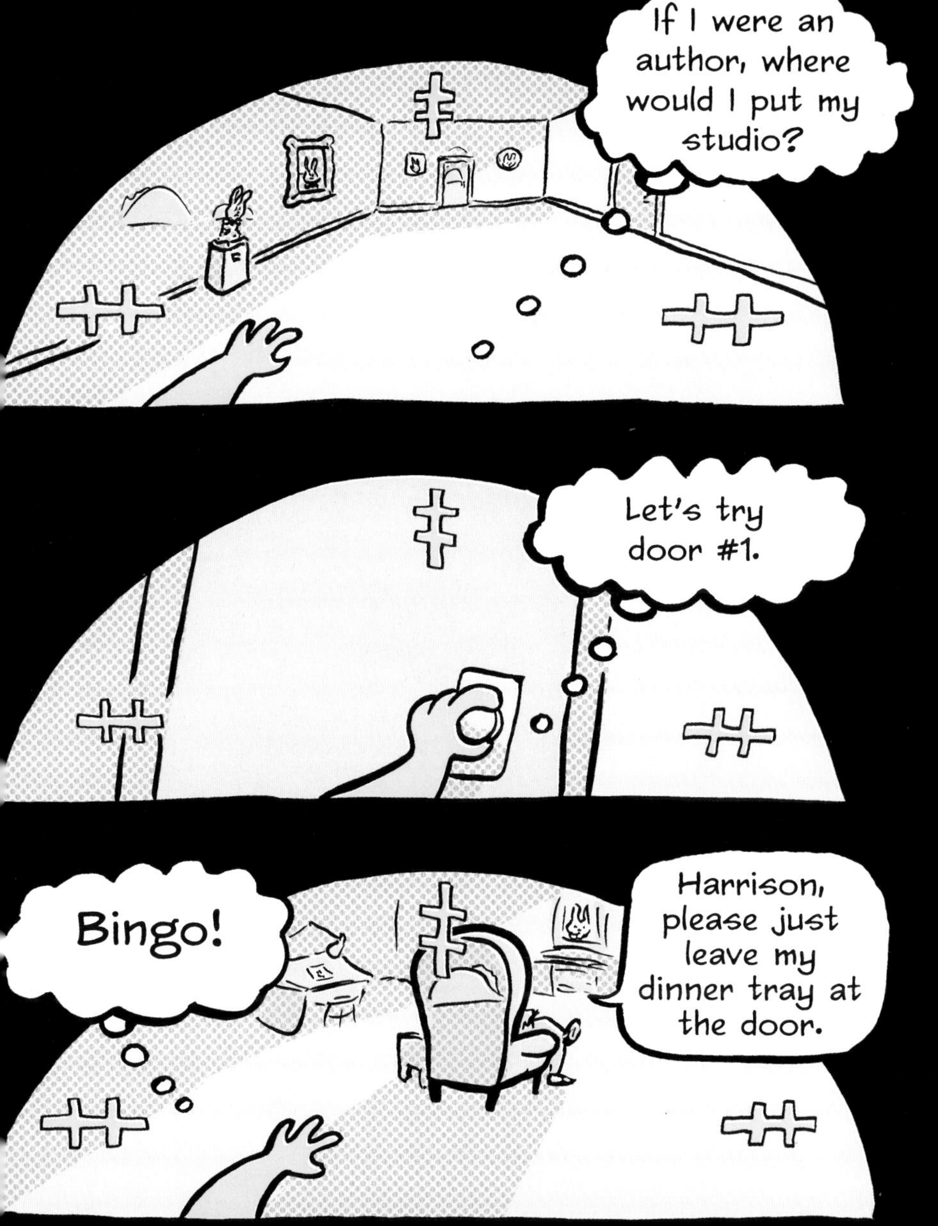
If I were an author, where would I put my studio?
Let's try door #1.
Bingo!
Harrison, please just leave my dinner tray at the door.

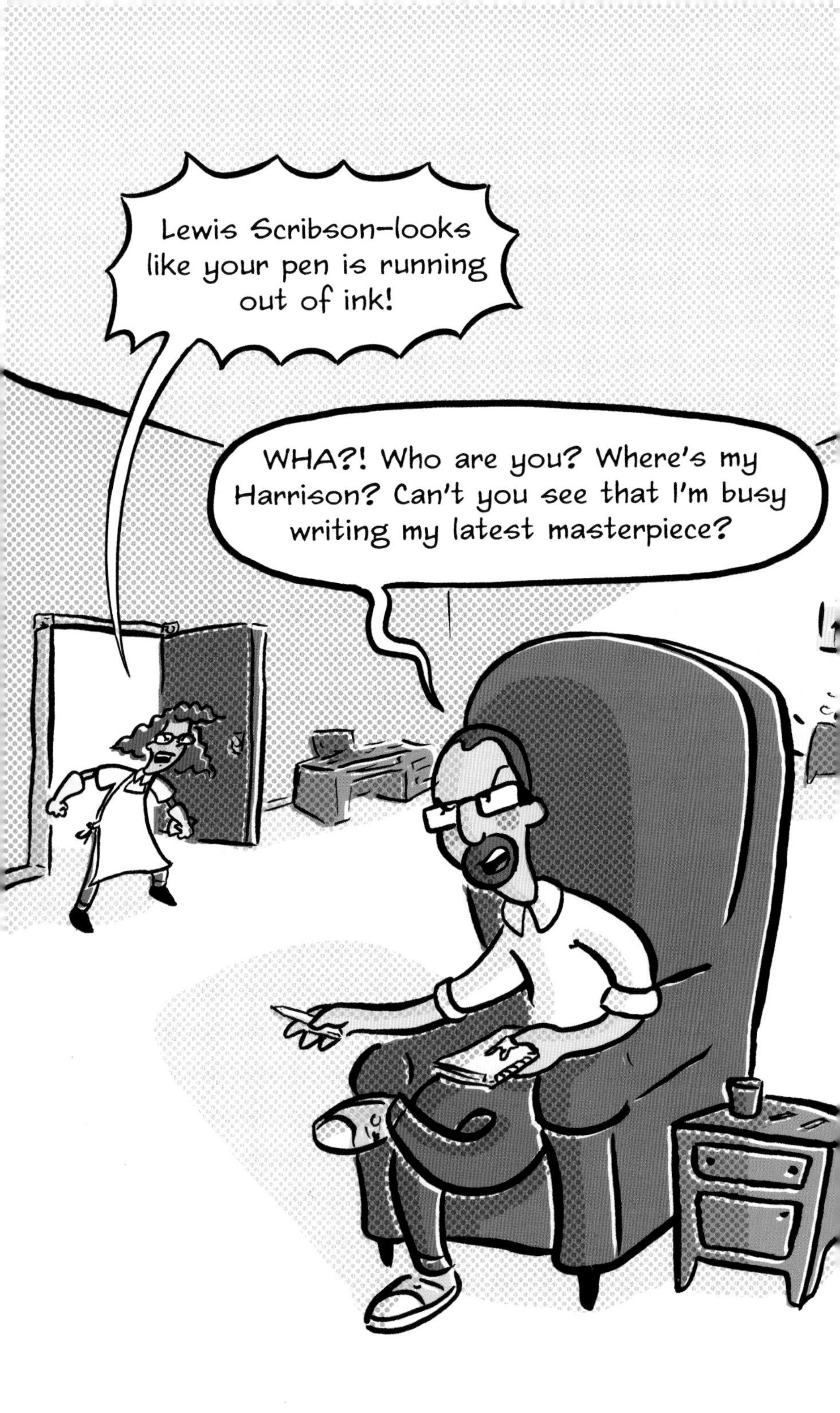
Lewis Scribson—looks like your pen is running out of ink!
WHA?! Who are you? Where's my Harrison? Can't you see that I'm busy writing my latest masterpiece?

Where's Coach Birkby?!

Wait—I recognize you—you're that lunch lady from that school yesterday. . . .

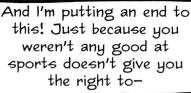

And I'm putting an end to this! Just because you weren't any good at sports doesn't give you the right to—

It's not about that!

You kidnapped phys-ed teachers because you lacked athletic skills as a kid!

You're ruining the story! Leave it to the professional!

You see, as a kid I was terrible at sports.

Do you know the pain of
being picked last for teams?

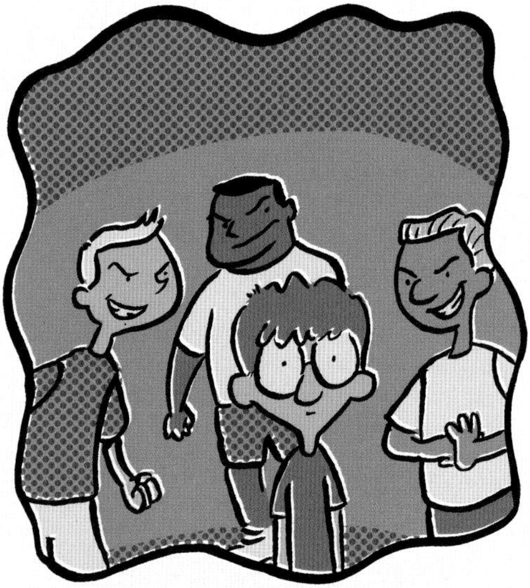

My gym teacher, Mr. Zatyrka,
only made it worse.

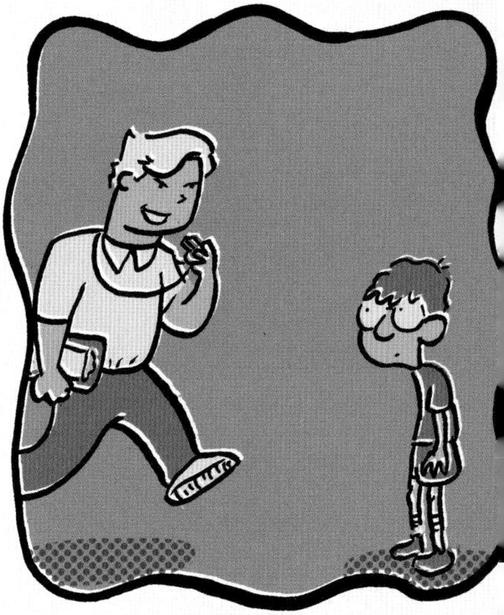

He made me play
dodgeball . . .

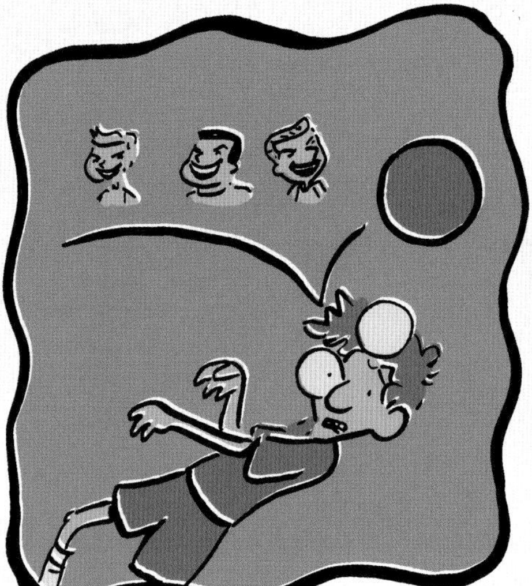

. . . and football.
It was dreadful!

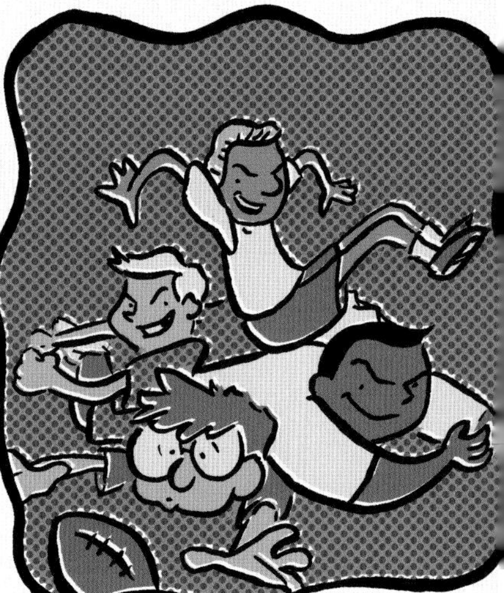

I had to climb the ropes . . .

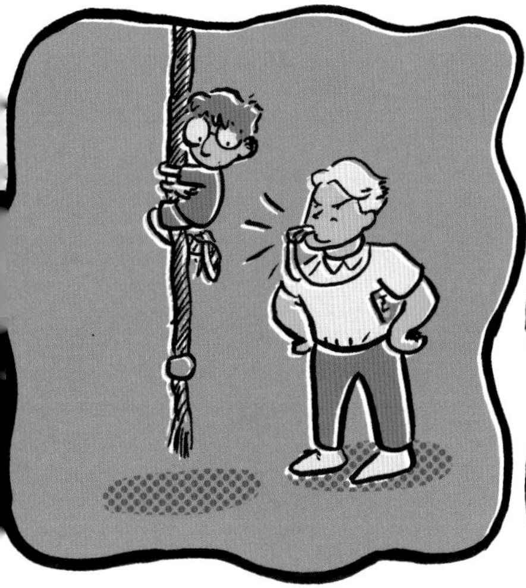

. . . and when I would fall . . .

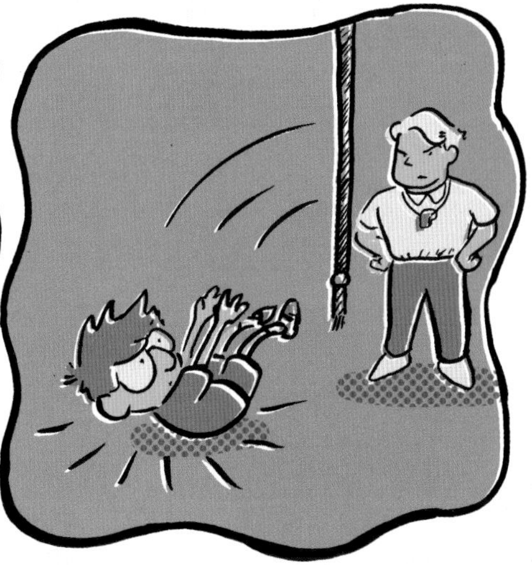

. . . he would make fun of me with all the other kids.

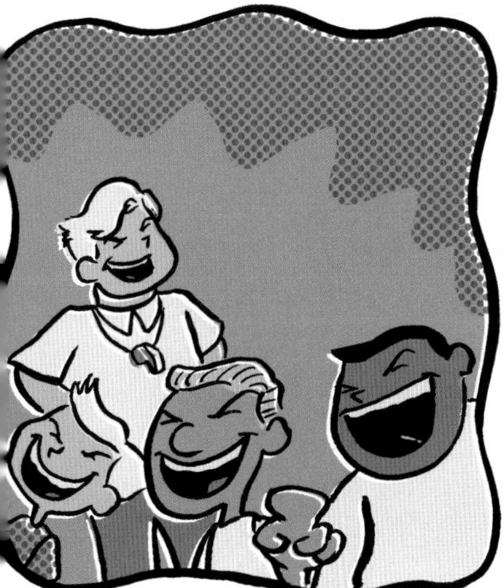

How I *hated* him.

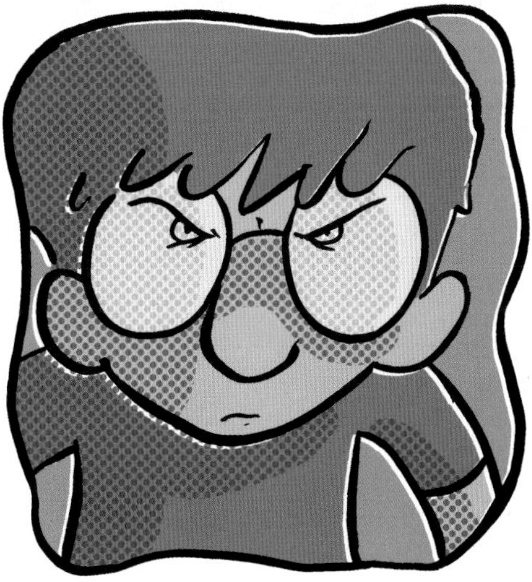

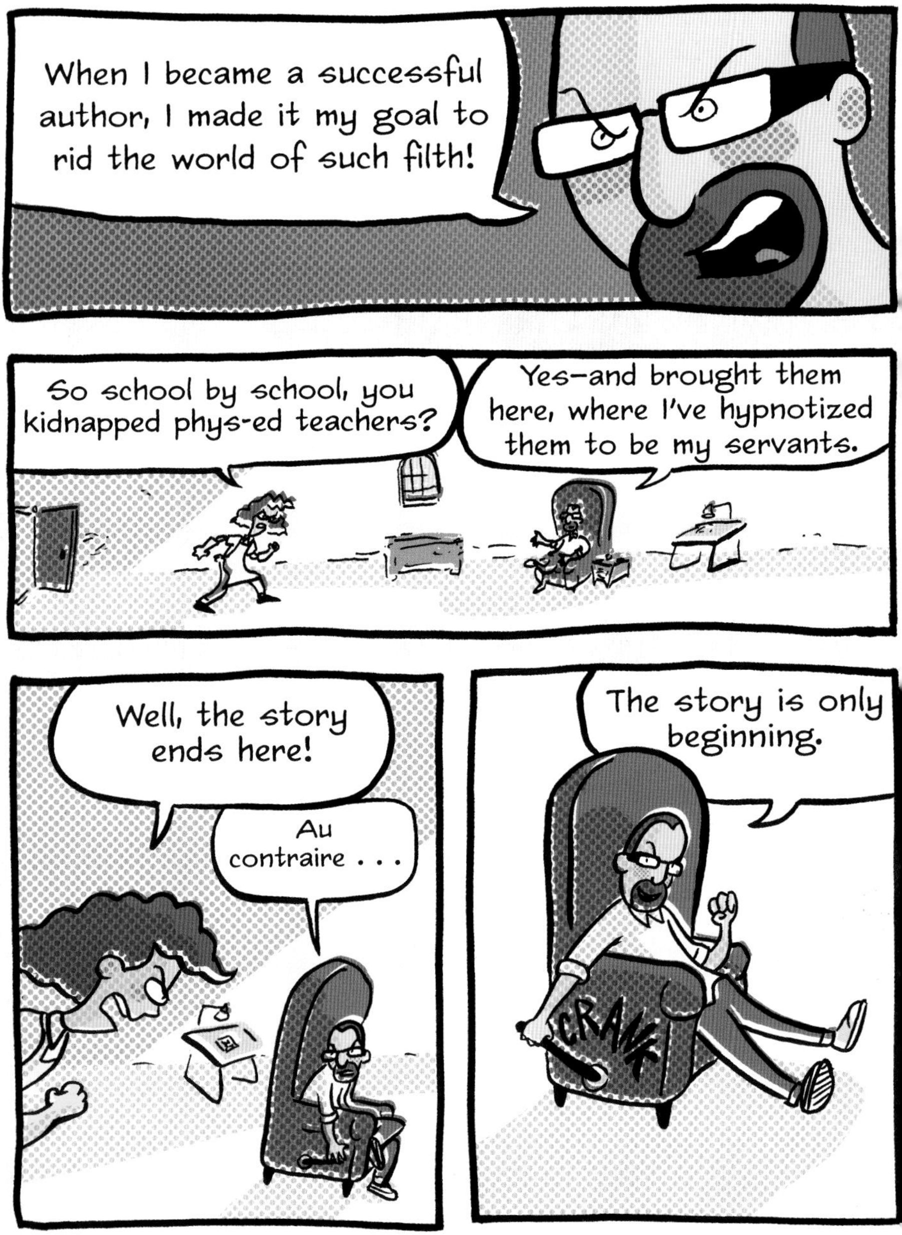
When I became a successful author, I made it my goal to rid the world of such filth!
So school by school, you kidnapped phys-ed teachers?
Yes—and brought them here, where I've hypnotized them to be my servants.
Well, the story ends here!
Au contraire . . .
The story is only beginning.
CRANK

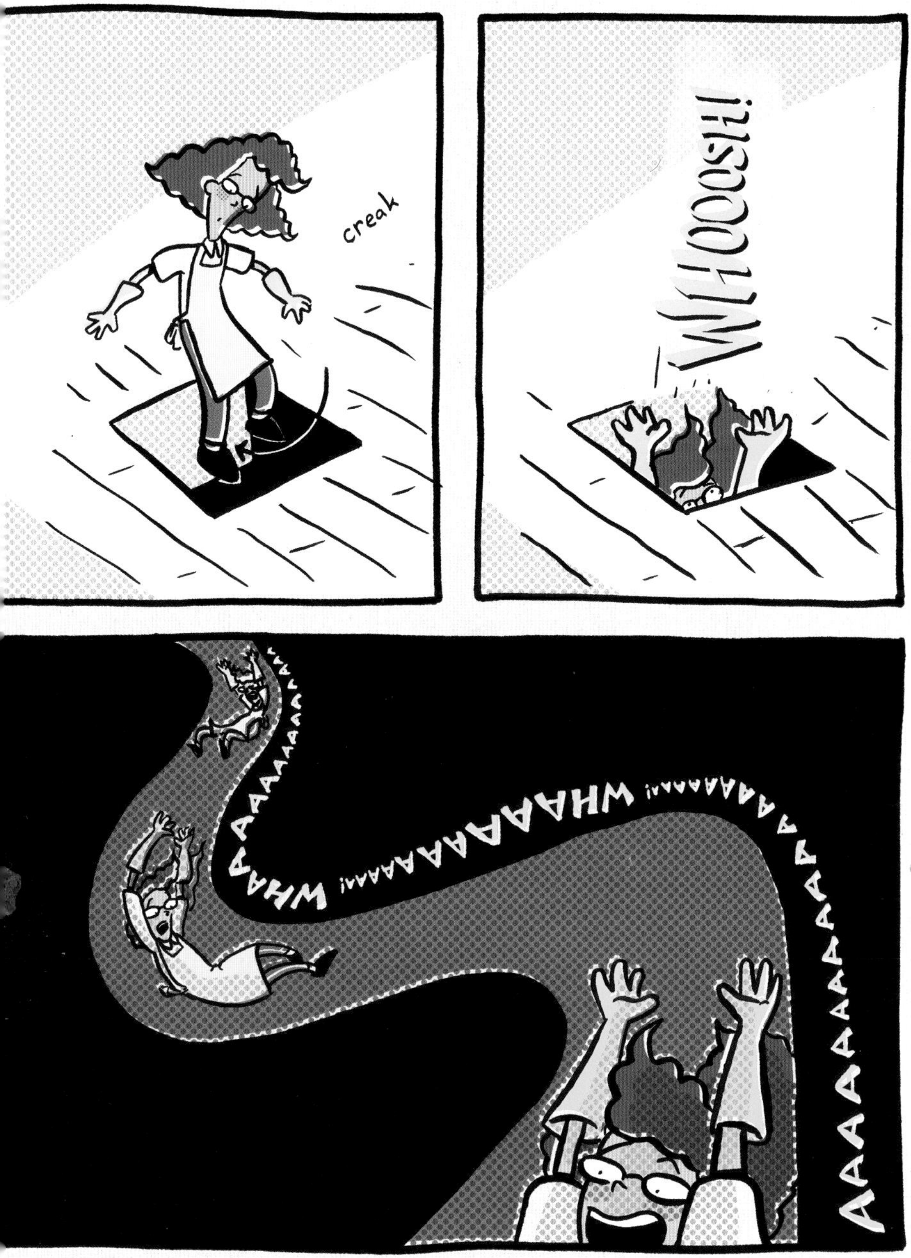
creak
WHOOOSH!
WHAAAAAAAAAAAAA!!!
WHAAAAAAAAAAA!!!
AAAAAAAAAAAAAAAAAA

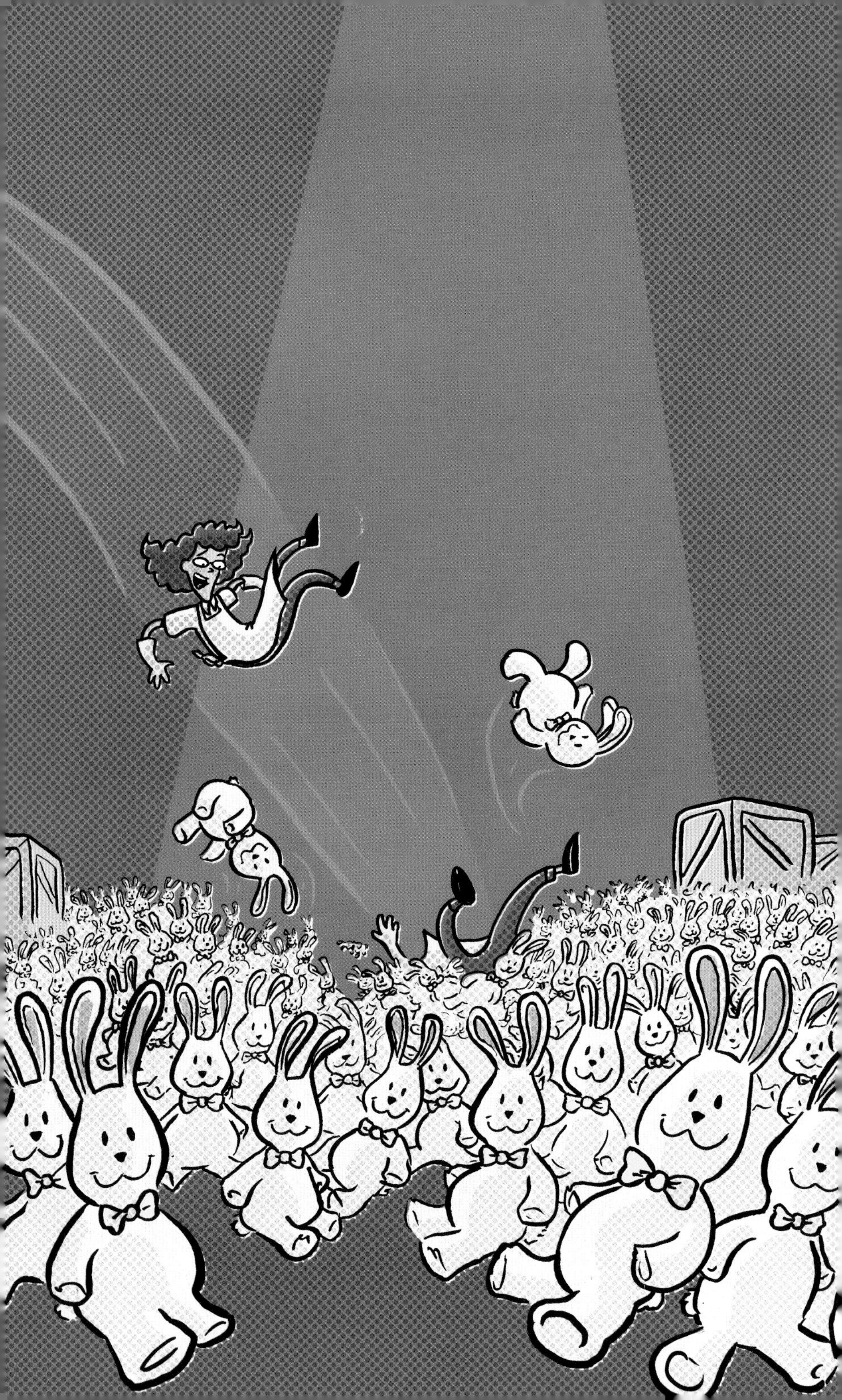

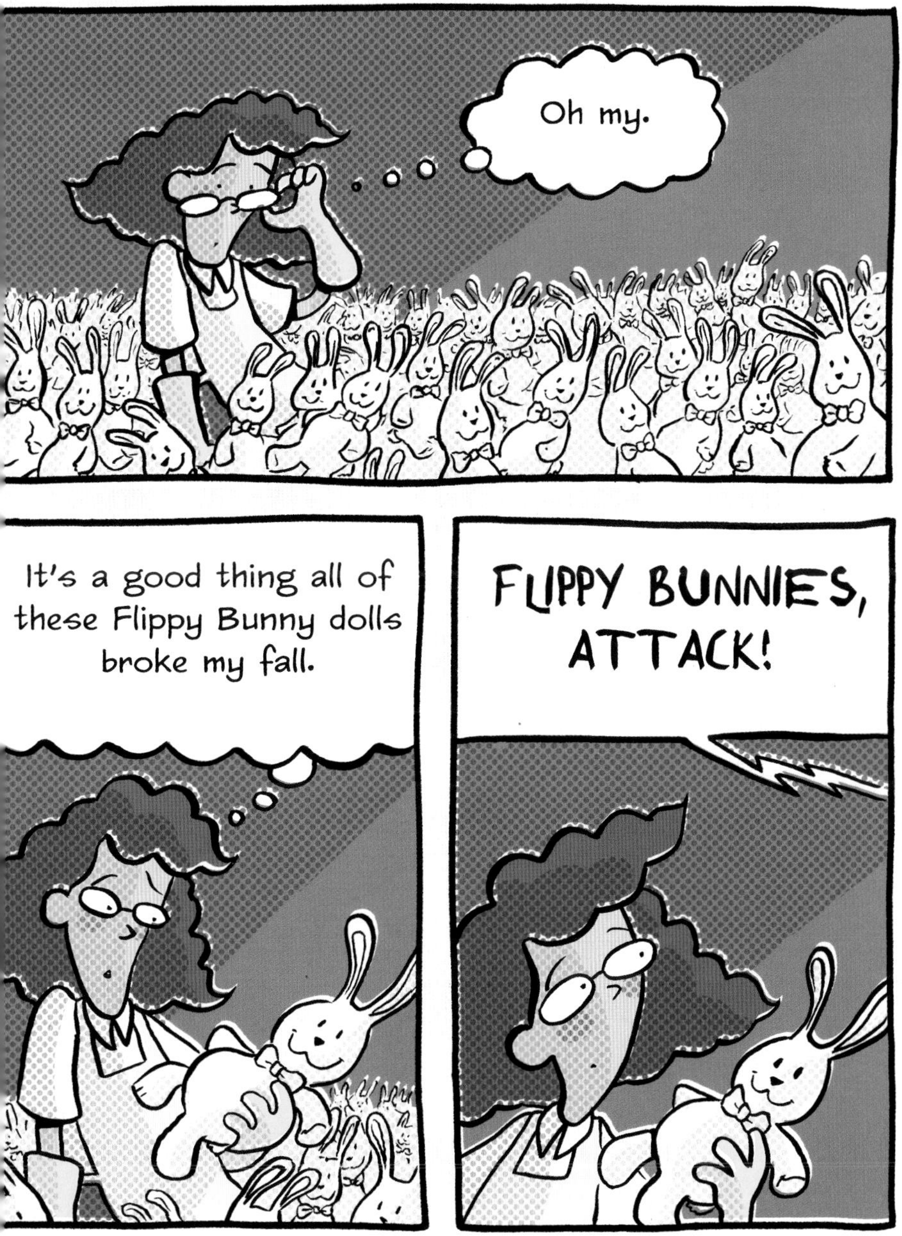
Oh my.
It's a good thing all of these Flippy Bunny dolls broke my fall.
FLIPPY BUNNIES, ATTACK!

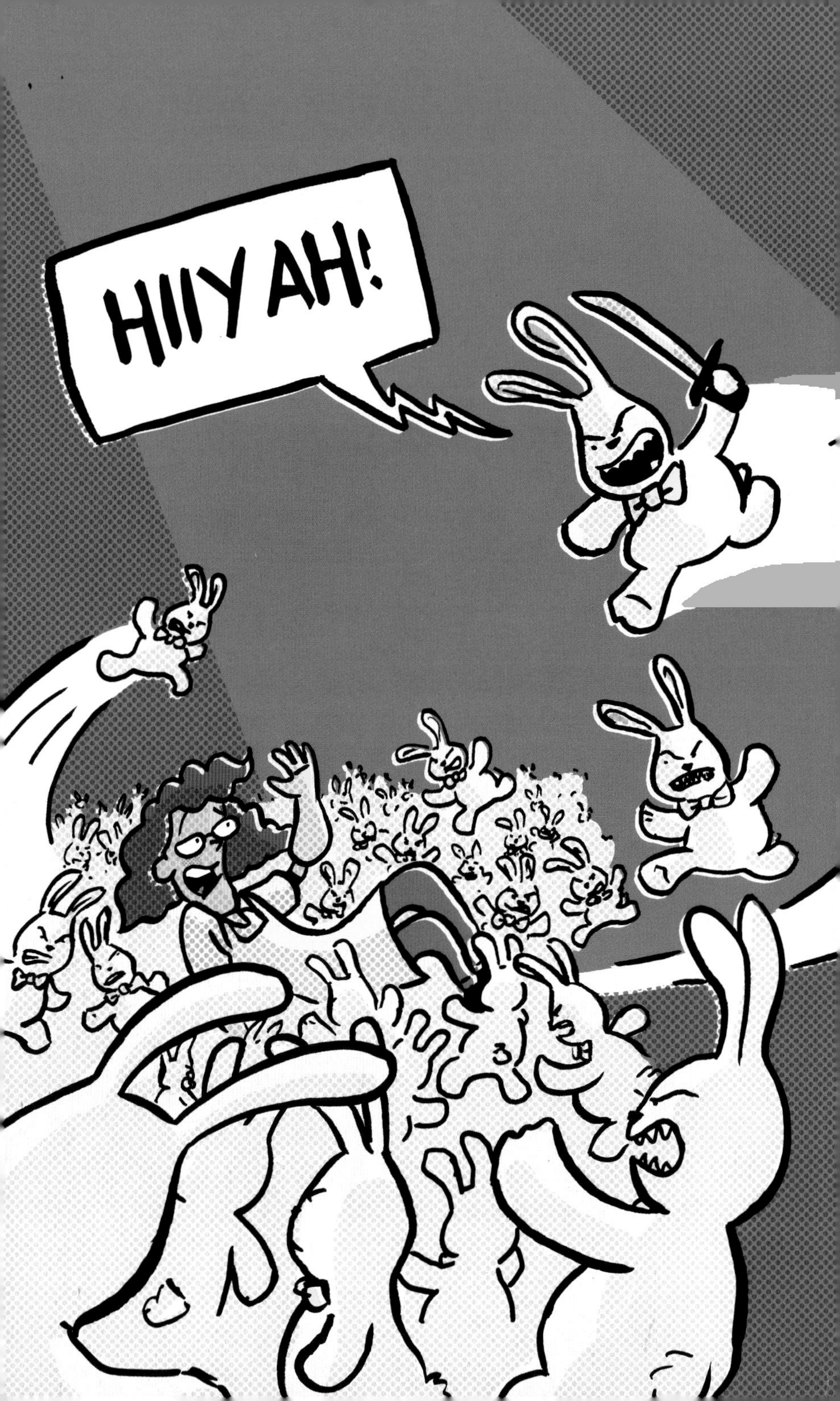
HIIYAH!

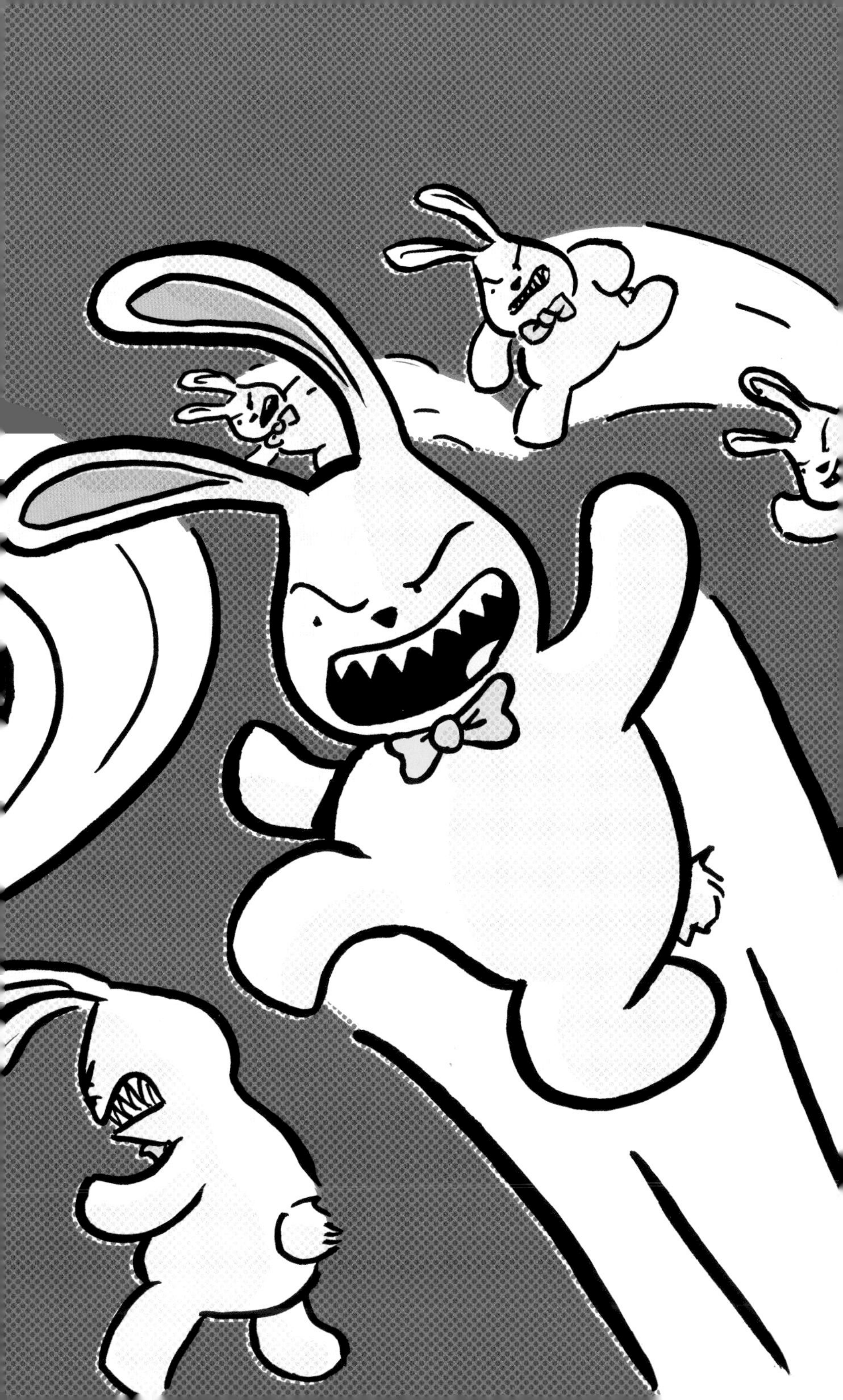

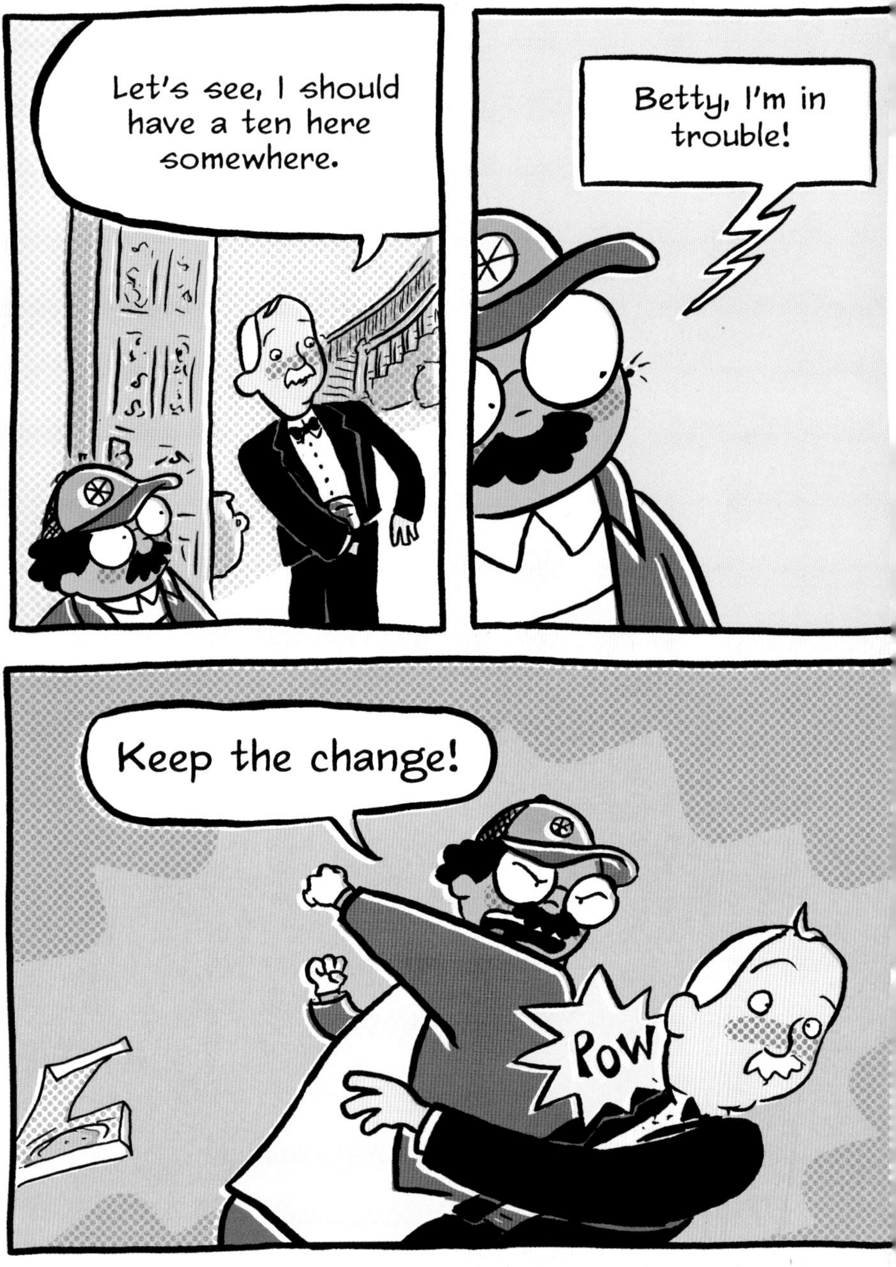
Let's see, I should have a ten here somewhere.
Betty, I'm in trouble!
Keep the change!
POW

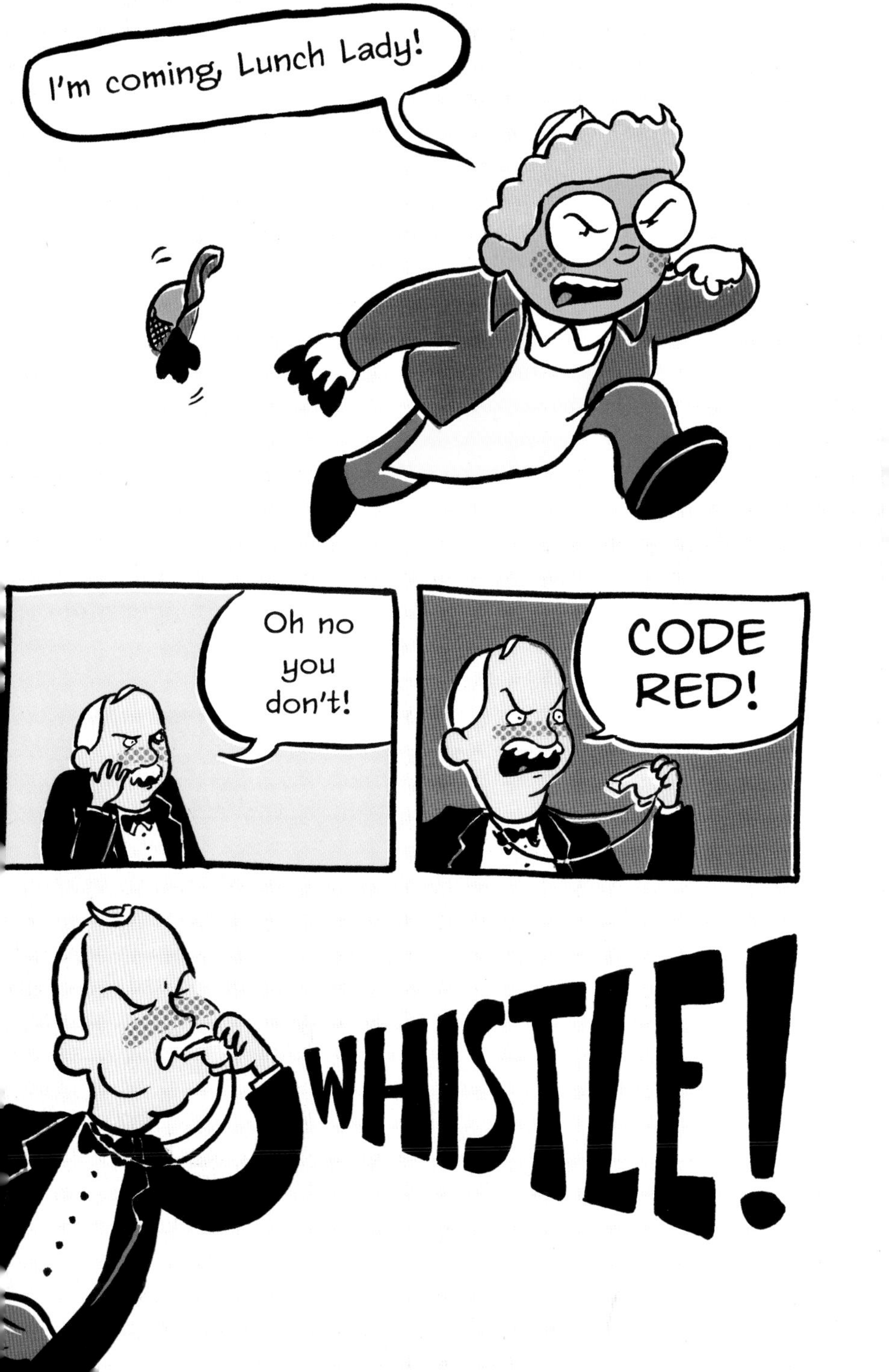
I'm coming, Lunch Lady!
Oh no you don't!
CODE RED!
WHISTLE!

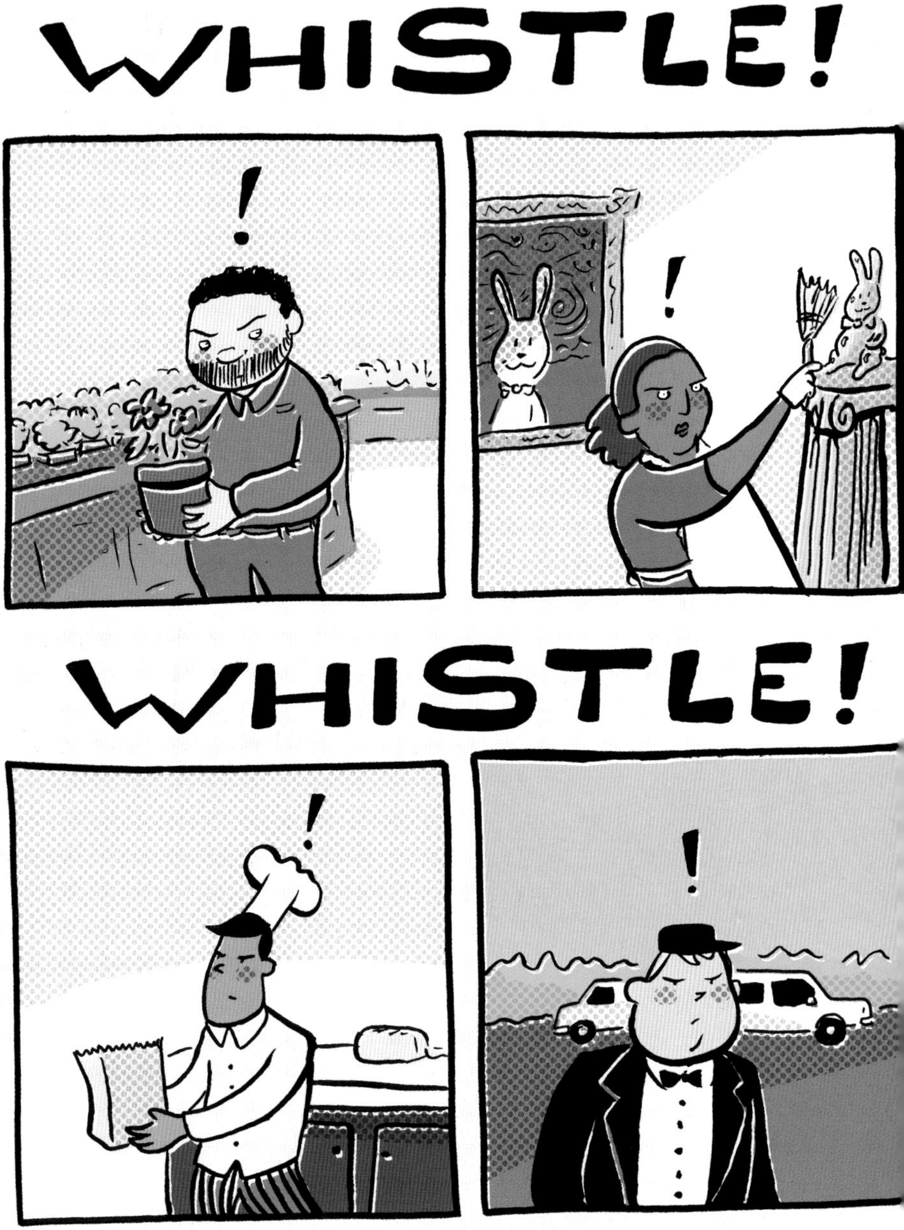
WHISTLE!
WHISTLE!

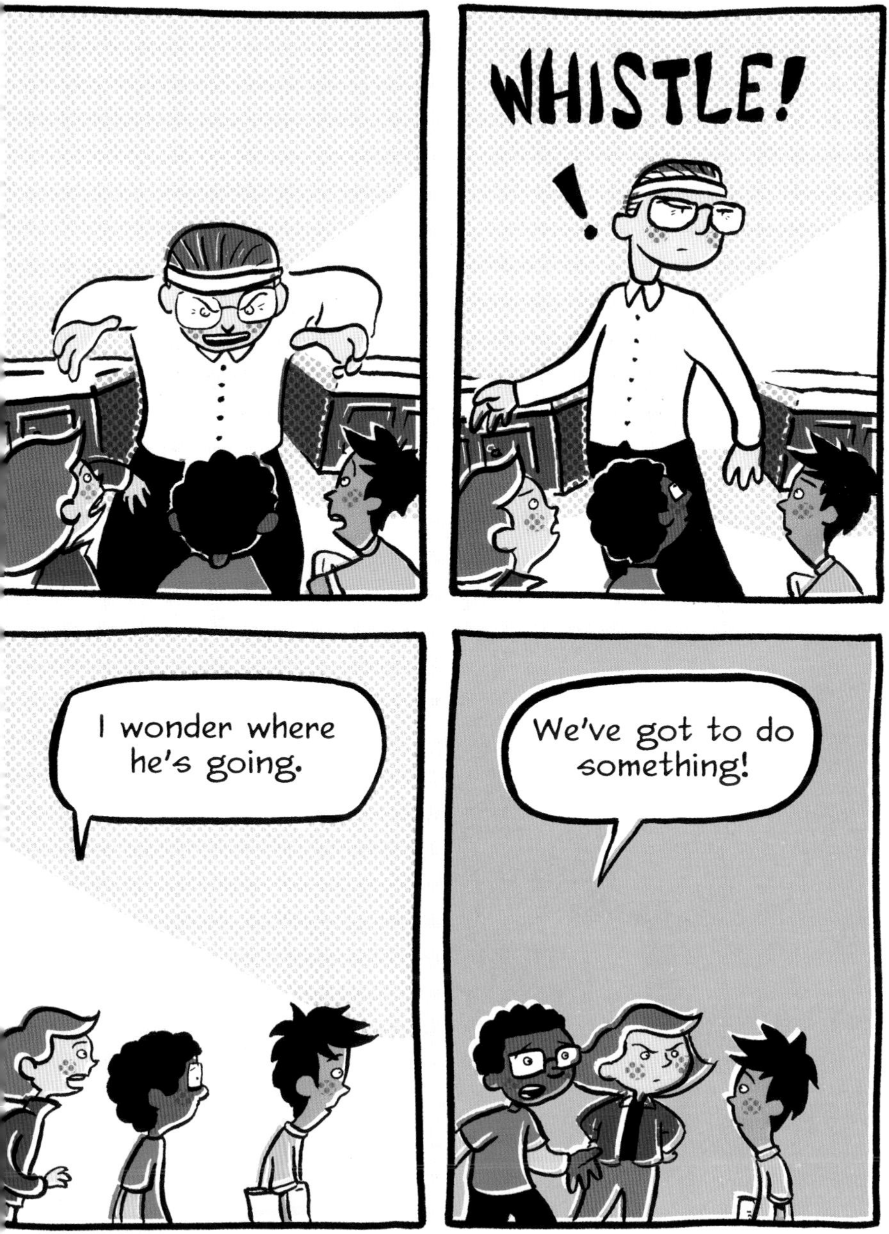
WHISTLE!
!
I wonder where he's going.
We've got to do something!

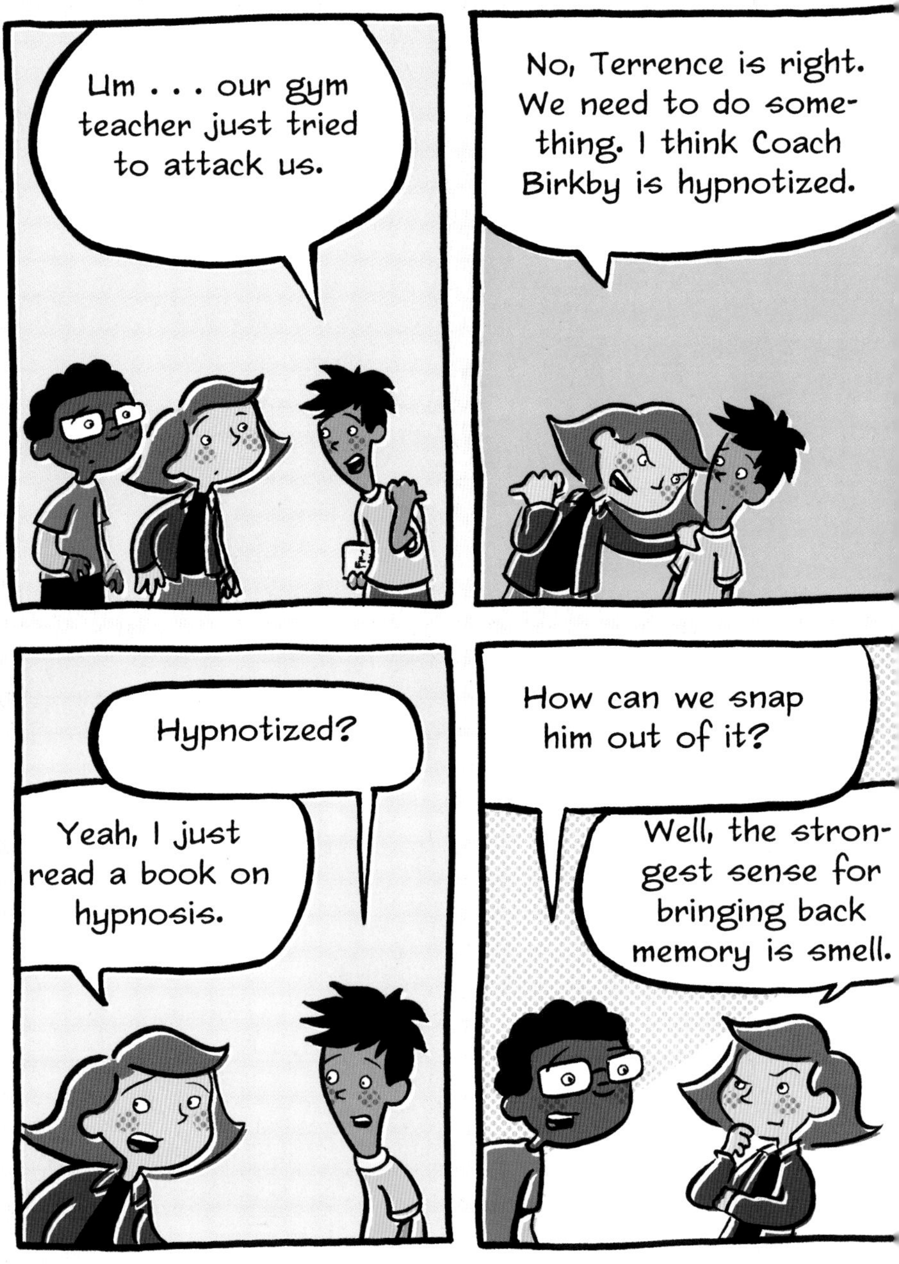
Um . . . our gym teacher just tried to attack us.
No, Terrence is right. We need to do something. I think Coach Birkby is hypnotized.
Hypnotized?
Yeah, I just read a book on hypnosis.
How can we snap him out of it?
Well, the strongest sense for bringing back memory is smell.

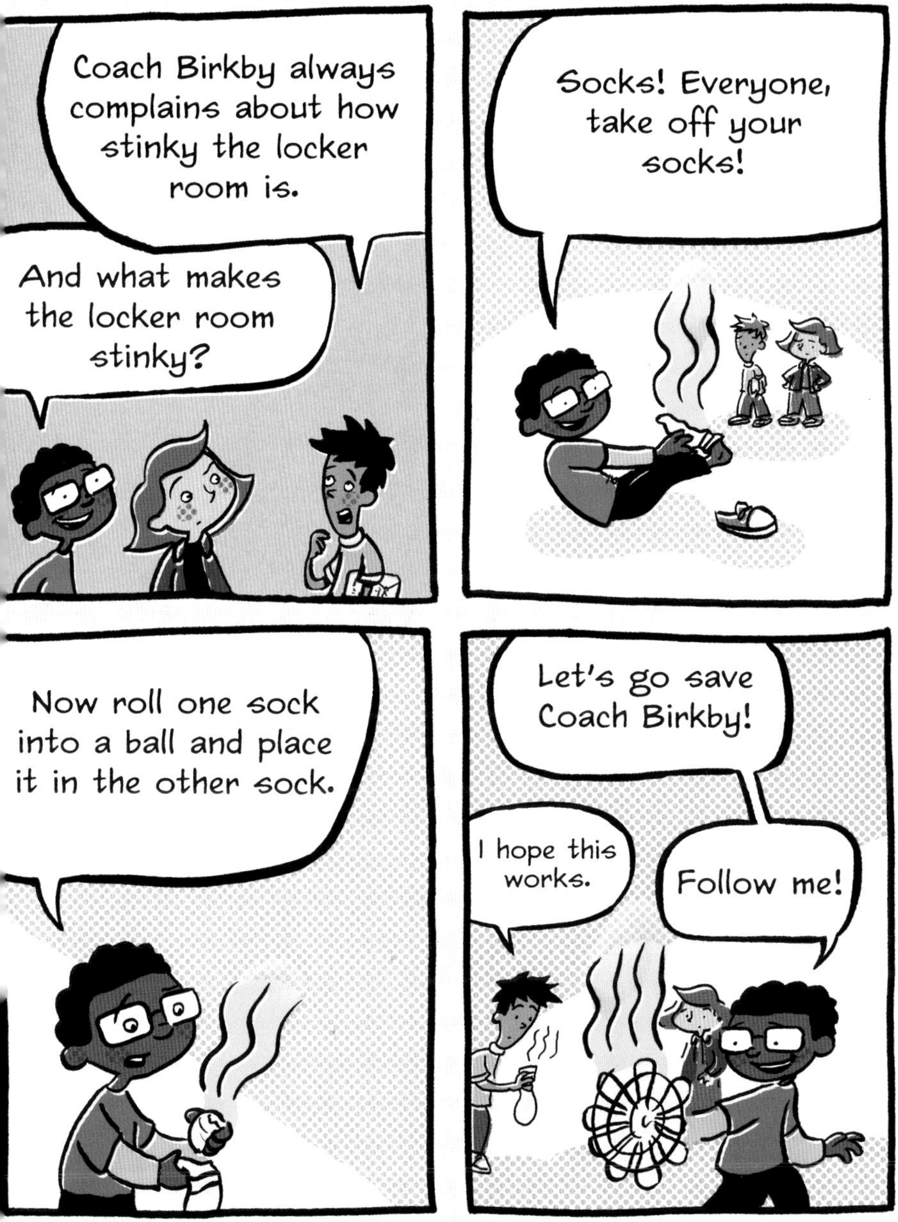
Coach Birkby always complains about how stinky the locker room is.
And what makes the locker room stinky?
Socks! Everyone, take off your socks!
Now roll one sock into a ball and place it in the other sock.
Let's go save Coach Birkby!
I hope this works.
Follow me!

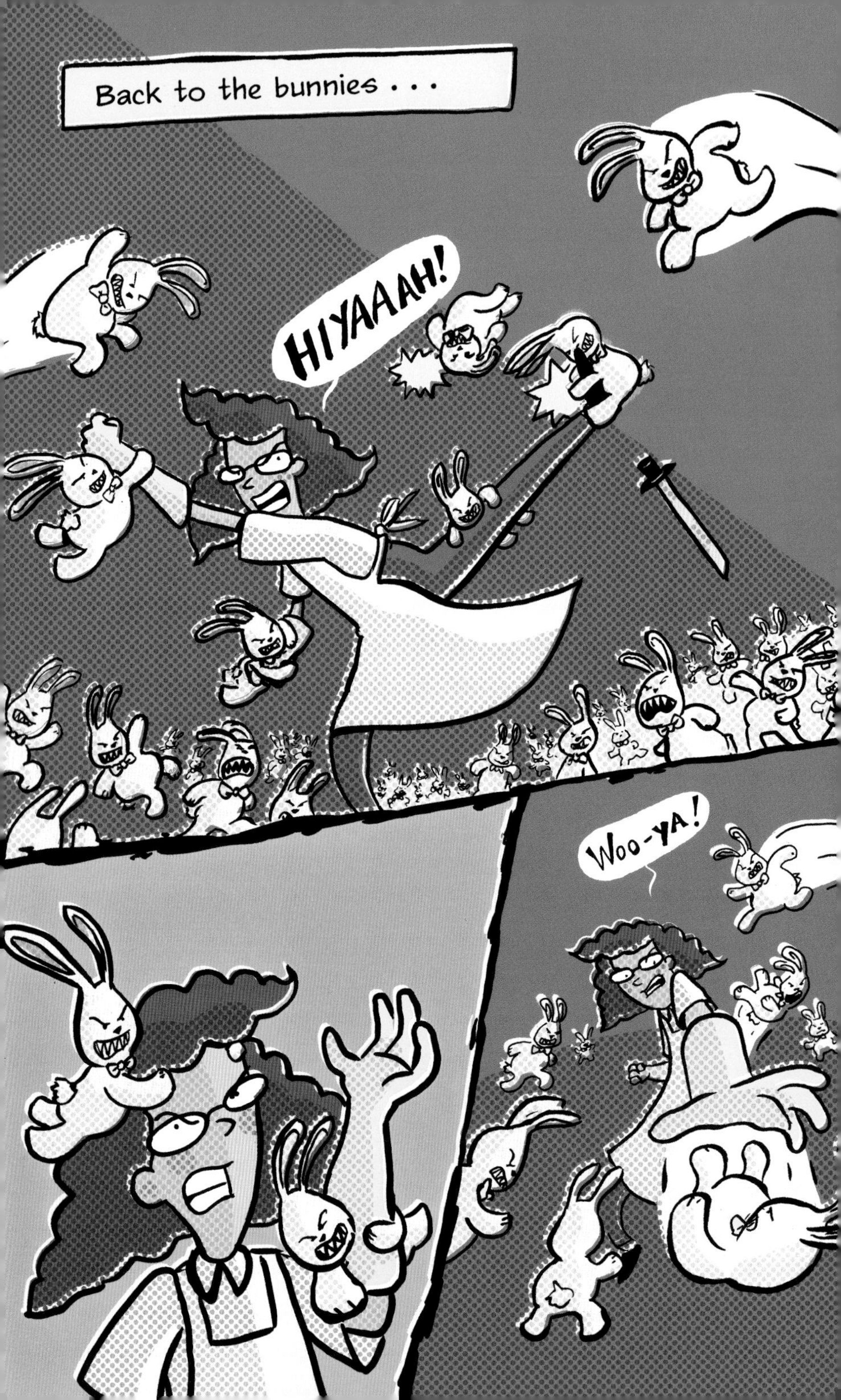
Back to the bunnies . . .
HIYAAAH!
Woo-YA!

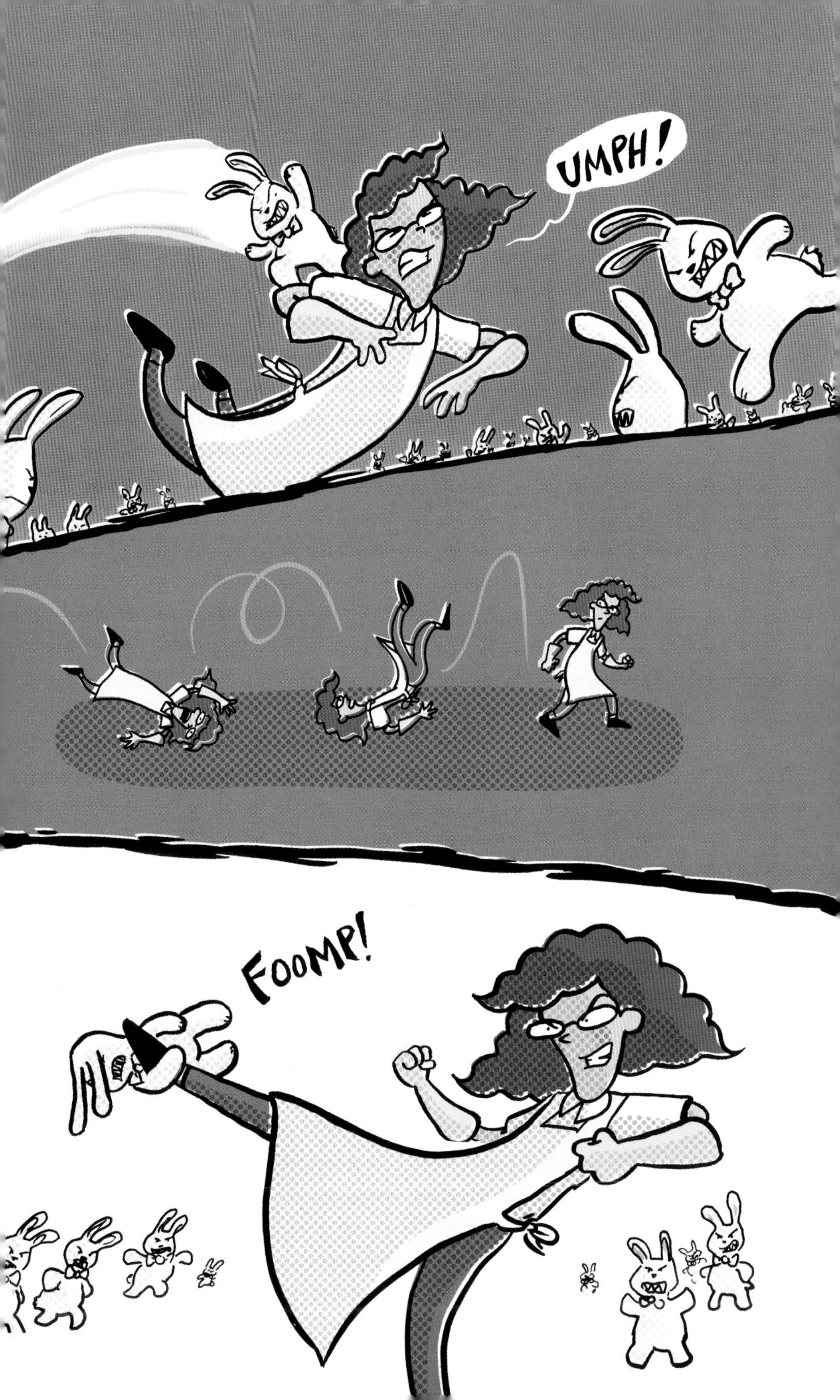
UMPH!
FOOMP!

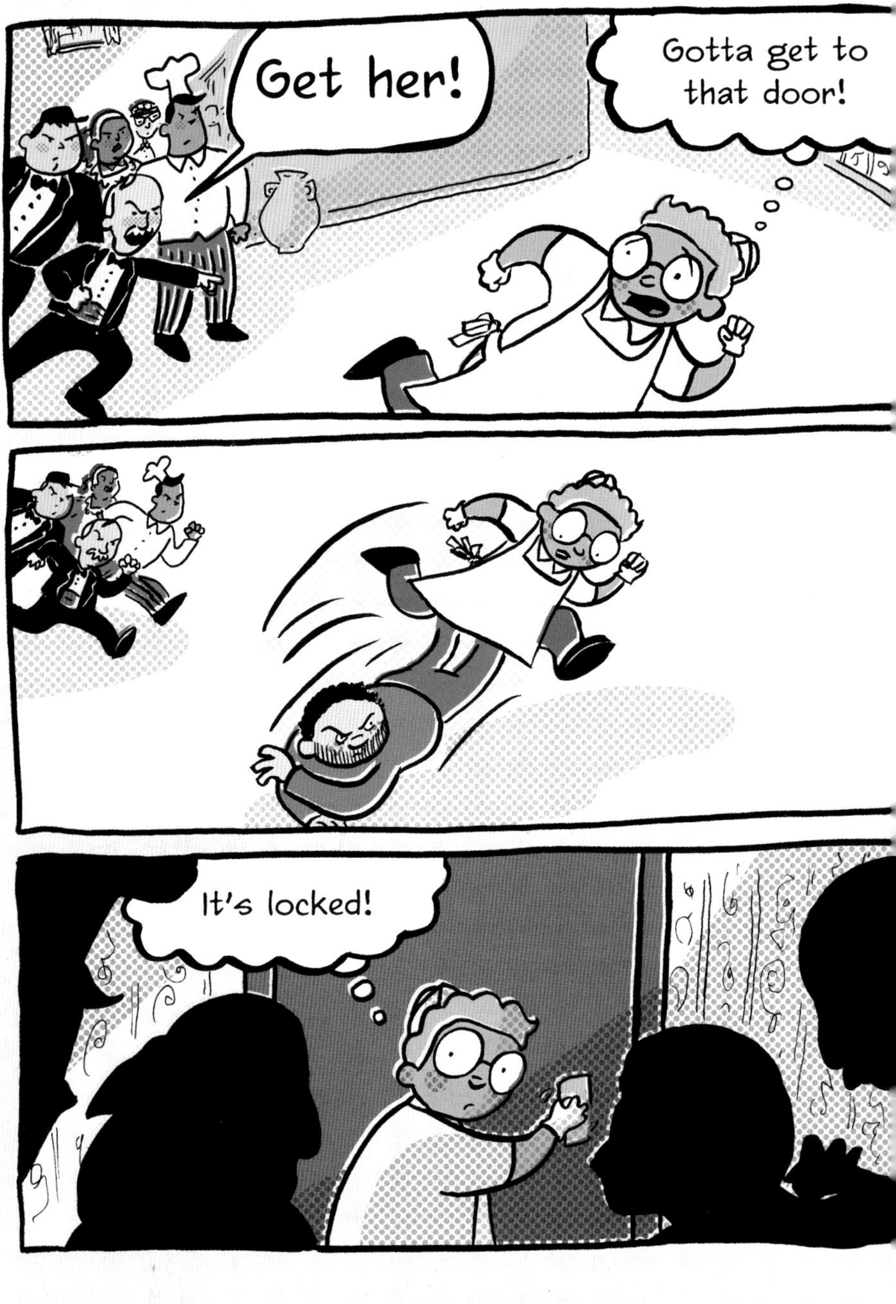
Get her!
Gotta get to that door!
It's locked!

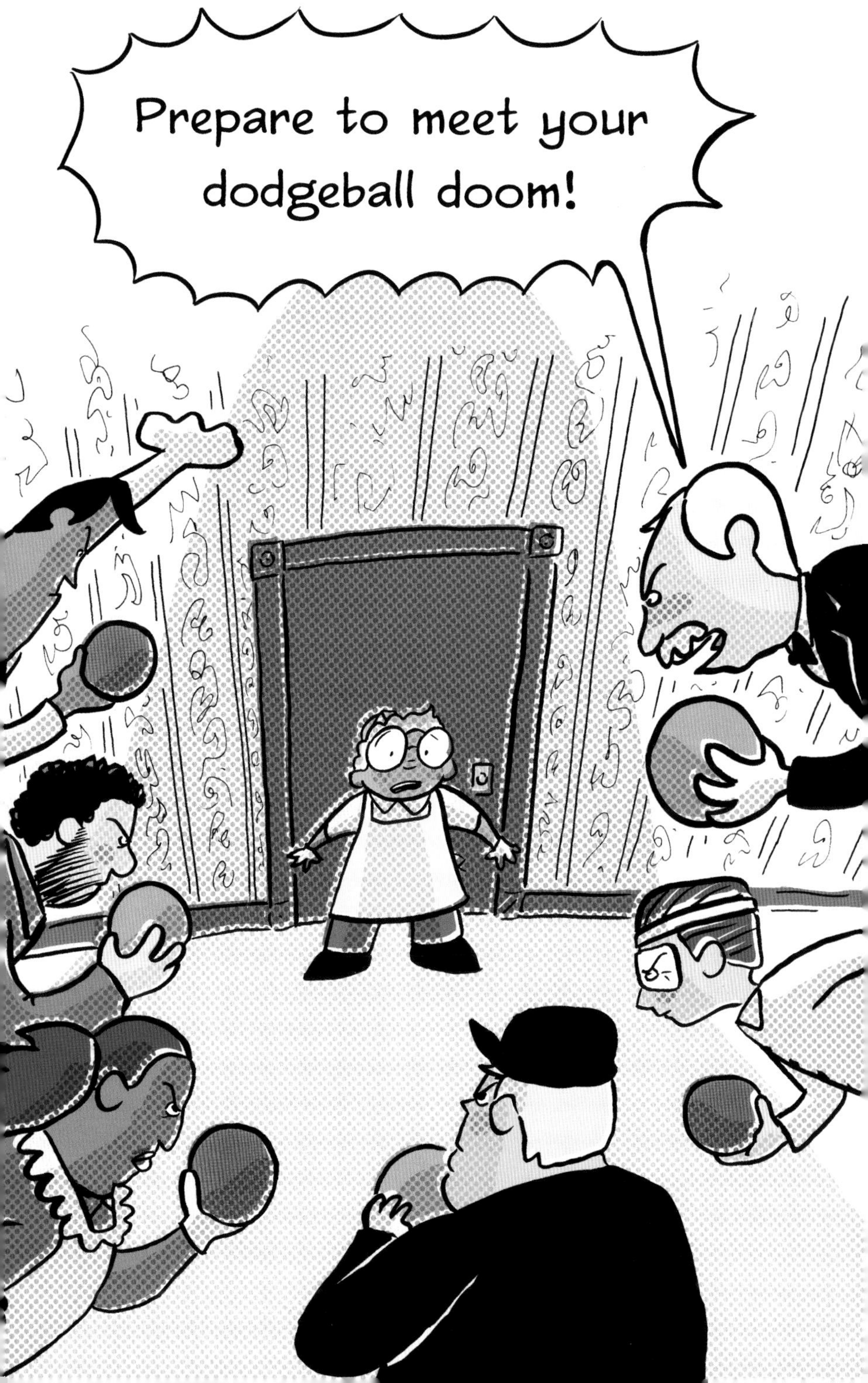
Prepare to meet your dodgeball doom!

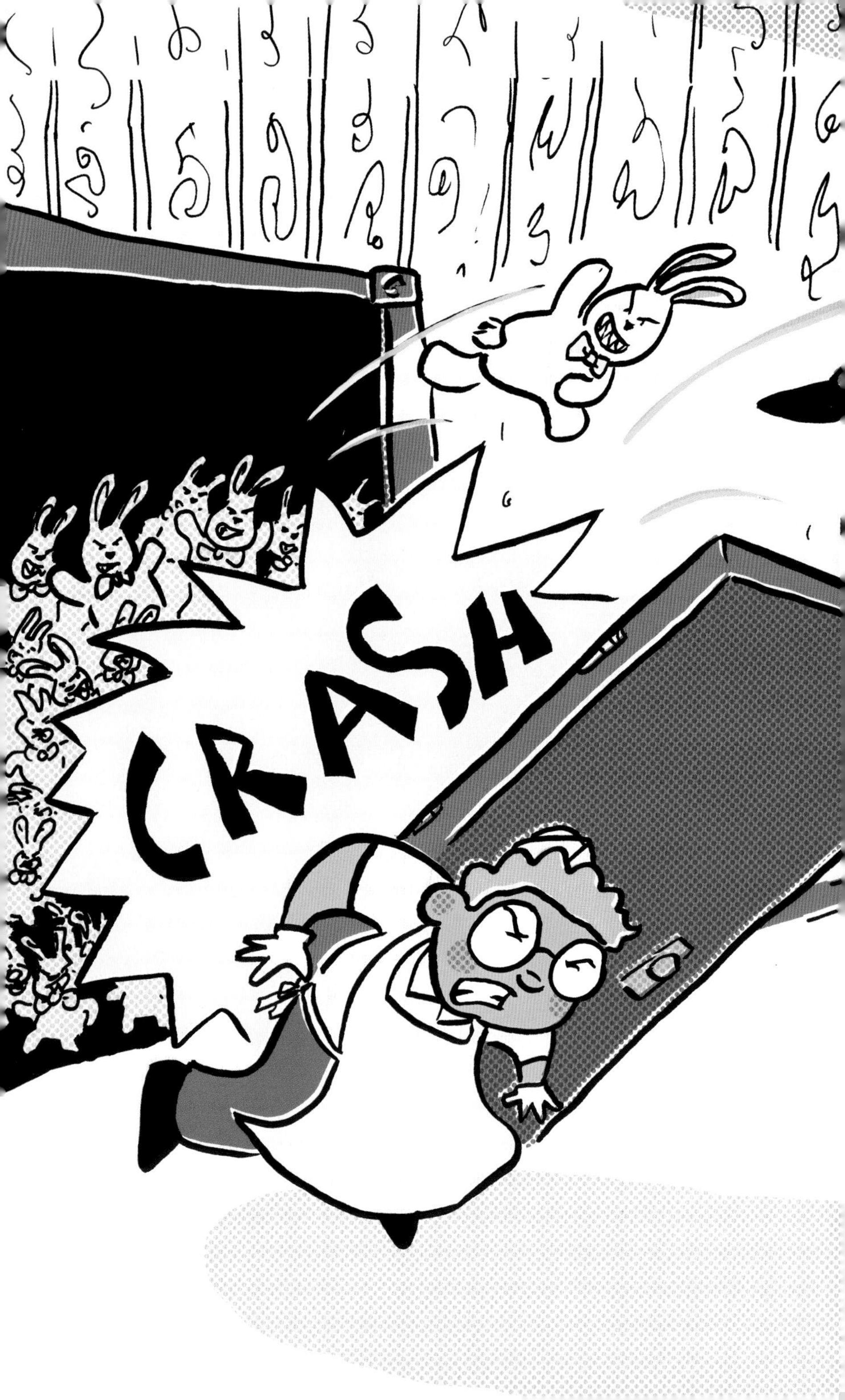
CRASH

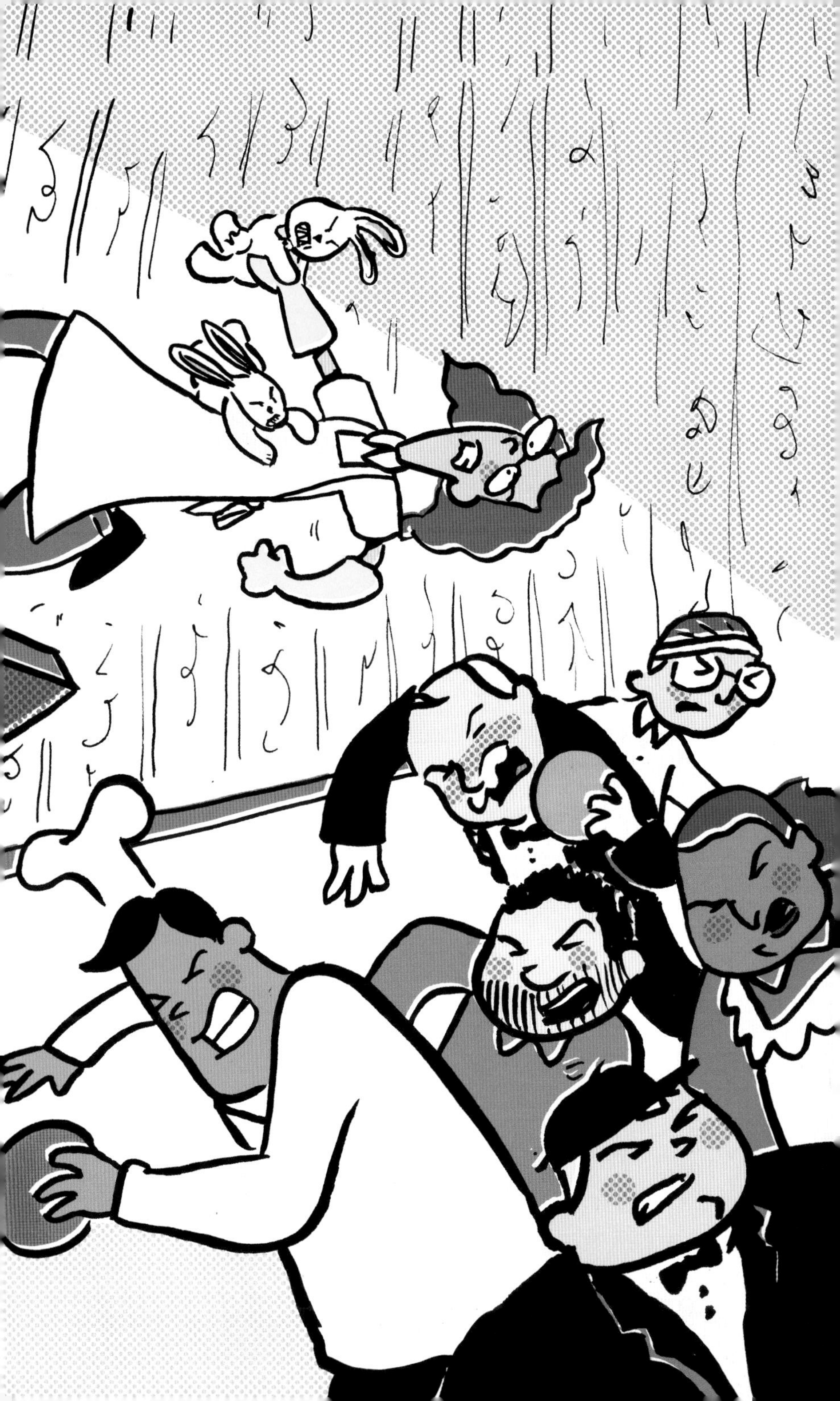

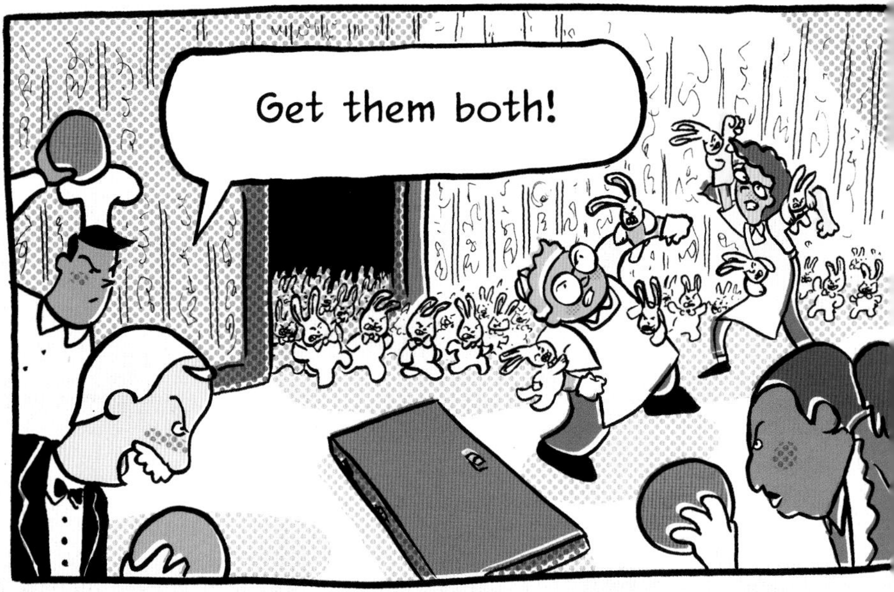
Get them both!

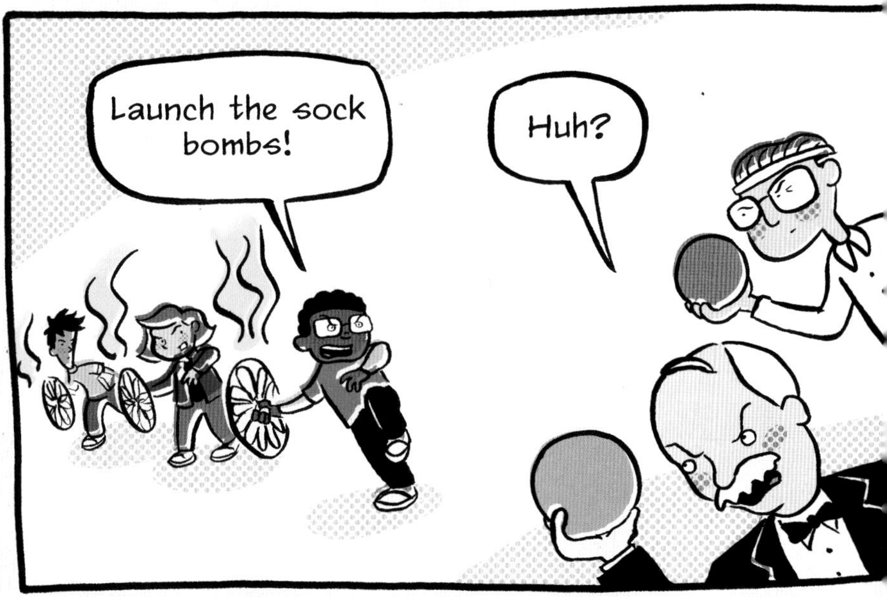
Launch the sock bombs!
Huh?

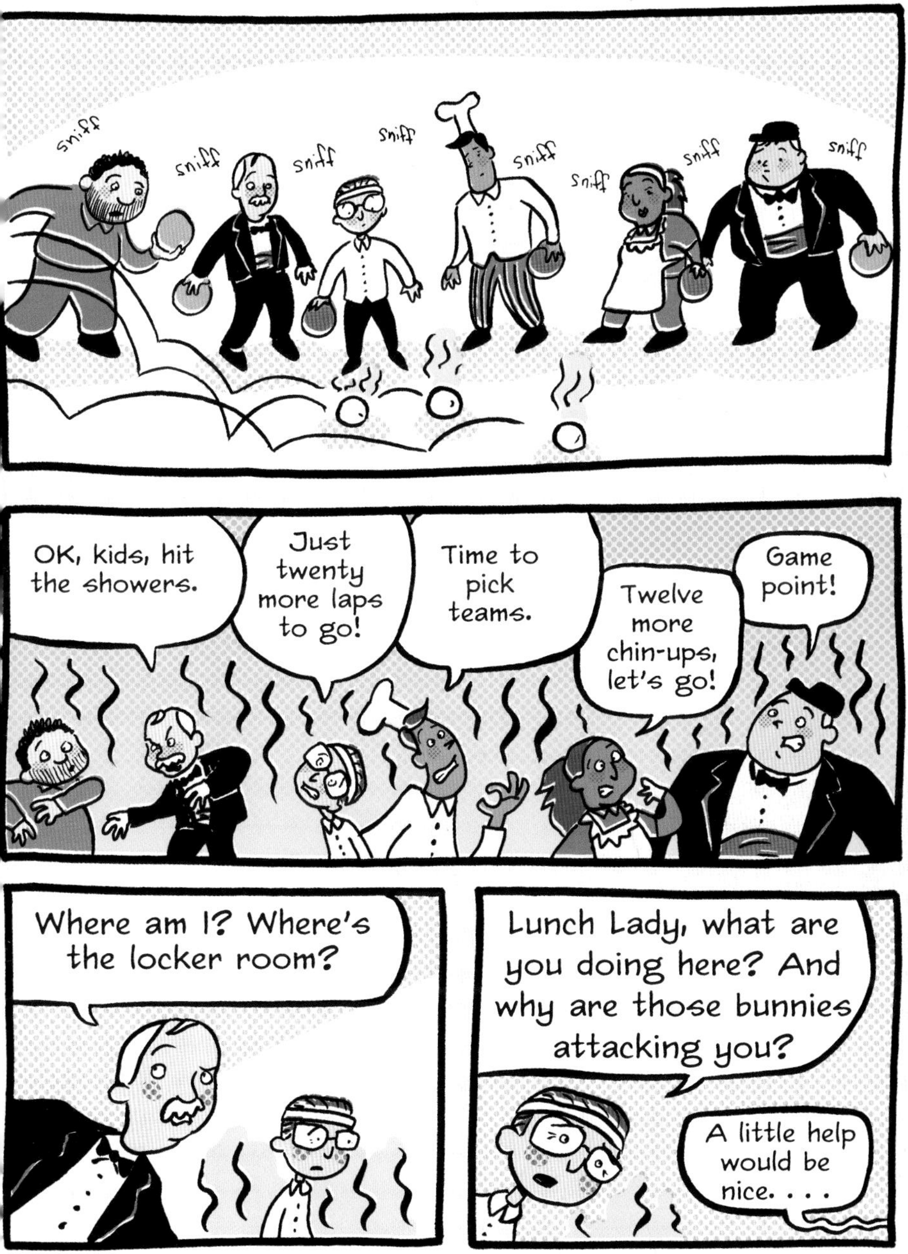
sniff
sniff
sniff
sniff
sniff
sniff
sniff
sniff
OK, kids, hit the showers.
Just twenty more laps to go!
Time to pick teams.
Twelve more chin-ups, let's go!
Game point!
Where am I? Where's the locker room?
Lunch Lady, what are you doing here? And why are those bunnies attacking you?
A little help would be nice. . . .

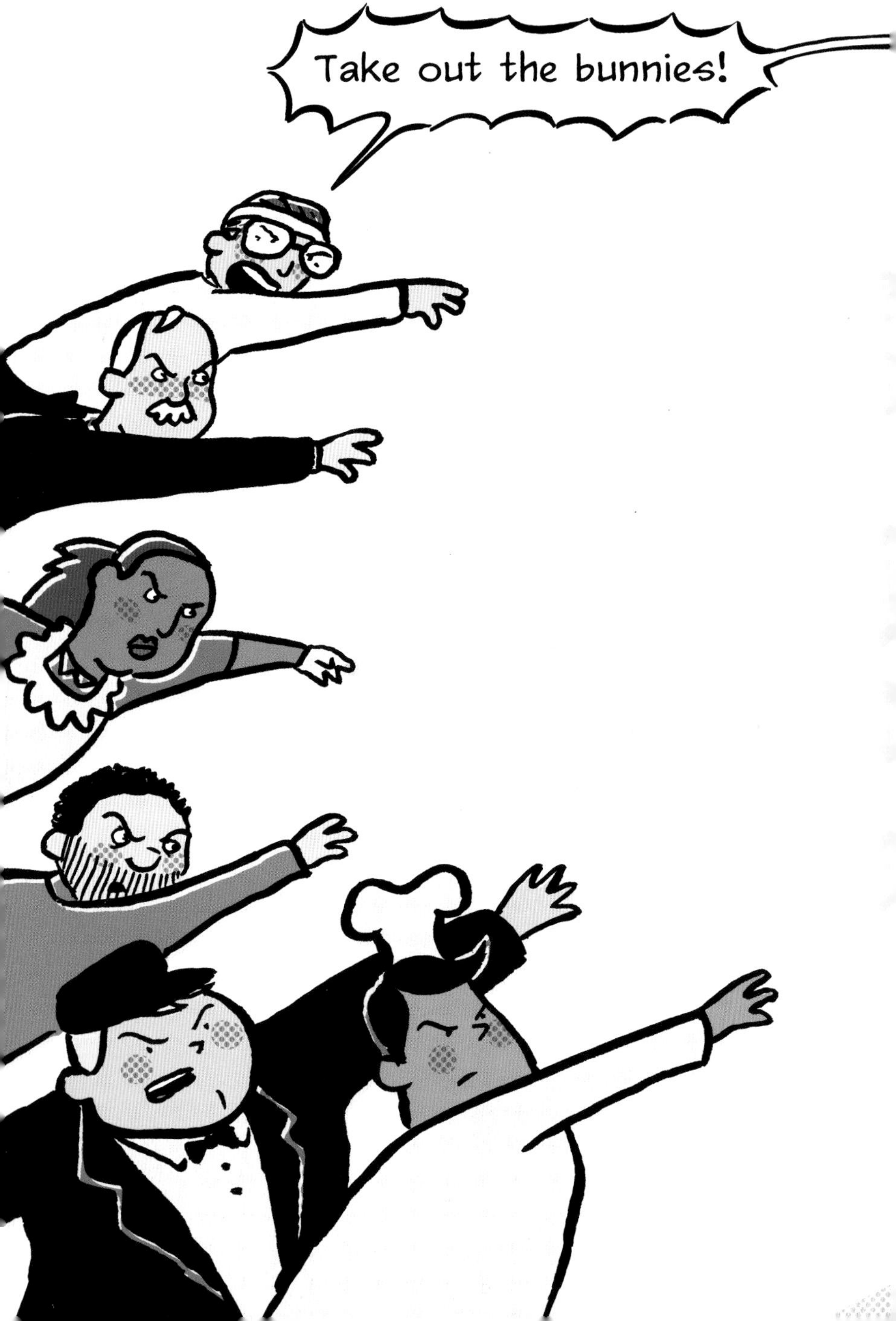
Take out the bunnies!

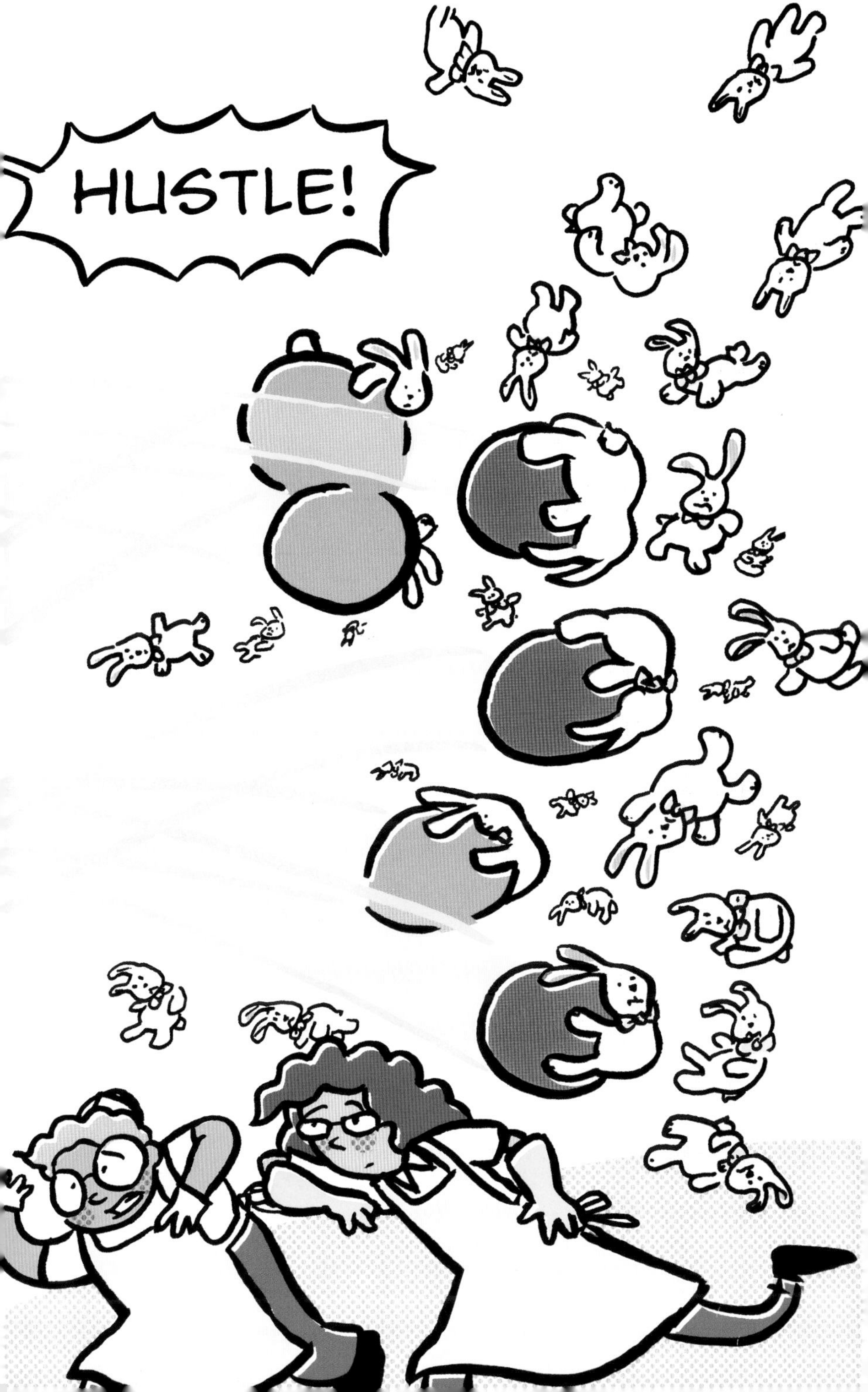
HUSTLE!

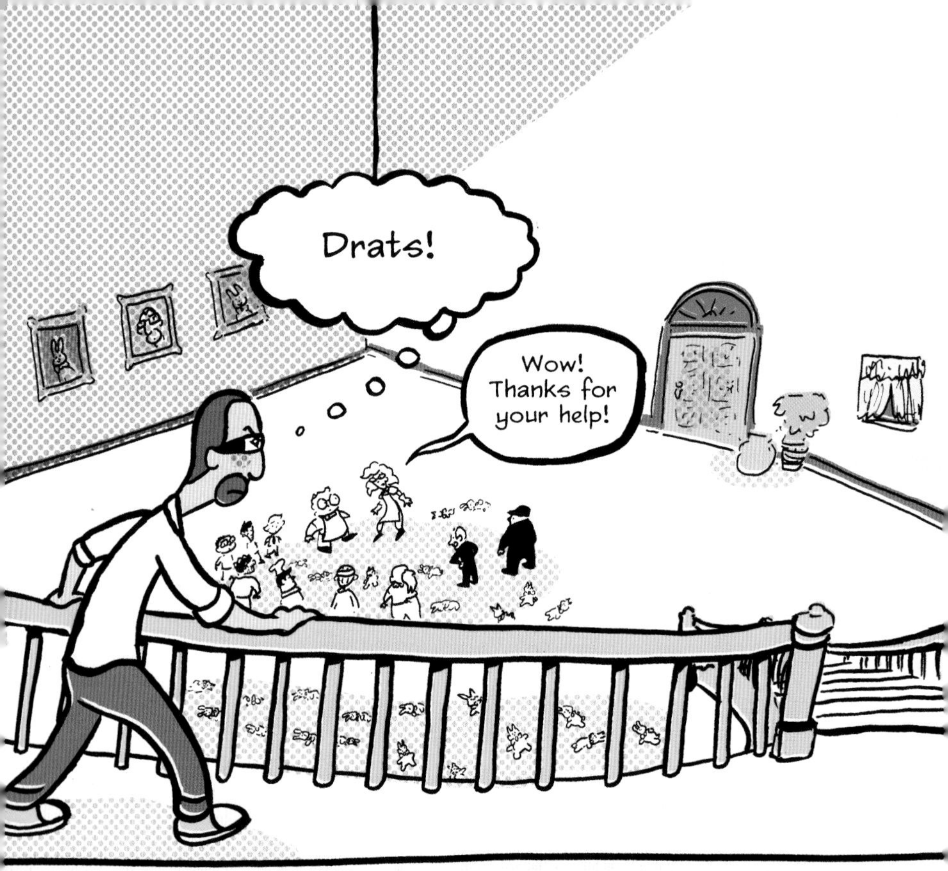
Drats!
Wow! Thanks for your help!

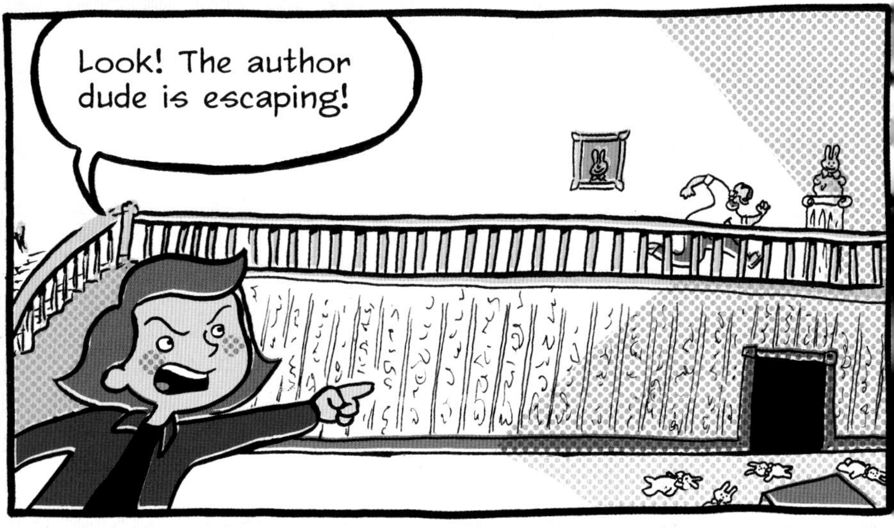
Look! The author dude is escaping!

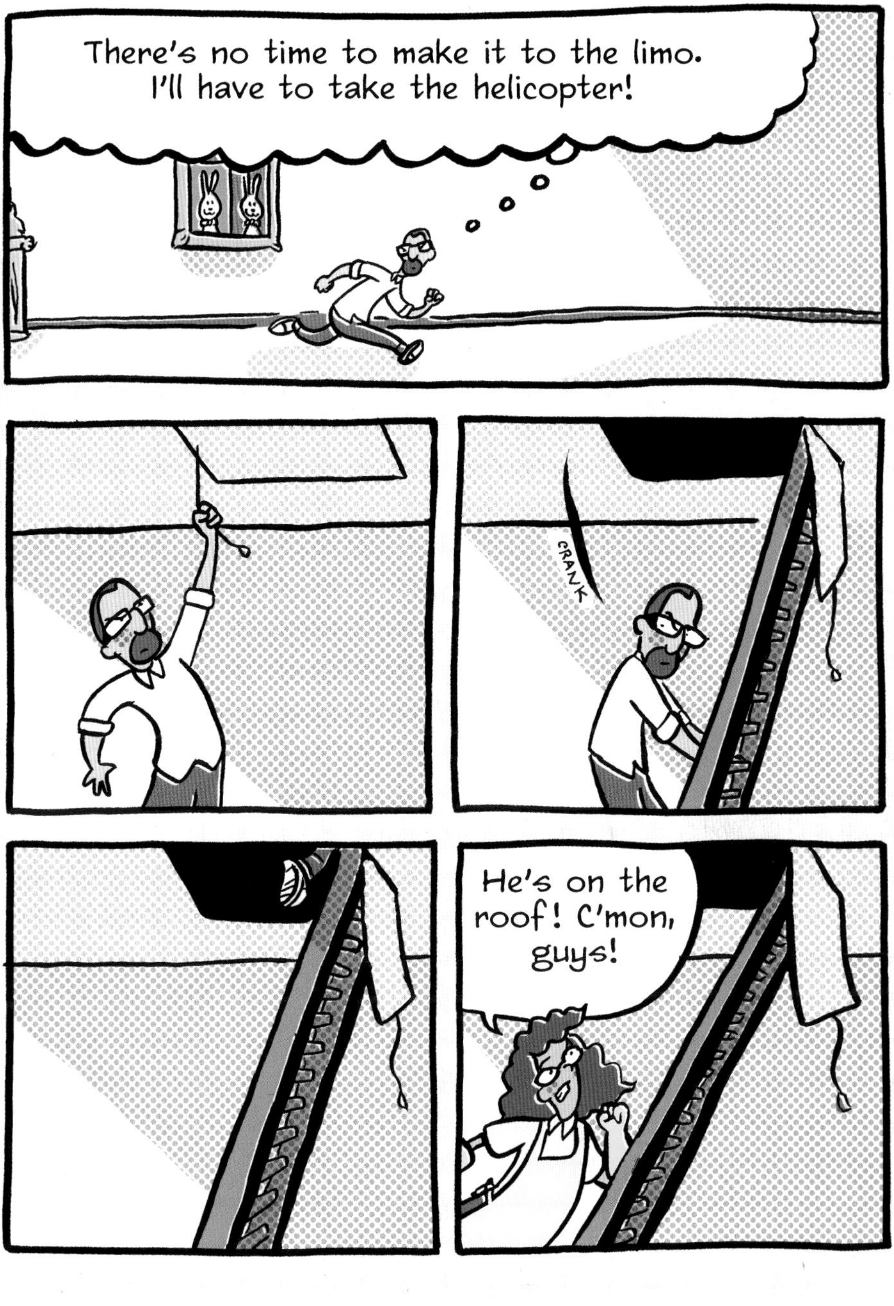
There's no time to make it to the limo. I'll have to take the helicopter!
CRANK
He's on the roof! C'mon, guys!

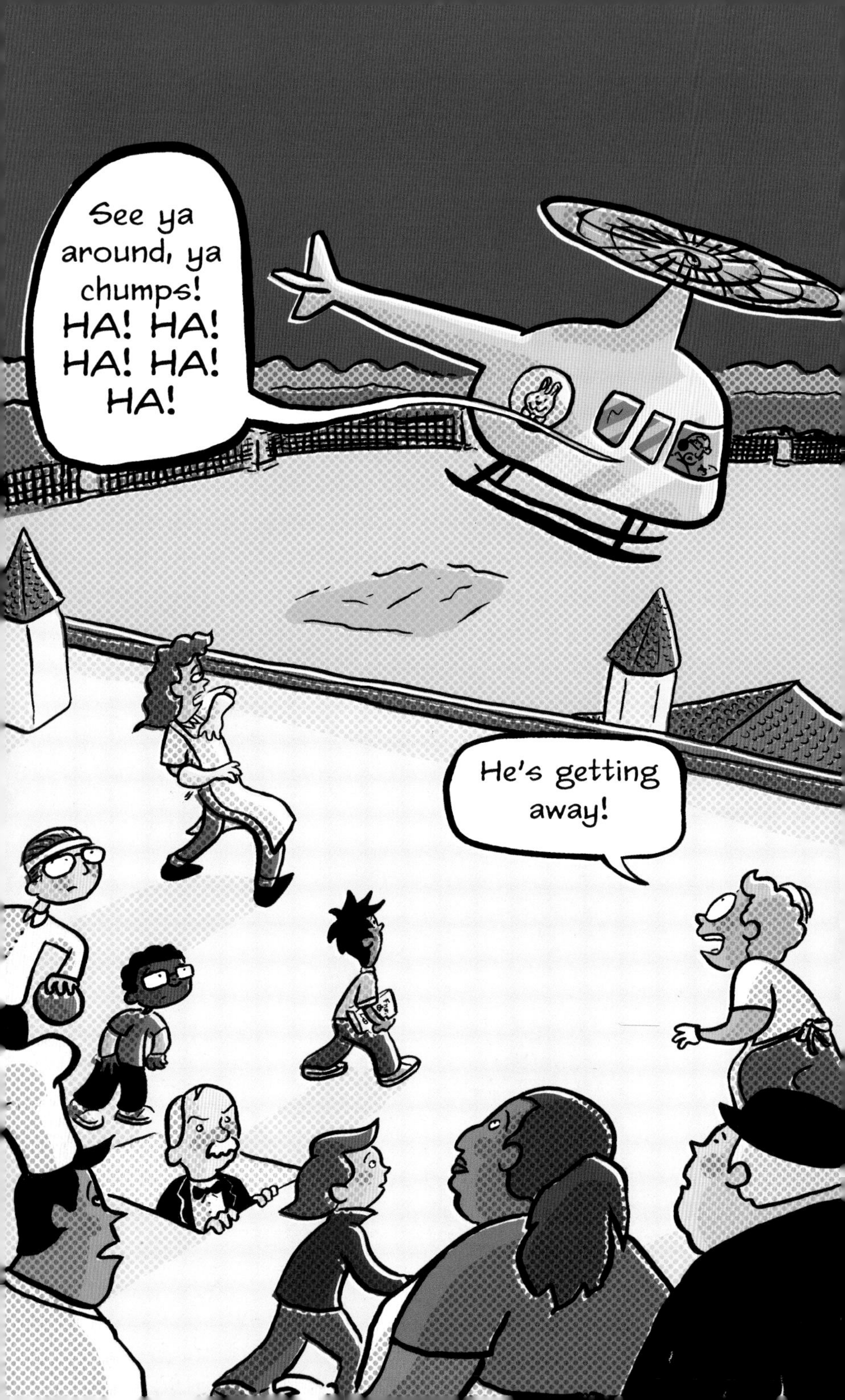
See ya around, ya chumps! HA! HA! HA! HA! HA!
He's getting away!

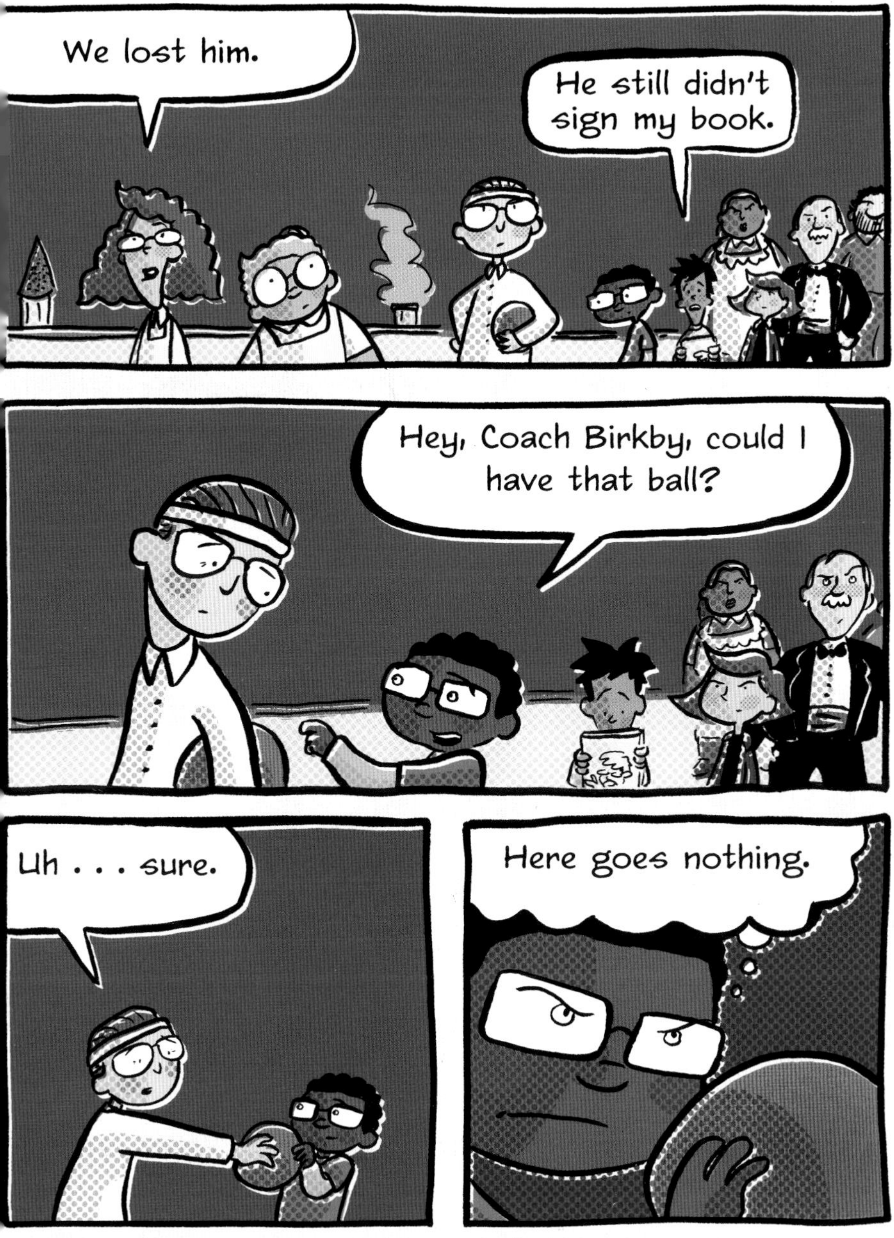
We lost him.
He still didn't sign my book.
Hey, Coach Birkby, could I have that ball?
Uh . . . sure.
Here goes nothing.

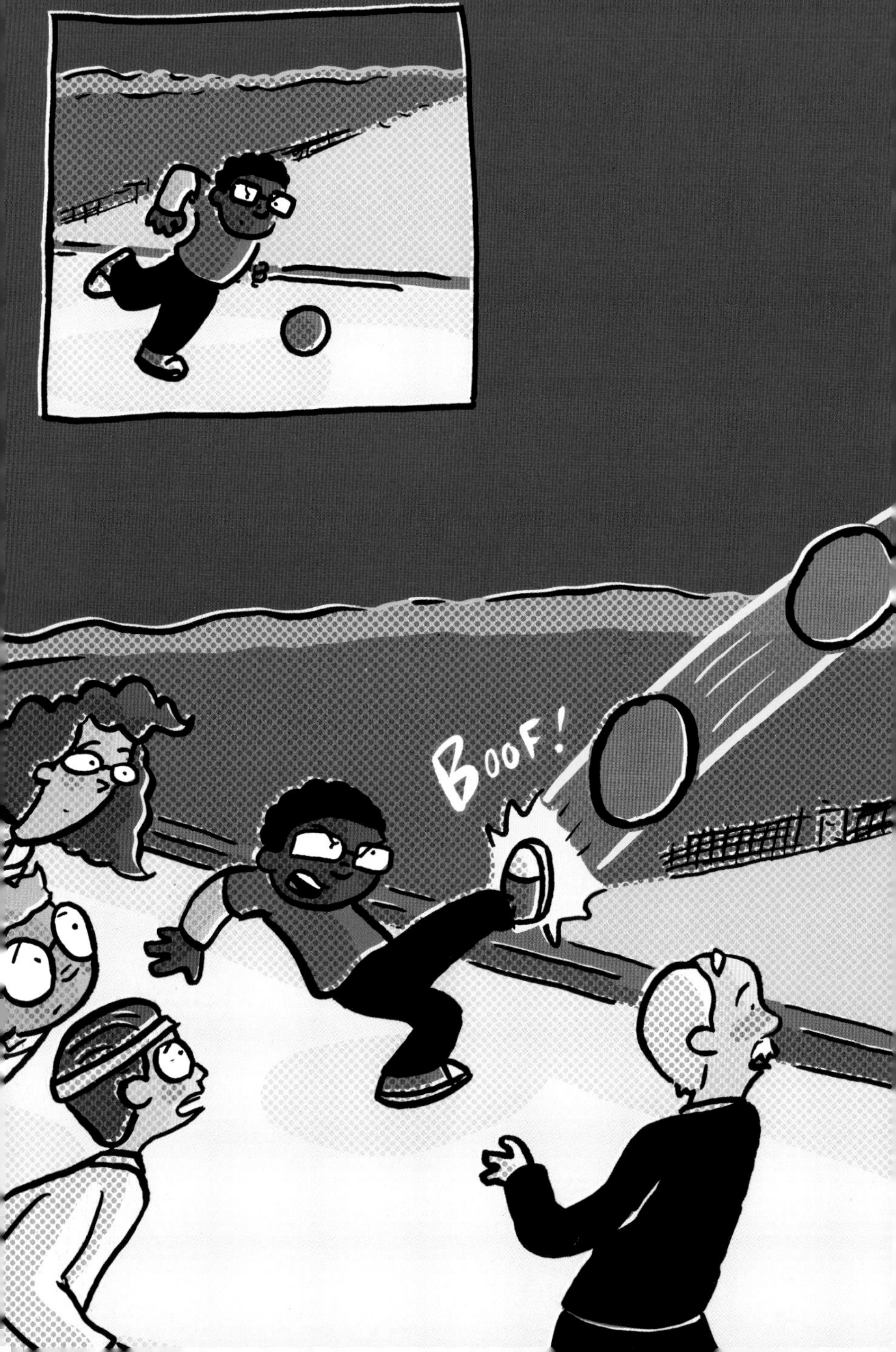
BOOF!

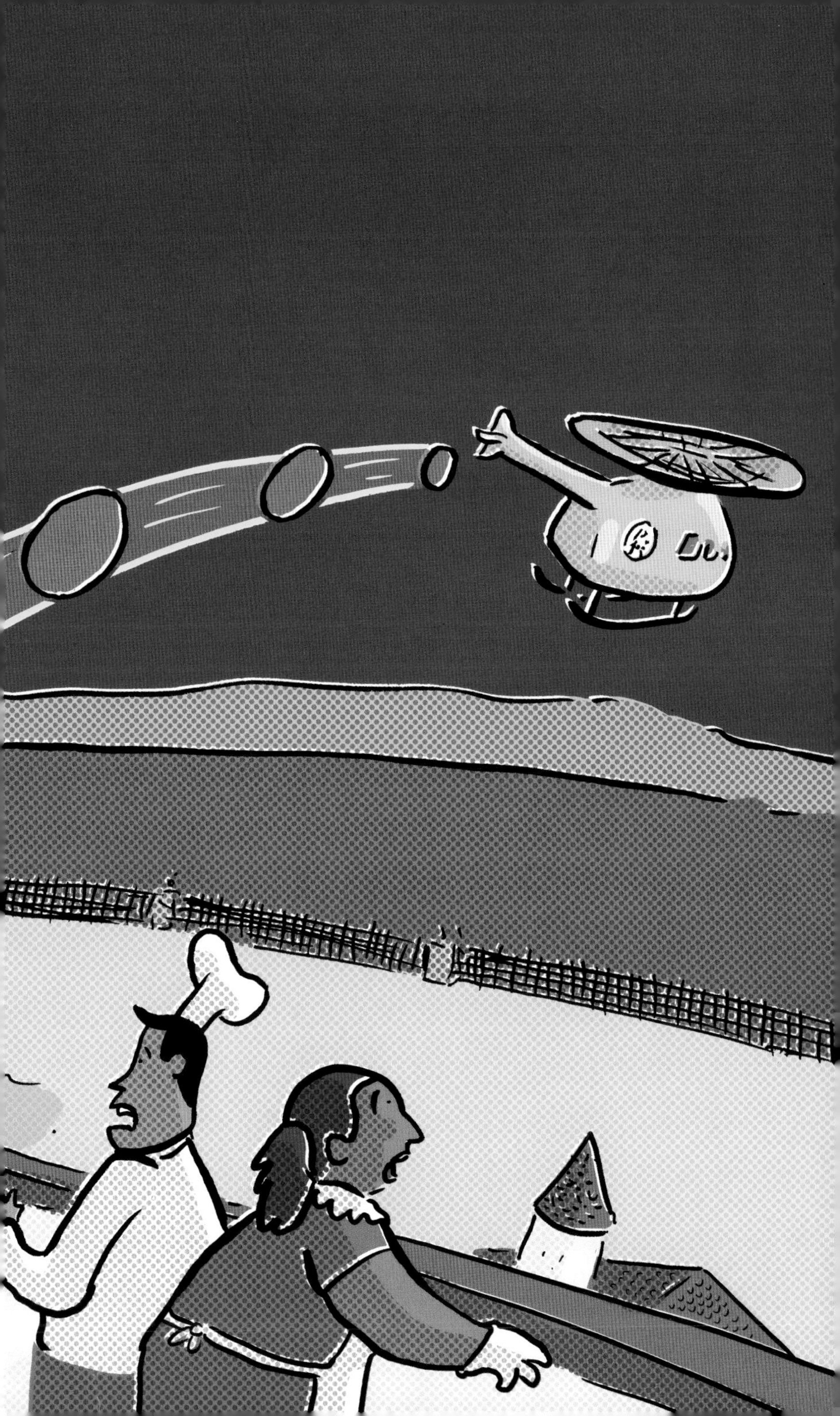

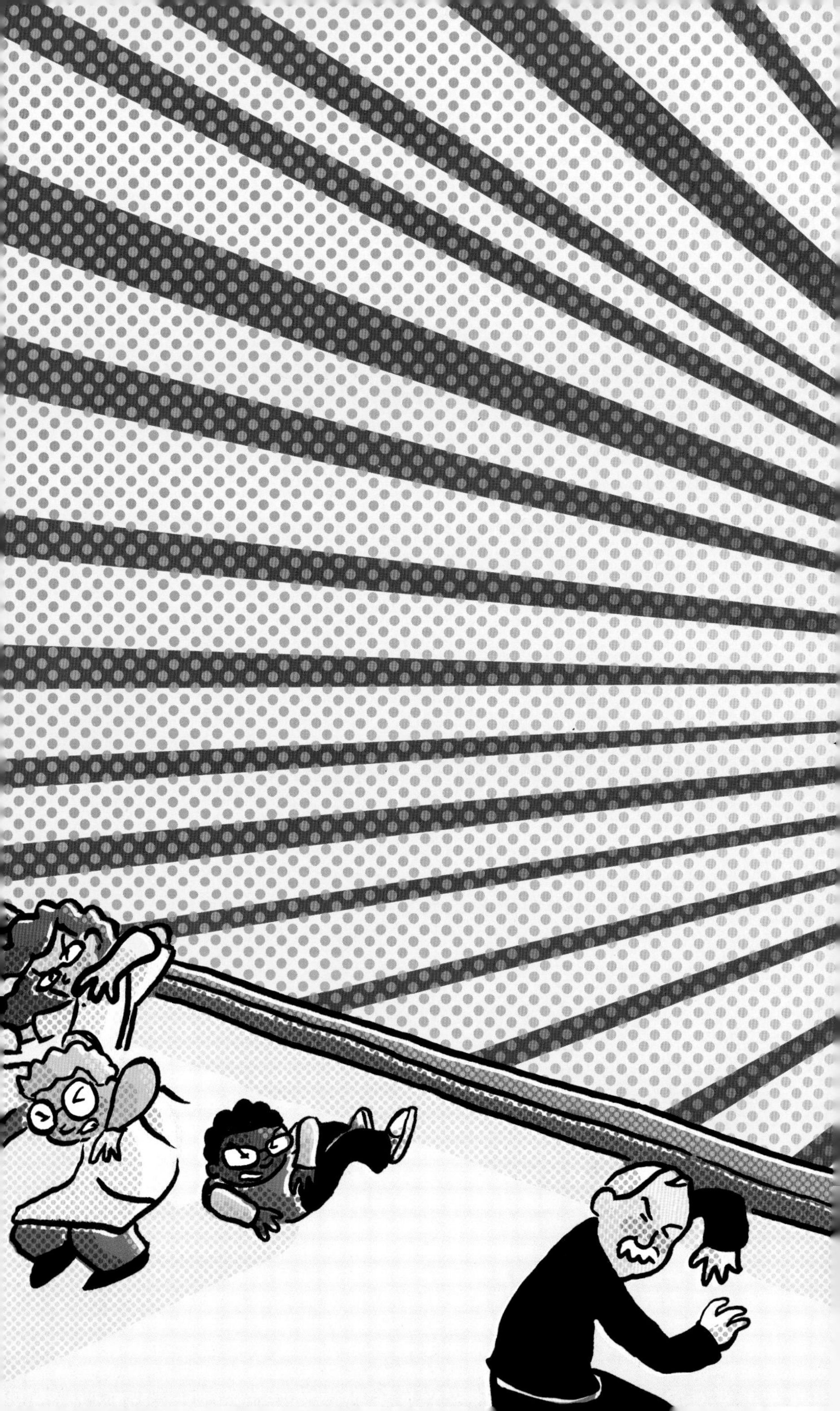

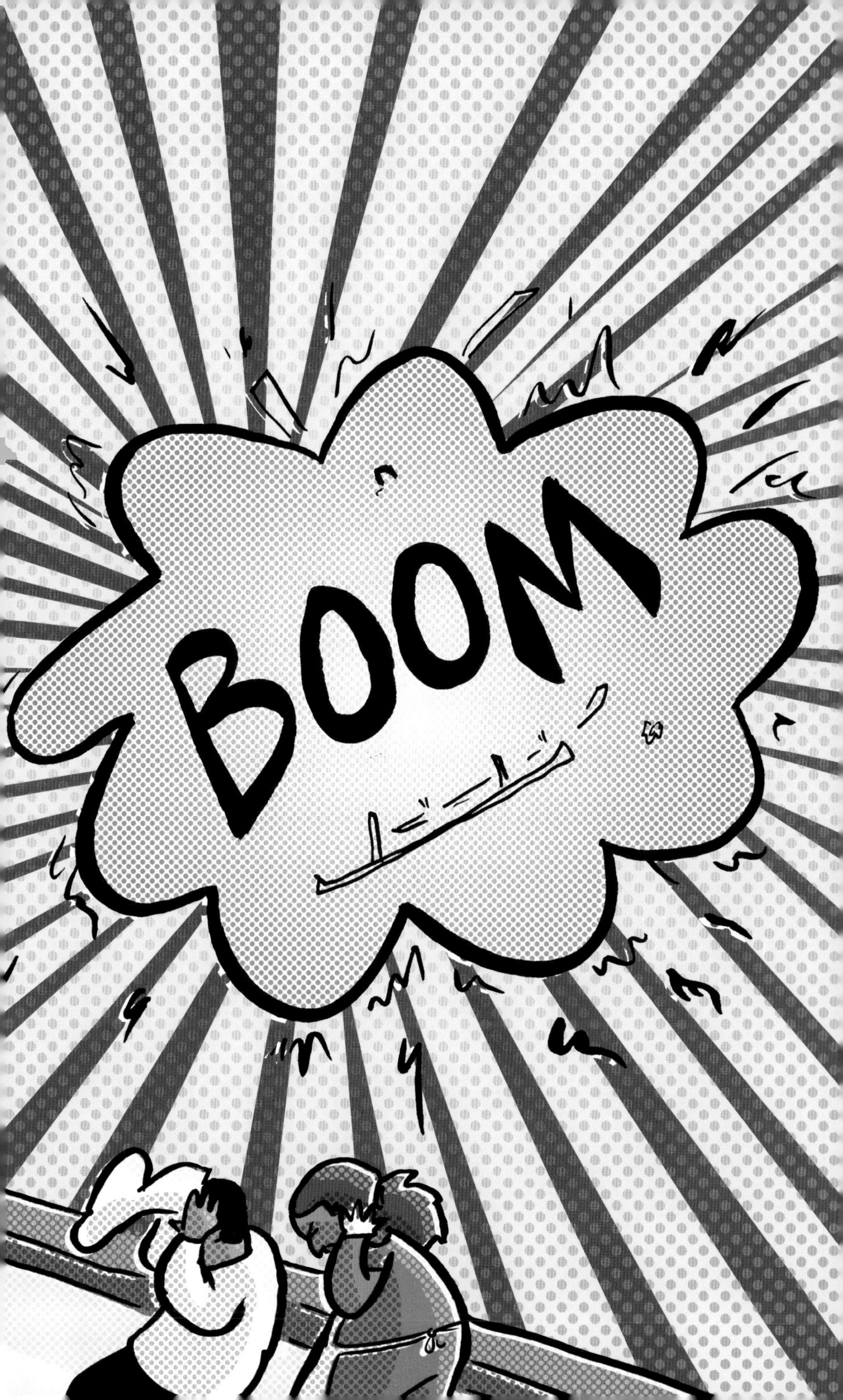
BOOM

Well, well, well. Look what we have here.

Get me down!

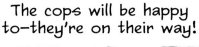

The cops will be happy to—they're on their way!

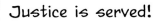

Justice is served!

So, Lunch Lady, explain to me again how we all got here.

The author kidnapped all of the gym teachers, plus Betty and me!

Whoa!

These kids saved us all, then!

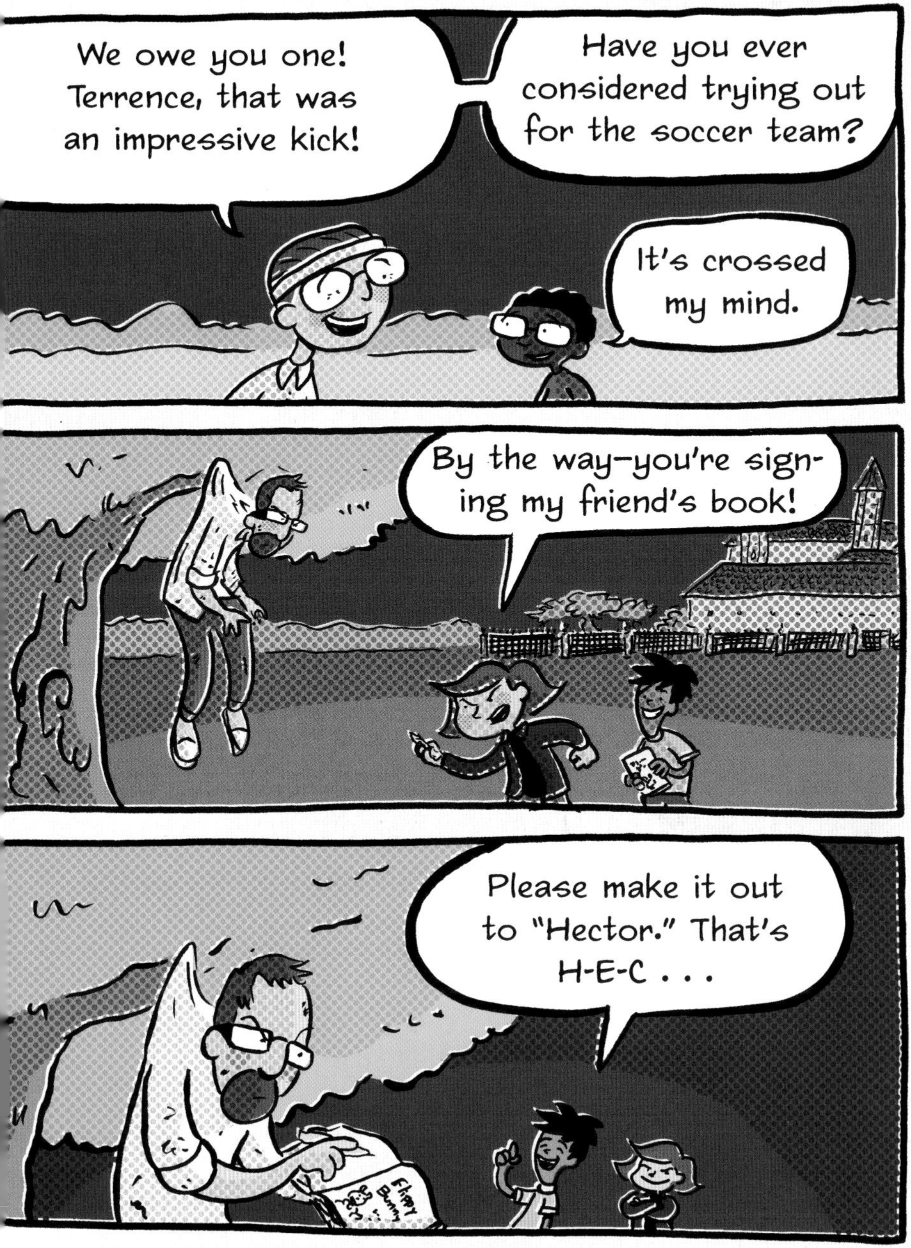
We owe you one! Terrence, that was an impressive kick!
Have you ever considered trying out for the soccer team?
It's crossed my mind.
By the way—you're sign-ing my friend's book!
Please make it out to "Hector." That's H-E-C . . .

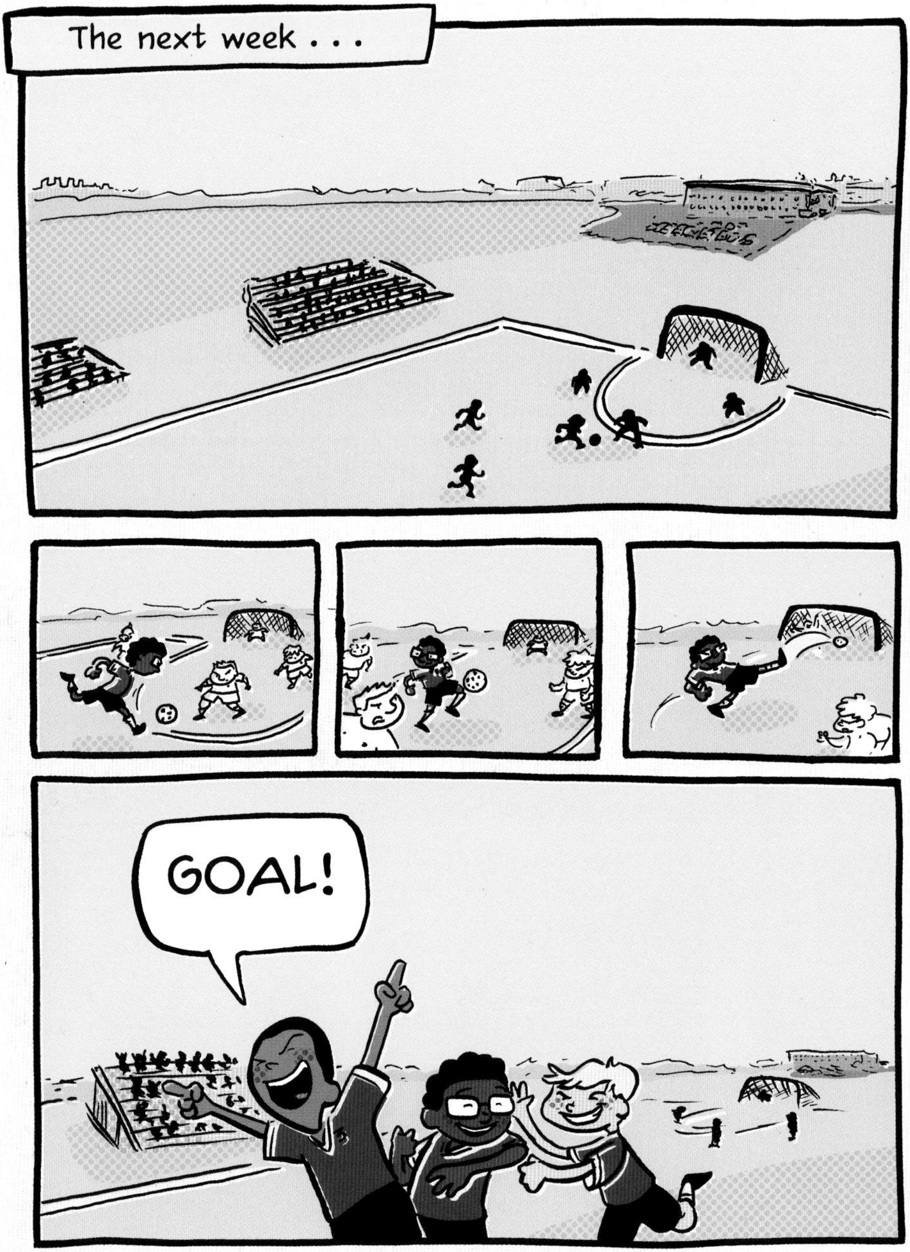
The next week . . .
GOAL!

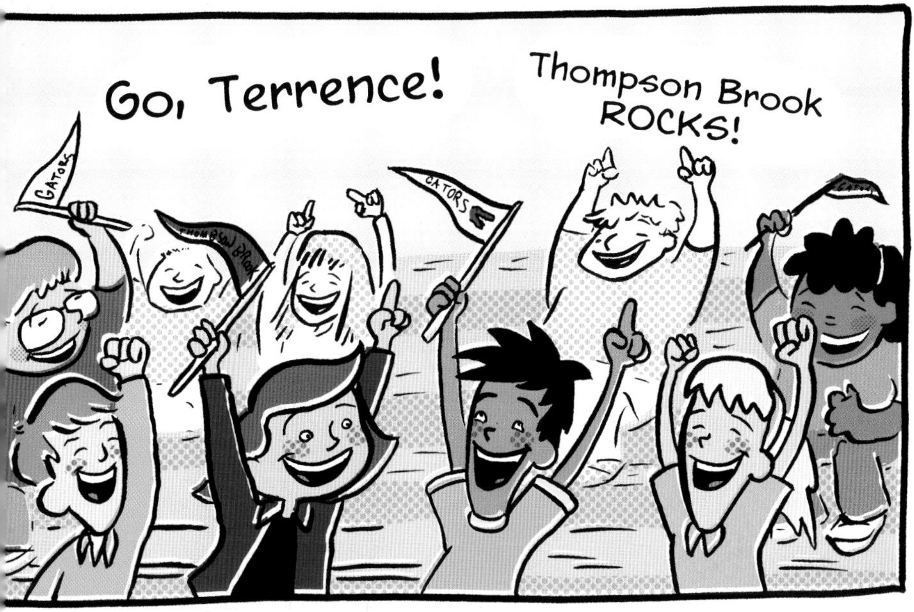
Go, Terrence!
Thompson Brook ROCKS!
GATORS
THOMPSON BROOK
GATORS

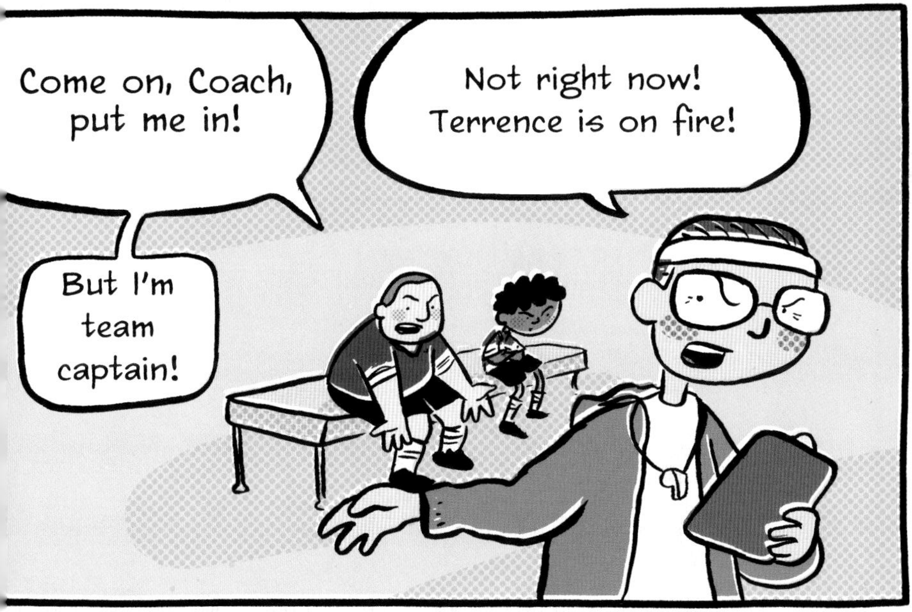
Come on, Coach, put me in!
Not right now! Terrence is on fire!
But I'm team captain!

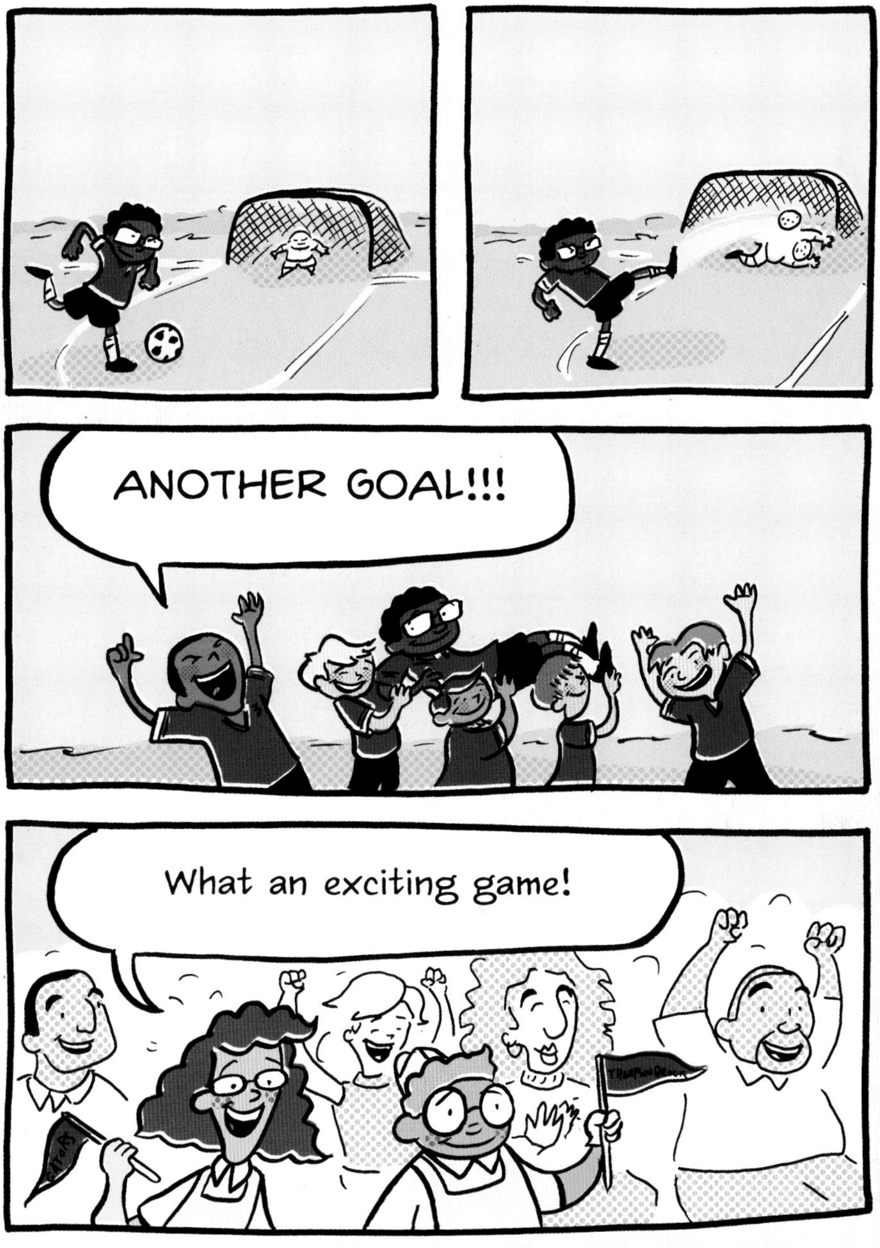
ANOTHER GOAL!!!
What an exciting game!

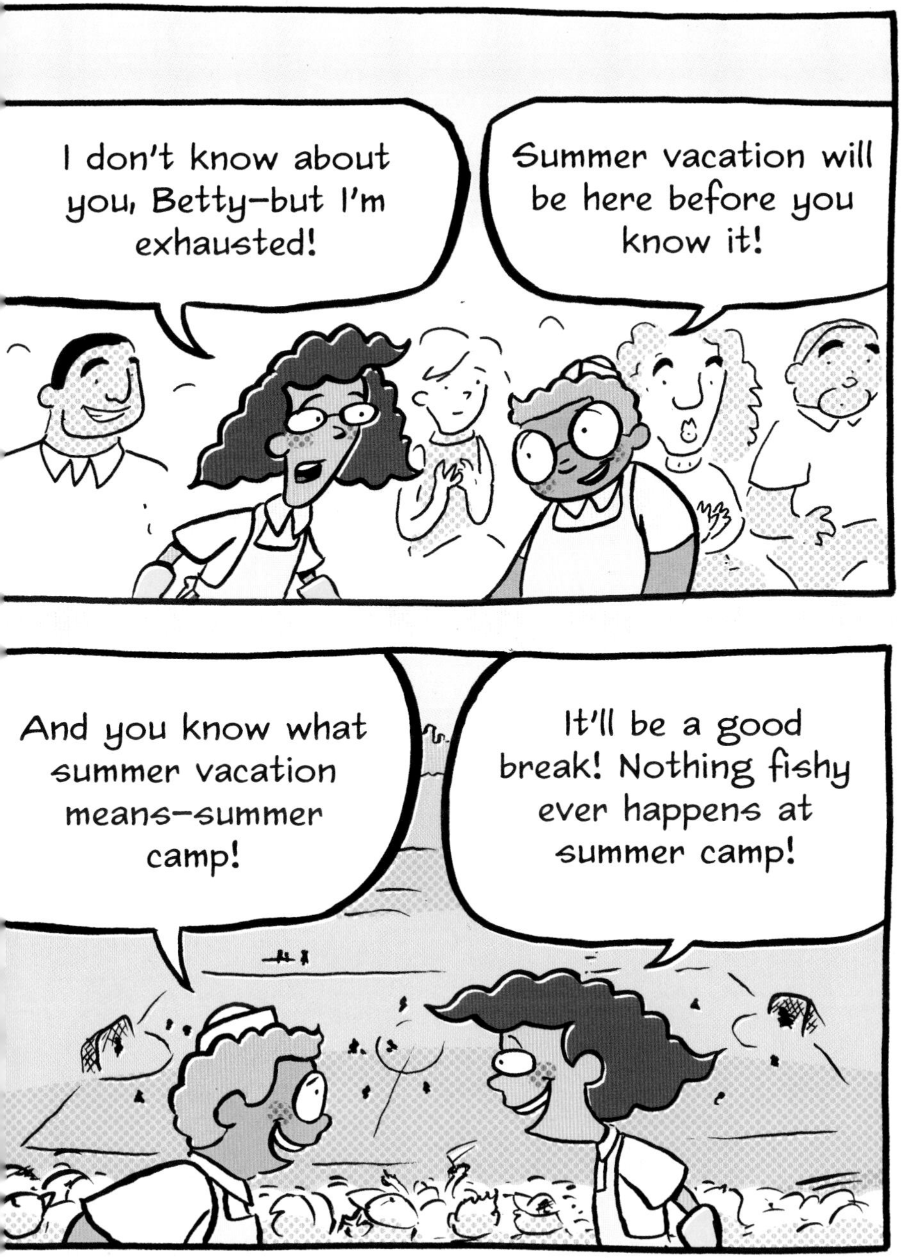
I don't know about you, Betty—but I'm exhausted!
Summer vacation will be here before you know it!
And you know what summer vacation means—summer camp!
It'll be a good break! Nothing fishy ever happens at summer camp!

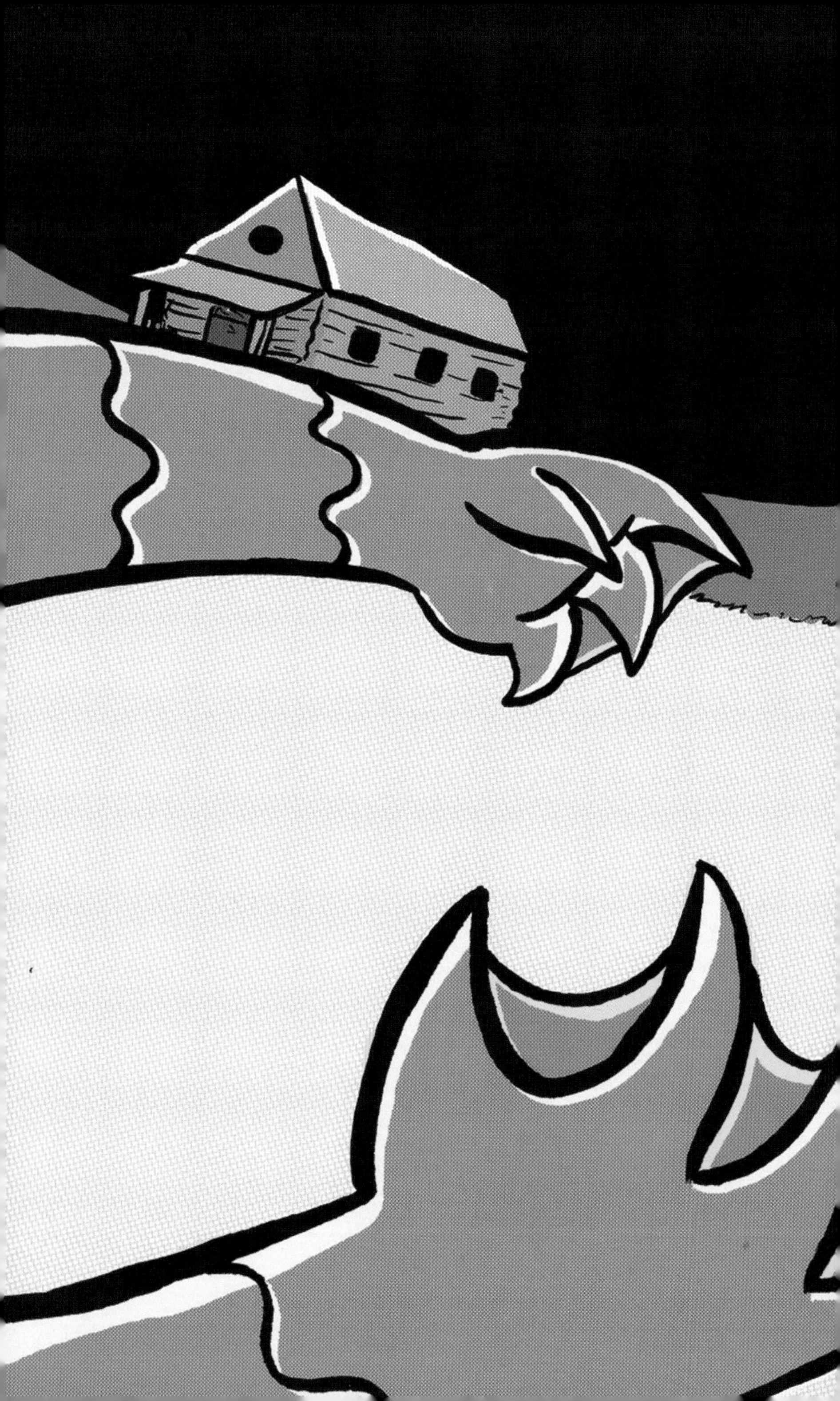

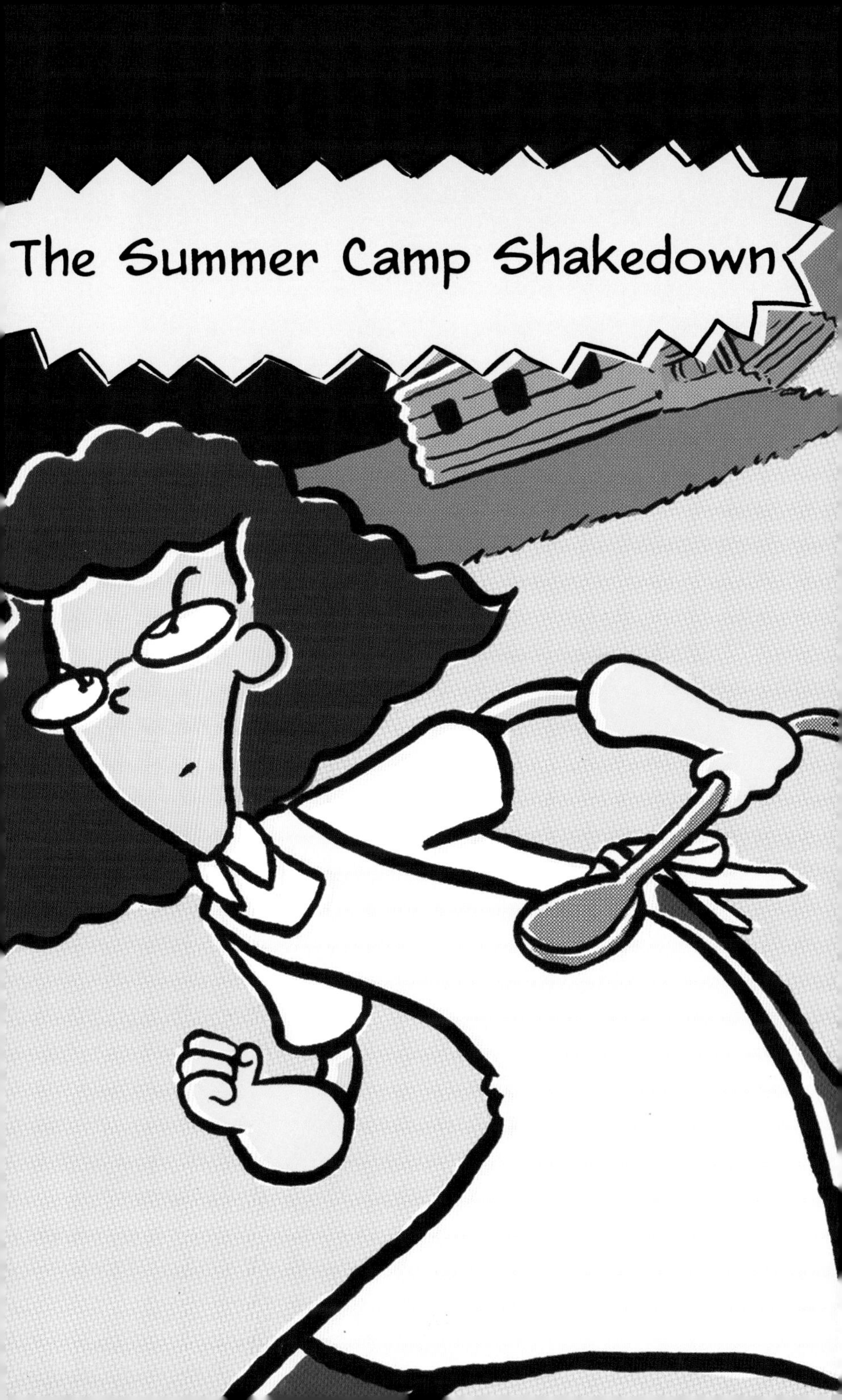
The Summer Camp Shakedown

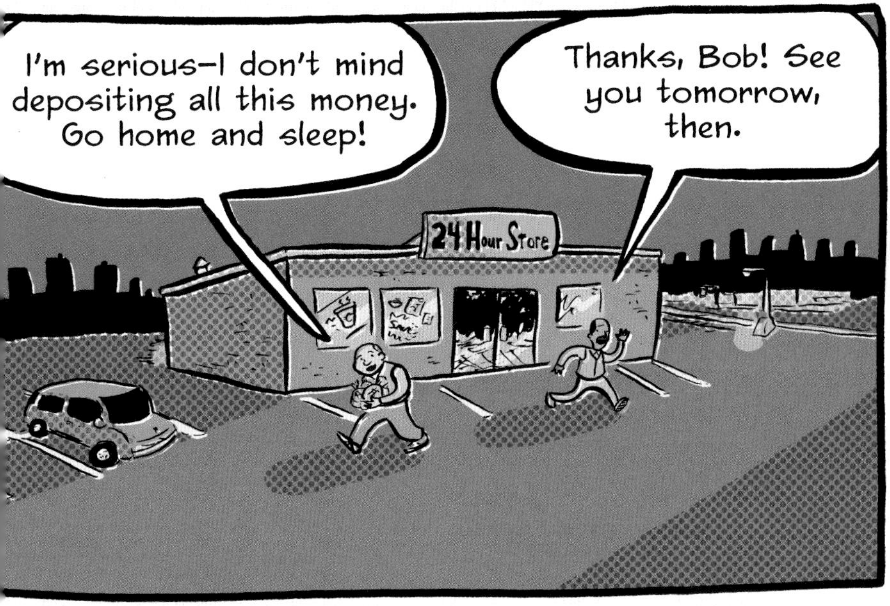

I'm serious—I don't mind depositing all this money. Go home and sleep!
Thanks, Bob! See you tomorrow, then.
24 Hour Store

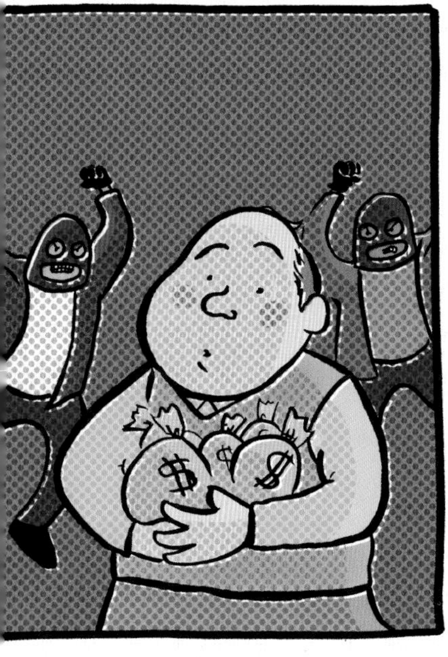

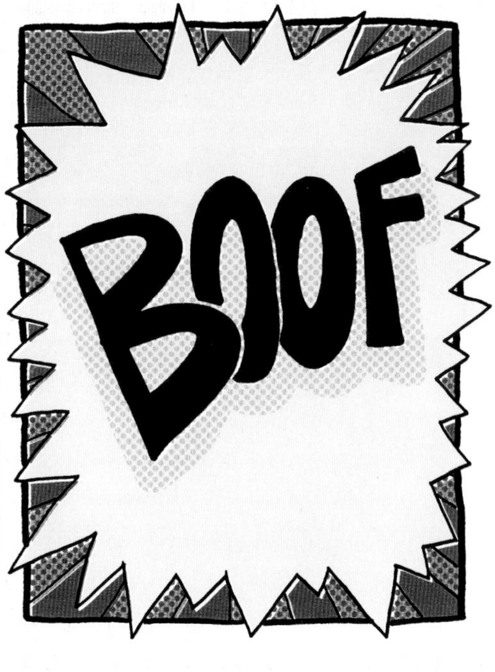

BOOF

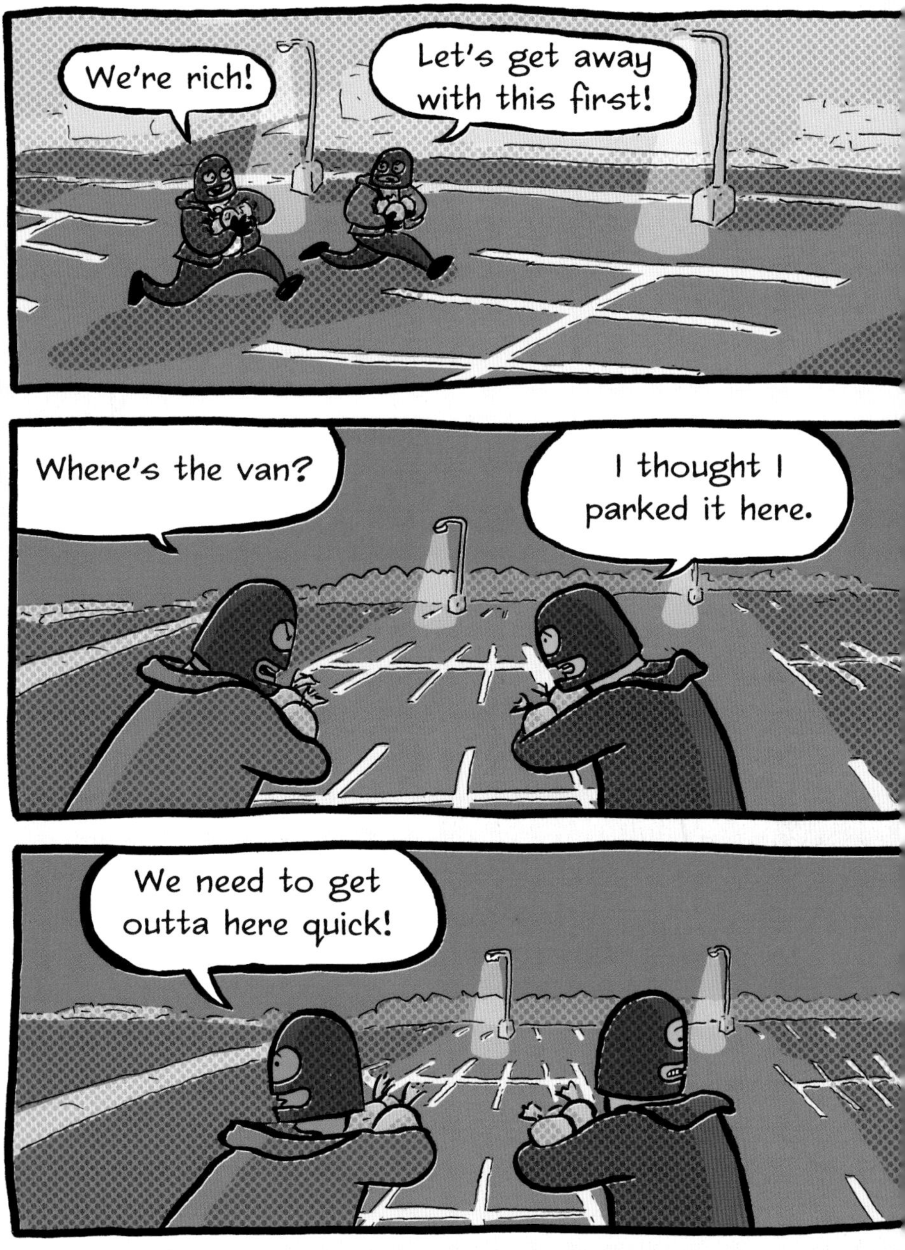
We're rich!
Let's get away with this first!
Where's the van?
I thought I parked it here.
We need to get outta here quick!

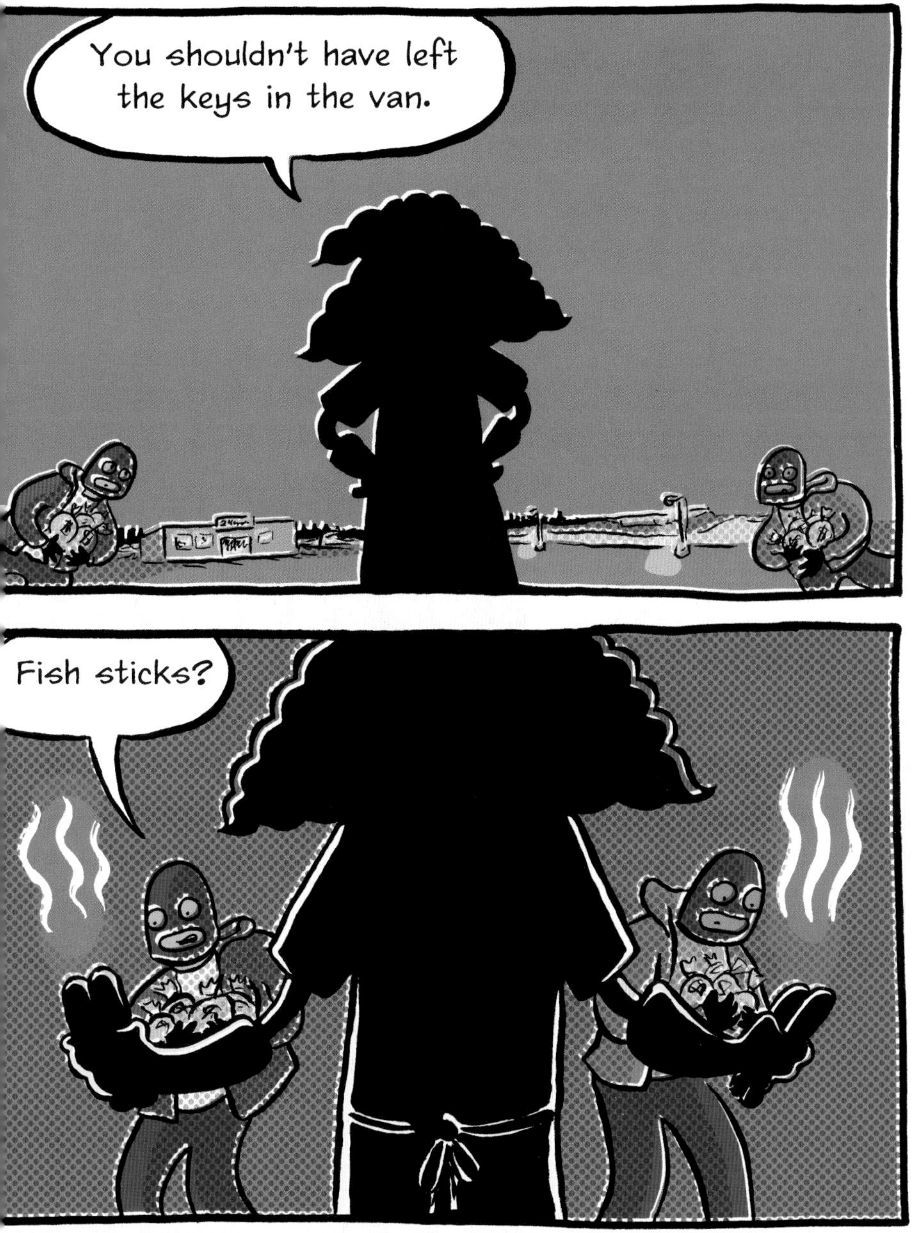
You shouldn't have left the keys in the van.
Fish sticks?

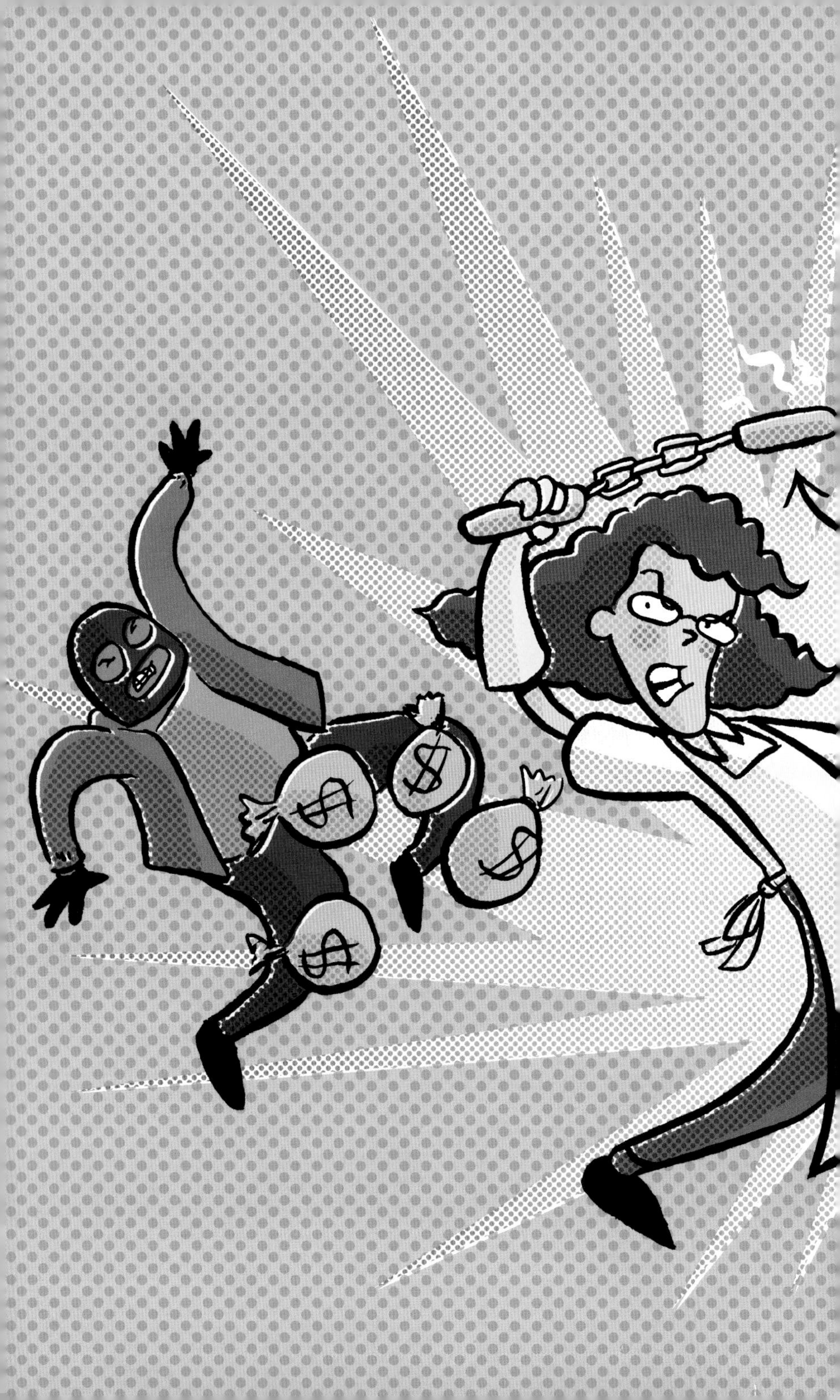

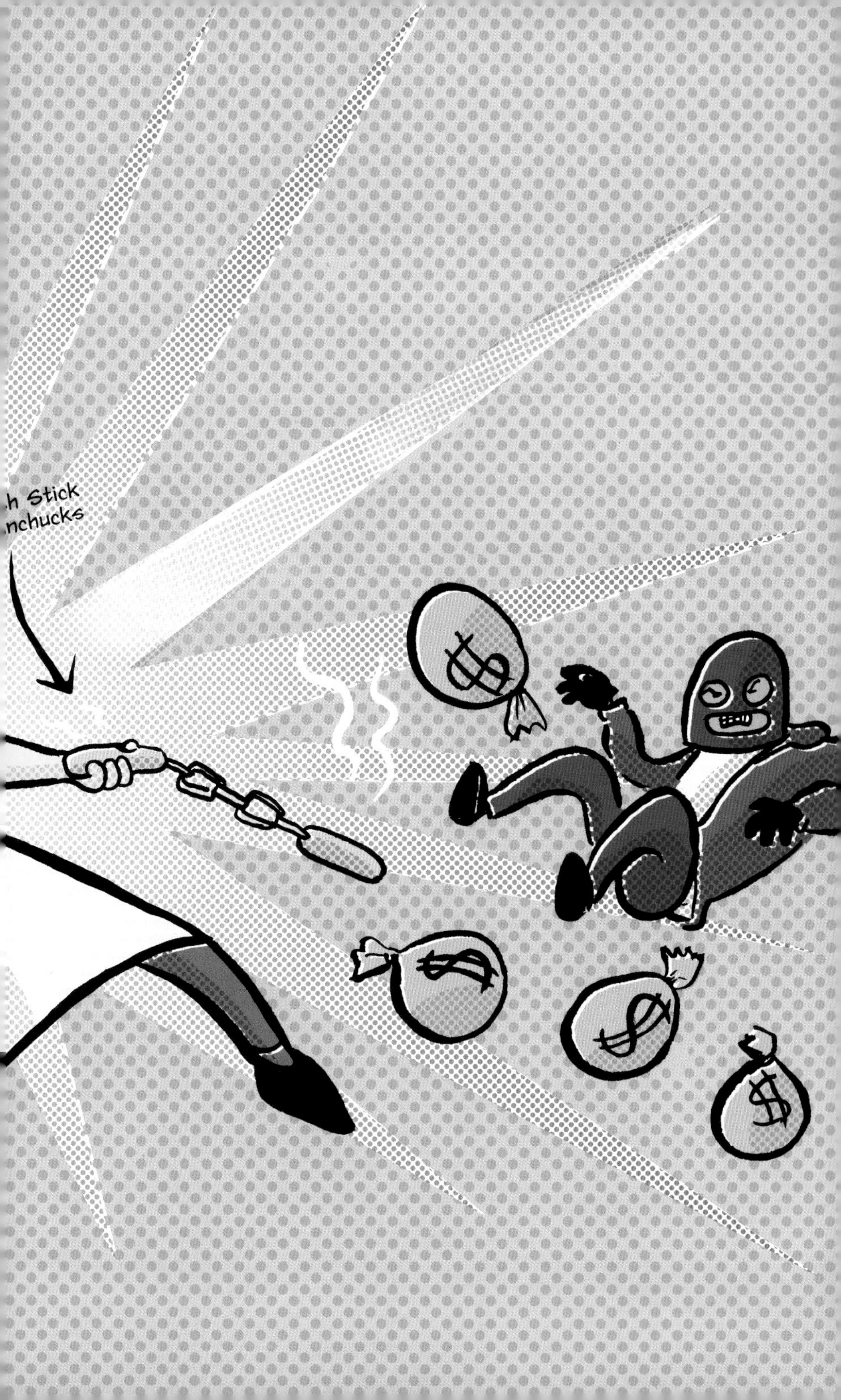
h Stick
nchucks

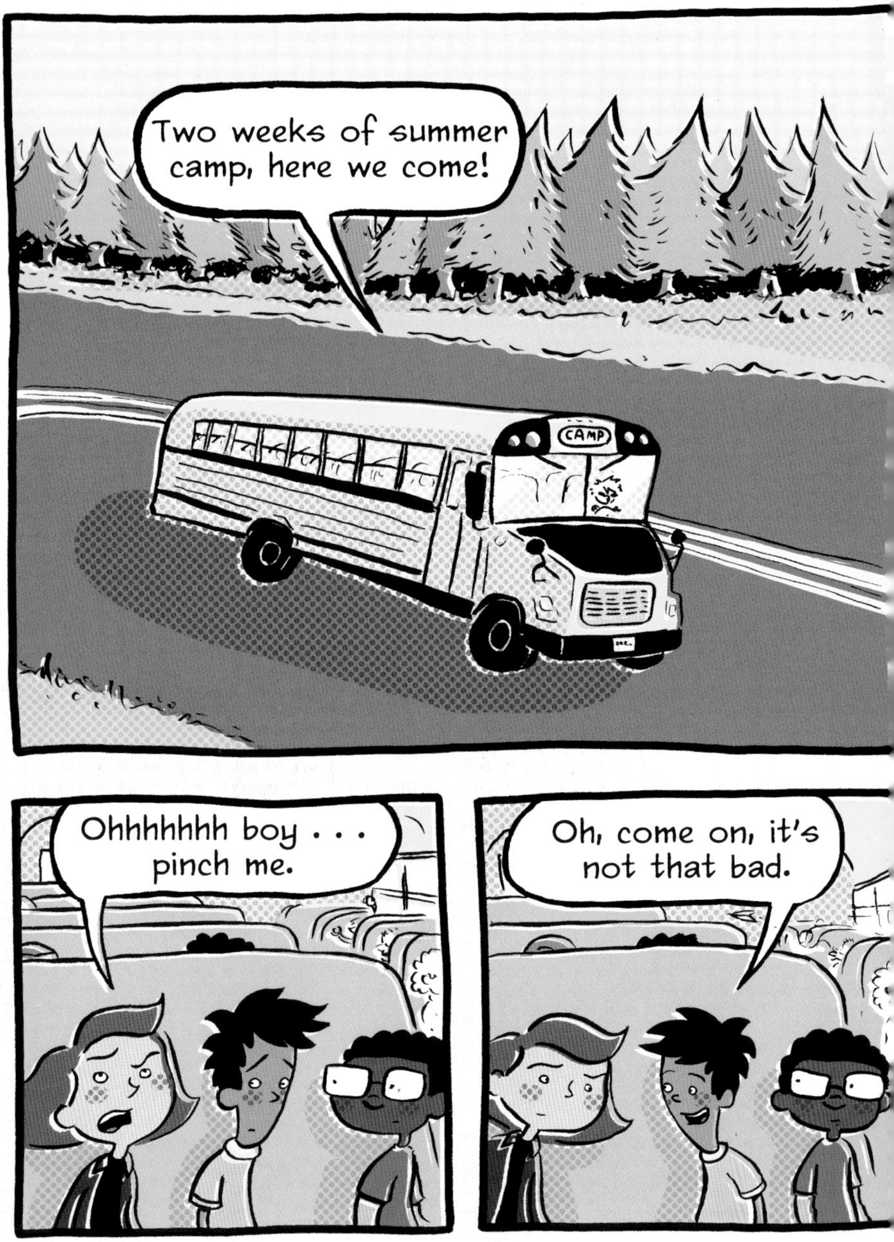
Two weeks of summer camp, here we come!
CAMP
Ohhhhhhh boy . . . pinch me.
Oh, come on, it's not that bad.

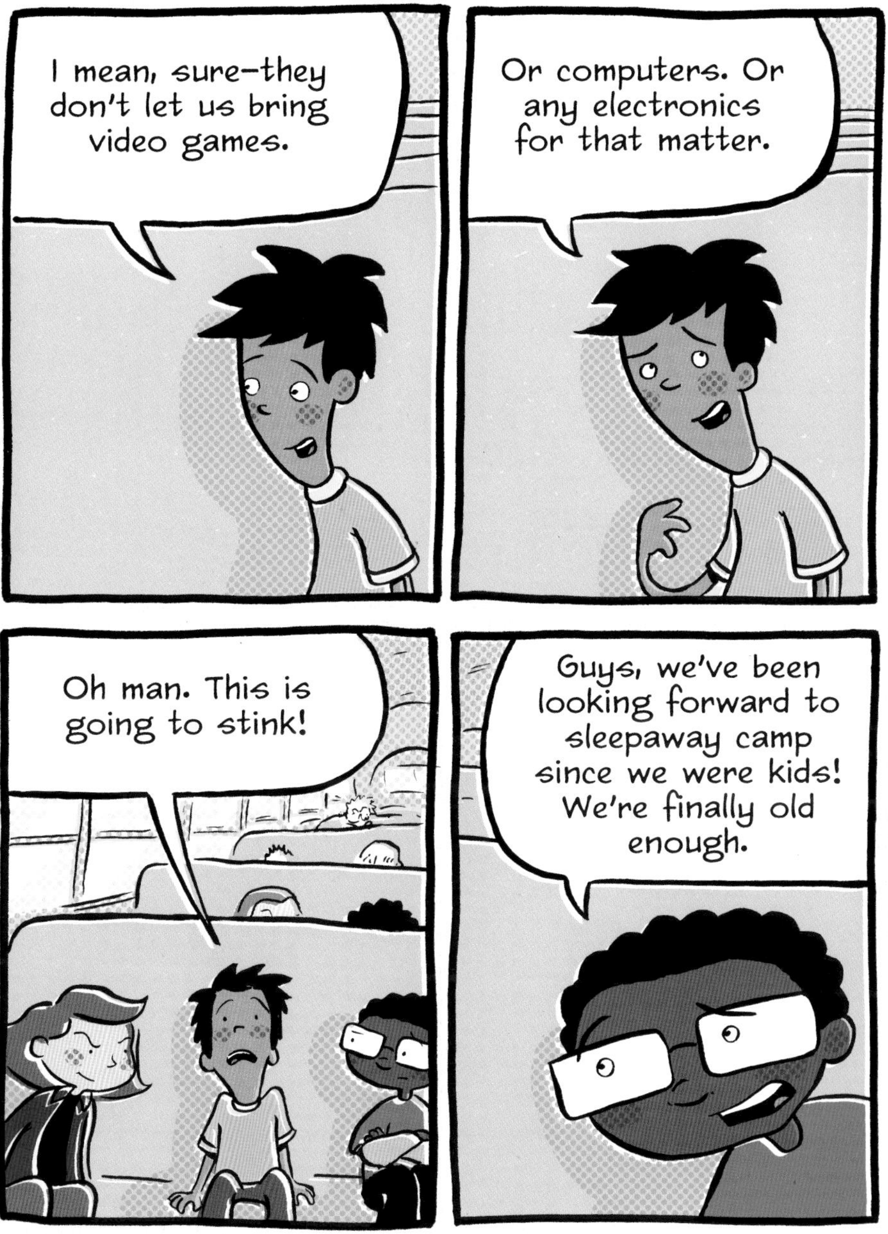

I mean, sure–they don't let us bring video games.
Or computers. Or any electronics for that matter.
Oh man. This is going to stink!
Guys, we've been looking forward to sleepaway camp since we were kids! We're finally old enough.

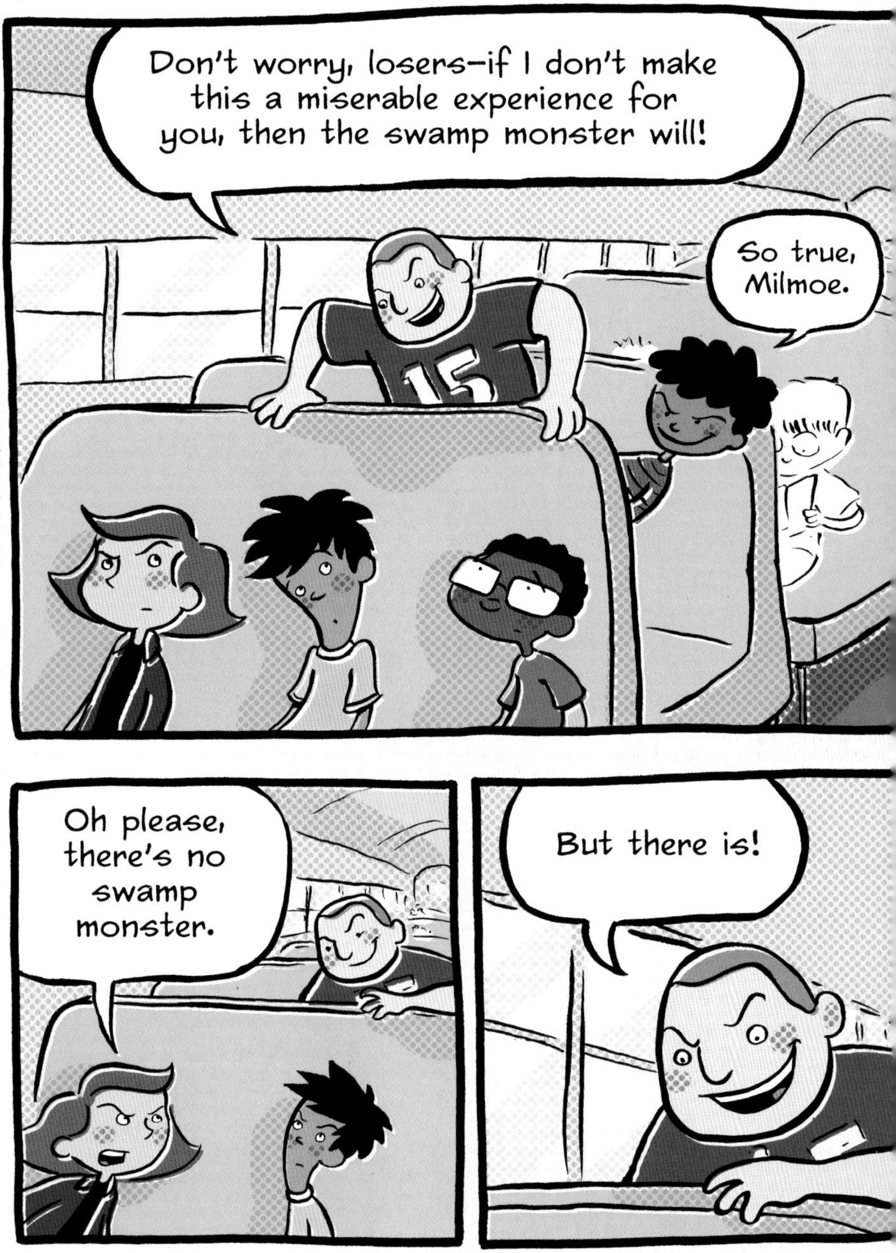
Don't worry, losers–if I don't make this a miserable experience for you, then the swamp monster will!
So true, Milmoe.
Oh please, there's no swamp monster.
But there is!

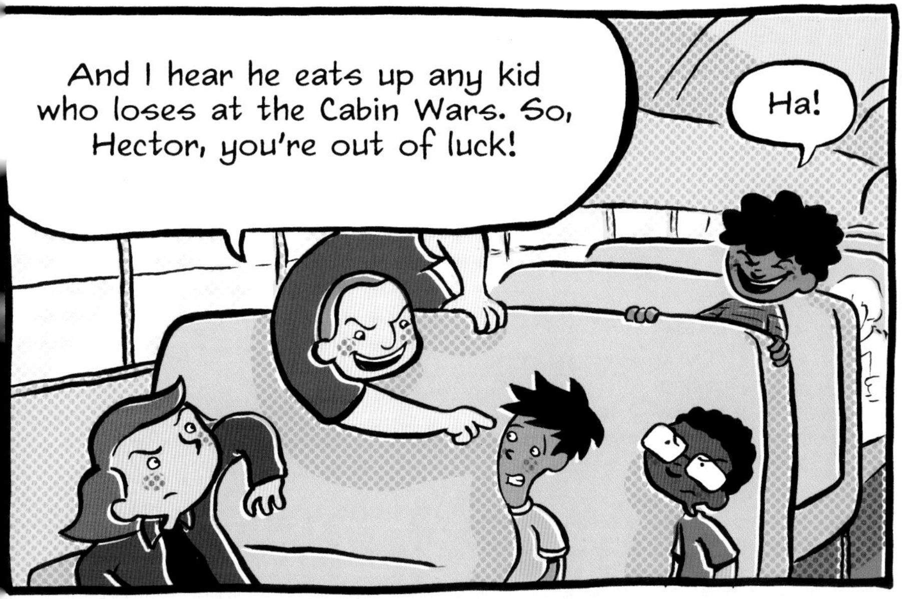
And I hear he eats up any kid who loses at the Cabin Wars. So, Hector, you're out of luck!
Ha!

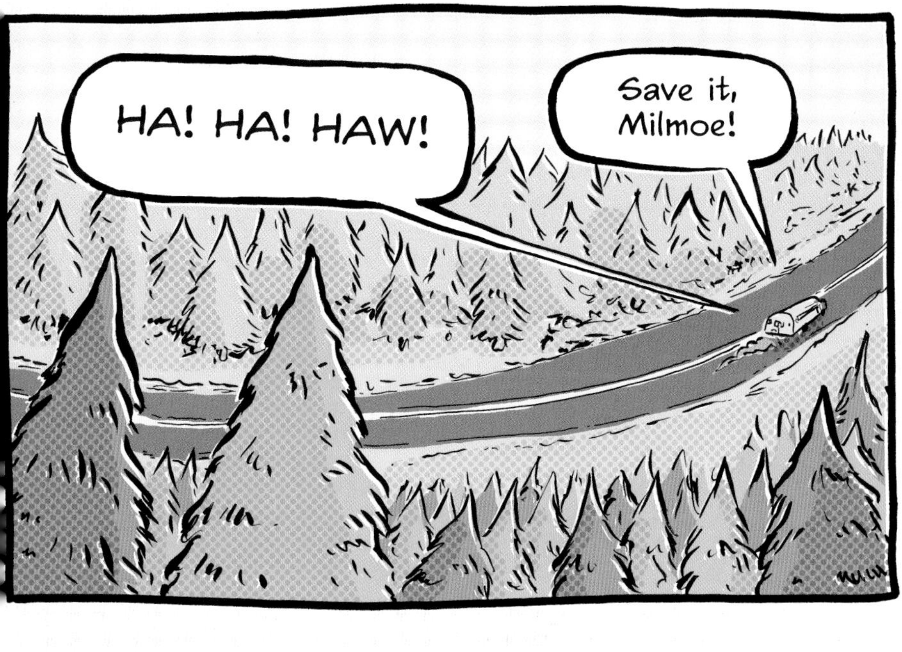
HA! HA! HAW!
Save it, Milmoe!

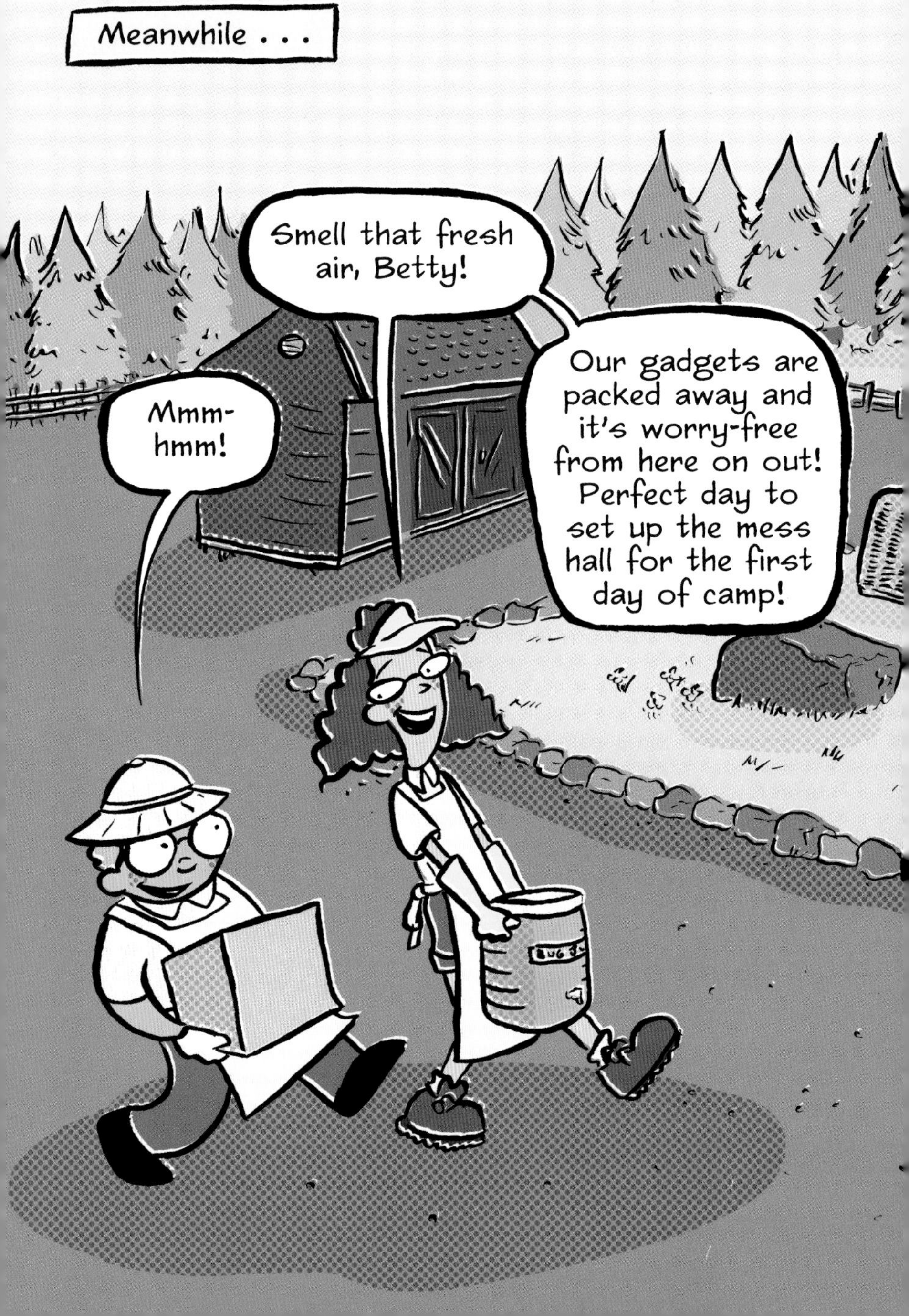
Meanwhile . . .
Smell that fresh air, Betty!
Mmm-hmm!
Our gadgets are packed away and it's worry-free from here on out! Perfect day to set up the mess hall for the first day of camp!

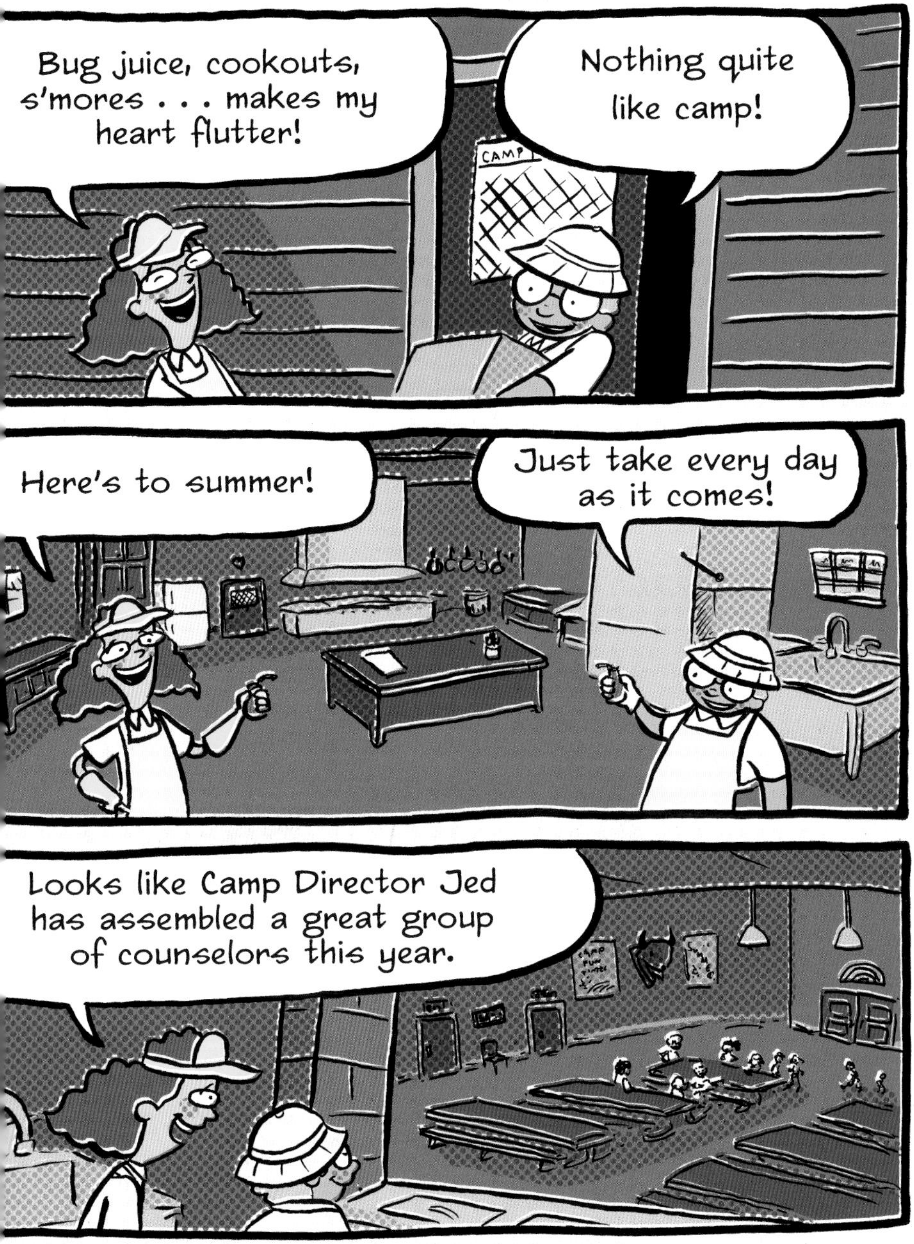
Bug juice, cookouts, s'mores . . . makes my heart flutter!
Nothing quite like camp!
CAMP
Here's to summer!
Just take every day as it comes!
Looks like Camp Director Jed has assembled a great group of counselors this year.

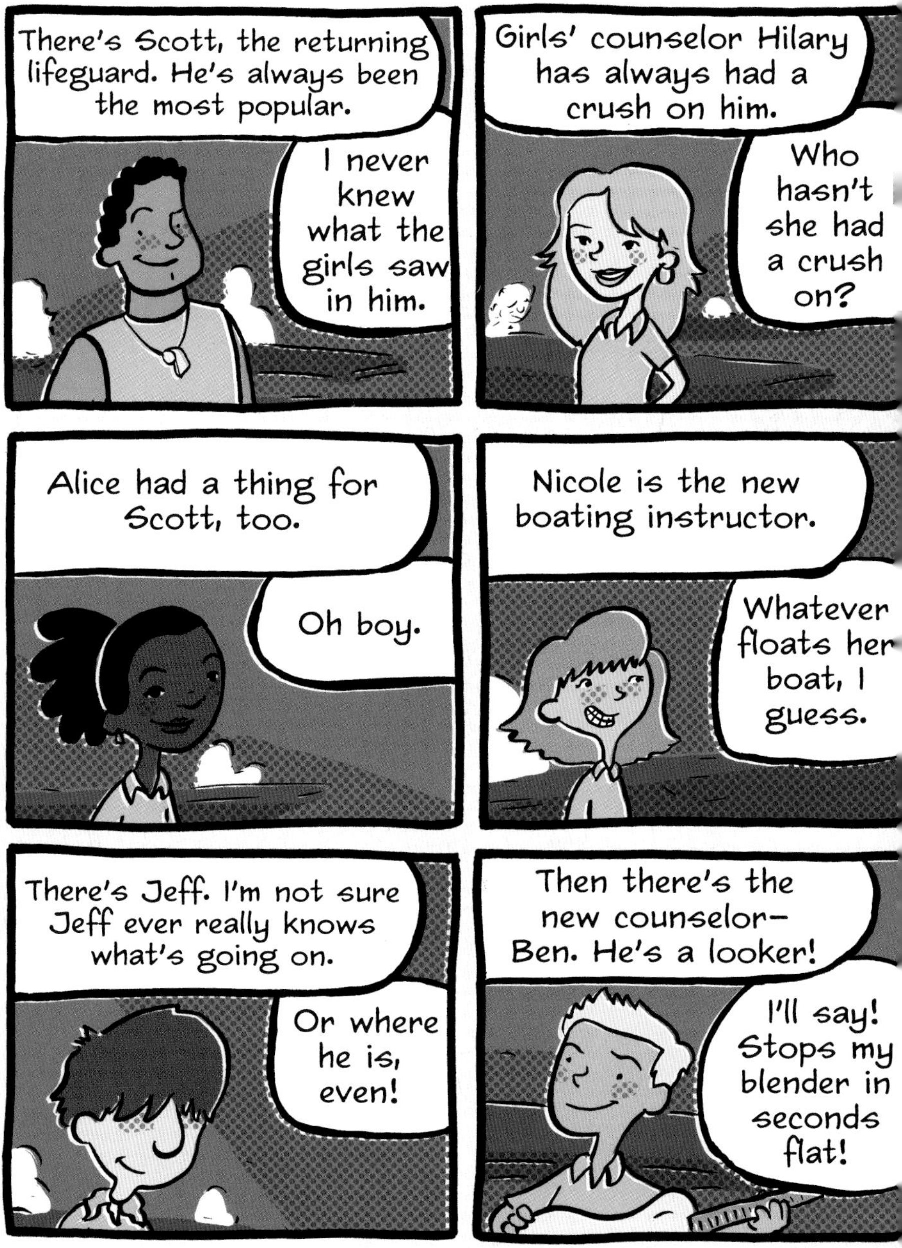

There's Scott, the returning lifeguard. He's always been the most popular.
I never knew what the girls saw in him.
Girls' counselor Hilary has always had a crush on him.
Who hasn't she had a crush on?
Alice had a thing for Scott, too.
Oh boy.
Nicole is the new boating instructor.
Whatever floats her boat, I guess.
There's Jeff. I'm not sure Jeff ever really knows what's going on.
Or where he is, even!
Then there's the new counselor–Ben. He's a looker!
I'll say! Stops my blender in seconds flat!

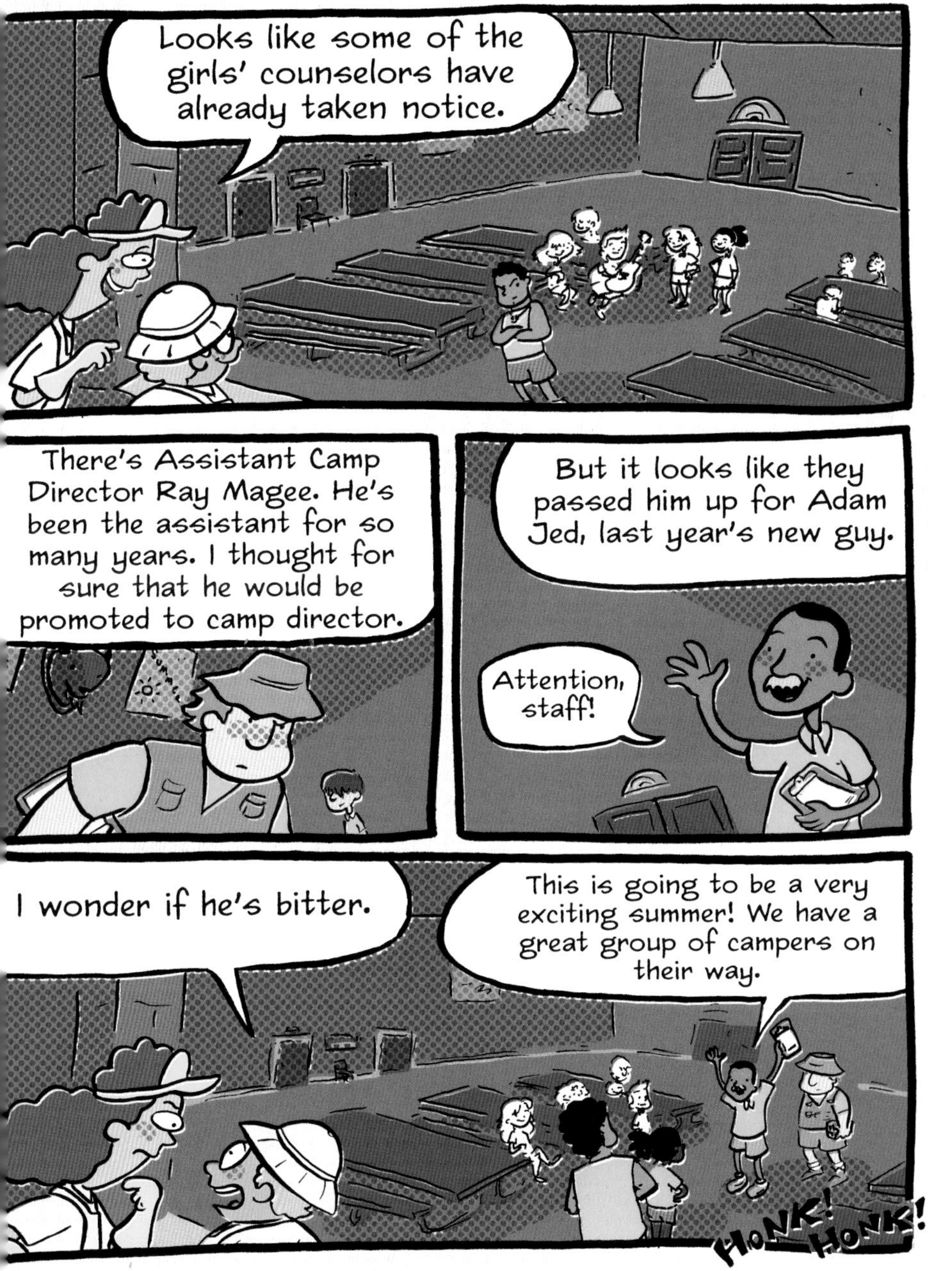

Looks like some of the girls' counselors have already taken notice.
There's Assistant Camp Director Ray Magee. He's been the assistant for so many years. I thought for sure that he would be promoted to camp director.
But it looks like they passed him up for Adam Jed, last year's new guy.
Attention, staff!
I wonder if he's bitter.
This is going to be a very exciting summer! We have a great group of campers on their way.
HONK! HONK!

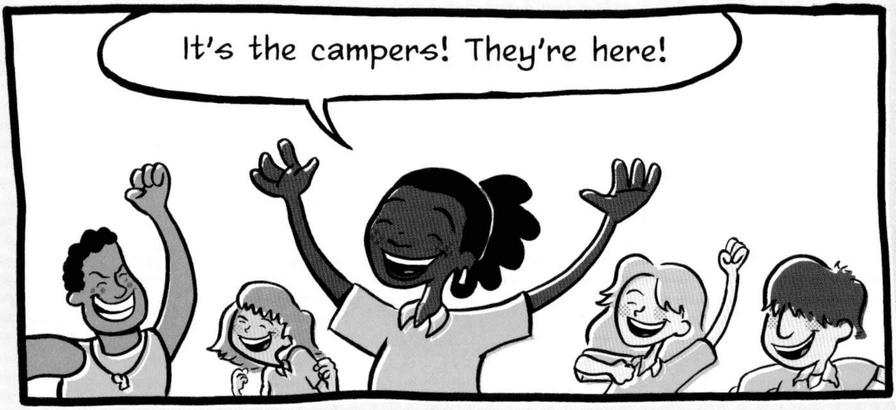
It's the campers! They're here!

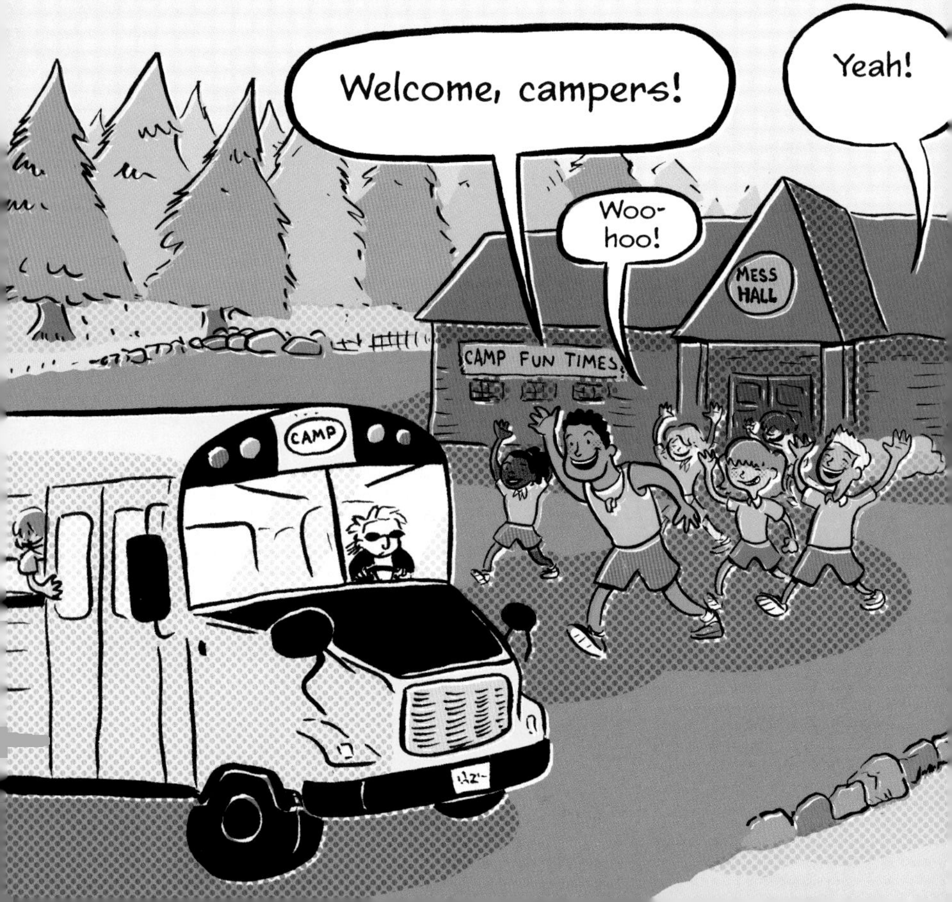
Welcome, campers!
Yeah!
Woo-hoo!
CAMP FUN TIMES
MESS HALL
CAMP

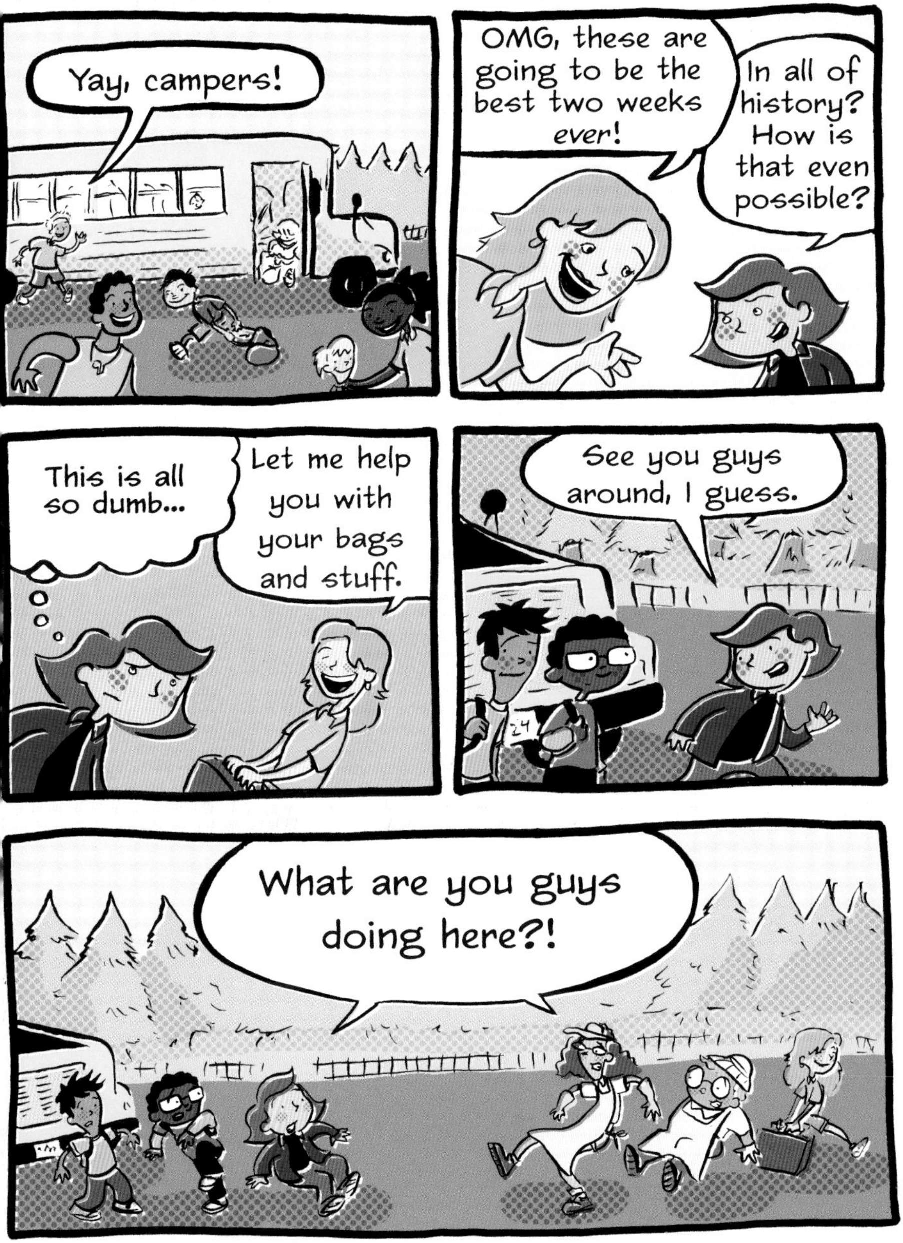
Yay, campers!
OMG, these are going to be the best two weeks ever!
In all of history? How is that even possible?
This is all so dumb...
Let me help you with your bags and stuff.
See you guys around, I guess.
What are you guys doing here?!

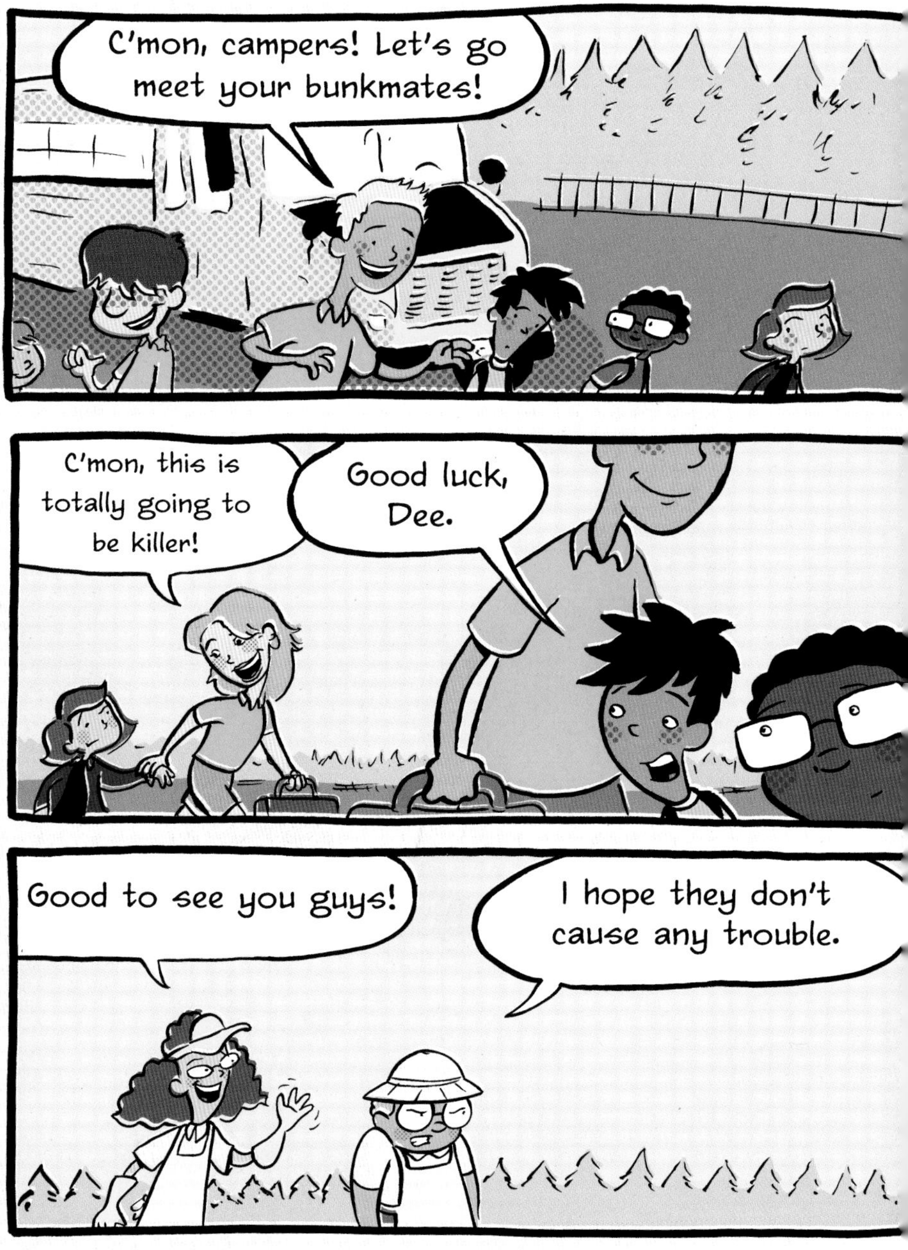
C'mon, campers! Let's go meet your bunkmates!
C'mon, this is totally going to be killer!
Good luck, Dee.
Good to see you guys!
I hope they don't cause any trouble.

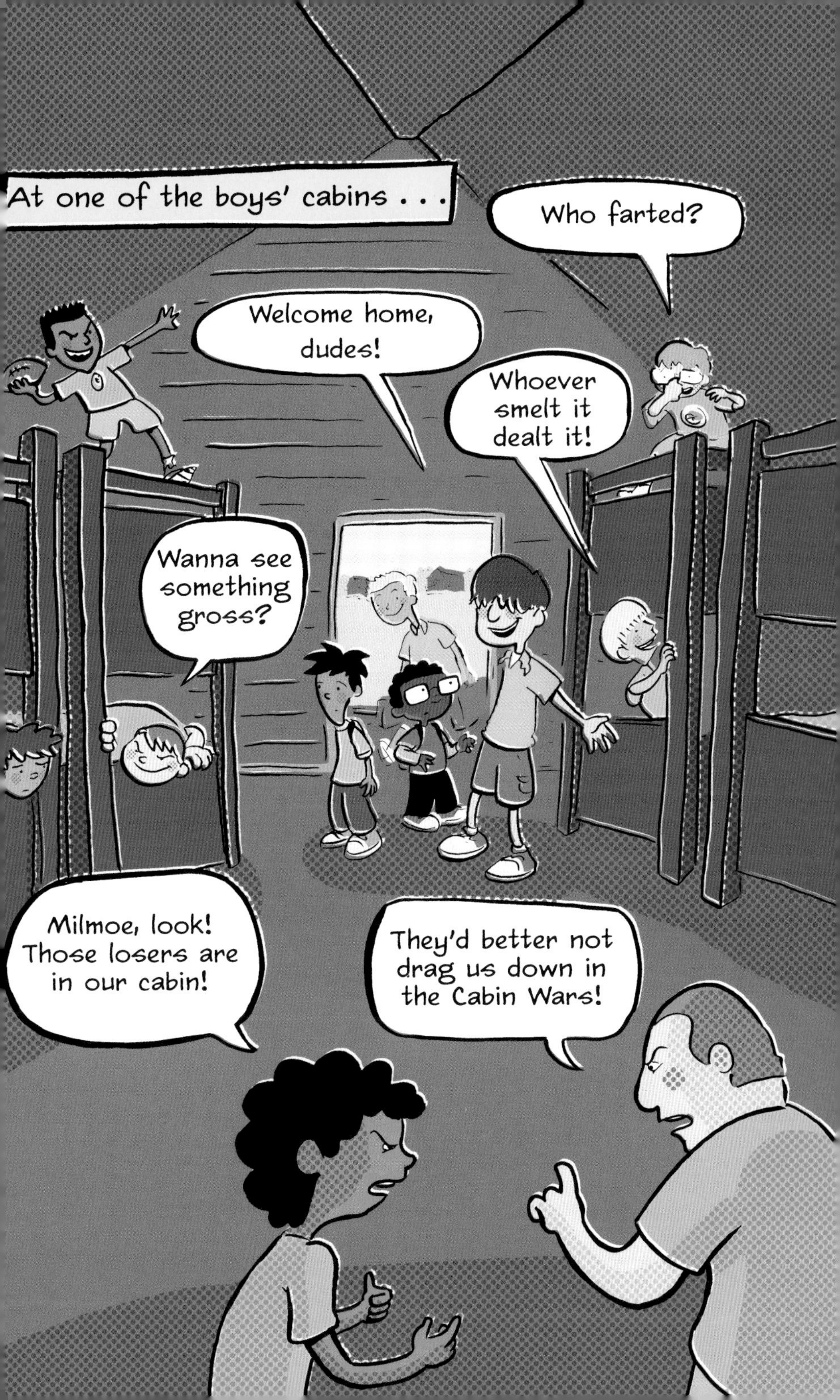
At one of the boys' cabins . . .
Who farted?
Welcome home, dudes!
Whoever smelt it dealt it!
Wanna see something gross?
Milmoe, look! Those losers are in our cabin!
They'd better not drag us down in the Cabin Wars!

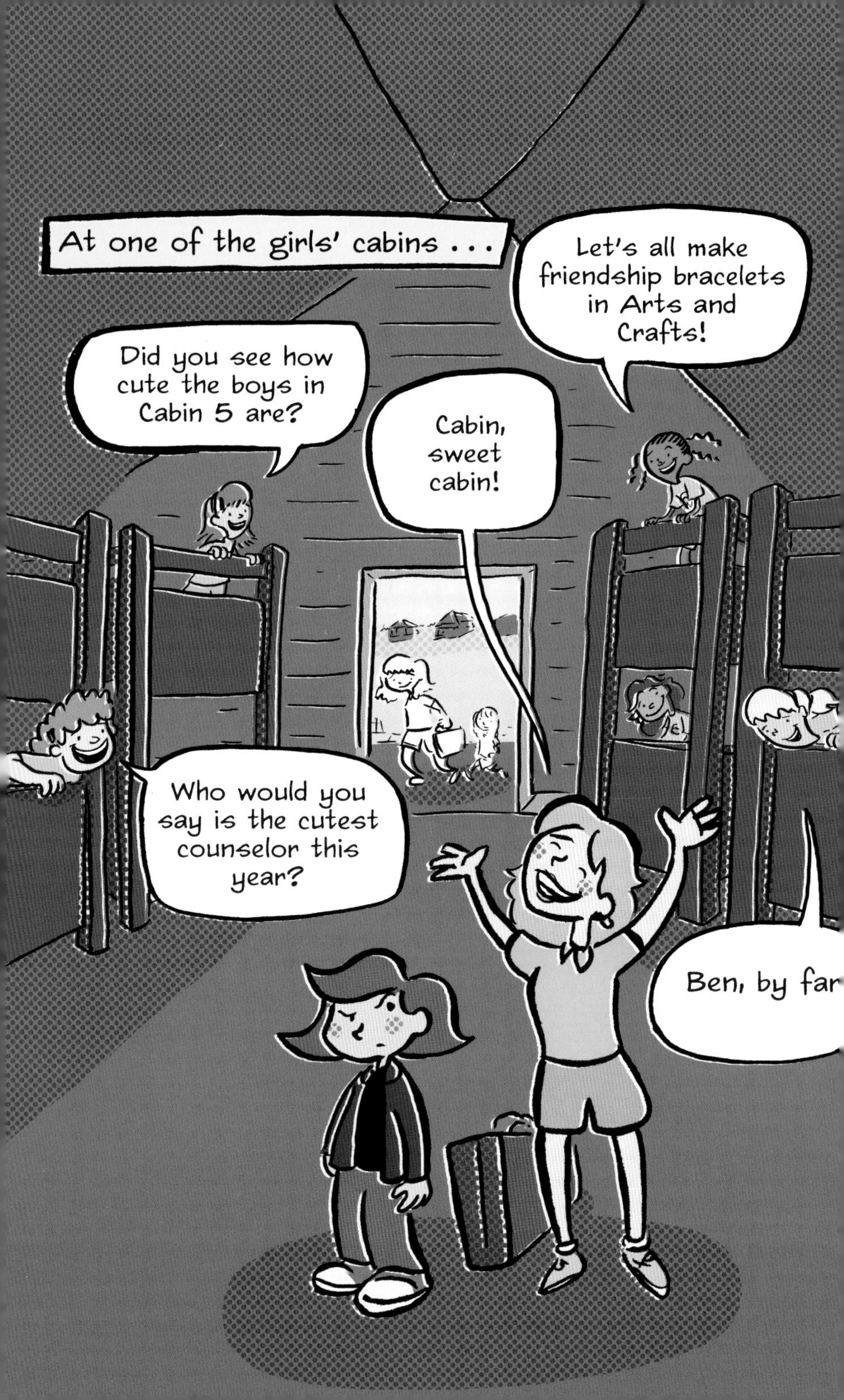
At one of the girls' cabins . . .
Did you see how cute the boys in Cabin 5 are?
Let's all make friendship bracelets in Arts and Crafts!
Cabin, sweet cabin!
Who would you say is the cutest counselor this year?
Ben, by far

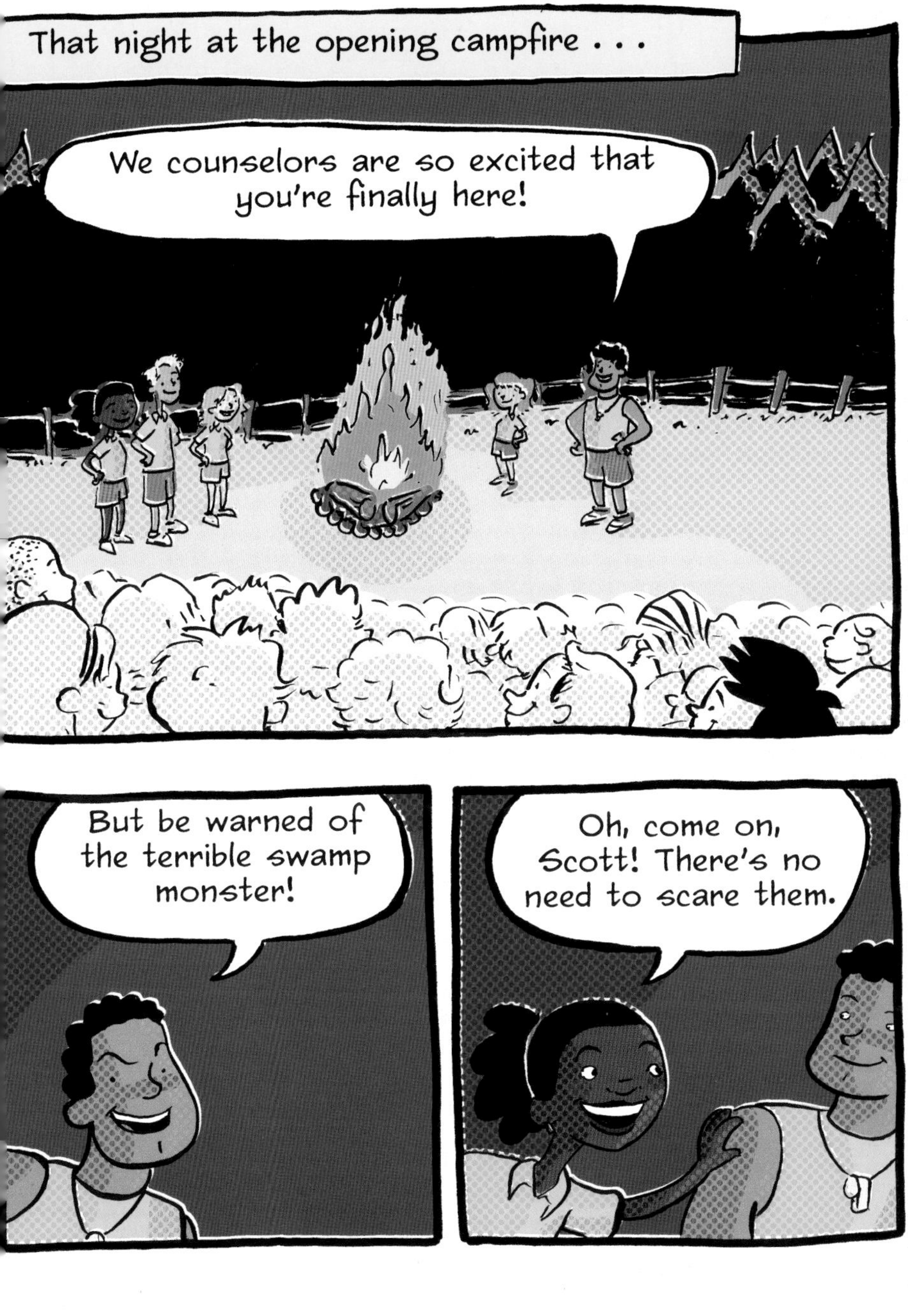
That night at the opening campfire . . .
We counselors are so excited that you're finally here!
But be warned of the terrible swamp monster!
Oh, come on, Scott! There's no need to scare them.

But they should know the story . . .

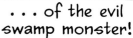

. . . of the evil swamp monster!

He lives at the bottom of the pond and eats squirrels for lunch!

He has legs the size of tree trunks!

And fangs as sharp as knives!

On the rare occasion a camper wanders off alone . . .

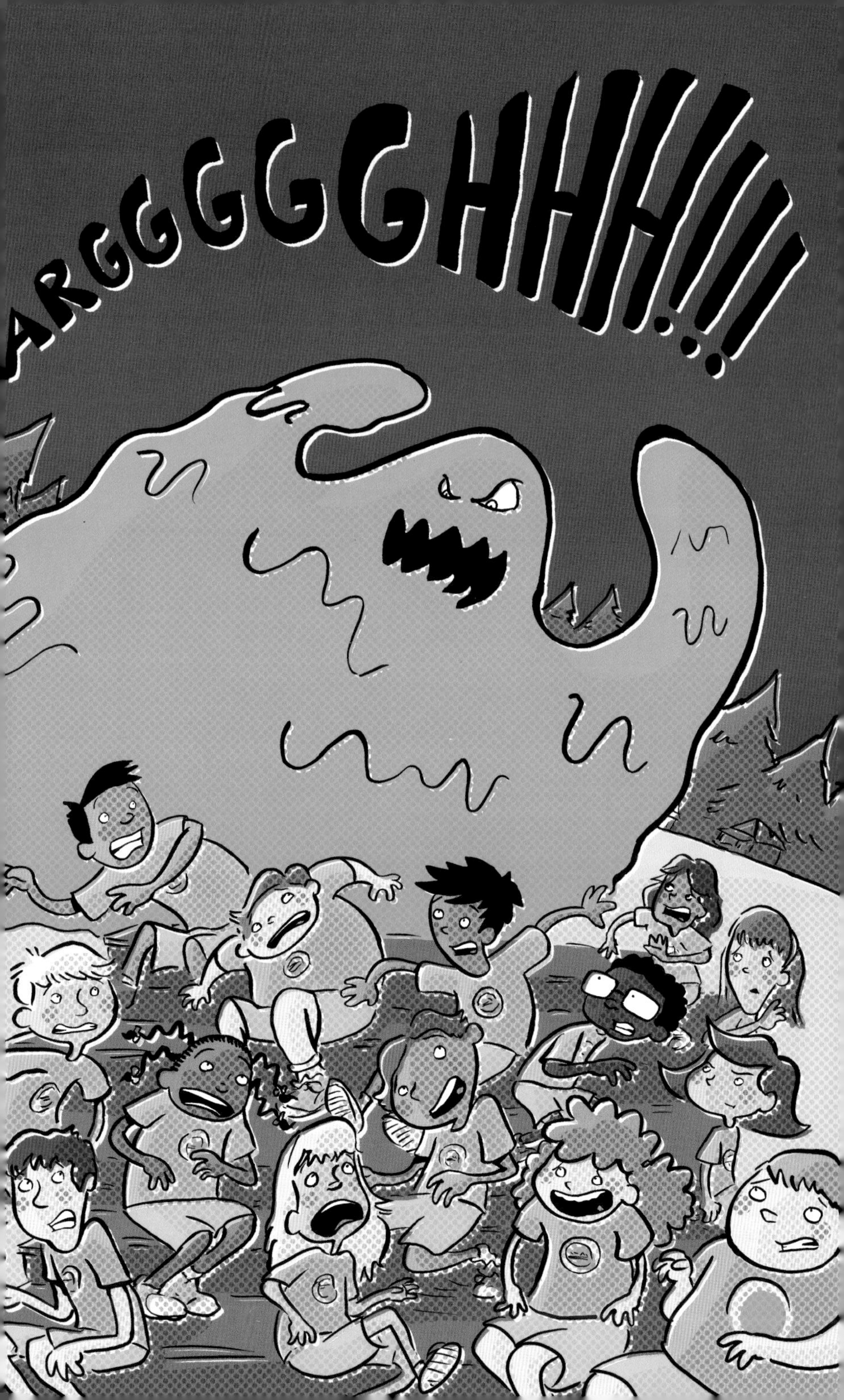
ARGGGGGGHHHH!!!

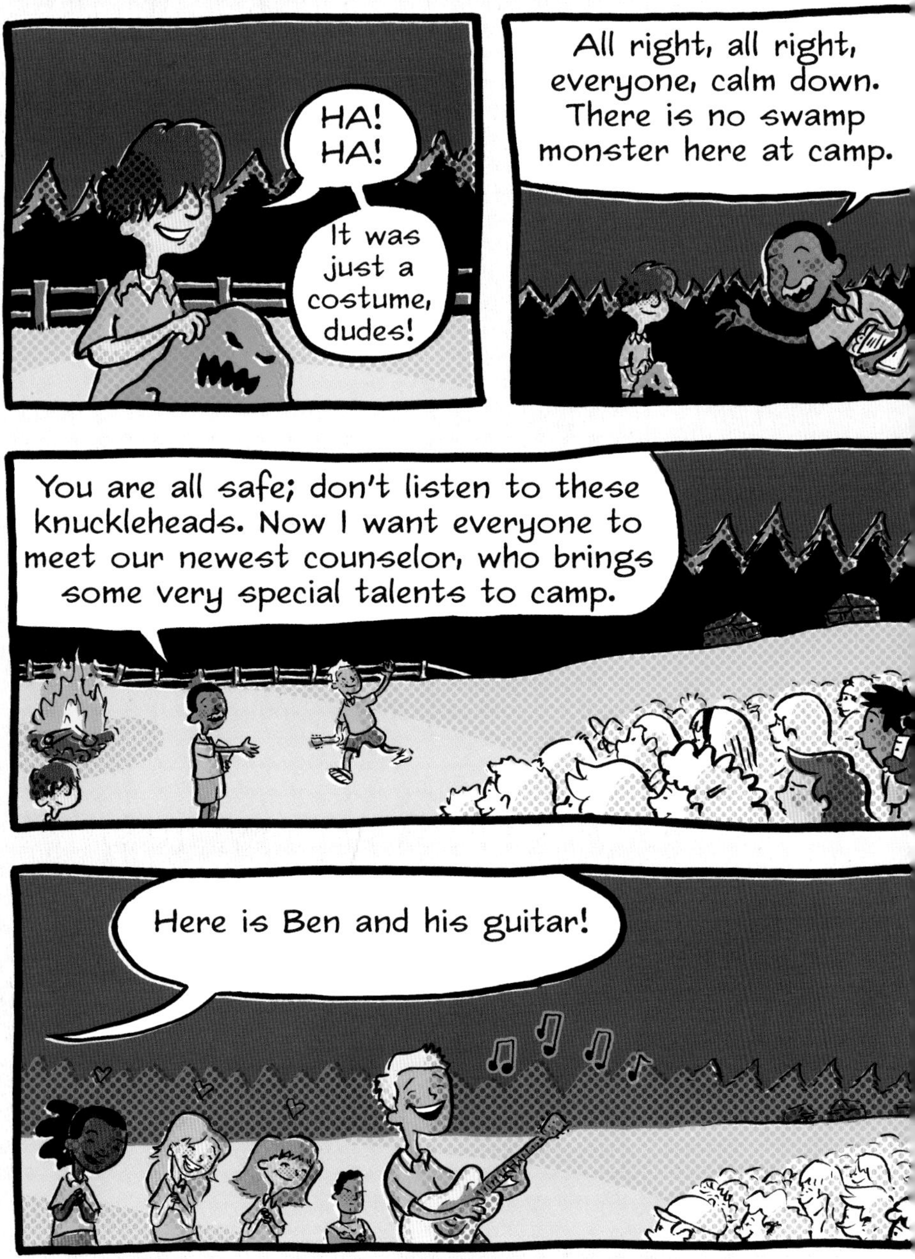
HA! HA!
It was just a costume, dudes!
All right, all right, everyone, calm down. There is no swamp monster here at camp.
You are all safe; don't listen to these knuckleheads. Now I want everyone to meet our newest counselor, who brings some very special talents to camp.
Here is Ben and his guitar!

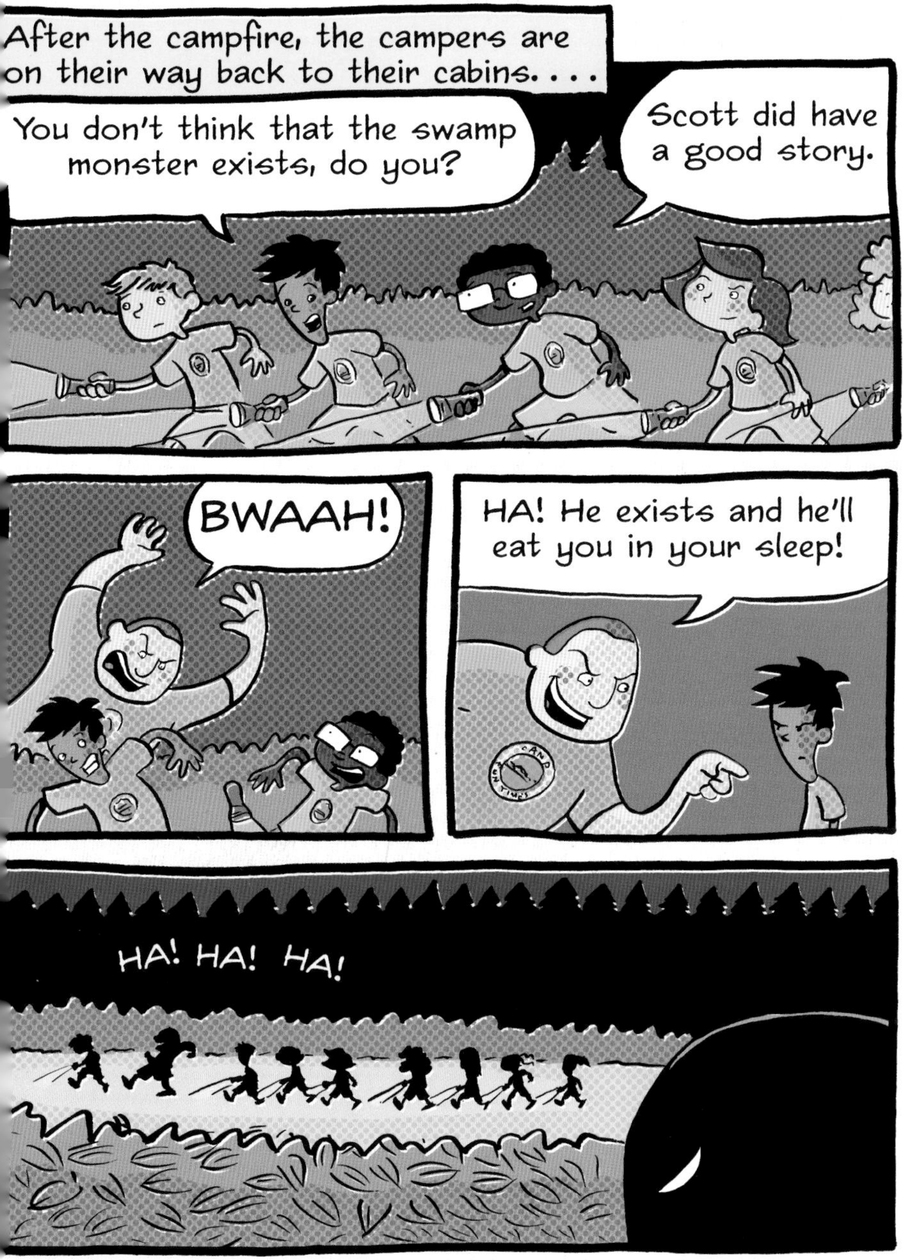
After the campfire, the campers are on their way back to their cabins. . . .
You don't think that the swamp monster exists, do you?
Scott did have a good story.
BWAAH!
HA! He exists and he'll eat you in your sleep!
HA! HA! HA!

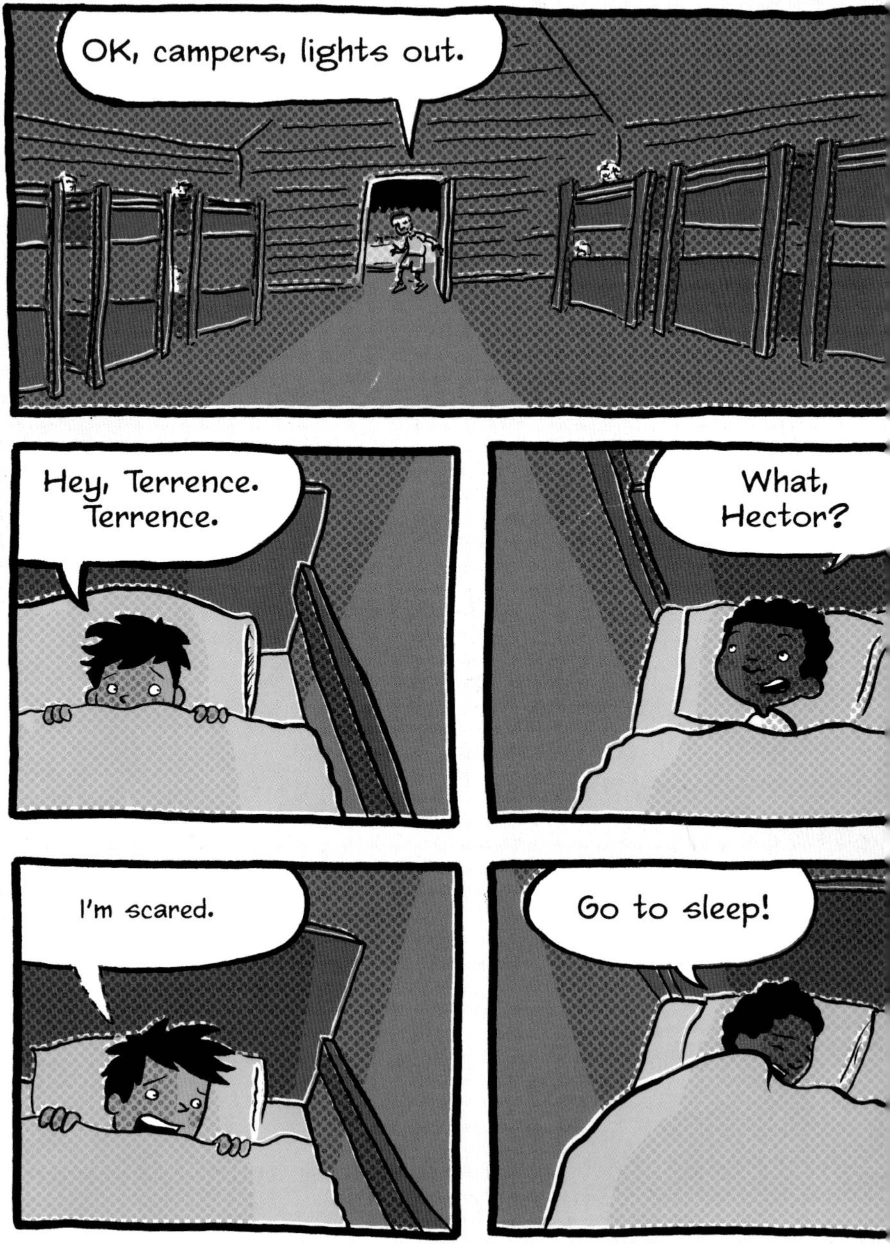
OK, campers, lights out.
Hey, Terrence. Terrence.
What, Hector?
I'm scared.
Go to sleep!

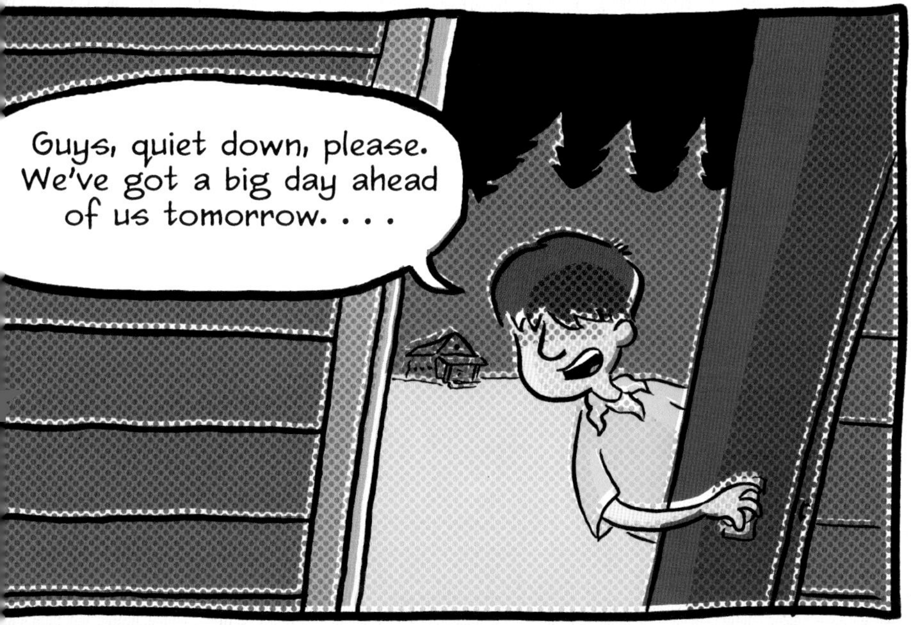
Guys, quiet down, please. We've got a big day ahead of us tomorrow. . . .

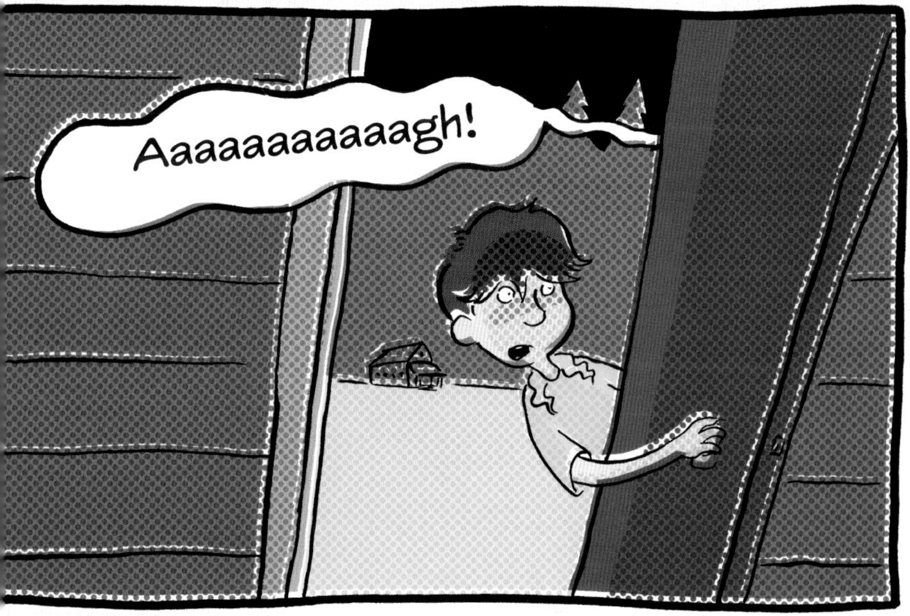
Aaaaaaaaaaagh!

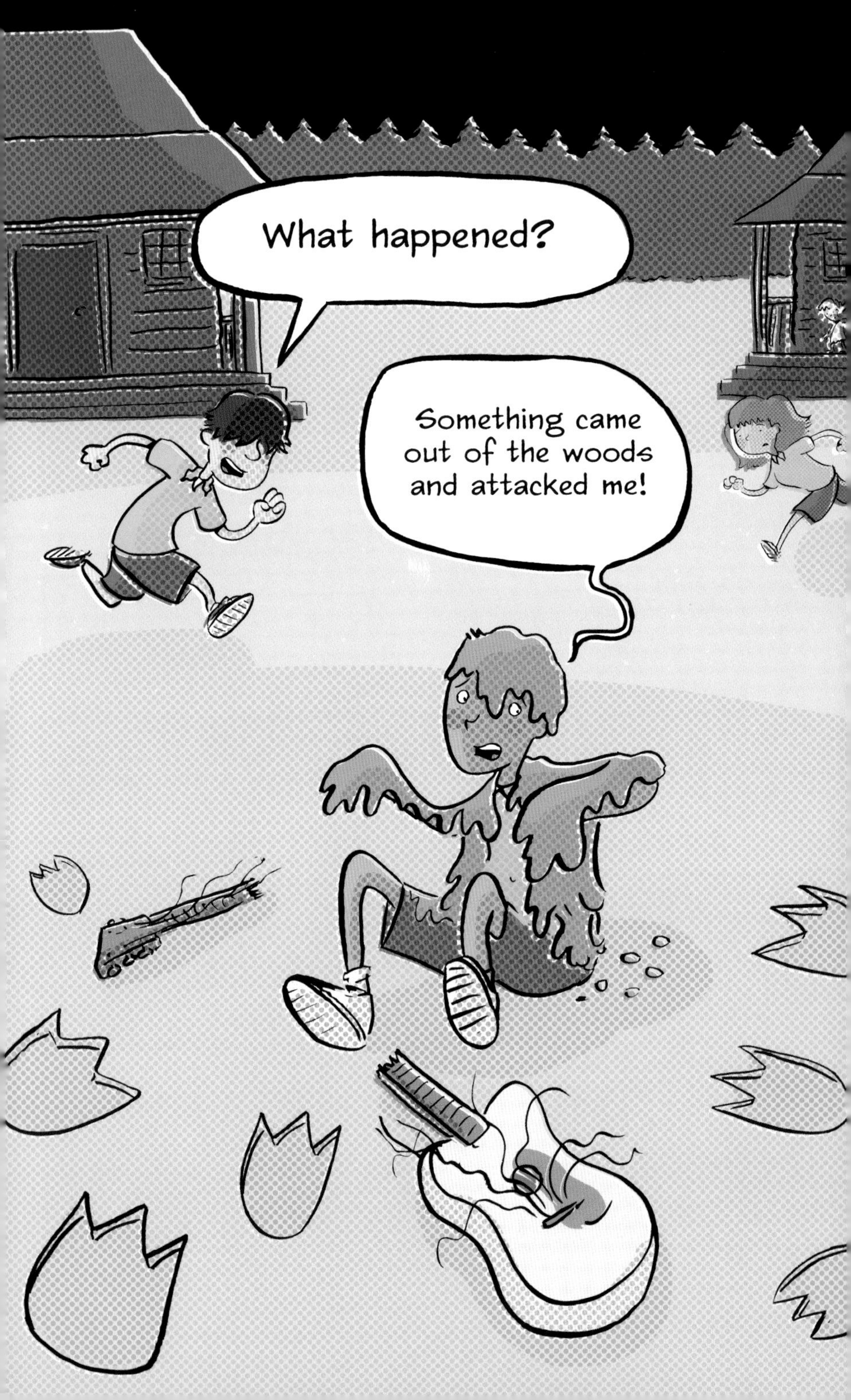
What happened?
Something came out of the woods and attacked me!

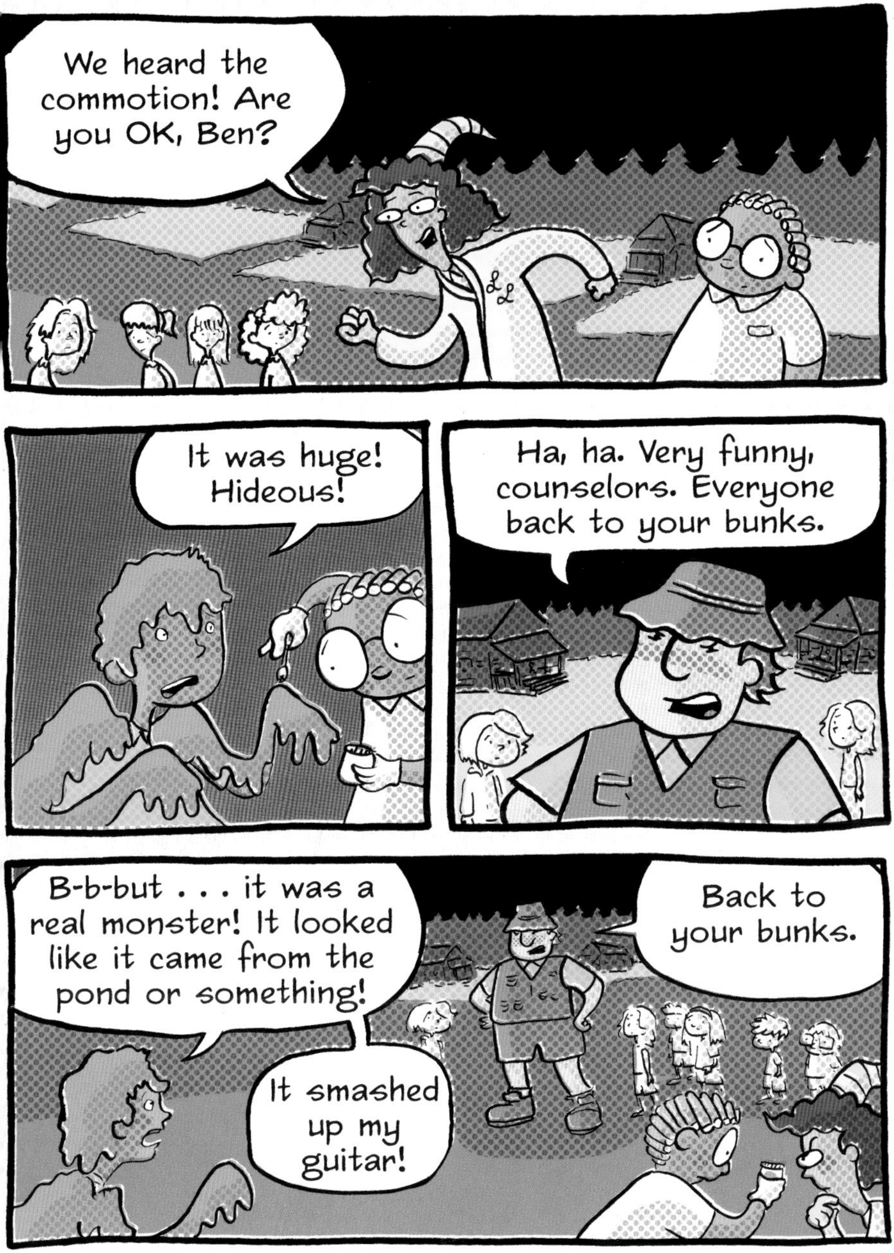

We heard the commotion! Are you OK, Ben?
It was huge! Hideous!
Ha, ha. Very funny, counselors. Everyone back to your bunks.
B-b-but . . . it was a real monster! It looked like it came from the pond or something!
It smashed up my guitar!
Back to your bunks.

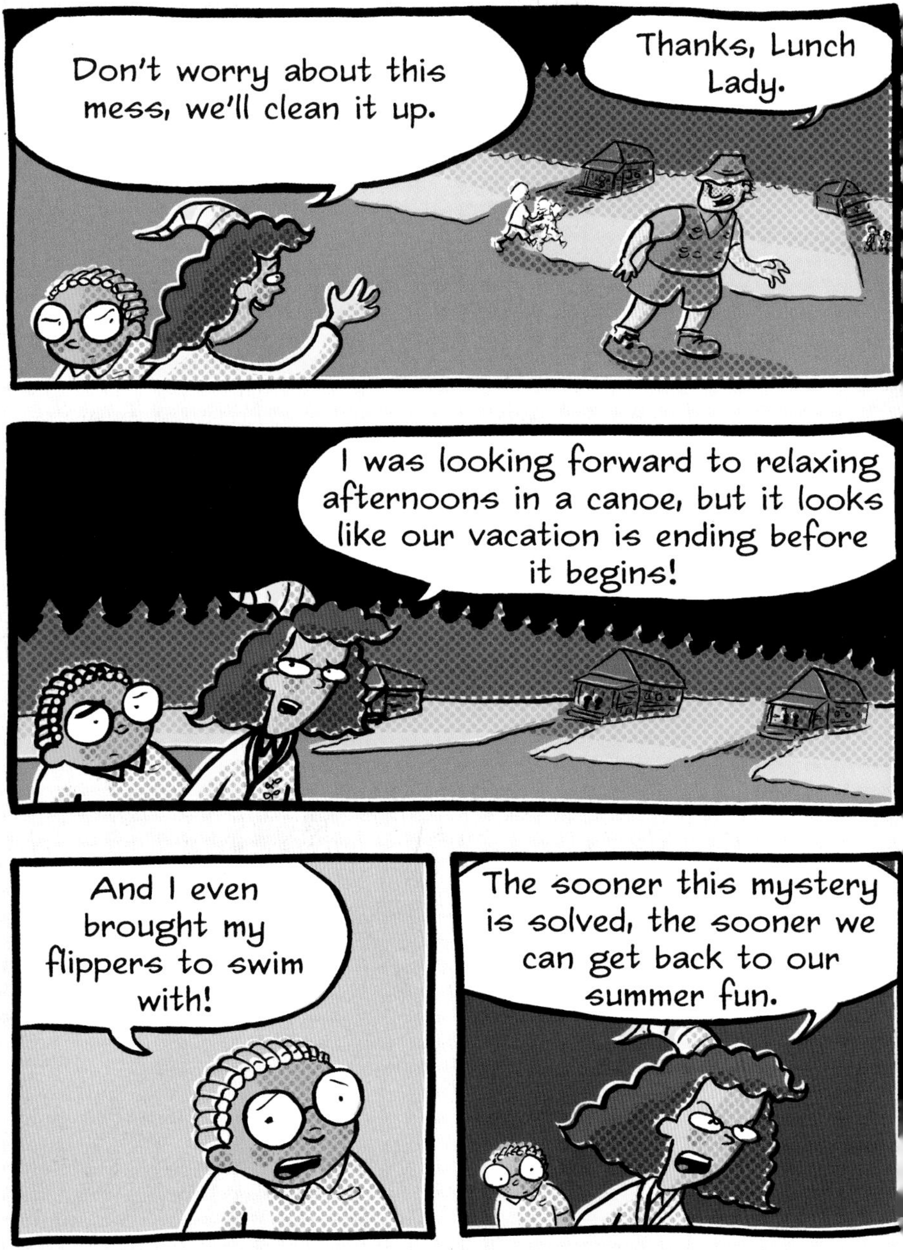
Don't worry about this mess, we'll clean it up.
Thanks, Lunch Lady.
I was looking forward to relaxing afternoons in a canoe, but it looks like our vacation is ending before it begins!
And I even brought my flippers to swim with!
The sooner this mystery is solved, the sooner we can get back to our summer fun.

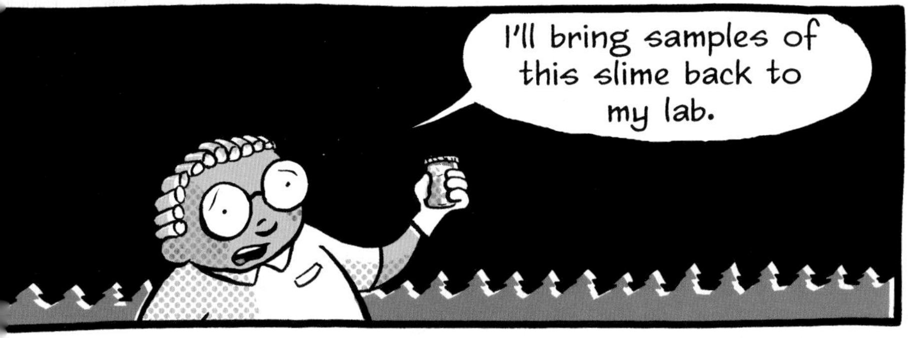
I'll bring samples of this slime back to my lab.

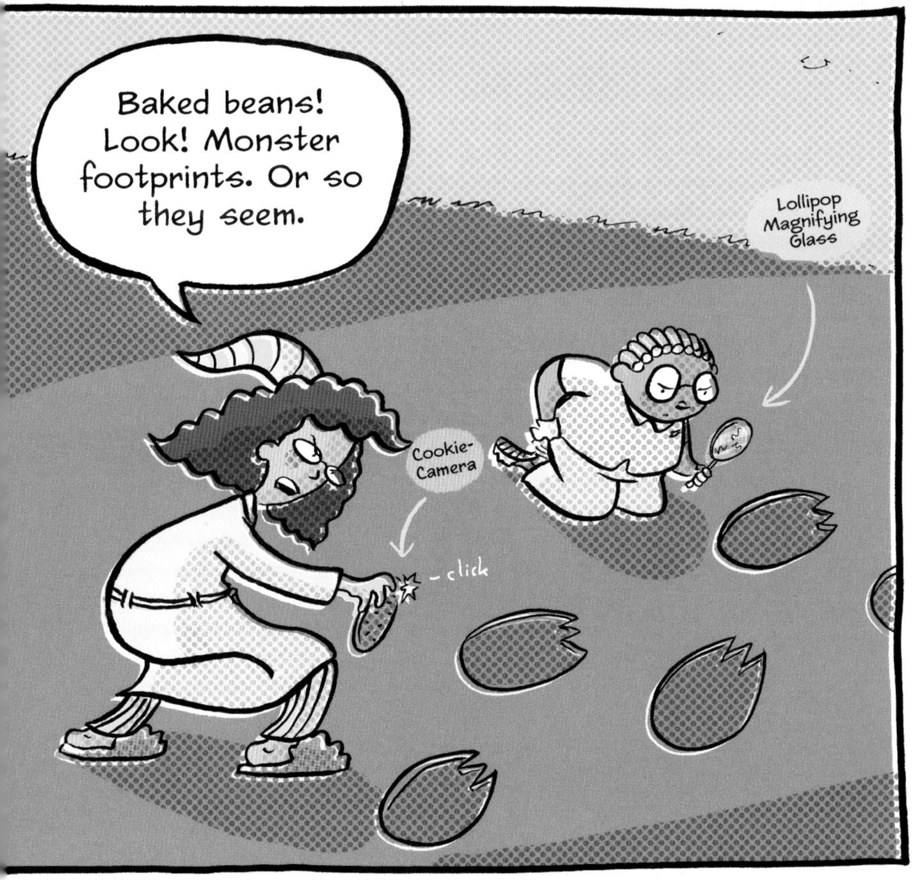
Baked beans! Look! Monster footprints. Or so they seem.
Lollipop Magnifying Glass
Cookie-Camera
-click

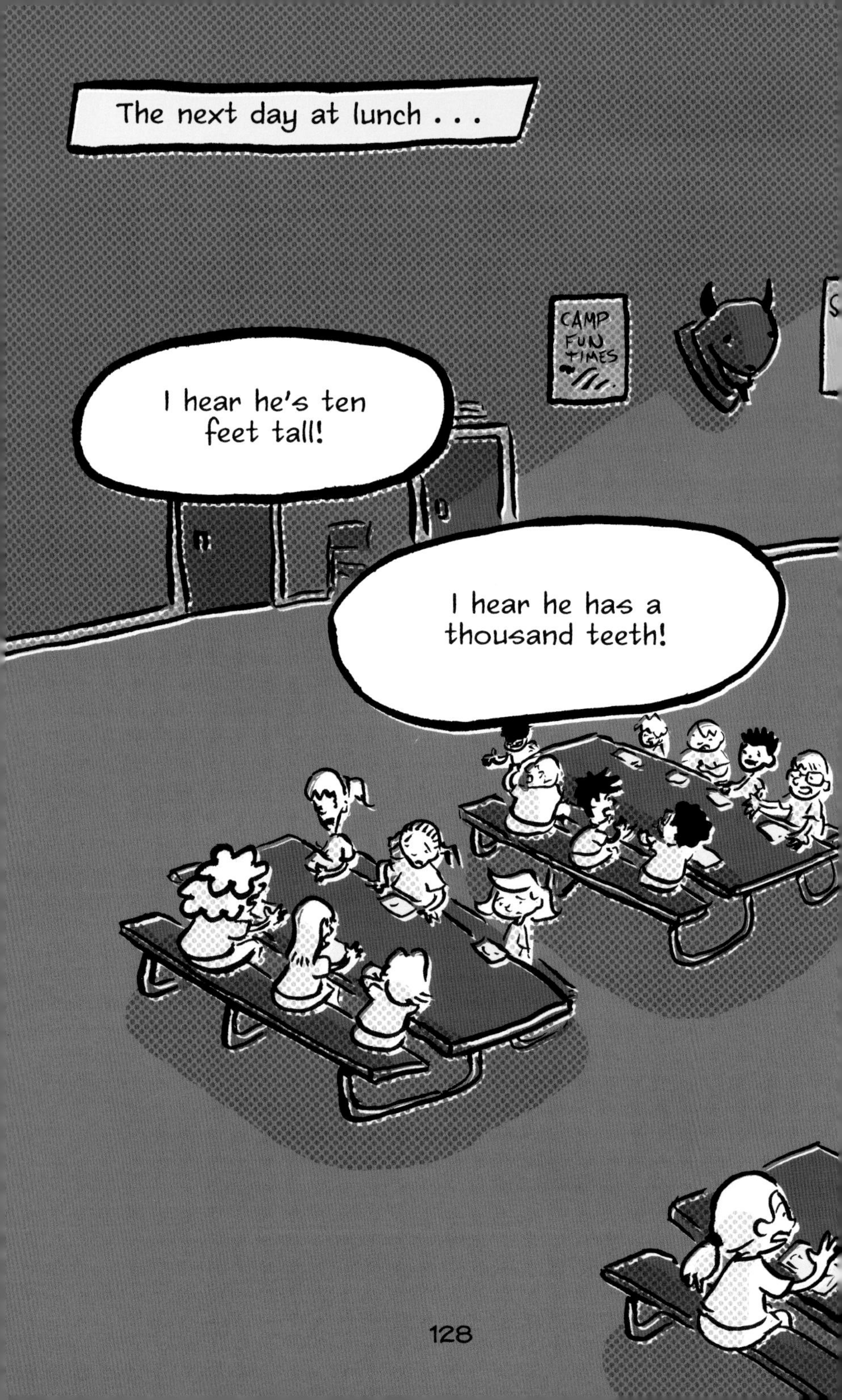

The next day at lunch . . .
CAMP FUN TIMES
I hear he's ten feet tall!
I hear he has a thousand teeth!

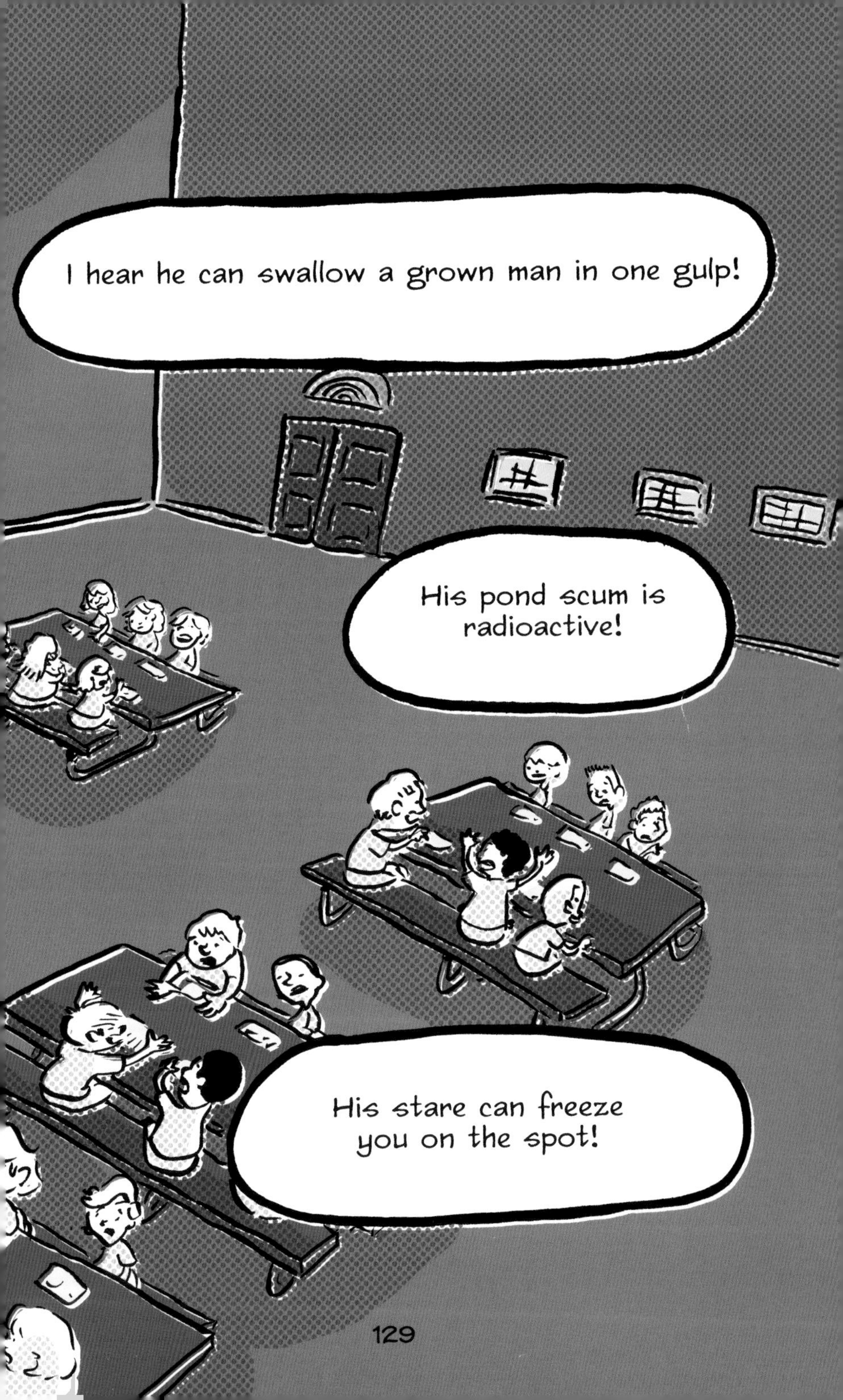
I hear he can swallow a grown man in one gulp!
His pond scum is radioactive!
His stare can freeze you on the spot!

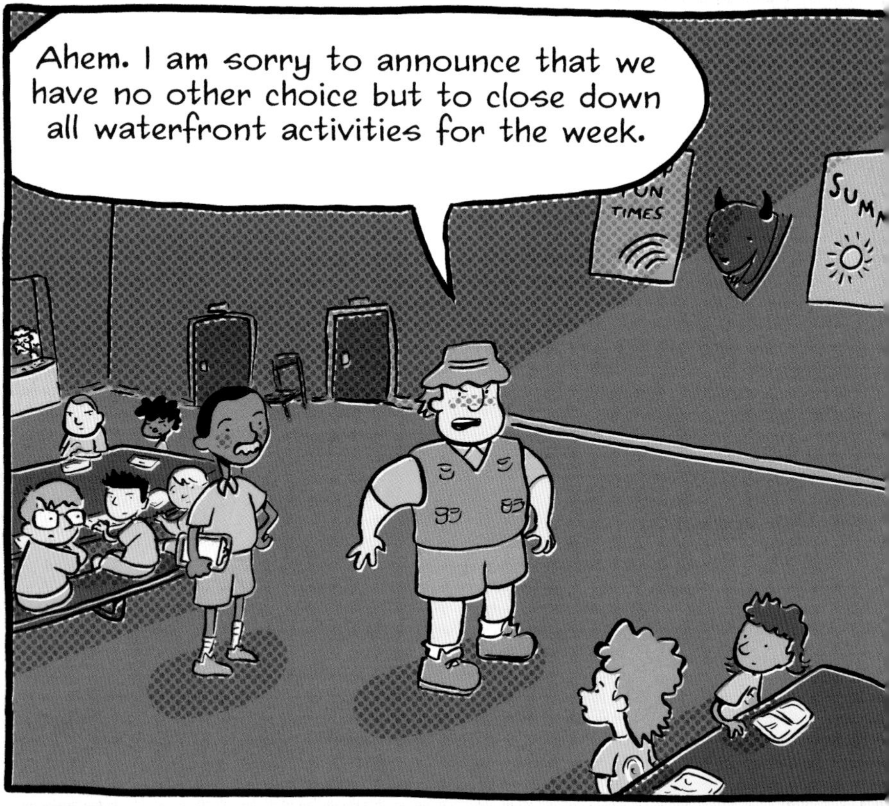
Ahem. I am sorry to announce that we have no other choice but to close down all waterfront activities for the week.
FUN
TIMES
SUM

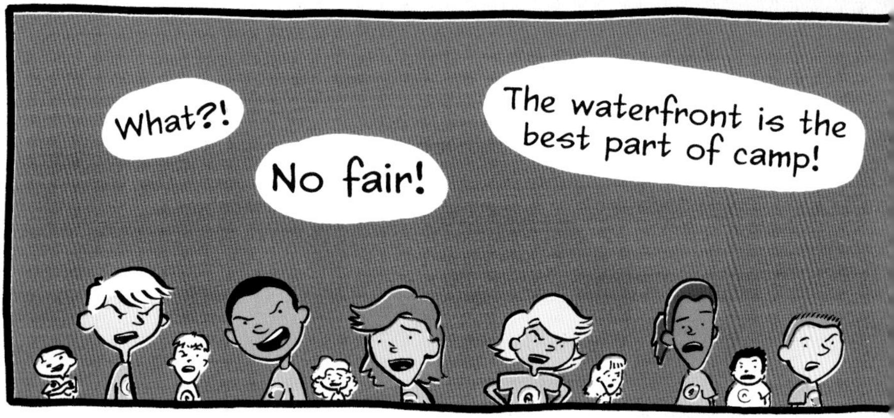
What?!
No fair!
The waterfront is the best part of camp!

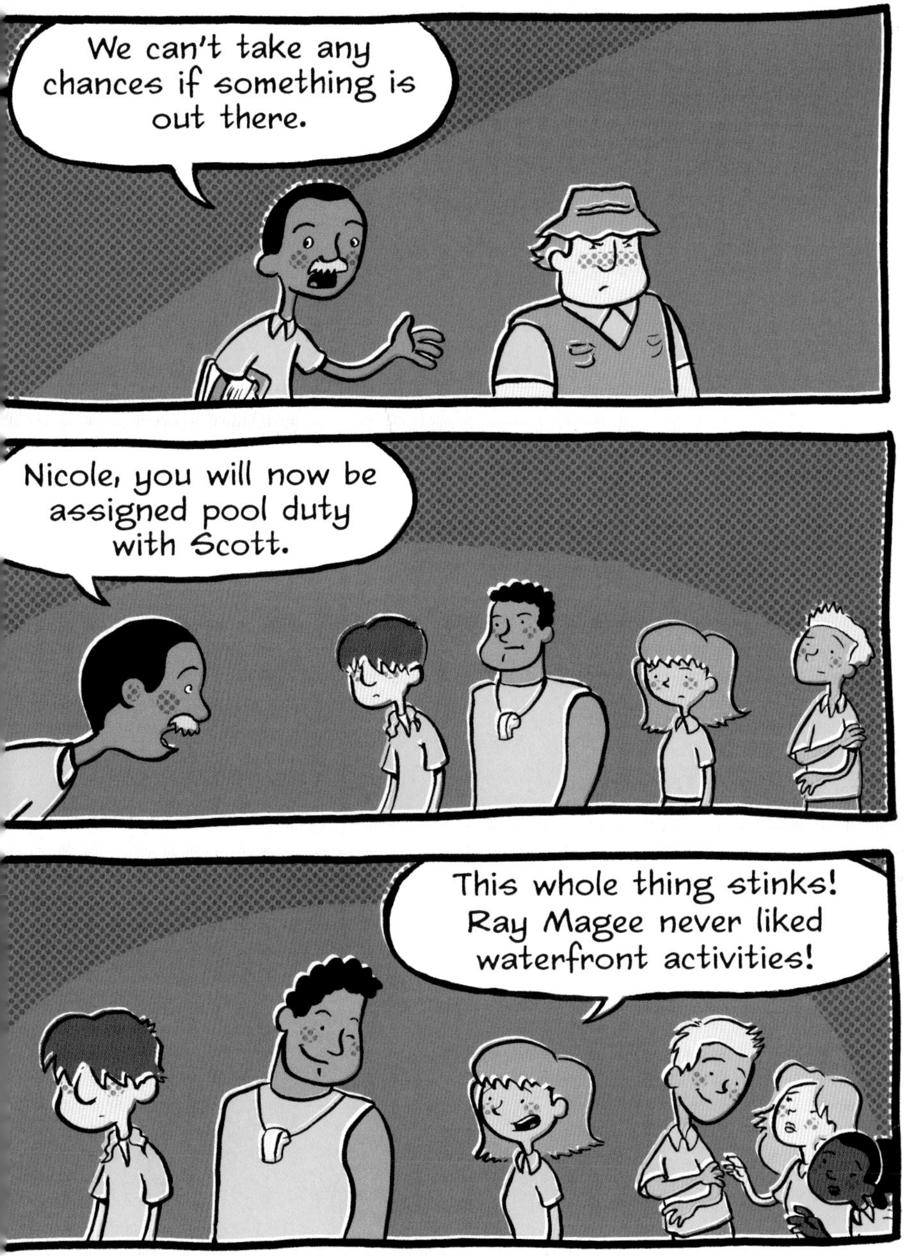
We can't take any chances if something is out there.
Nicole, you will now be assigned pool duty with Scott.
This whole thing stinks! Ray Magee never liked waterfront activities!

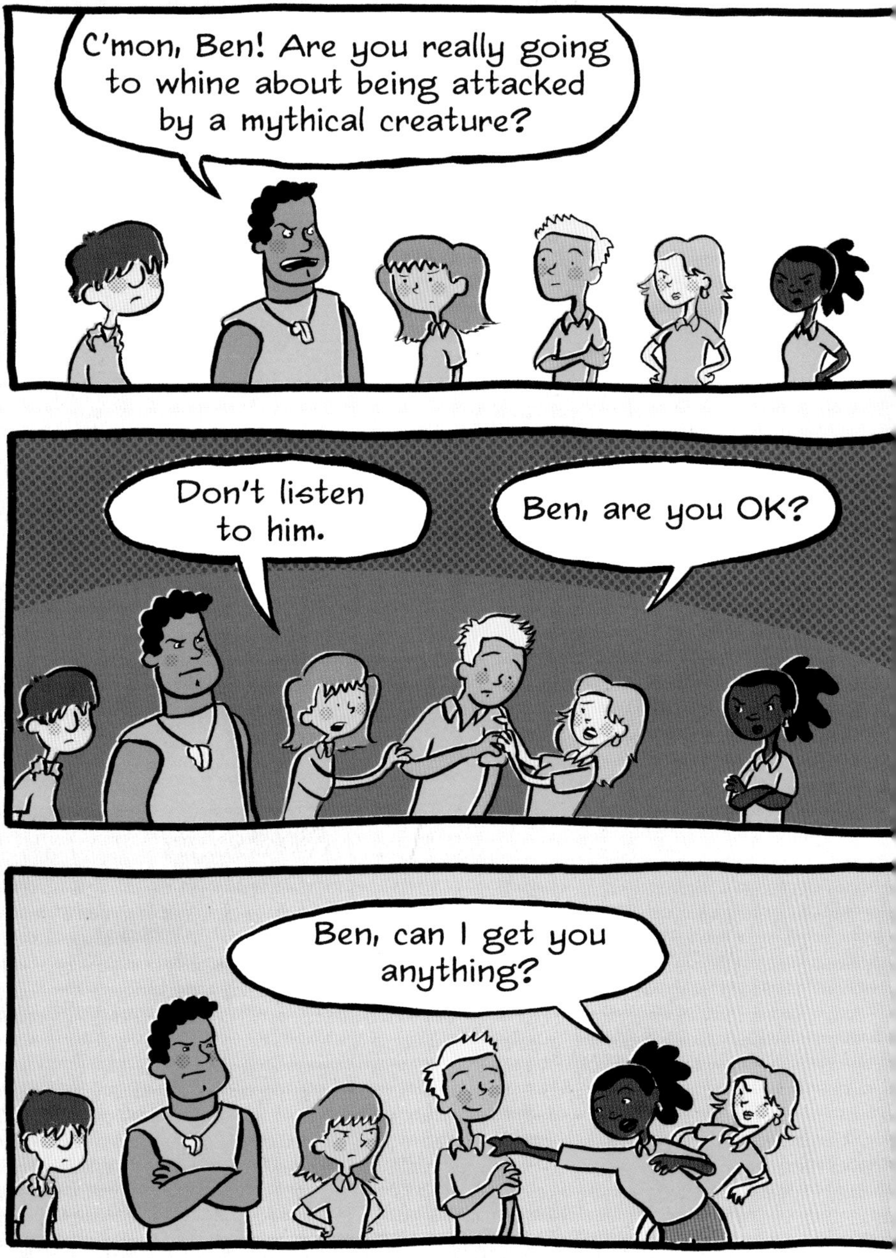
C'mon, Ben! Are you really going to whine about being attacked by a mythical creature?
Don't listen to him.
Ben, are you OK?
Ben, can I get you anything?

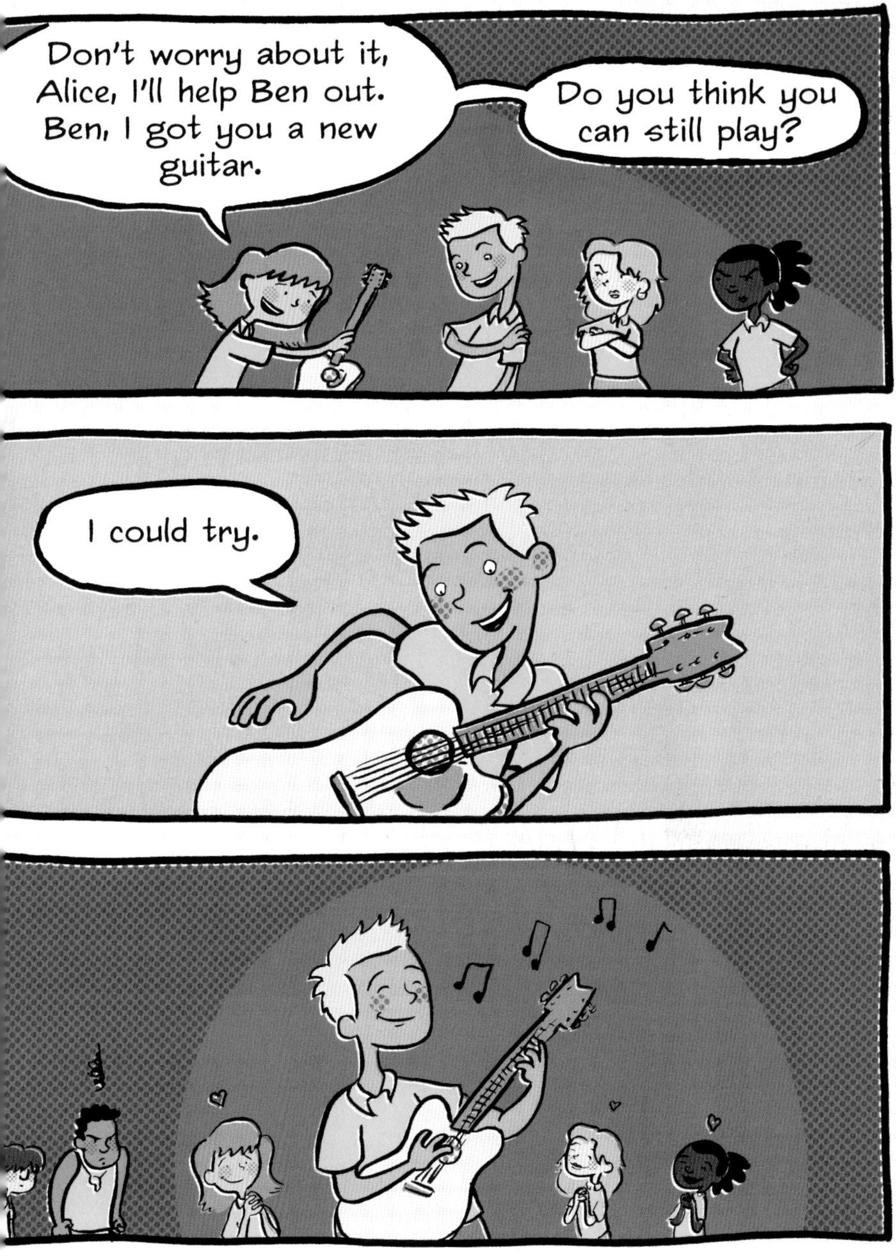

Don't worry about it, Alice, I'll help Ben out. Ben, I got you a new guitar.
Do you think you can still play?
I could try.

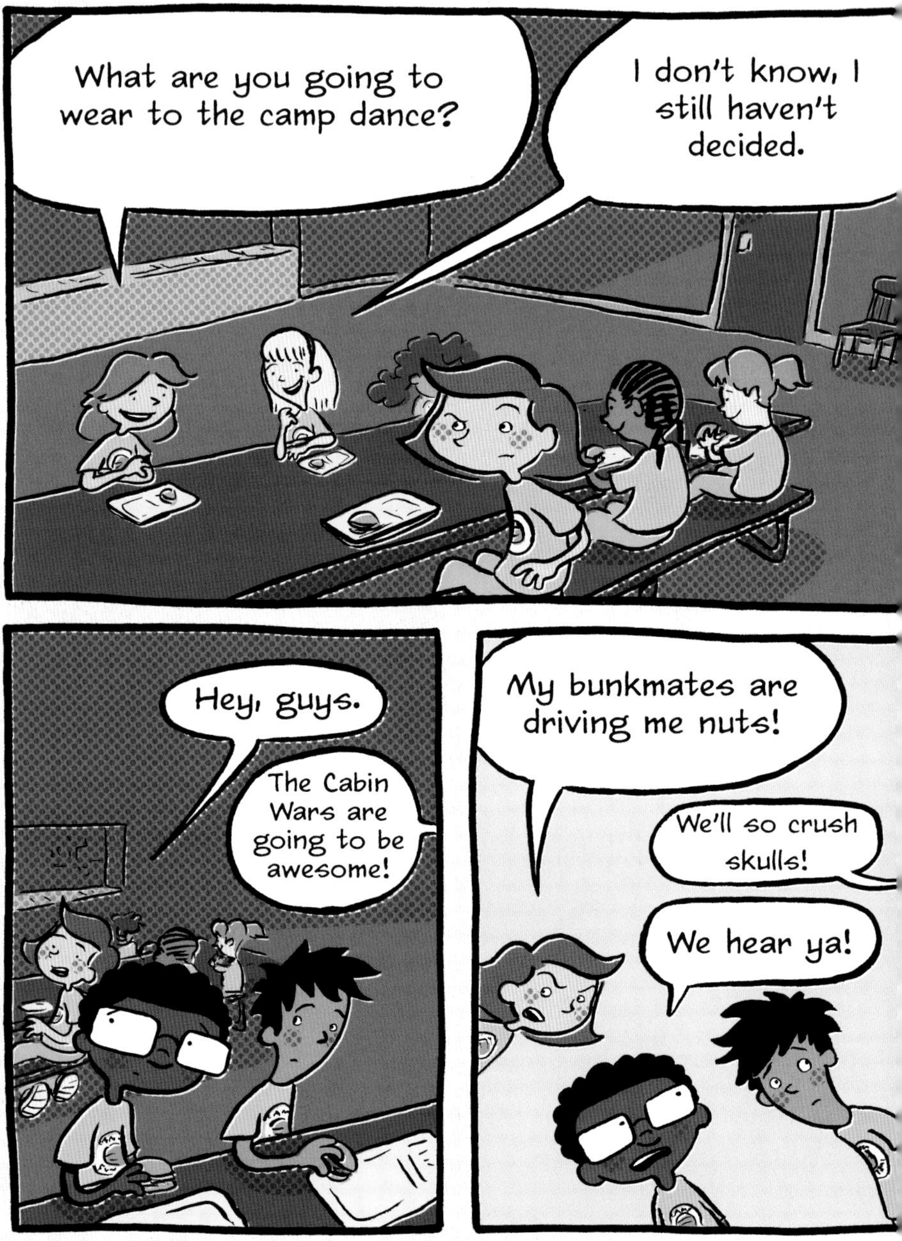
What are you going to wear to the camp dance?
I don't know, I still haven't decided.
Hey, guys.
The Cabin Wars are going to be awesome!
My bunkmates are driving me nuts!
We'll so crush skulls!
We hear ya!

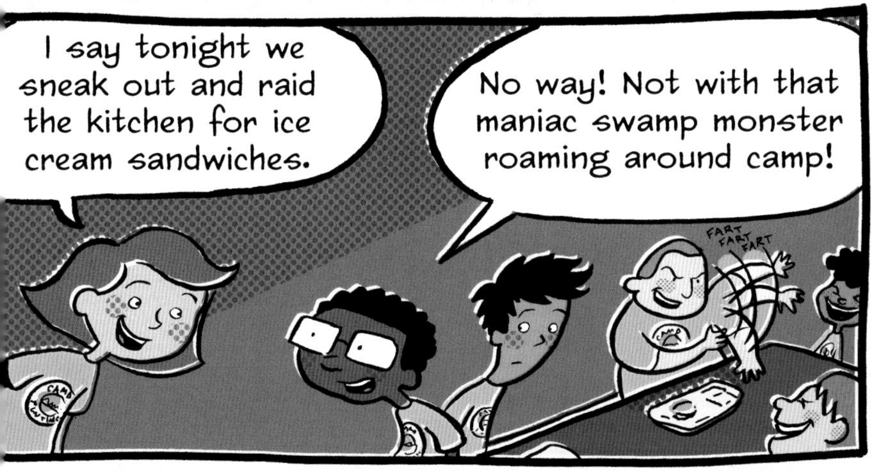
I say tonight we sneak out and raid the kitchen for ice cream sandwiches.
No way! Not with that maniac swamp monster roaming around camp!
FART FART FART

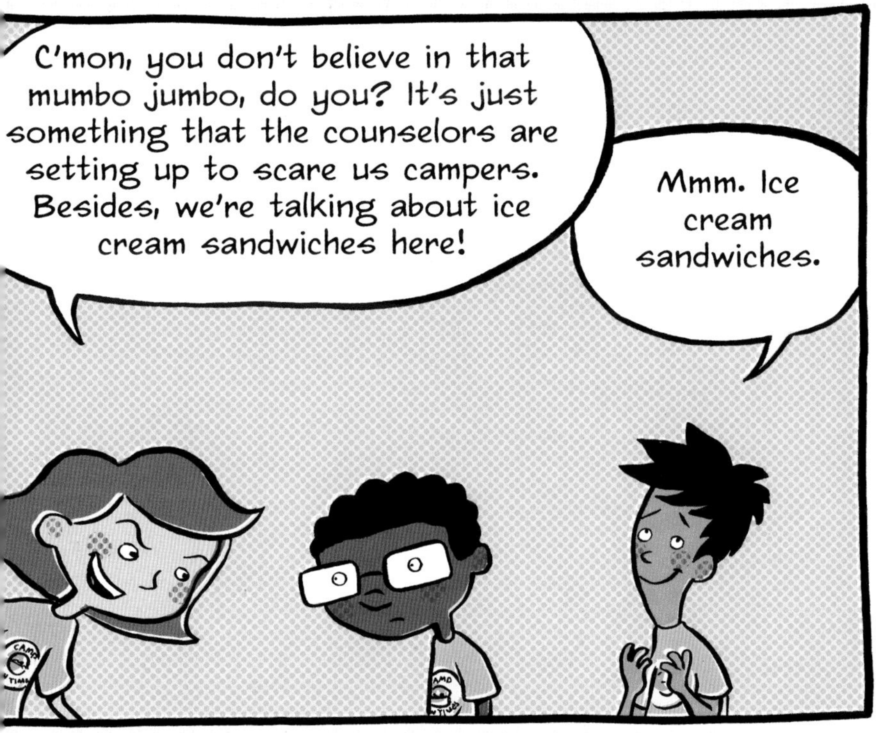
C'mon, you don't believe in that mumbo jumbo, do you? It's just something that the counselors are setting up to scare us campers. Besides, we're talking about ice cream sandwiches here!
Mmm. Ice cream sandwiches.

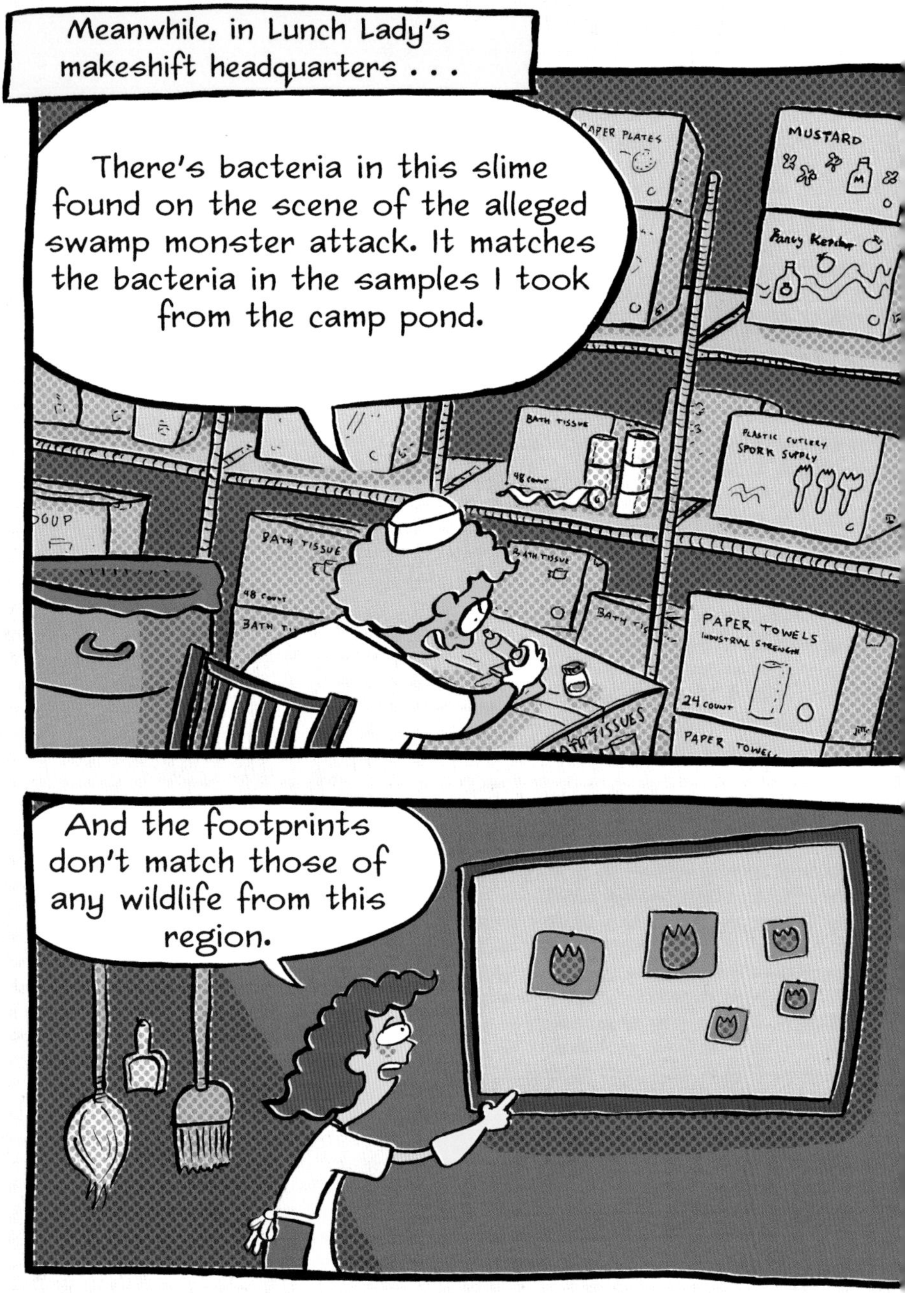
Meanwhile, in Lunch Lady's makeshift headquarters . . .
There's bacteria in this slime found on the scene of the alleged swamp monster attack. It matches the bacteria in the samples I took from the camp pond.
MUSTARD
Fancy Ketchup
BATH TISSUE
48 COUNT
PLASTIC CUTLERY
SPORK SUPPLY
PAPER TOWELS
INDUSTRIAL STRENGTH
24 COUNT
And the footprints don't match those of any wildlife from this region.

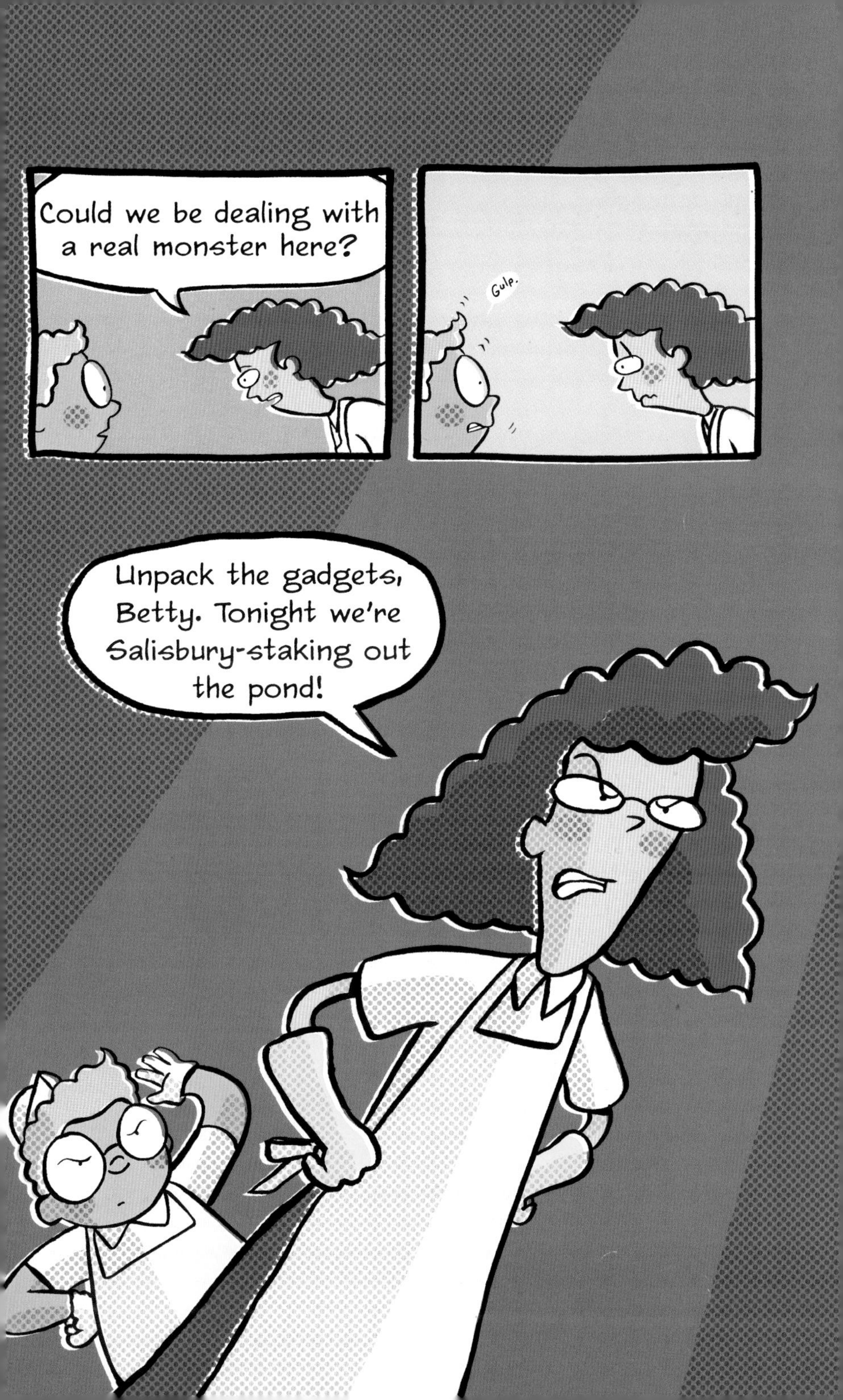
Could we be dealing with a real monster here?
Gulp.
Unpack the gadgets, Betty. Tonight we're Salisbury-staking out the pond!

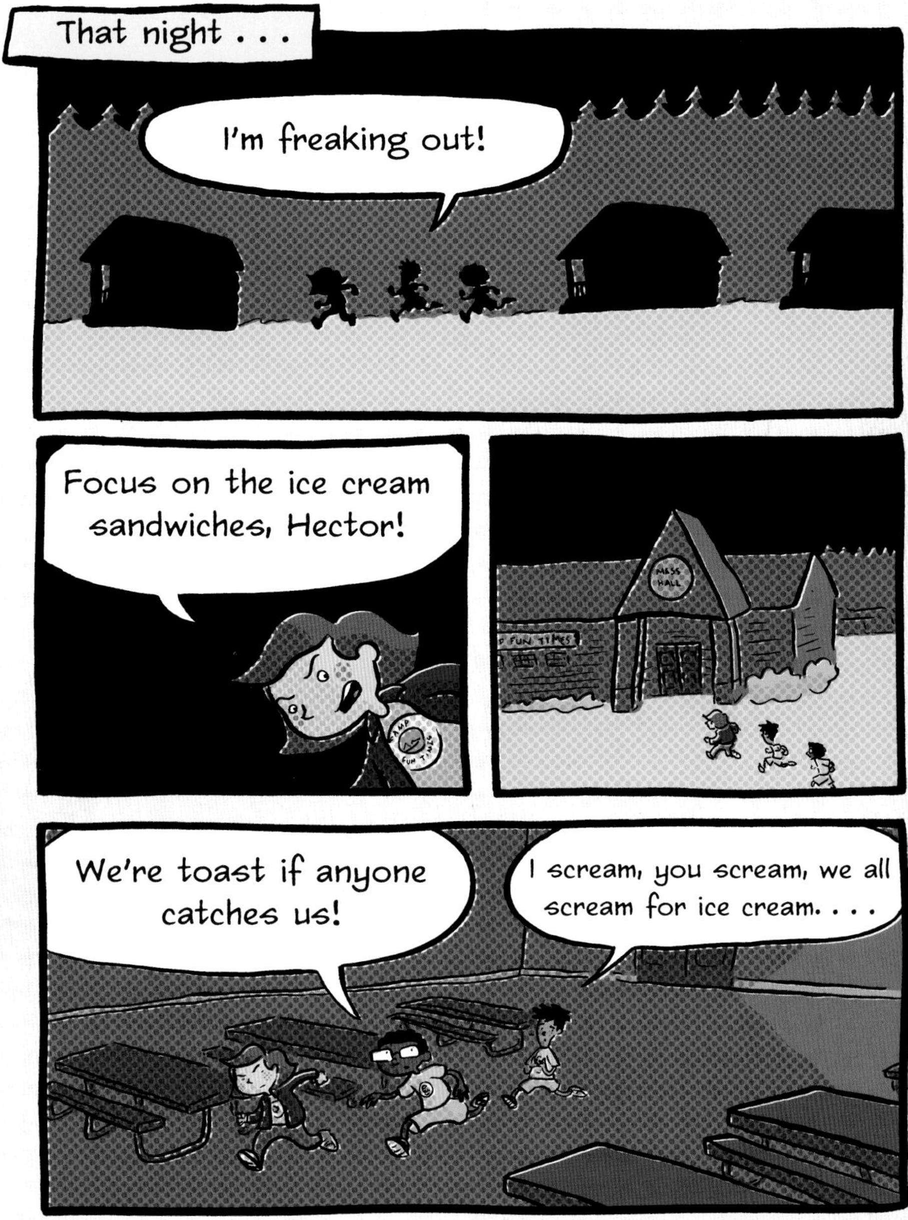
That night . . .
I'm freaking out!
Focus on the ice cream sandwiches, Hector!
MESS HALL
FUN TIMES
We're toast if anyone catches us!
I scream, you scream, we all scream for ice cream. . . .

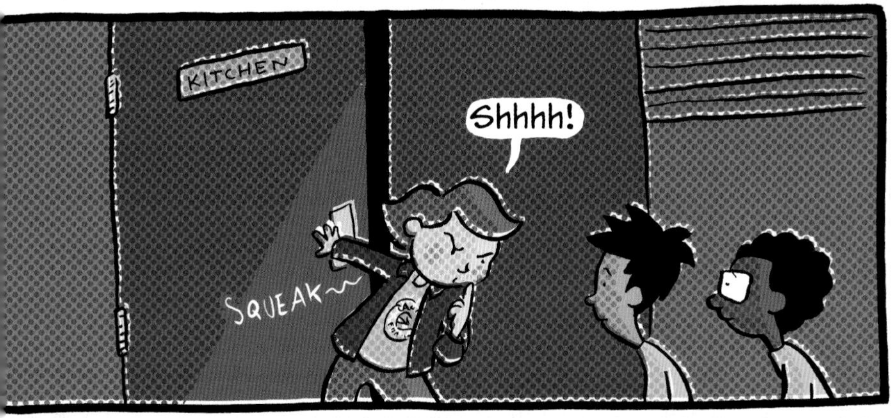
KITCHEN
Shhhh!
SQUEAK~

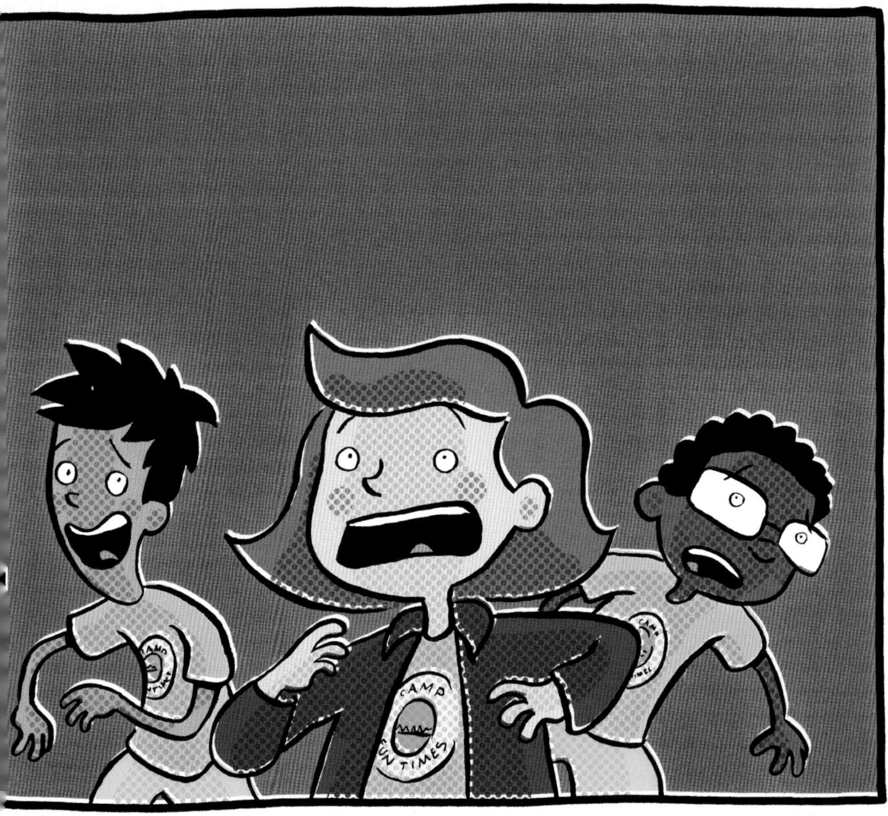
CAMP FUN TIMES

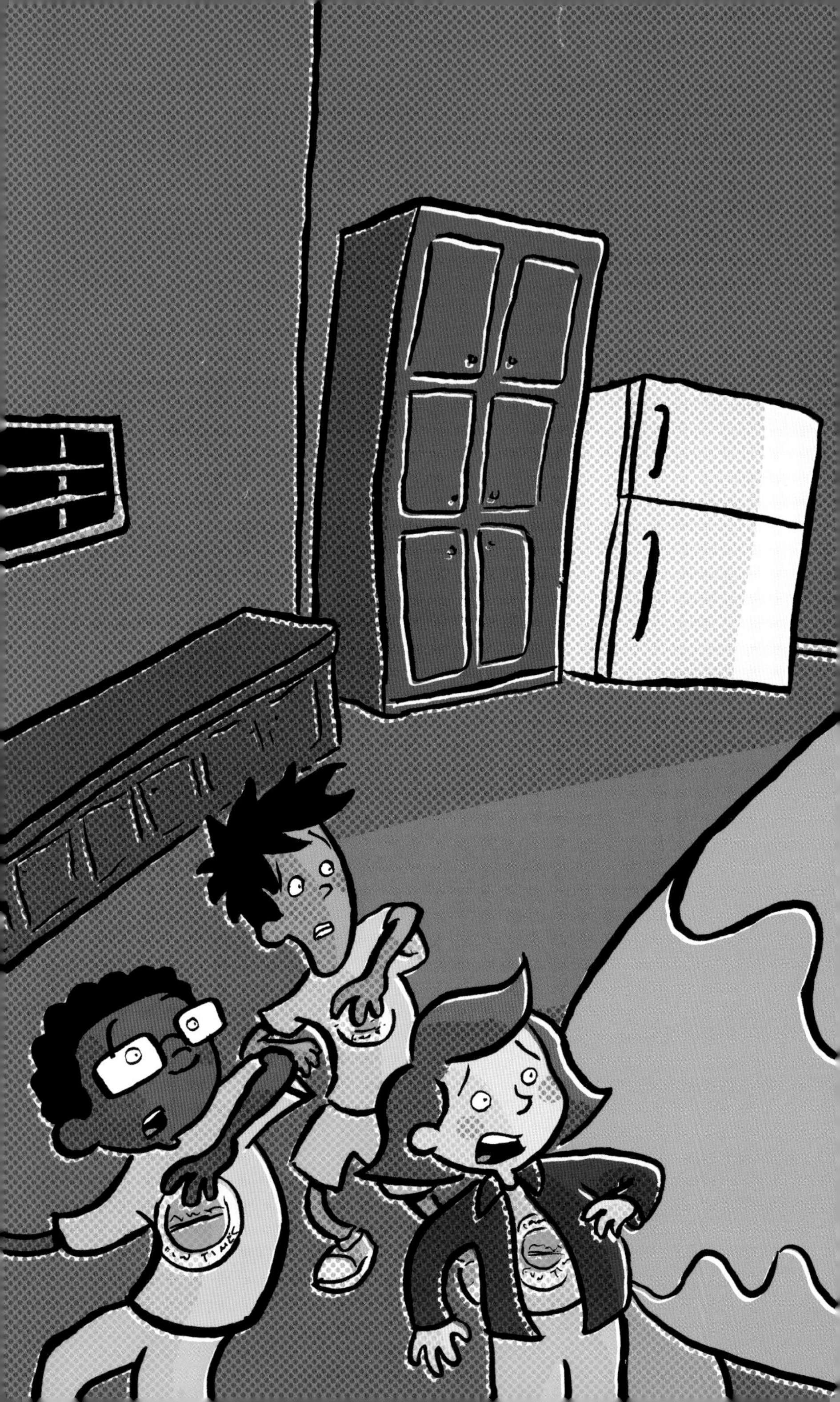

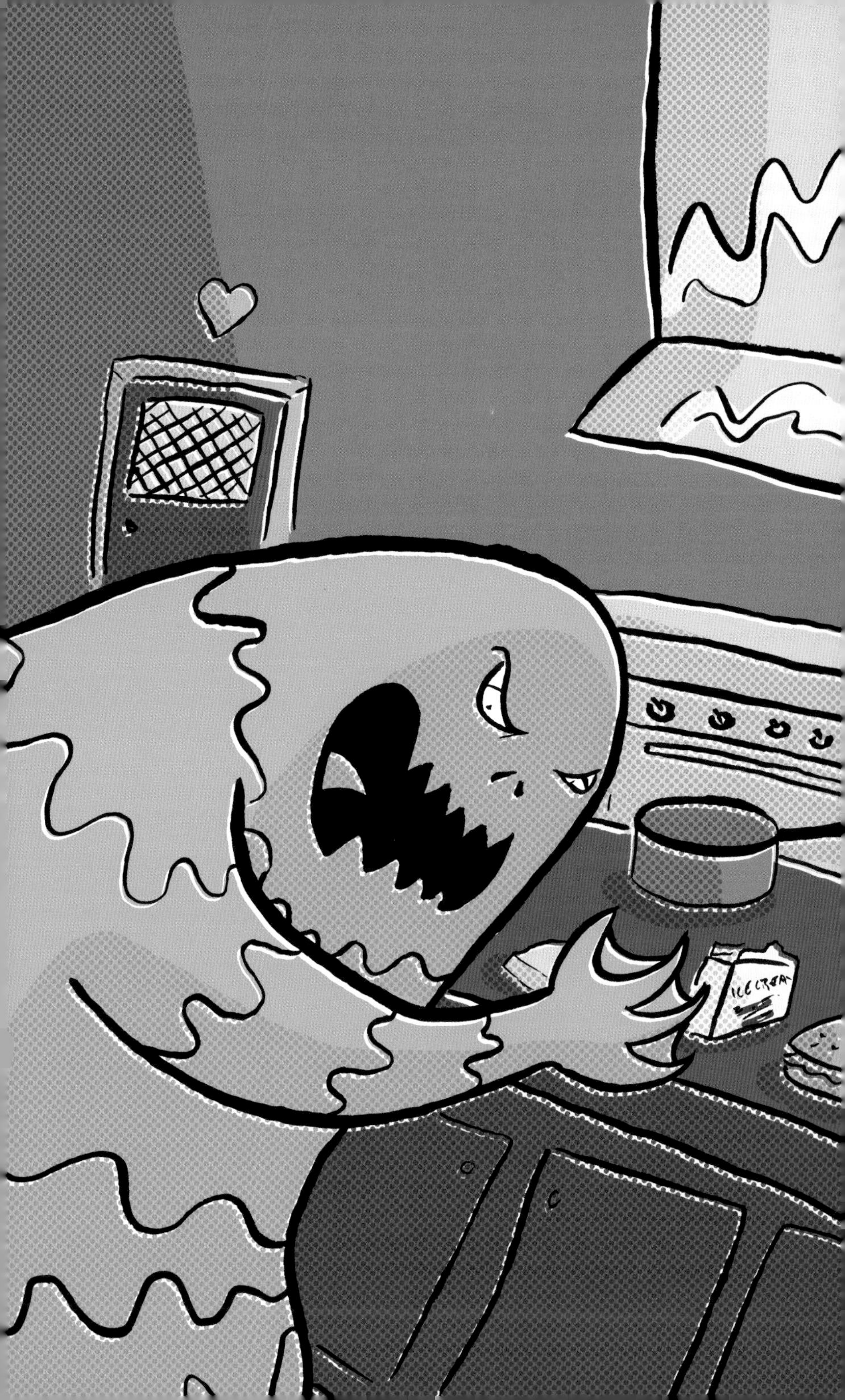
ICE CREA

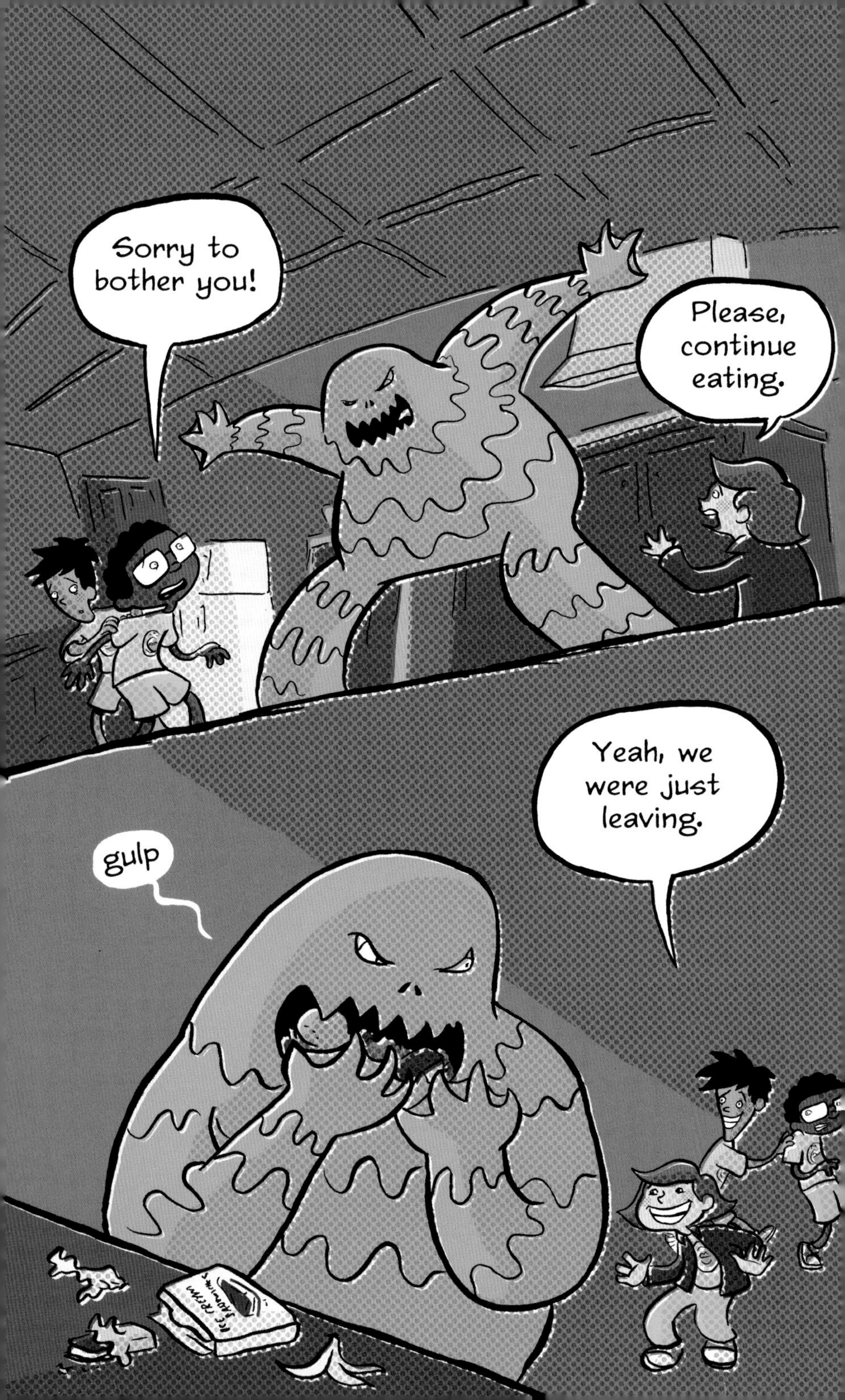
Sorry to bother you!
Please, continue eating.
Yeah, we were just leaving.
gulp

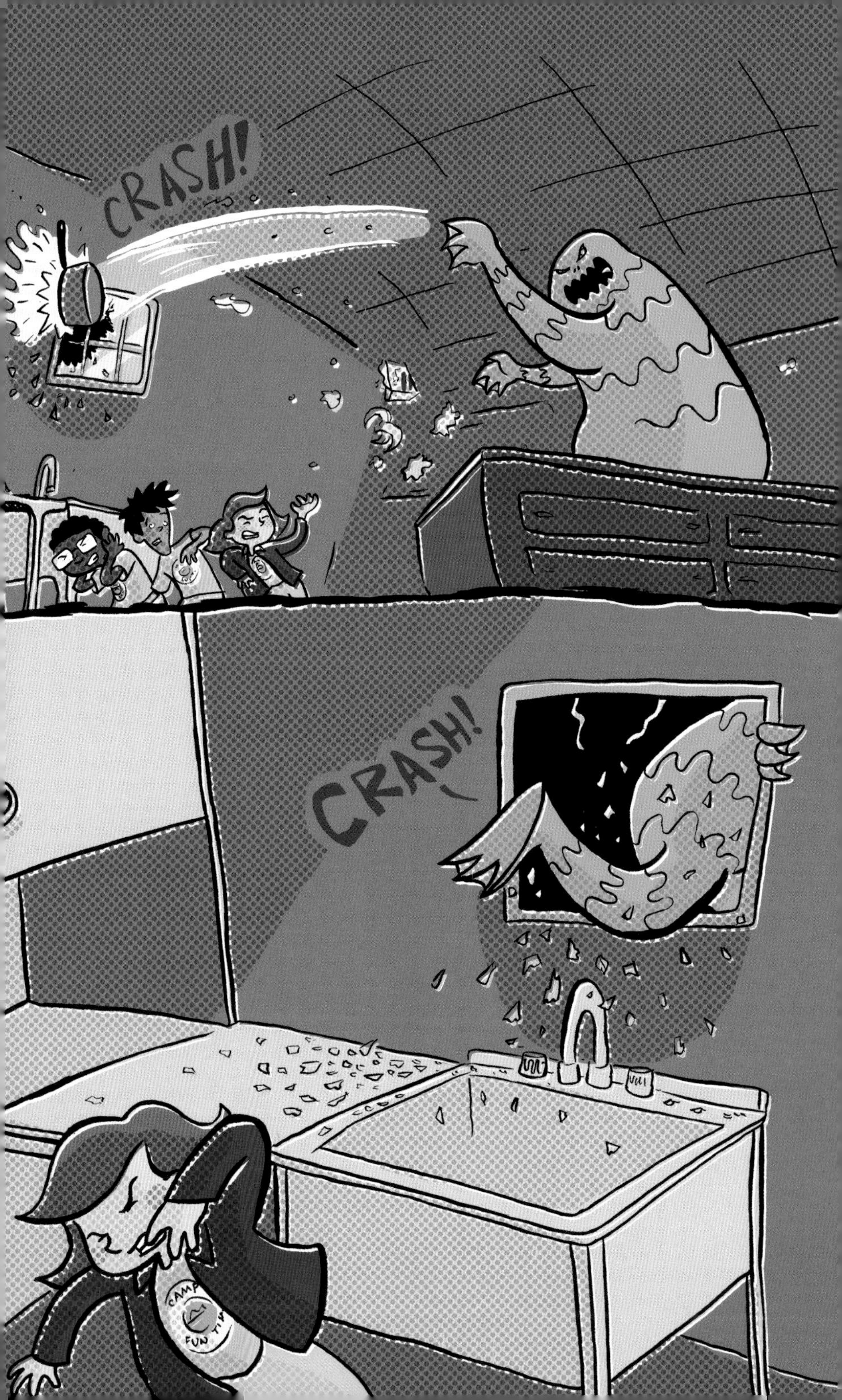
CRASH!
CRASH!

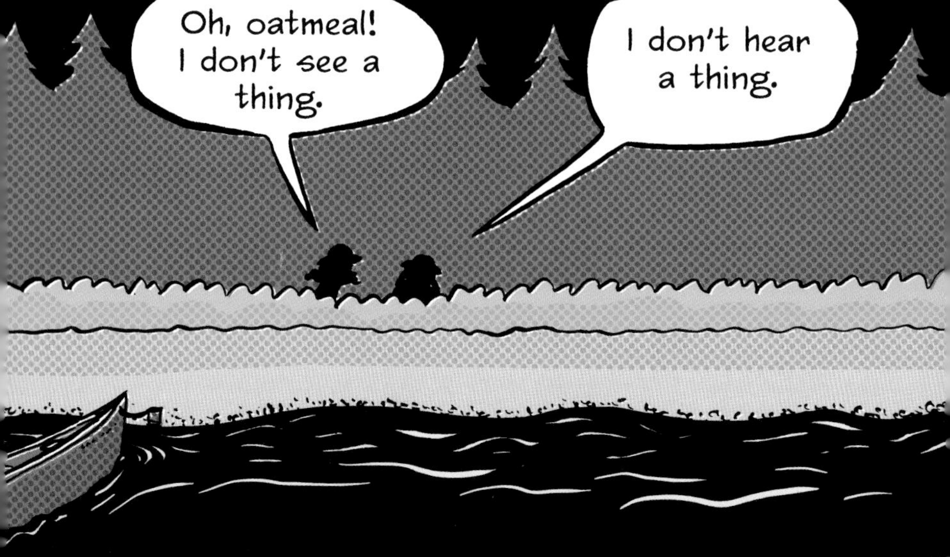
Oh, oatmeal! I don't see a thing.
I don't hear a thing.

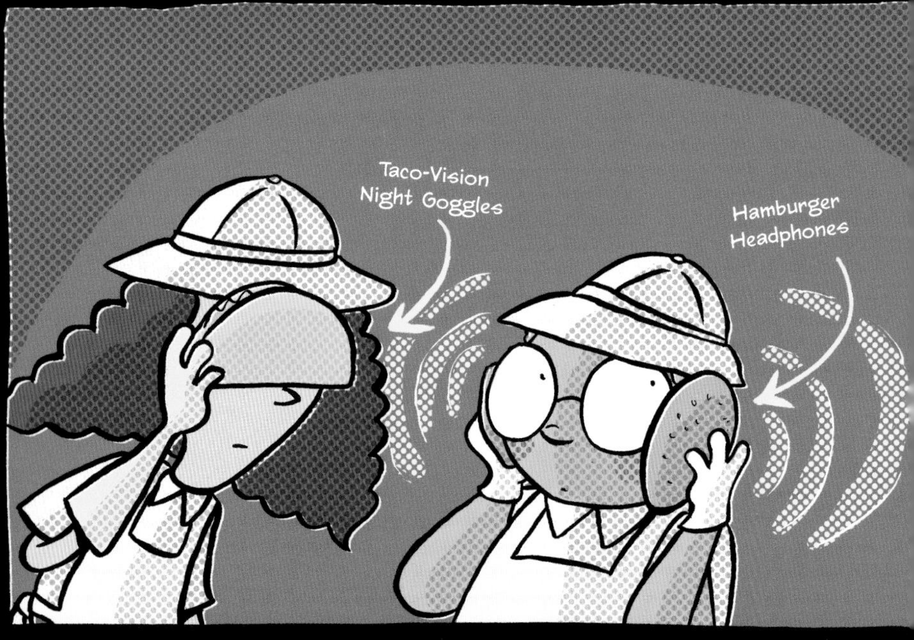
Taco-Vision Night Goggles
Hamburger Headphones

Wait!

I hear something.

I hear pots and pans!

The mess hall!
Let's go!

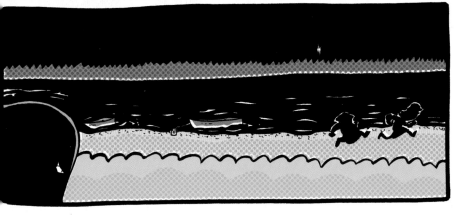

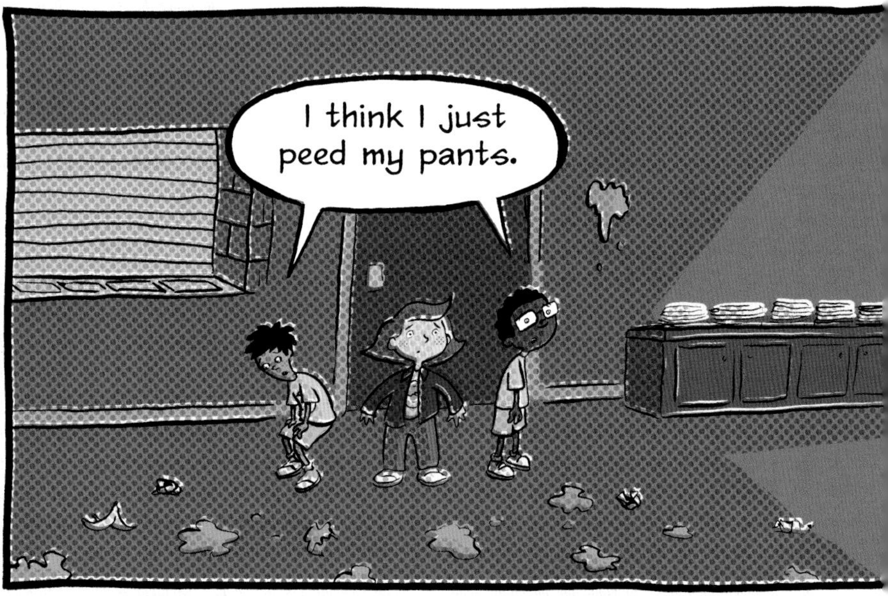
I think I just peed my pants.

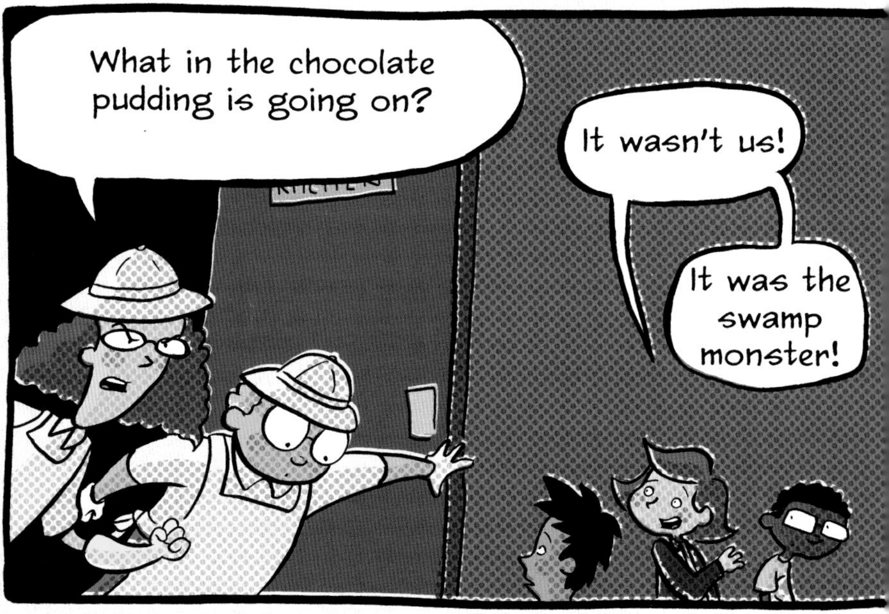
What in the chocolate pudding is going on?
It wasn't us!
It was the swamp monster!

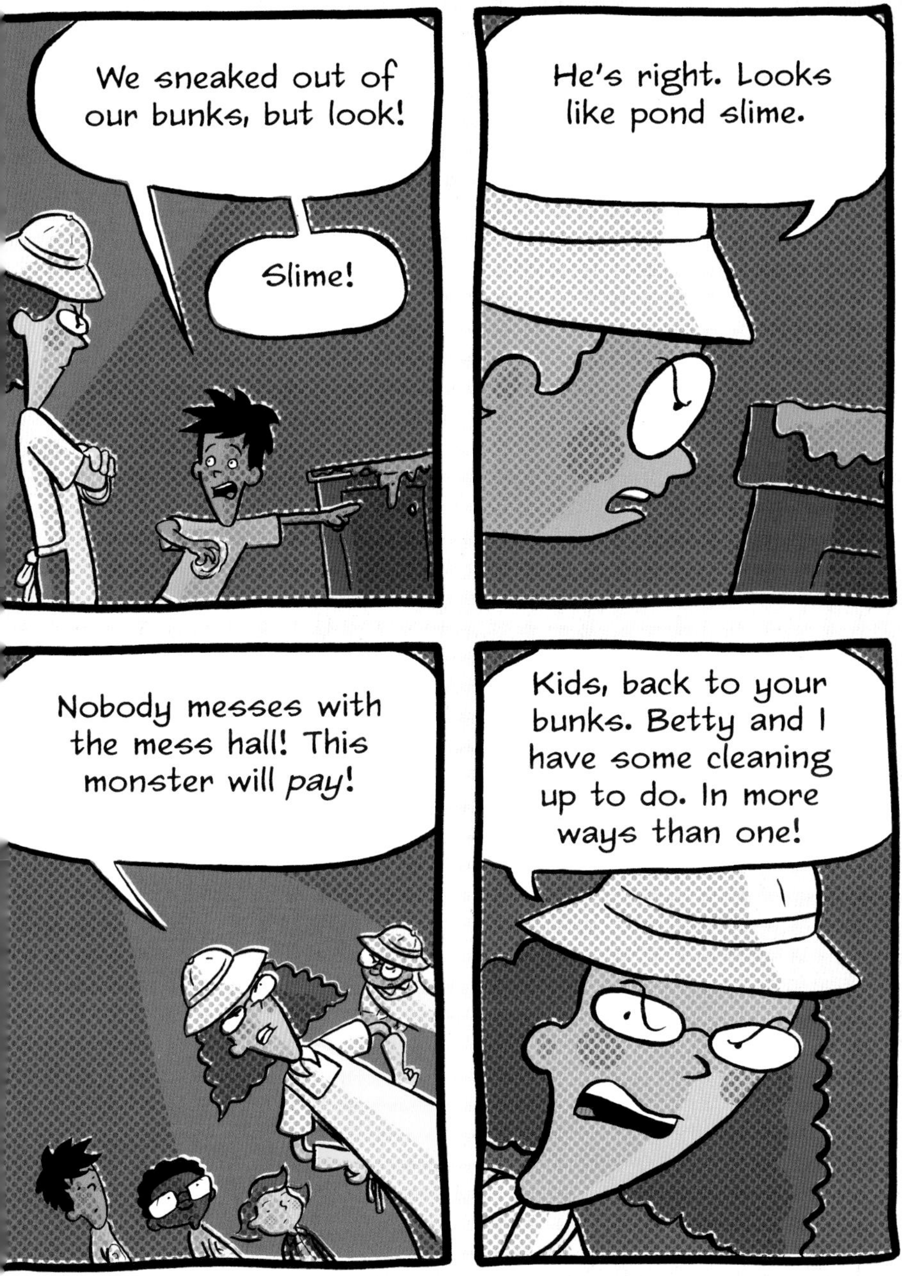
We sneaked out of our bunks, but look!
Slime!
He's right. Looks like pond slime.
Nobody messes with the mess hall! This monster will *pay*!
Kids, back to your bunks. Betty and I have some cleaning up to do. In more ways than one!

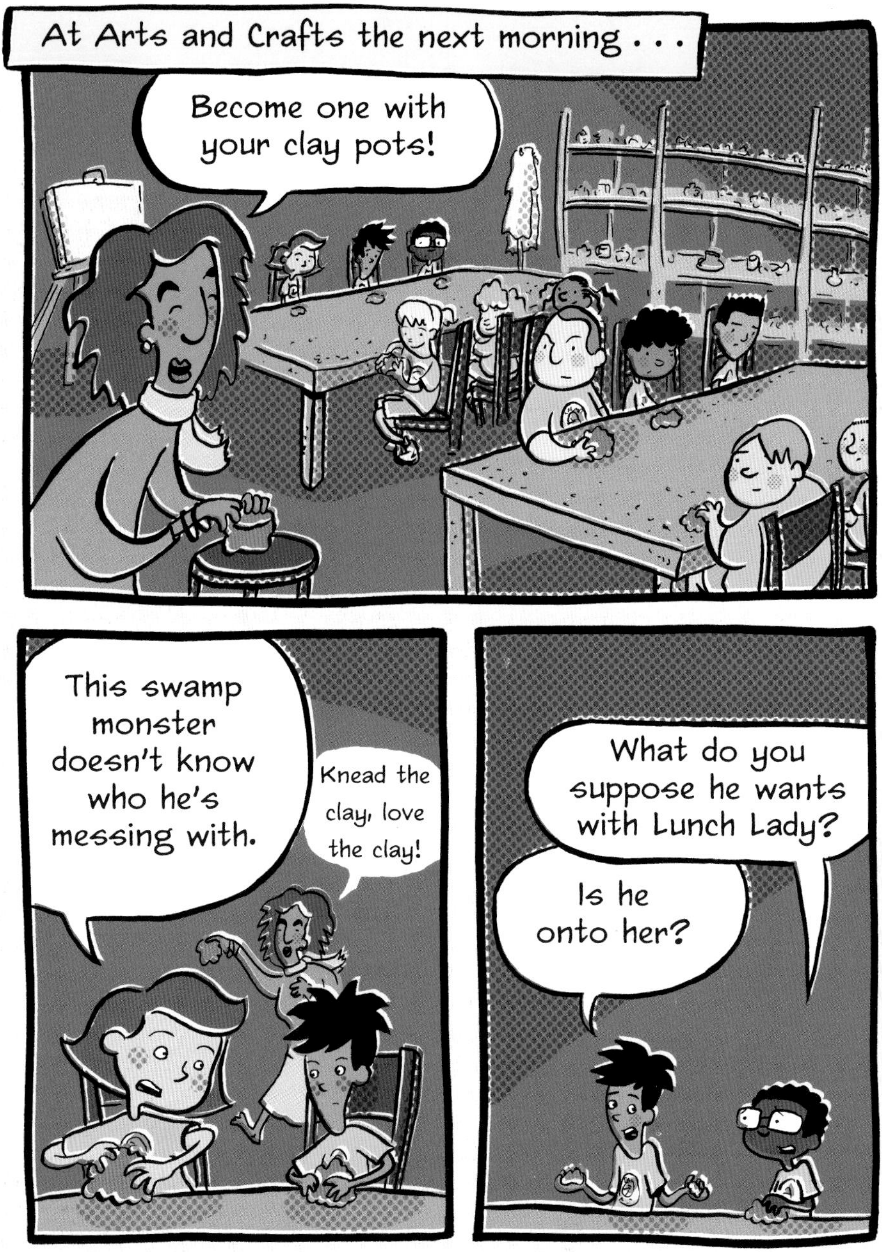
At Arts and Crafts the next morning . . .
Become one with your clay pots!
This swamp monster doesn't know who he's messing with.
Knead the clay, love the clay!
What do you suppose he wants with Lunch Lady?
Is he onto her?

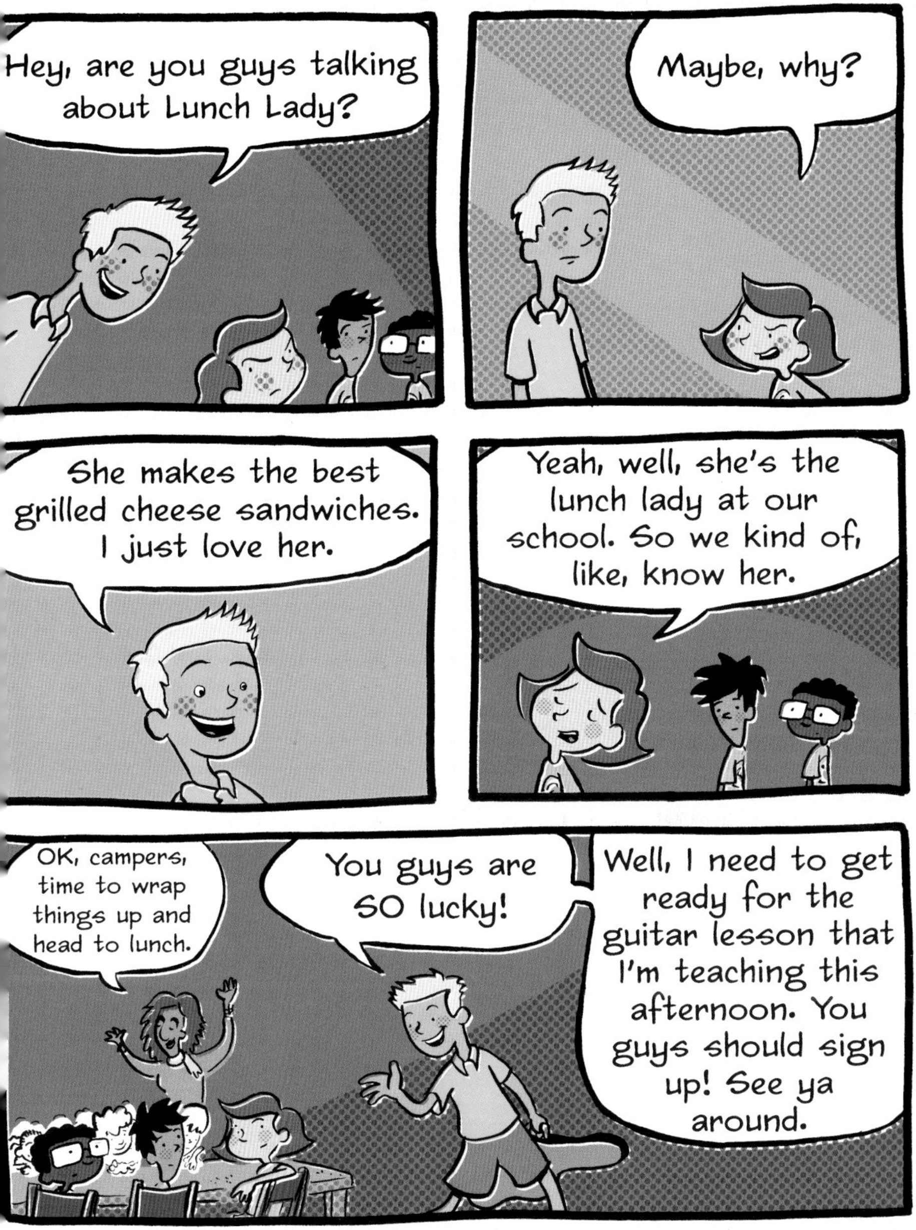
Hey, are you guys talking about Lunch Lady?
Maybe, why?
She makes the best grilled cheese sandwiches. I just love her.
Yeah, well, she's the lunch lady at our school. So we kind of, like, know her.
OK, campers, time to wrap things up and head to lunch.
You guys are SO lucky!
Well, I need to get ready for the guitar lesson that I'm teaching this afternoon. You guys should sign up! See ya around.

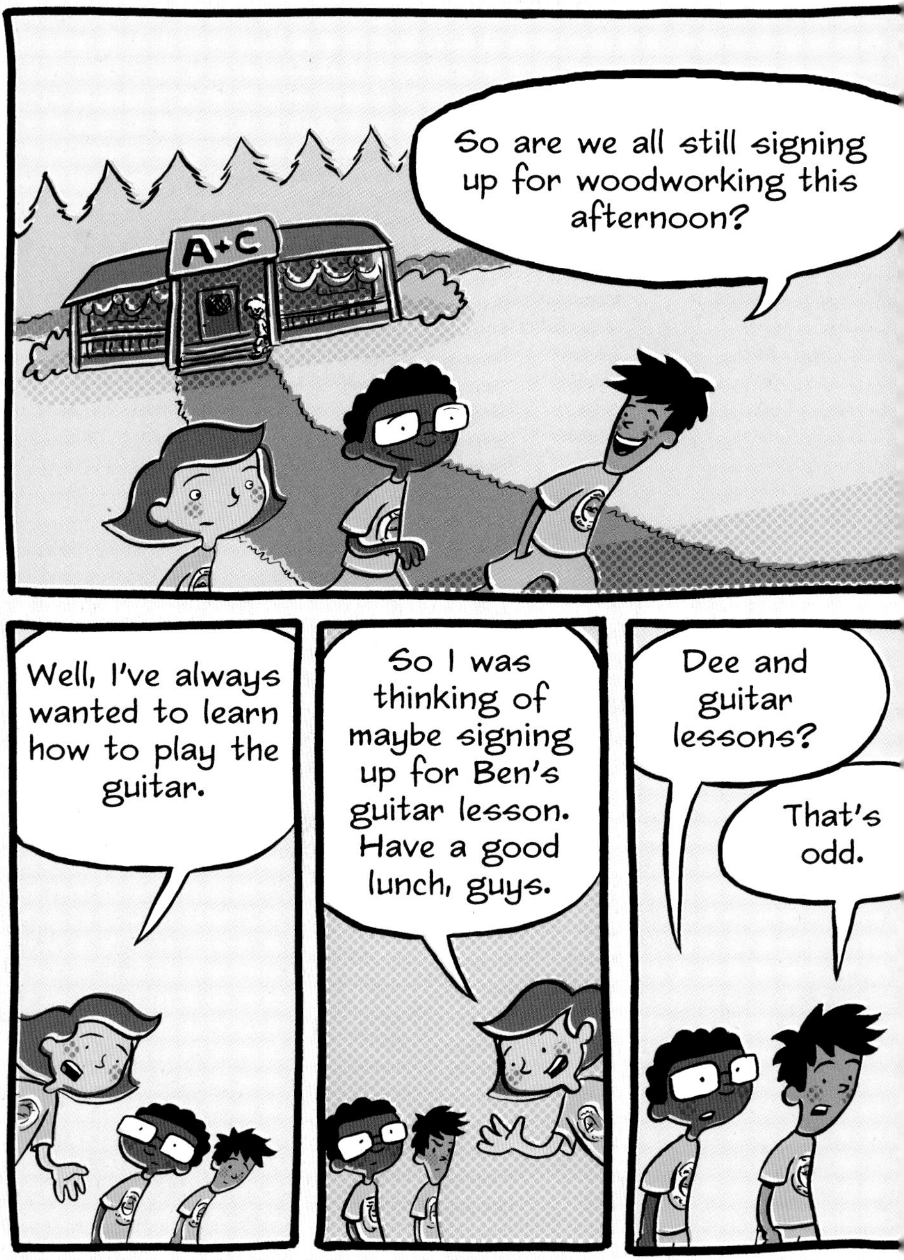
A+C
So are we all still signing up for woodworking this afternoon?
Well, I've always wanted to learn how to play the guitar.
So I was thinking of maybe signing up for Ben's guitar lesson. Have a good lunch, guys.
Dee and guitar lessons?
That's odd.

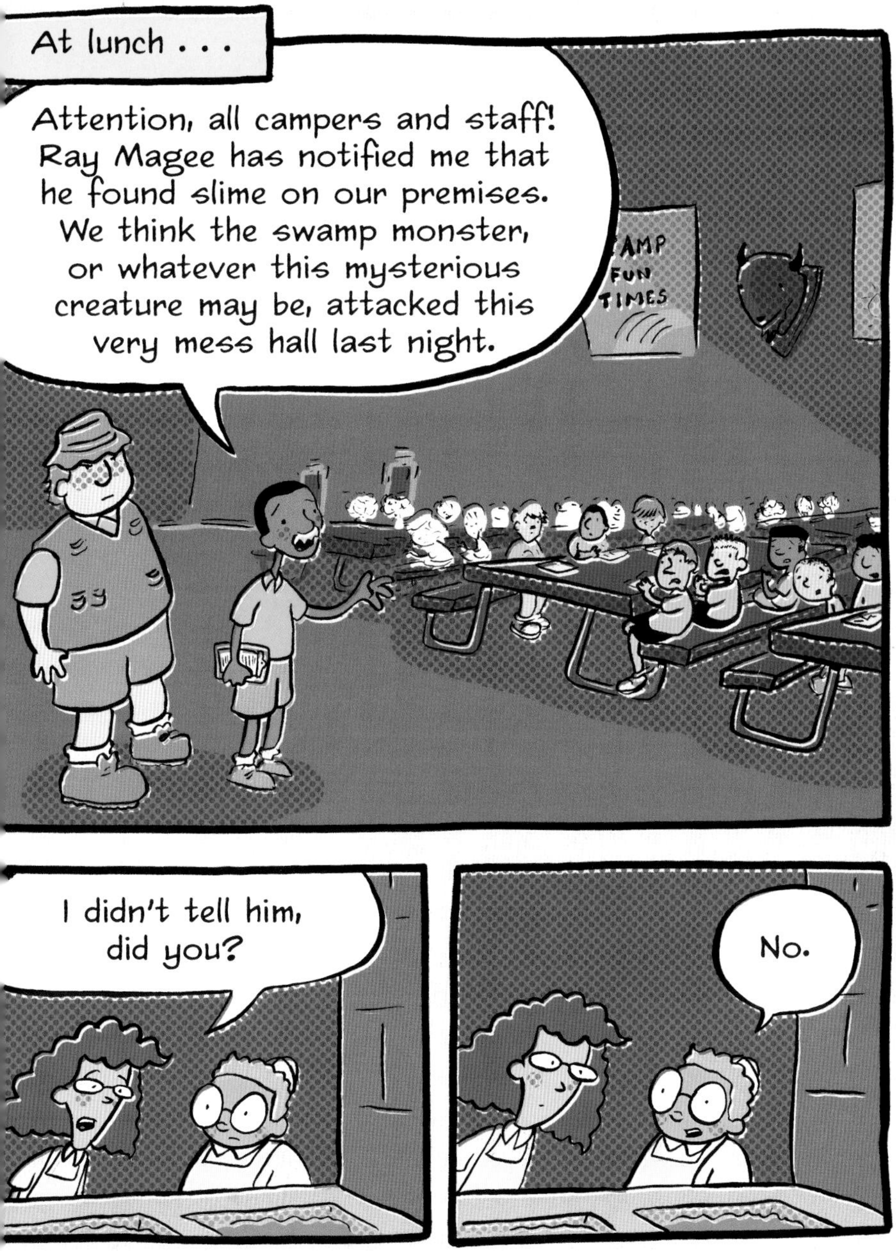
At lunch . . .
Attention, all campers and staff! Ray Magee has notified me that he found slime on our premises. We think the swamp monster, or whatever this mysterious creature may be, attacked this very mess hall last night.
AMP FUN TIMES
I didn't tell him, did you?
No.

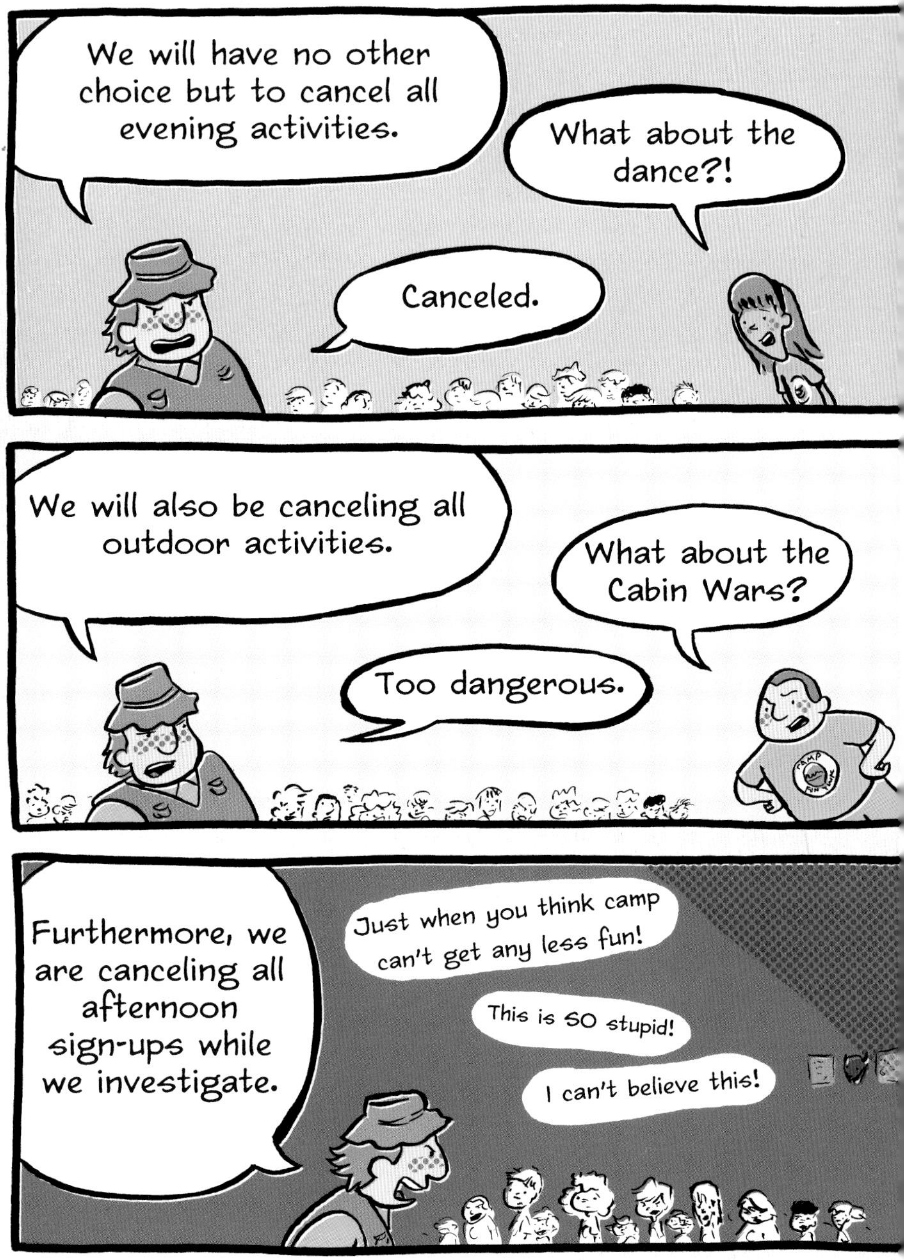
We will have no other choice but to cancel all evening activities.
What about the dance?!
Canceled.
We will also be canceling all outdoor activities.
What about the Cabin Wars?
Too dangerous.
Furthermore, we are canceling all afternoon sign-ups while we investigate.
Just when you think camp can't get any less fun!
This is SO stupid!
I can't believe this!

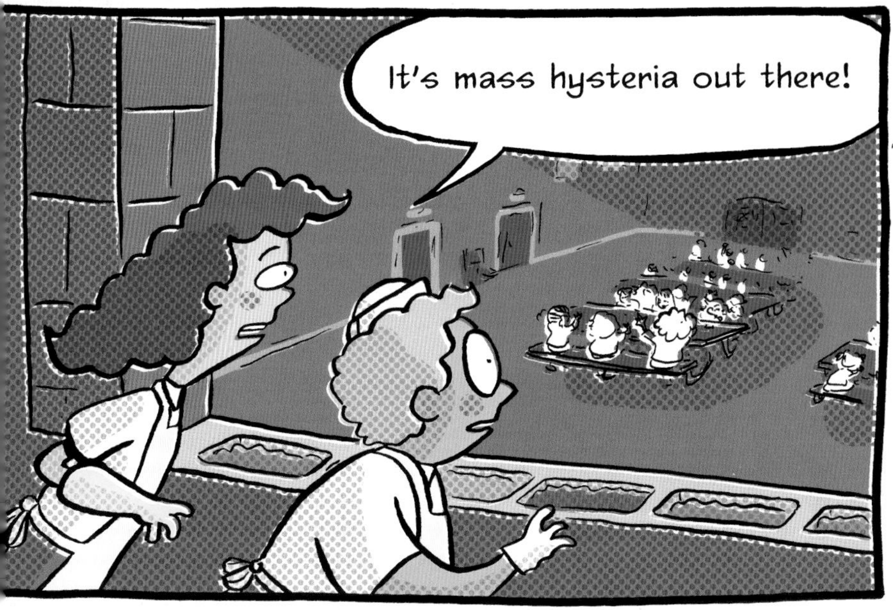
It's mass hysteria out there!

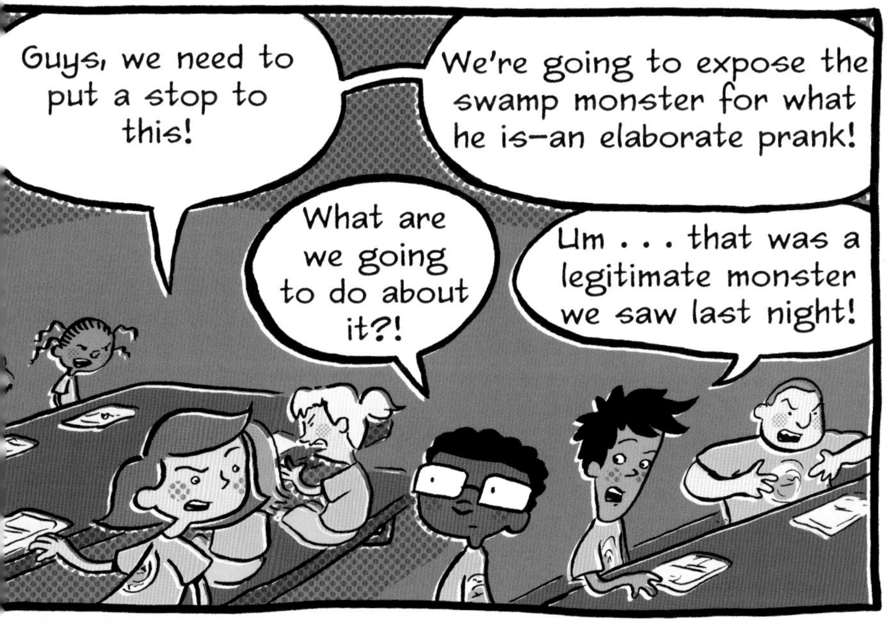
Guys, we need to put a stop to this!
We're going to expose the swamp monster for what he is—an elaborate prank!
What are we going to do about it?!
Um . . . that was a legitimate monster we saw last night!

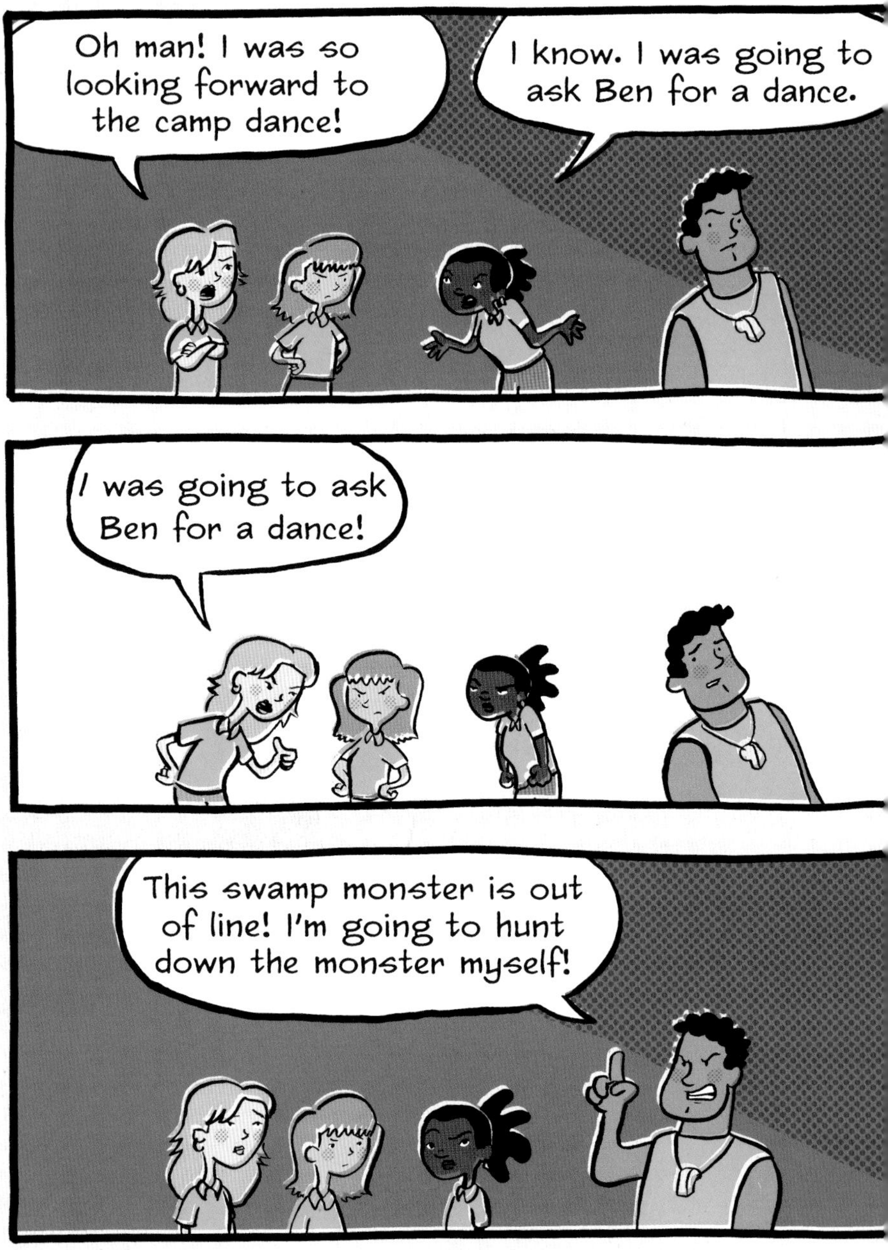

Oh man! I was so looking forward to the camp dance!
I know. I was going to ask Ben for a dance.
I was going to ask Ben for a dance!
This swamp monster is out of line! I'm going to hunt down the monster myself!

That sounds dangerous! Aren't you scared?
I'm not afraid of anything.
I'll see you ladies after I've defeated the monster and brought peace back to camp!
He's so brave!
Well, you can have Ben. I was going to ask Scott to dance anyhow.
No way, Scott is mine!

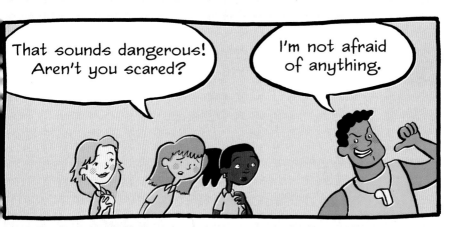

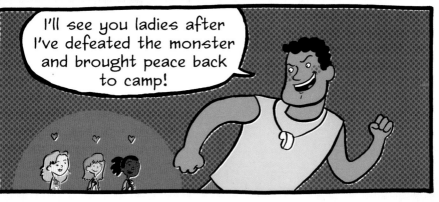

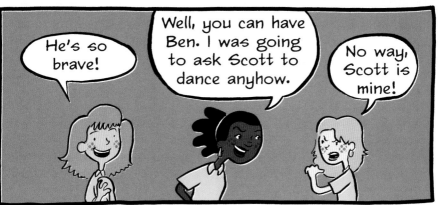

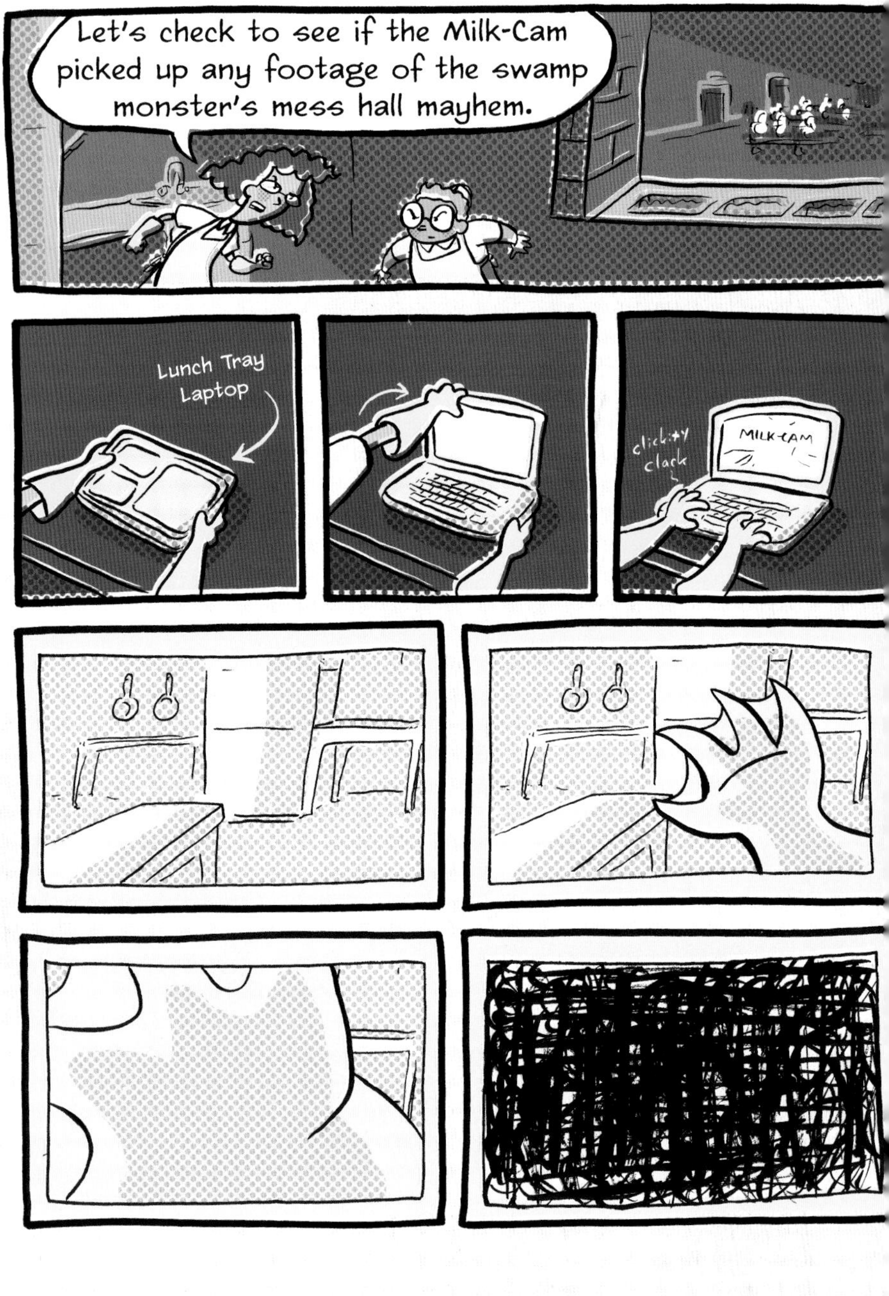
Let's check to see if the Milk-Cam picked up any footage of the swamp monster's mess hall mayhem.
Lunch Tray Laptop
clickity clack
MILK-CAM

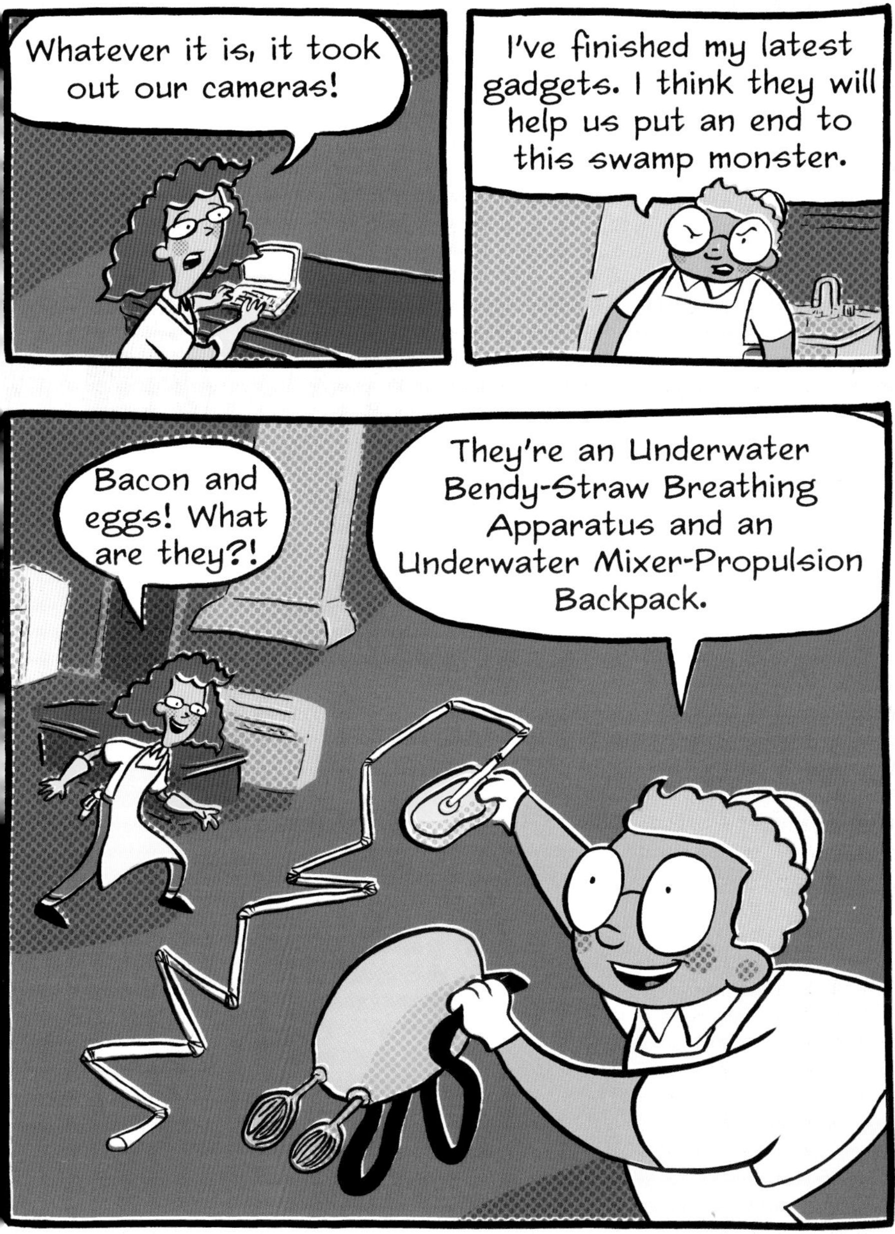
Whatever it is, it took out our cameras!
I've finished my latest gadgets. I think they will help us put an end to this swamp monster.
Bacon and eggs! What are they?!
They're an Underwater Bendy-Straw Breathing Apparatus and an Underwater Mixer-Propulsion Backpack.

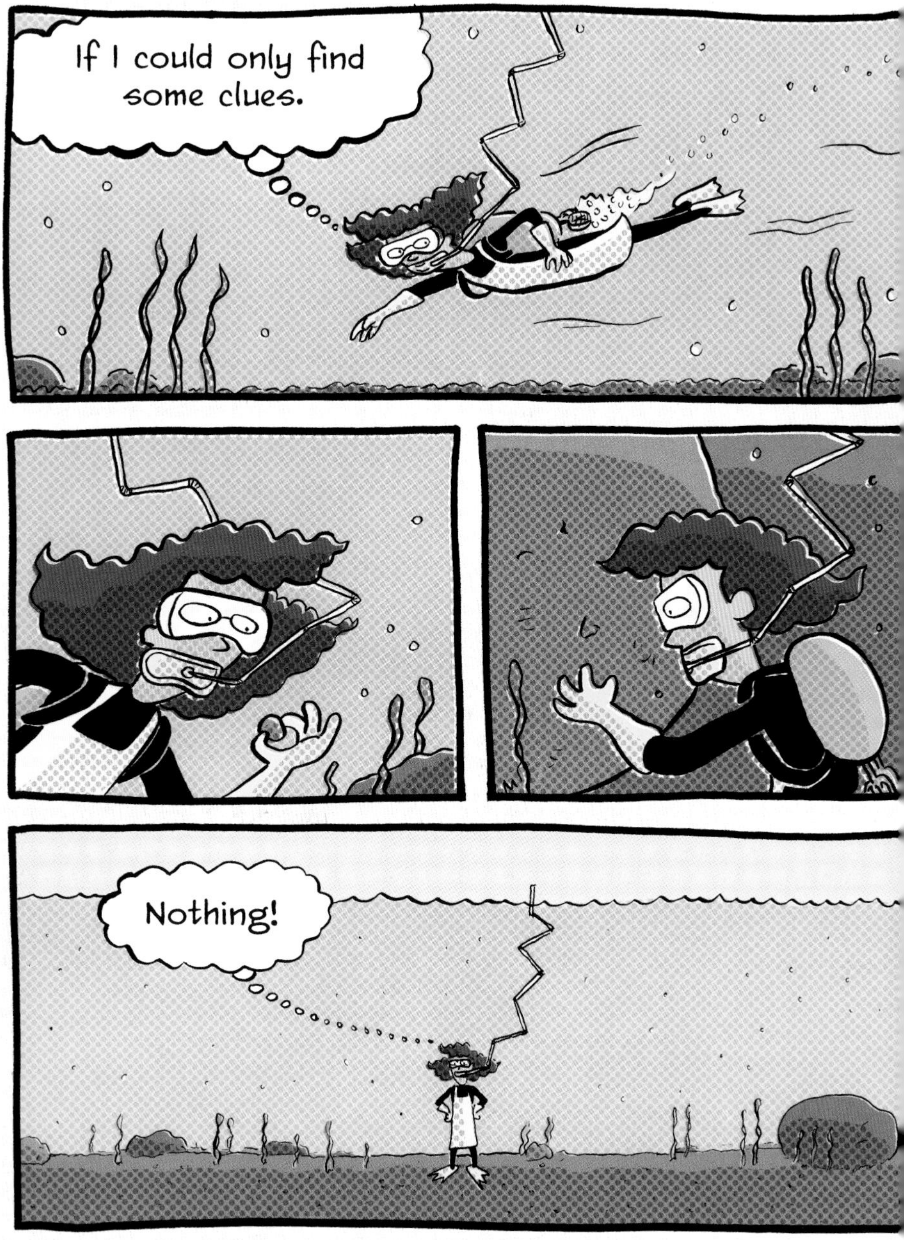
If I could only find some clues.
Nothing!

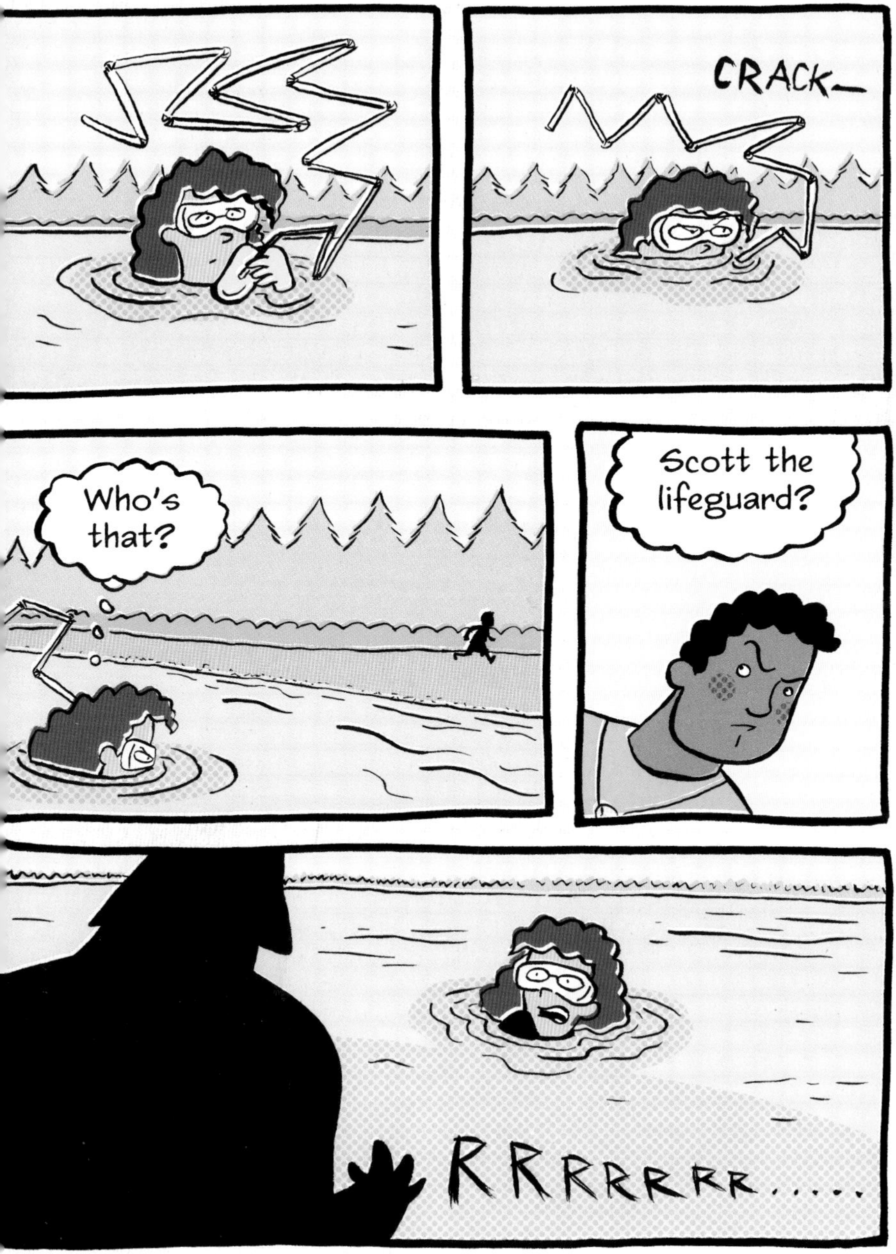
CRACK—
Who's that?
Scott the lifeguard?
RRRRRRR.....

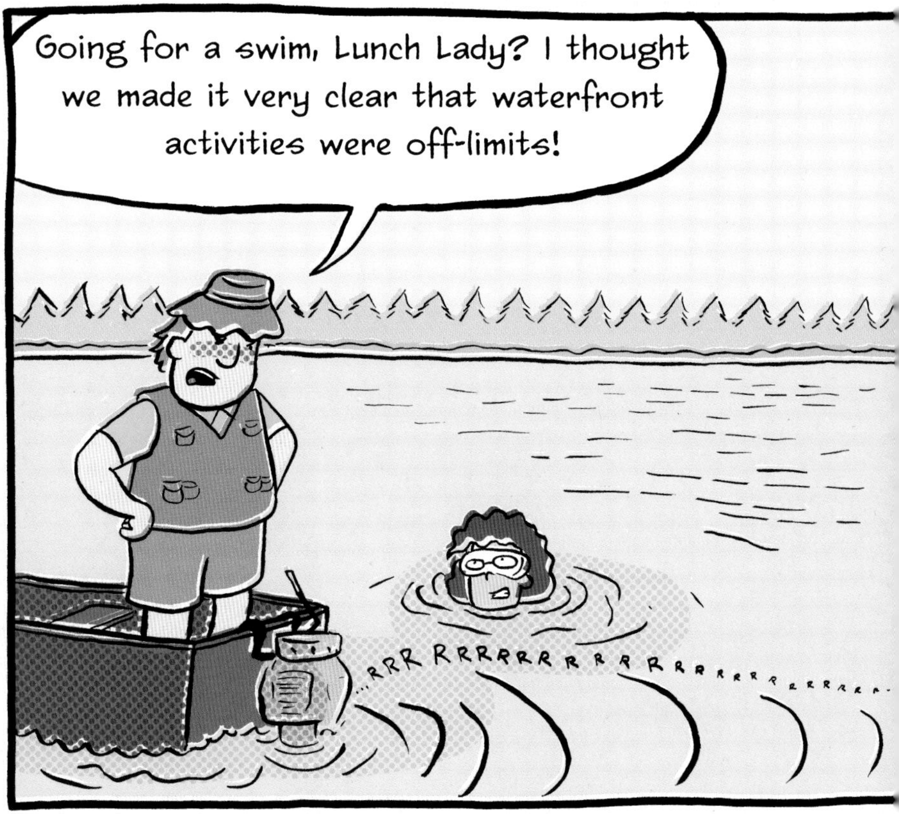
Going for a swim, Lunch Lady? I thought we made it very clear that waterfront activities were off-limits!
...RRR RRRRRRR R R R R R R R R R R R R R R R R R...

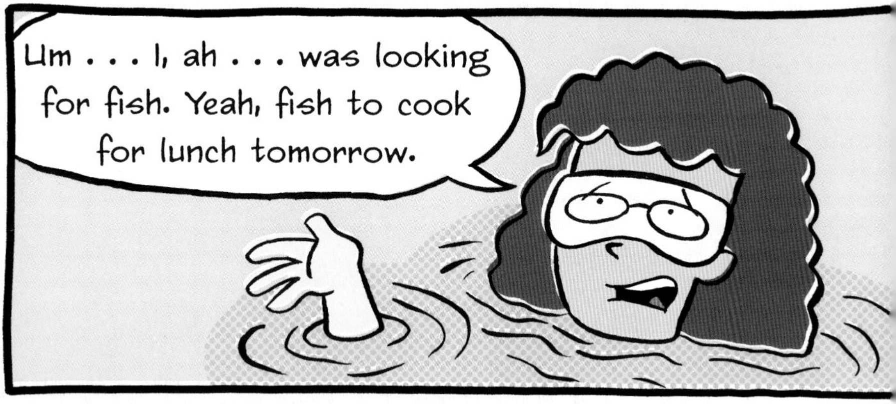
Um . . . I, ah . . . was looking for fish. Yeah, fish to cook for lunch tomorrow.

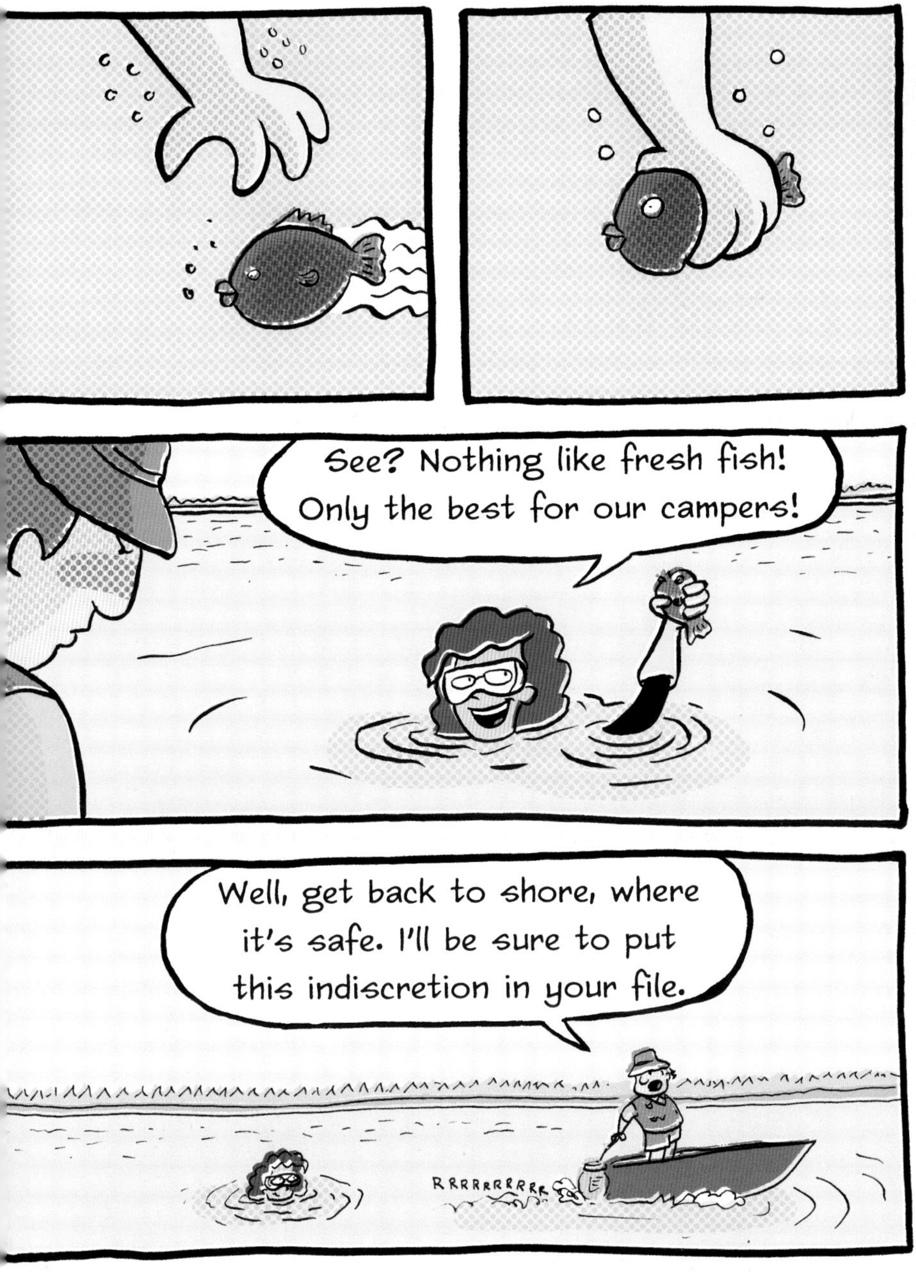
See? Nothing like fresh fish! Only the best for our campers!
Well, get back to shore, where it's safe. I'll be sure to put this indiscretion in your file.
RRRRRRRRRR

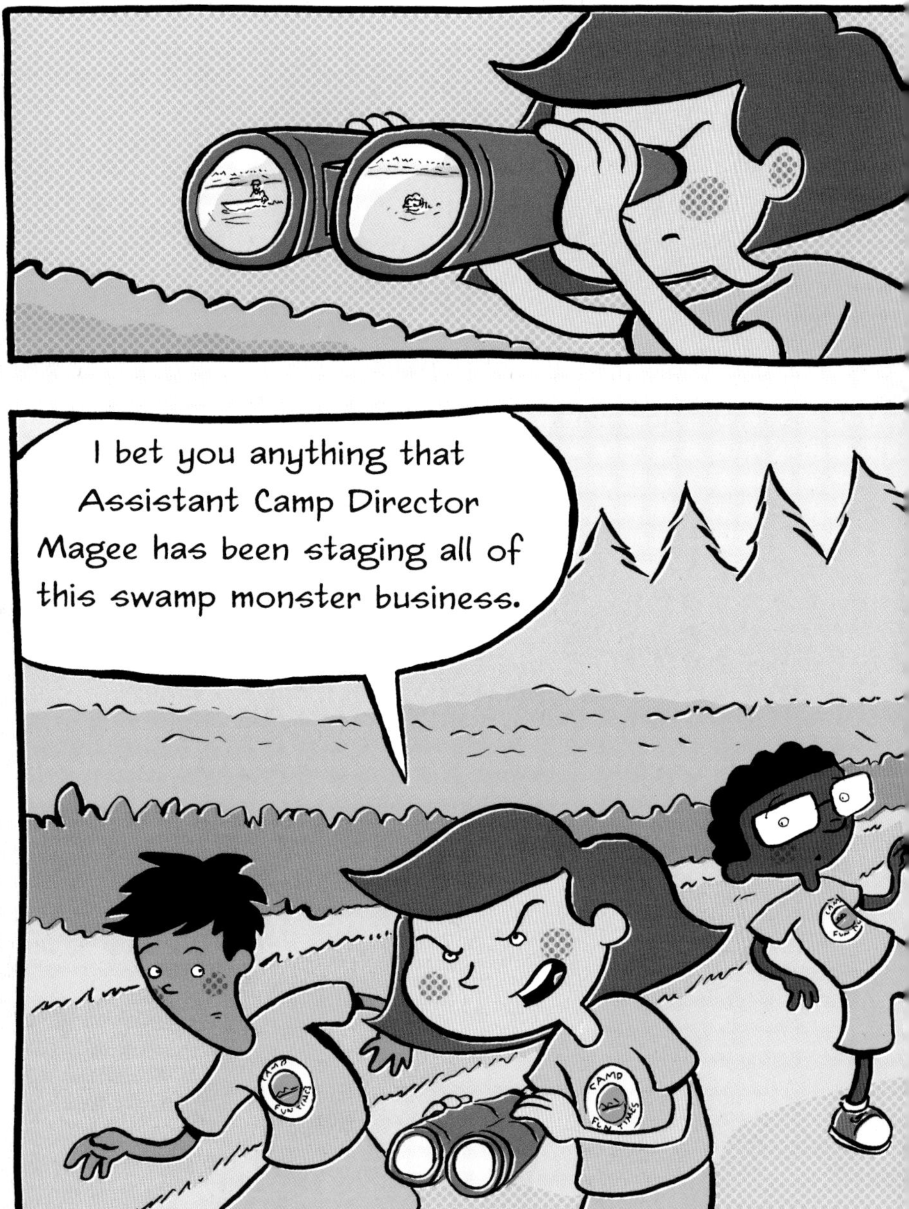
I bet you anything that Assistant Camp Director Magee has been staging all of this swamp monster business.

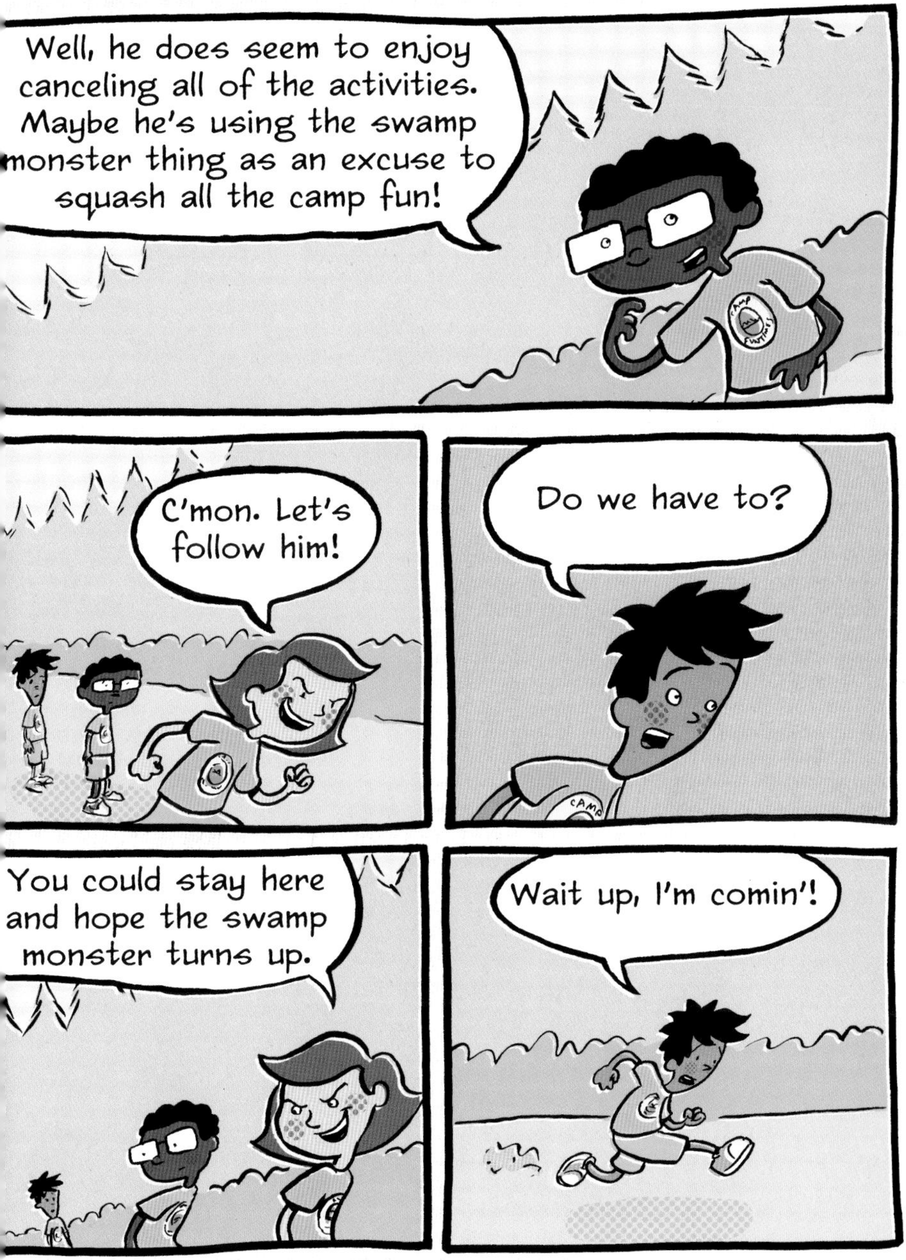
Well, he does seem to enjoy canceling all of the activities. Maybe he's using the swamp monster thing as an excuse to squash all the camp fun!
C'mon. Let's follow him!
Do we have to?
You could stay here and hope the swamp monster turns up.
Wait up, I'm comin'!

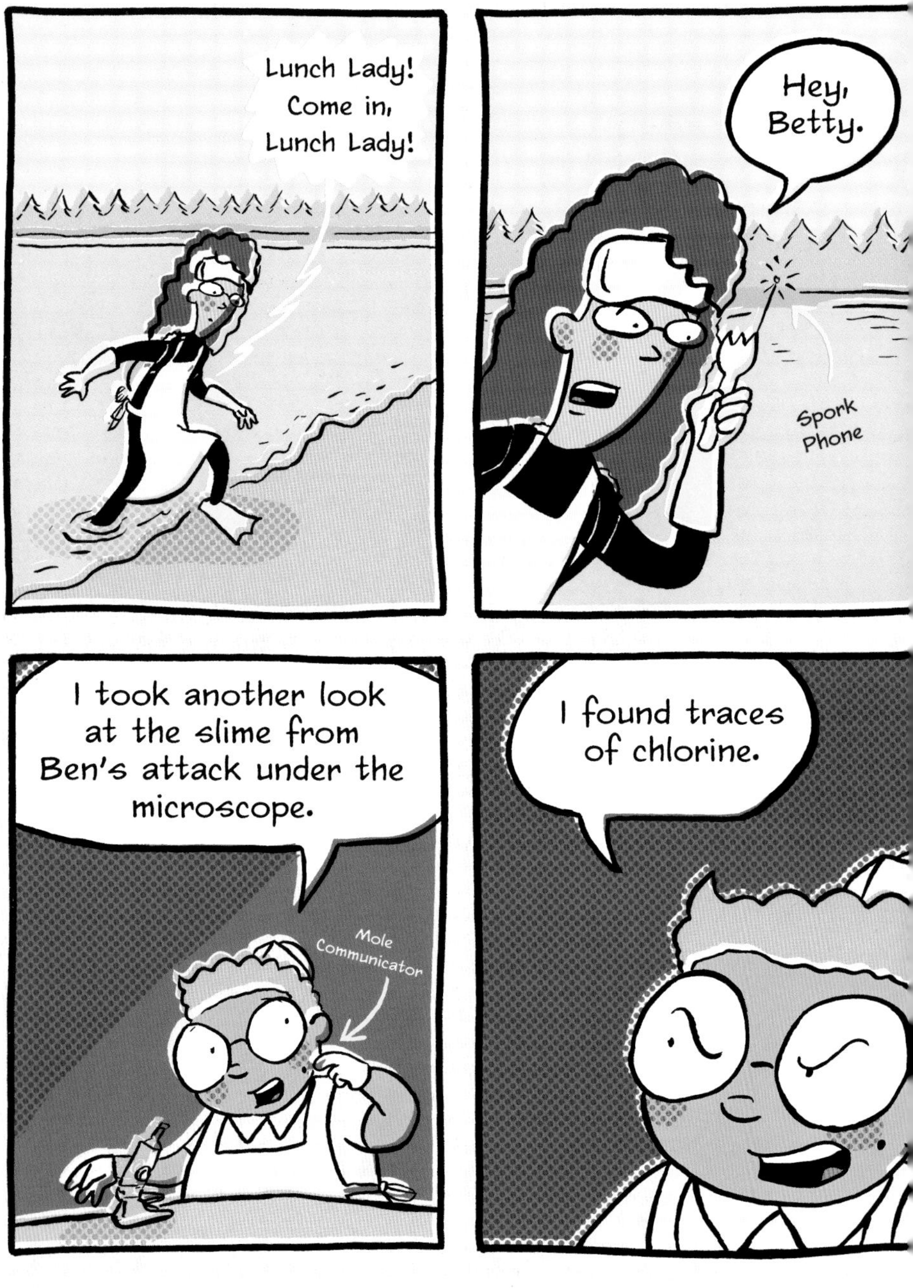
Lunch Lady! Come in, Lunch Lady!
Hey, Betty.
Spork Phone
I took another look at the slime from Ben's attack under the microscope.
Mole Communicator
I found traces of chlorine.

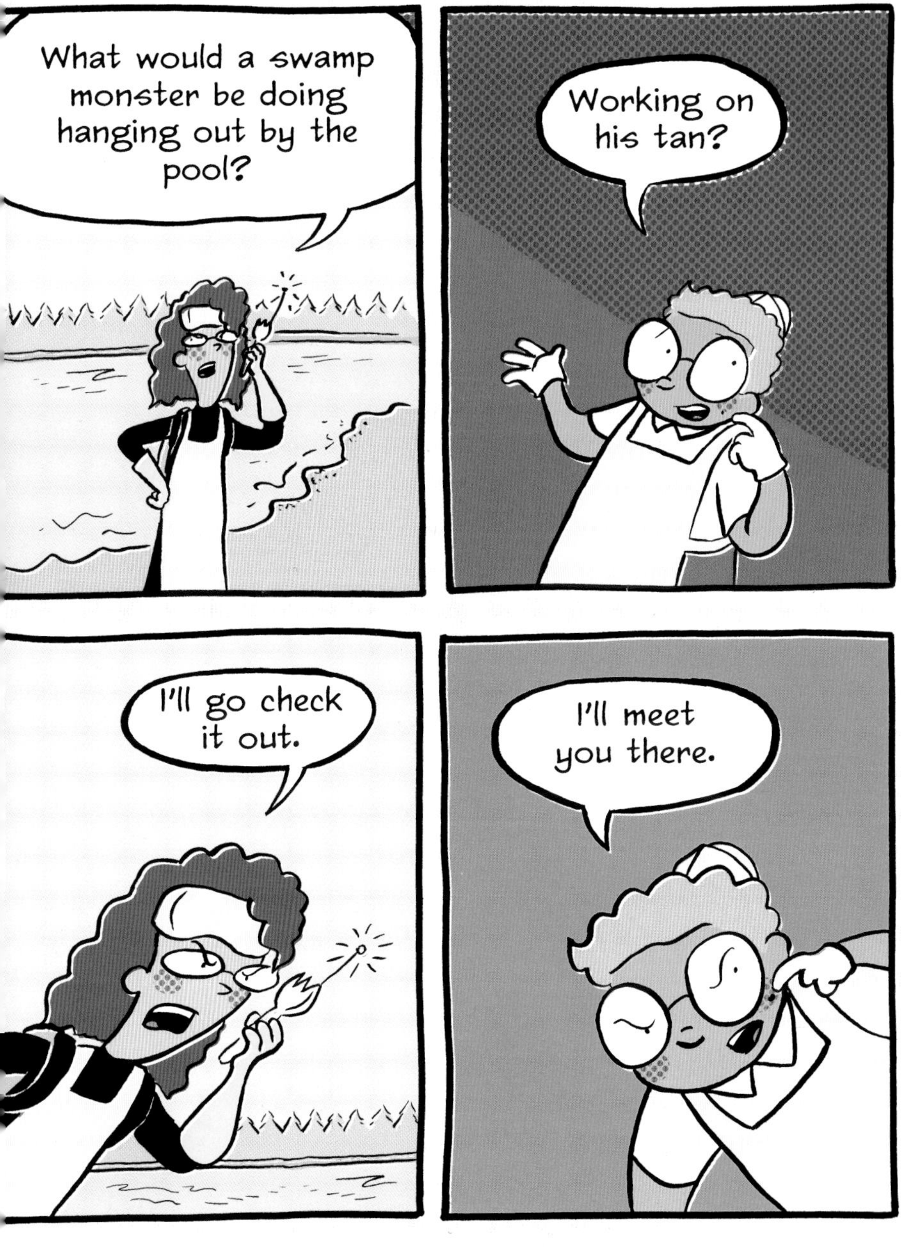
What would a swamp monster be doing hanging out by the pool?
Working on his tan?
I'll go check it out.
I'll meet you there.

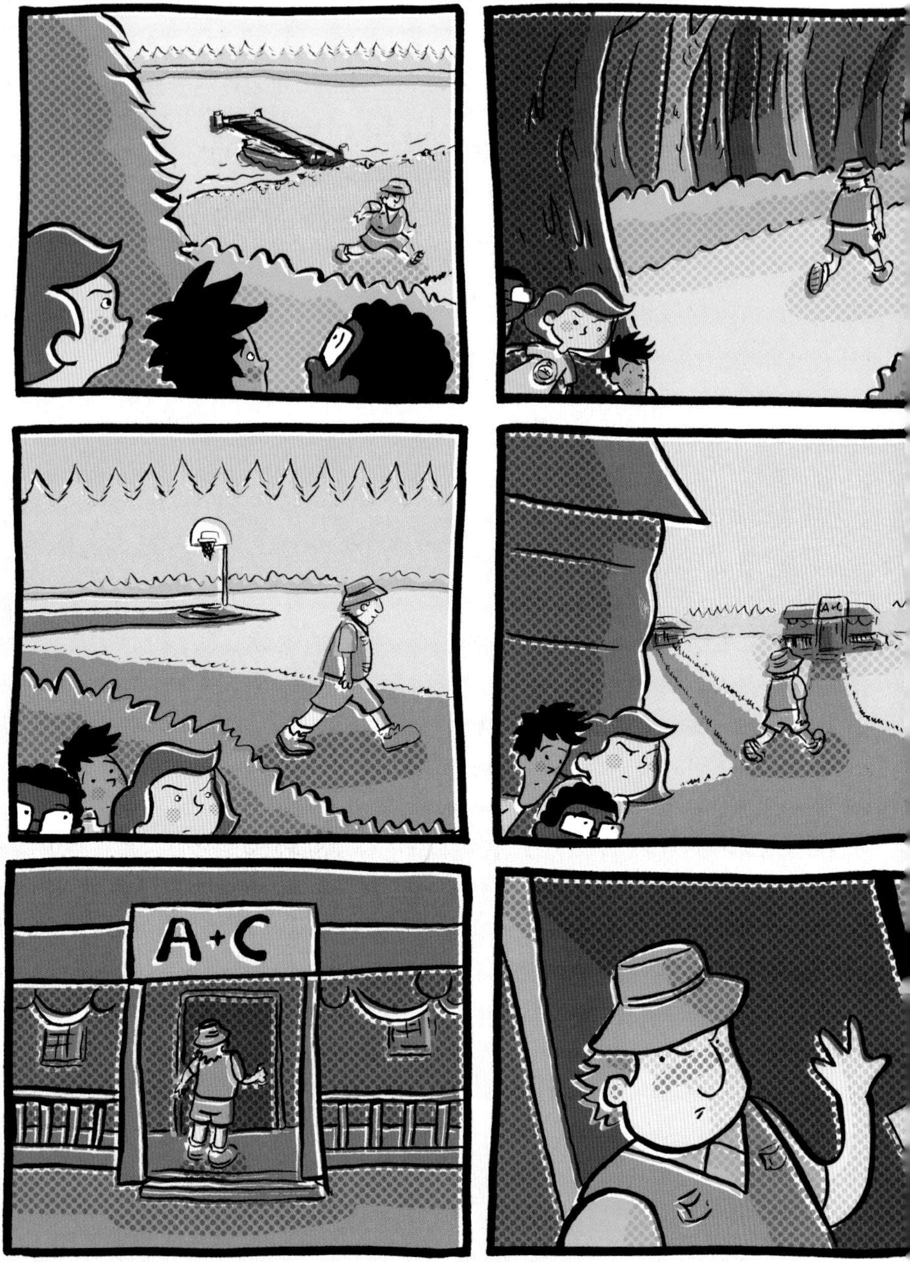
A+C
A+C

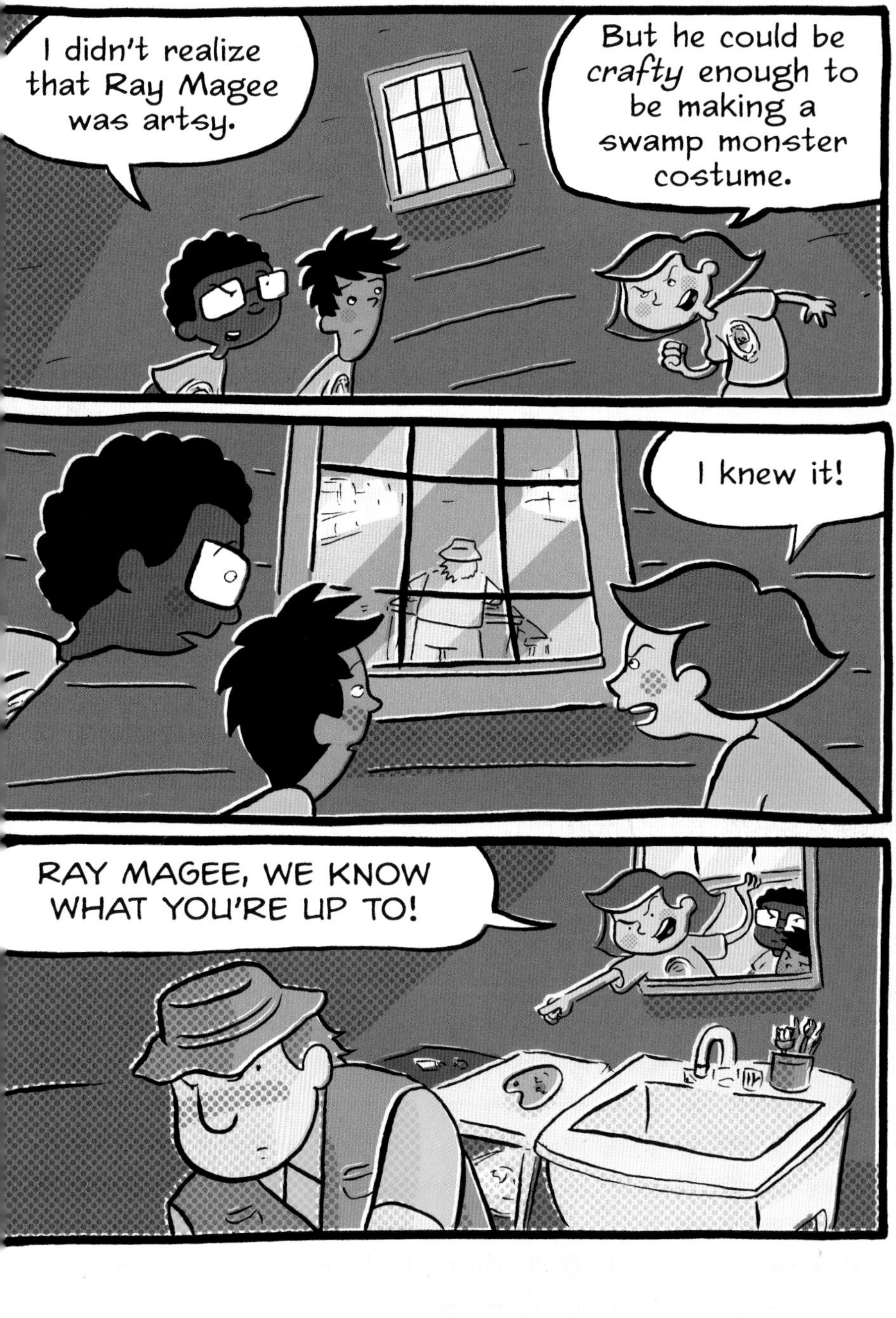
I didn't realize that Ray Magee was artsy.
But he could be *crafty* enough to be making a swamp monster costume.
I knew it!
RAY MAGEE, WE KNOW WHAT YOU'RE UP TO!

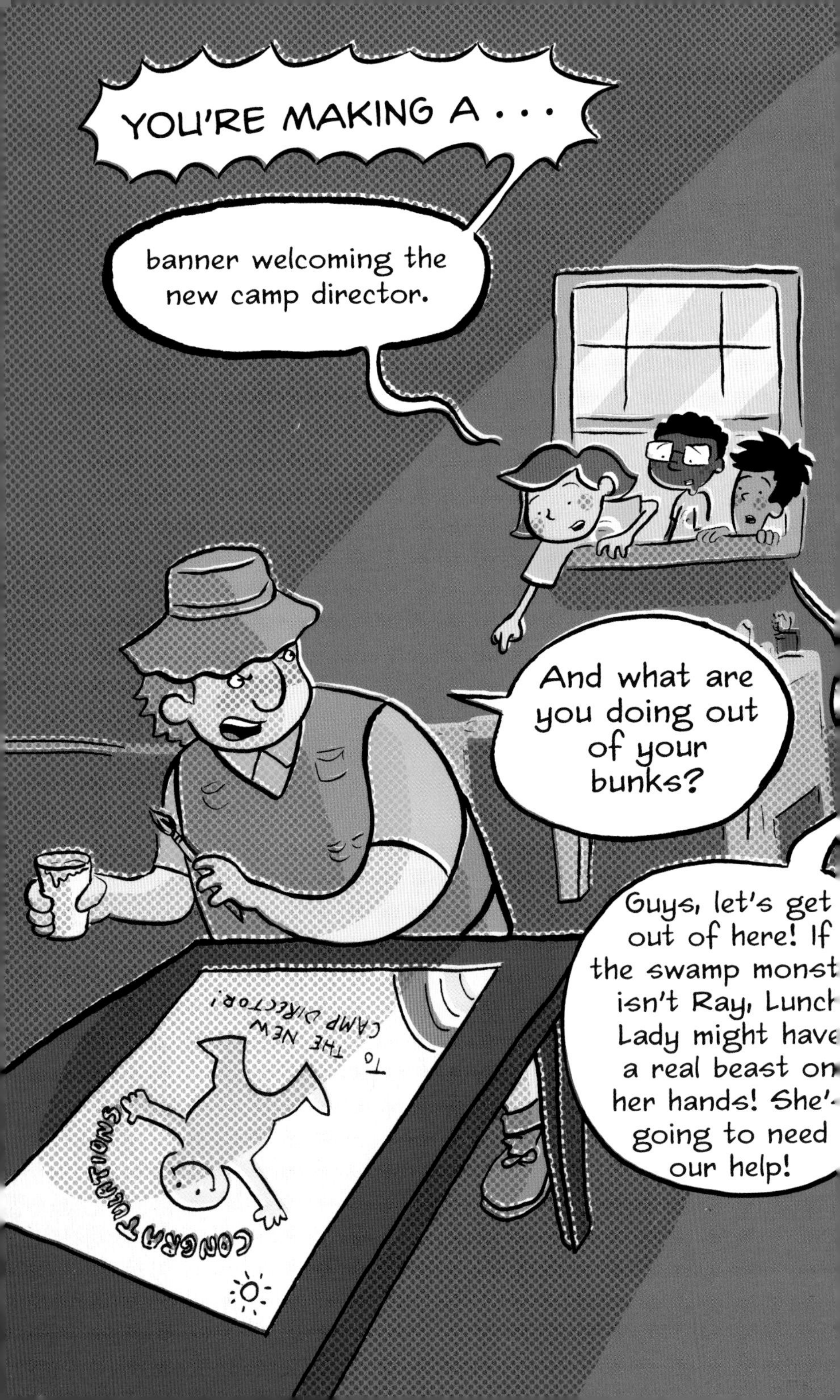
YOU'RE MAKING A . . .
banner welcoming the new camp director.
And what are you doing out of your bunks?
Guys, let's get out of here! If the swamp monst isn't Ray, Lunch Lady might have a real beast on her hands! She'- going to need our help!
CONGRATULATIONS
TO THE NEW CAMP DIRECTOR!

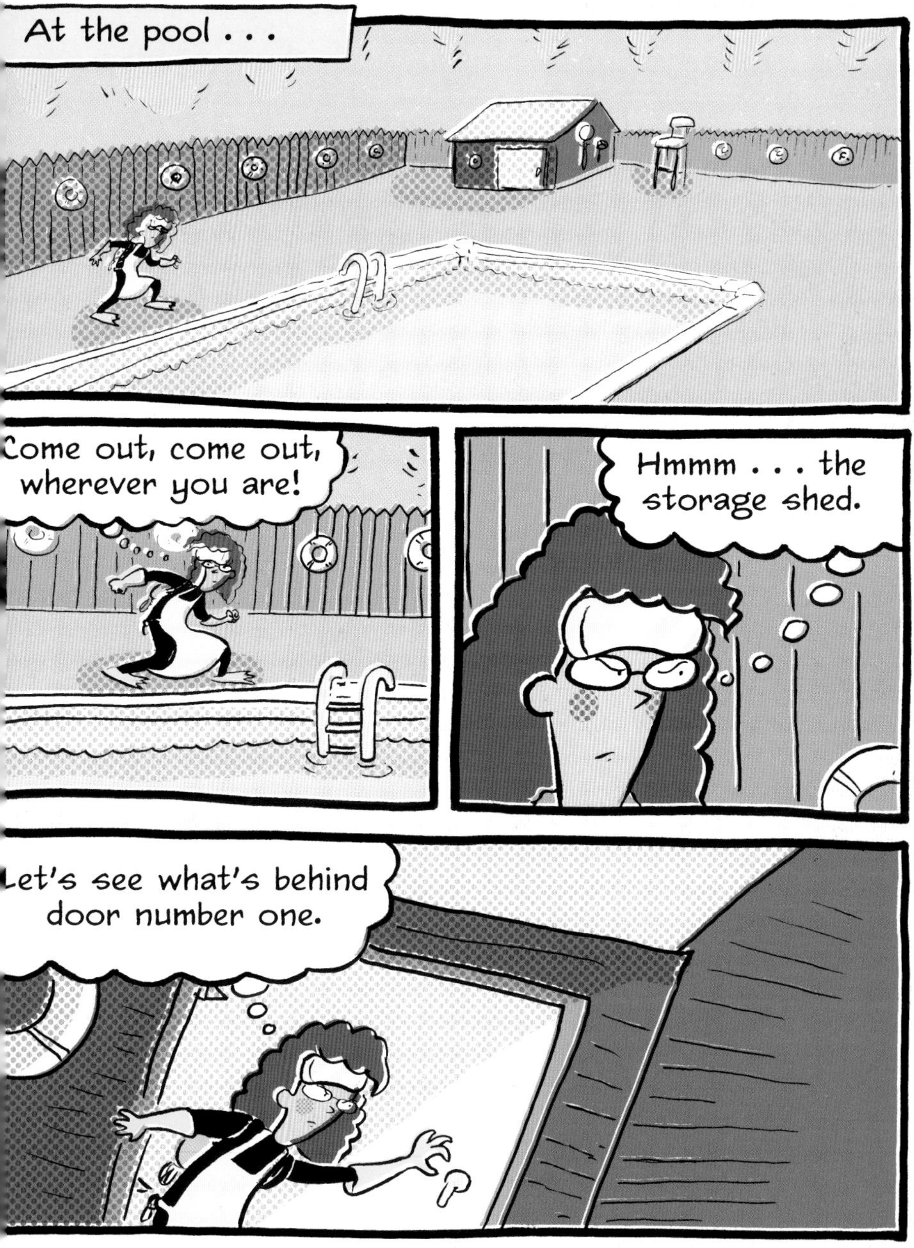
At the pool . . .
Come out, come out, wherever you are!
Hmmm . . . the storage shed.
Let's see what's behind door number one.

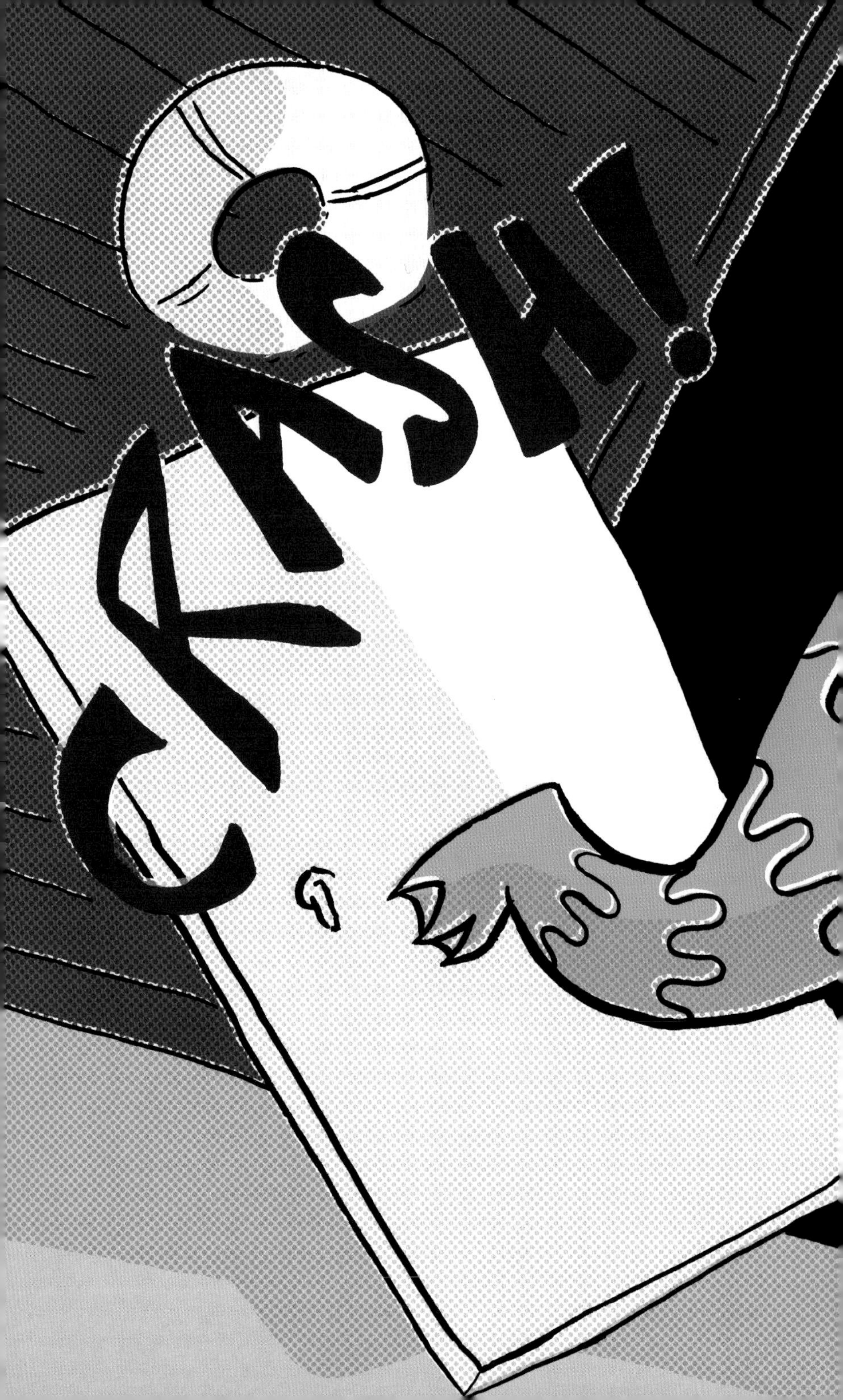
CRASH!

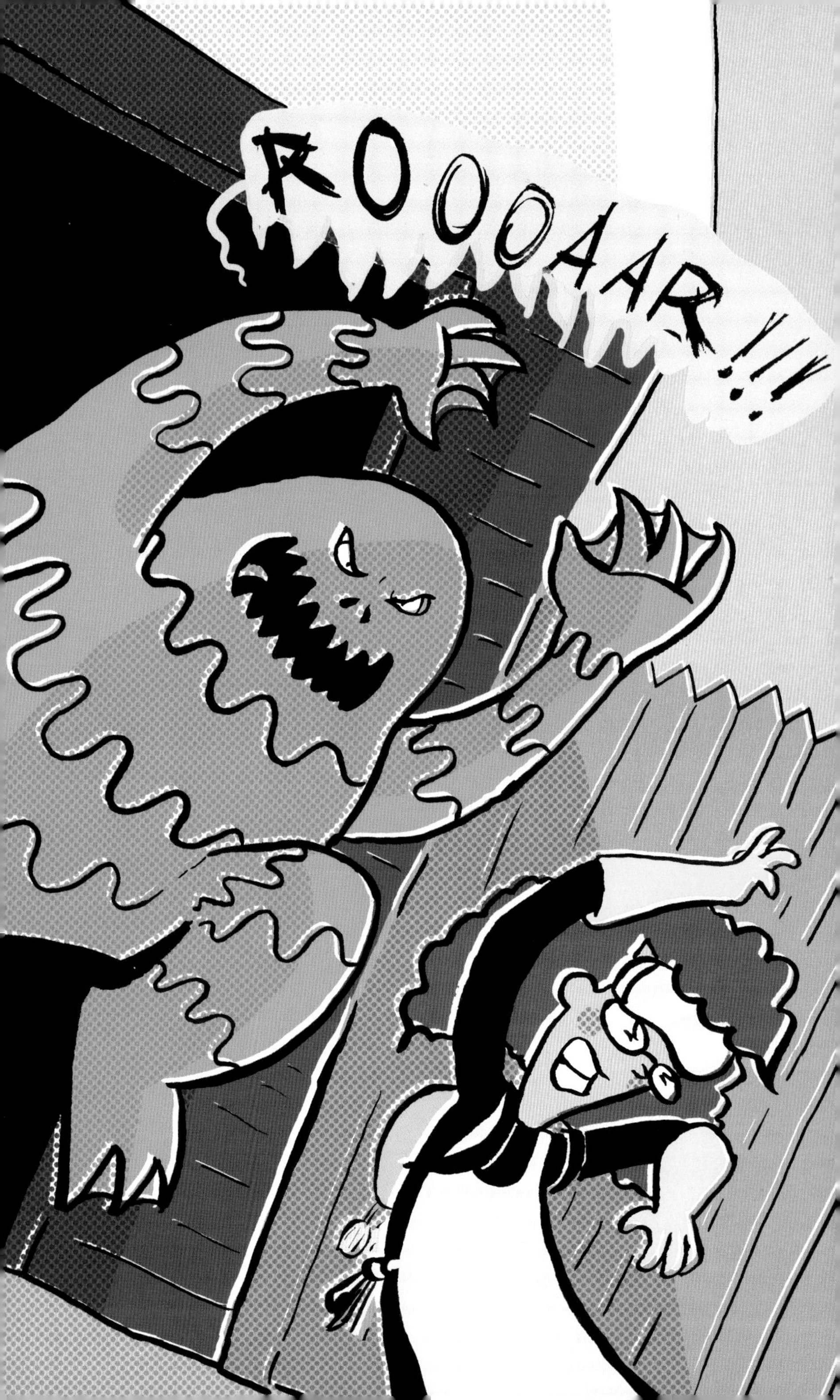
ROOOAAR!!!

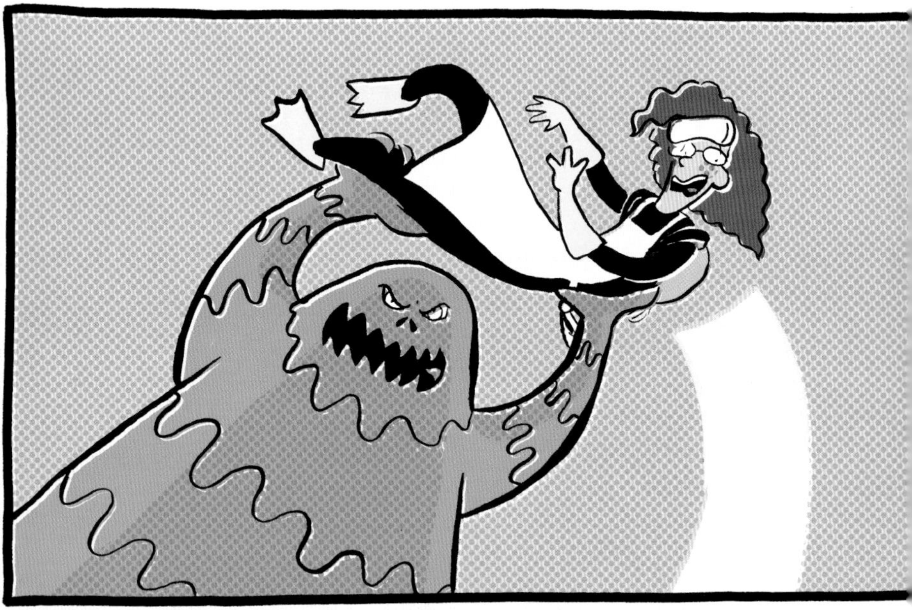

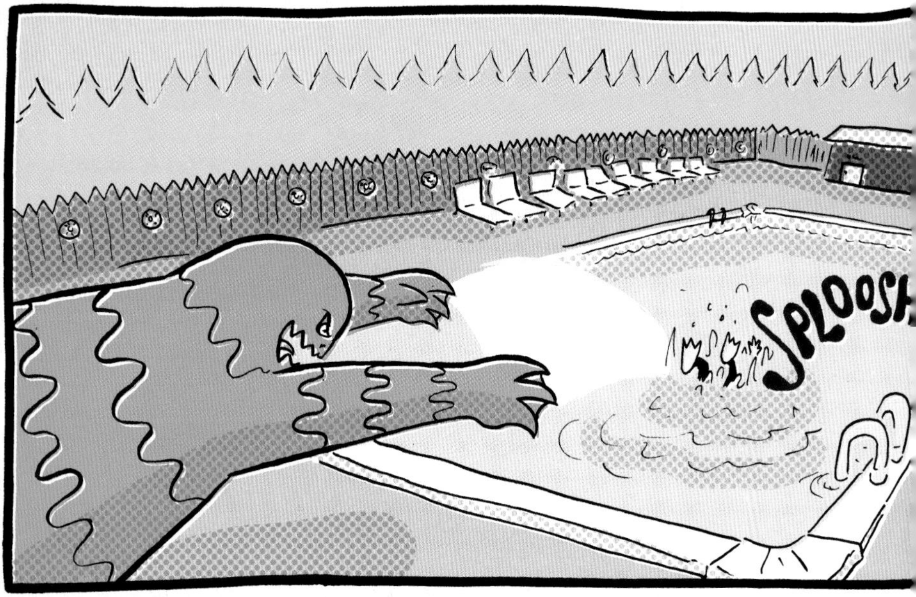
SPLOOSH

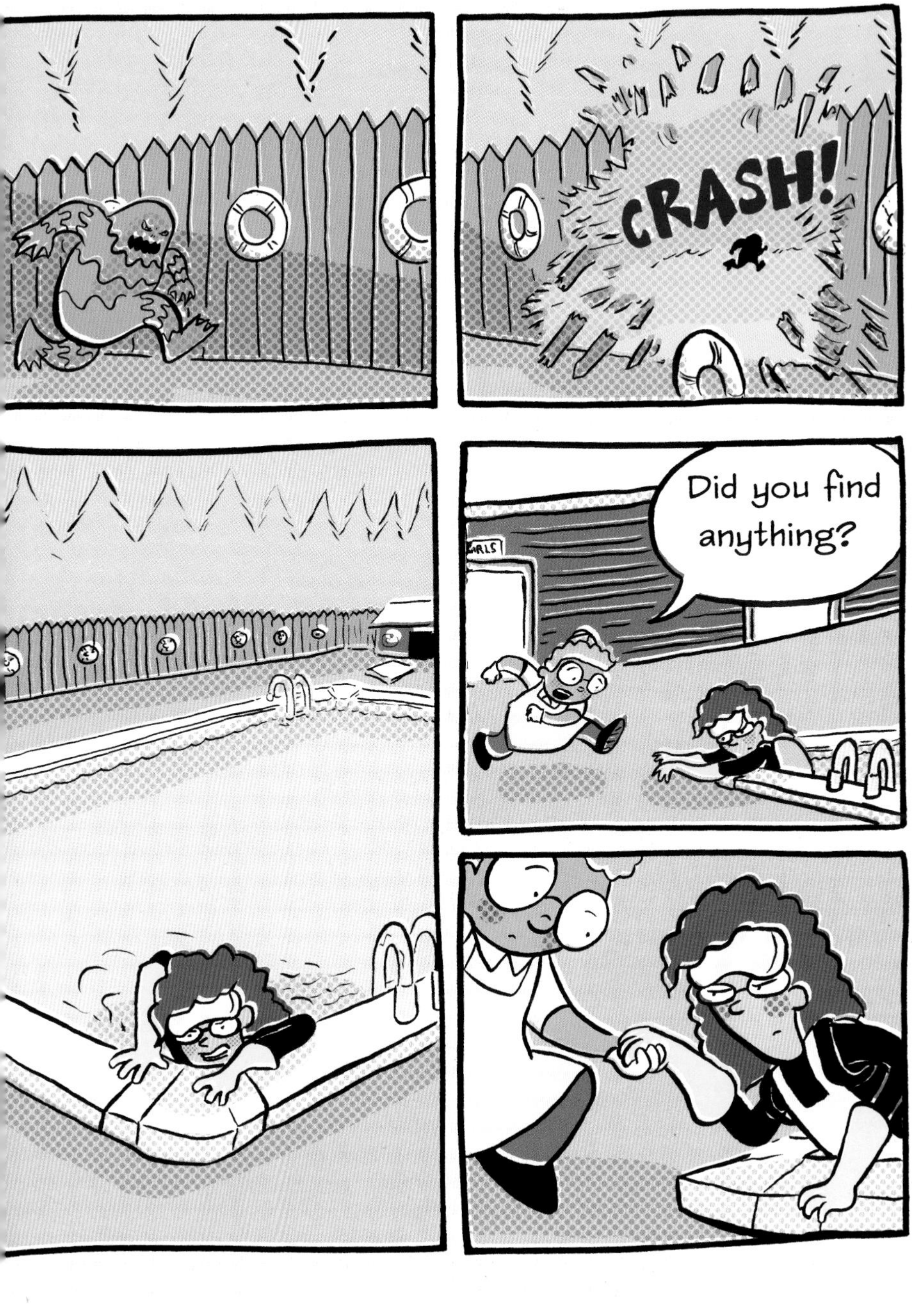
CRASH!
GIRLS
Did you find anything?

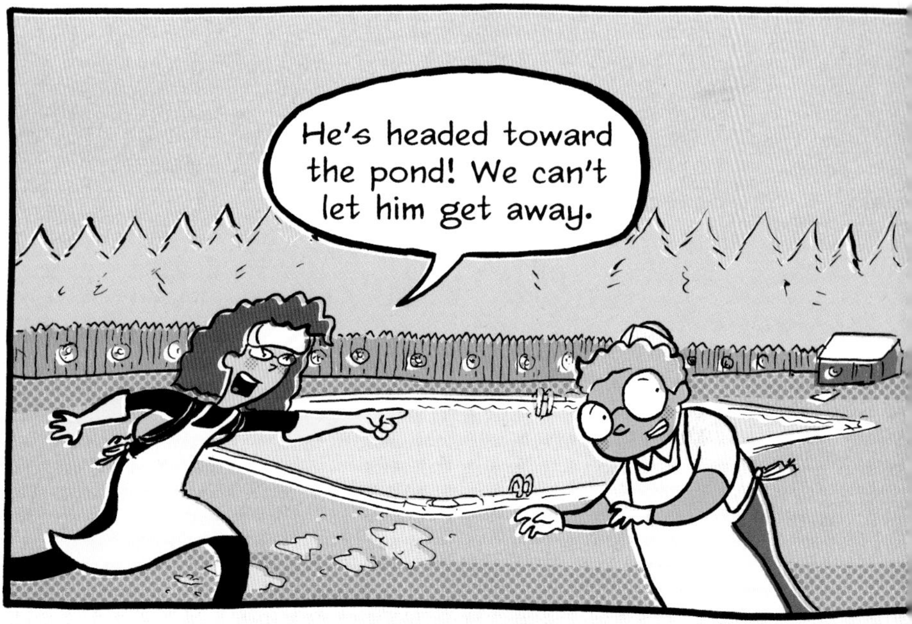
He's headed toward the pond! We can't let him get away.

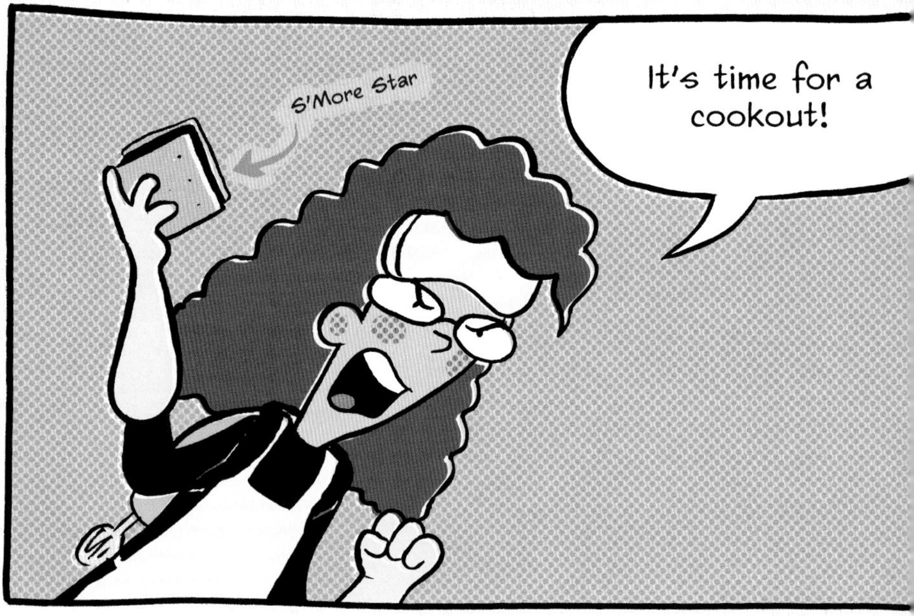
S'More Star
It's time for a cookout!

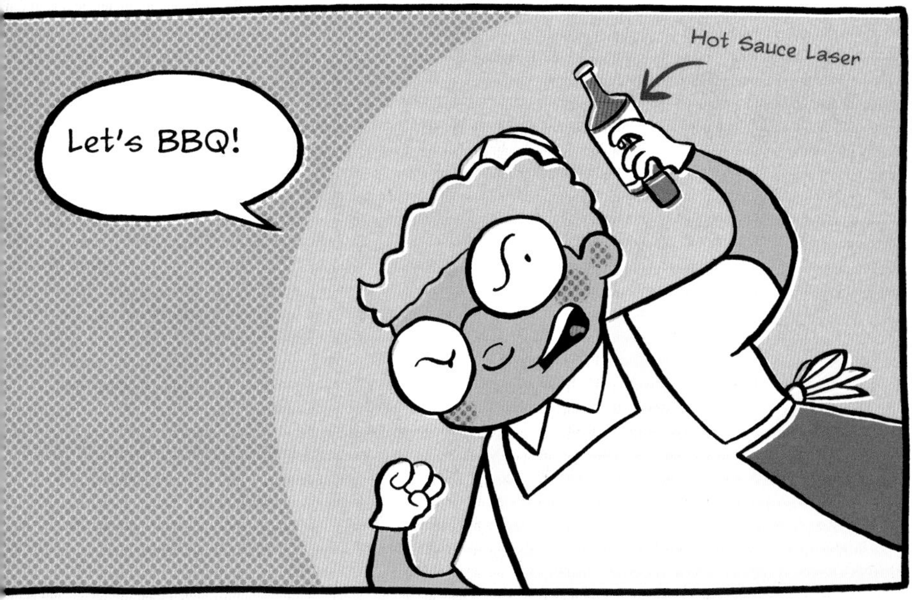
Let's BBQ!
Hot Sauce Laser

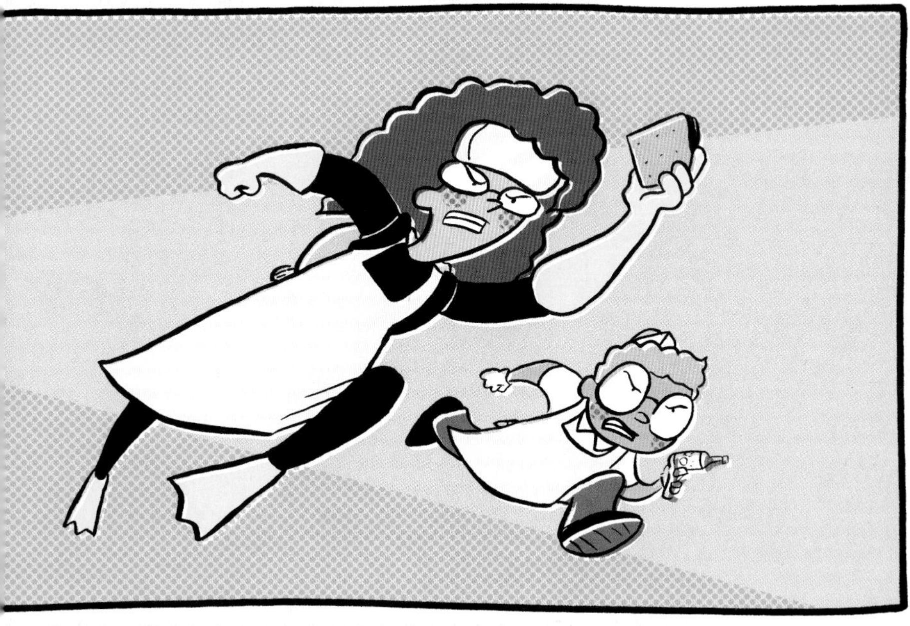

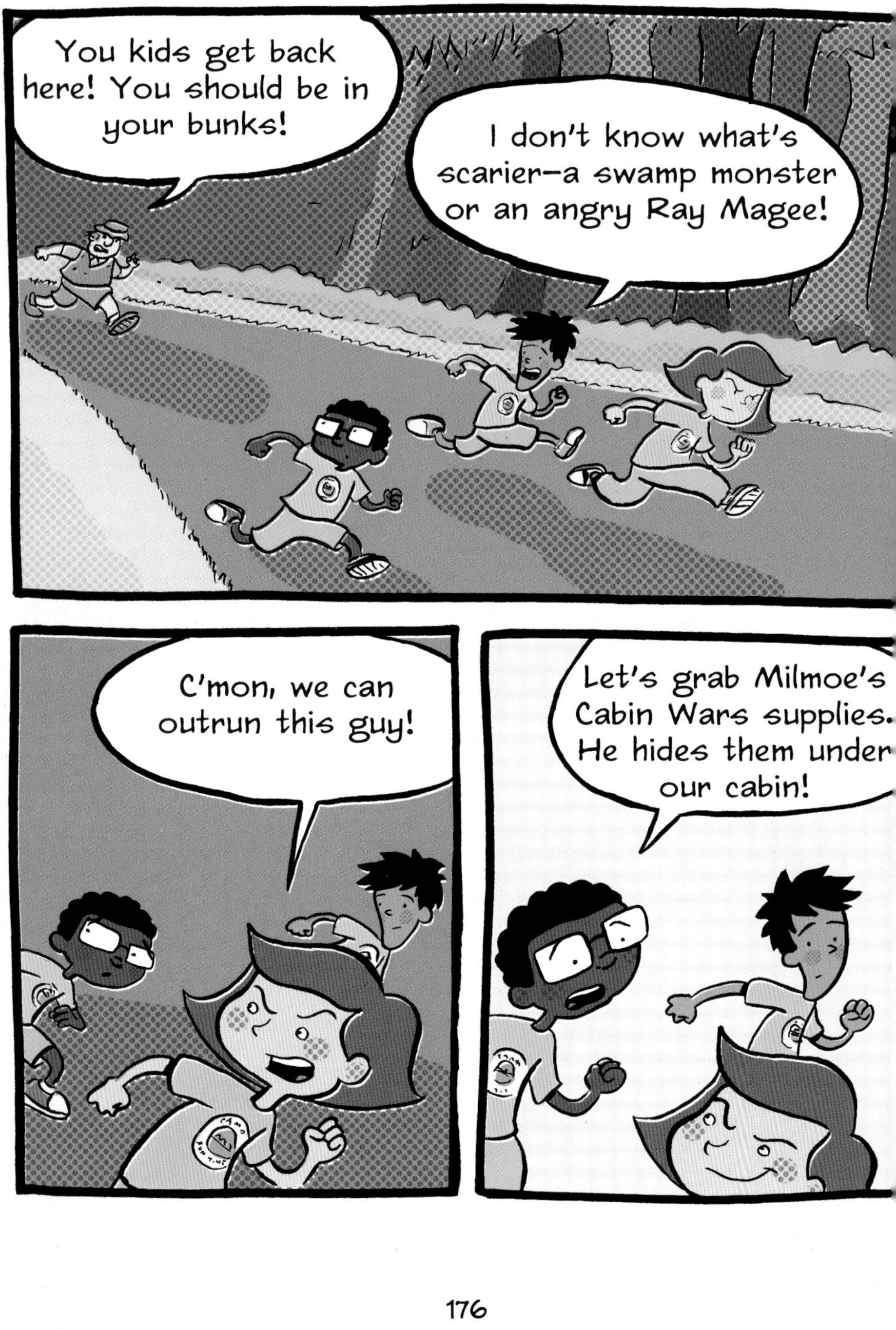
You kids get back here! You should be in your bunks!
I don't know what's scarier—a swamp monster or an angry Ray Magee!
C'mon, we can outrun this guy!
Let's grab Milmoe's Cabin Wars supplies. He hides them under our cabin!

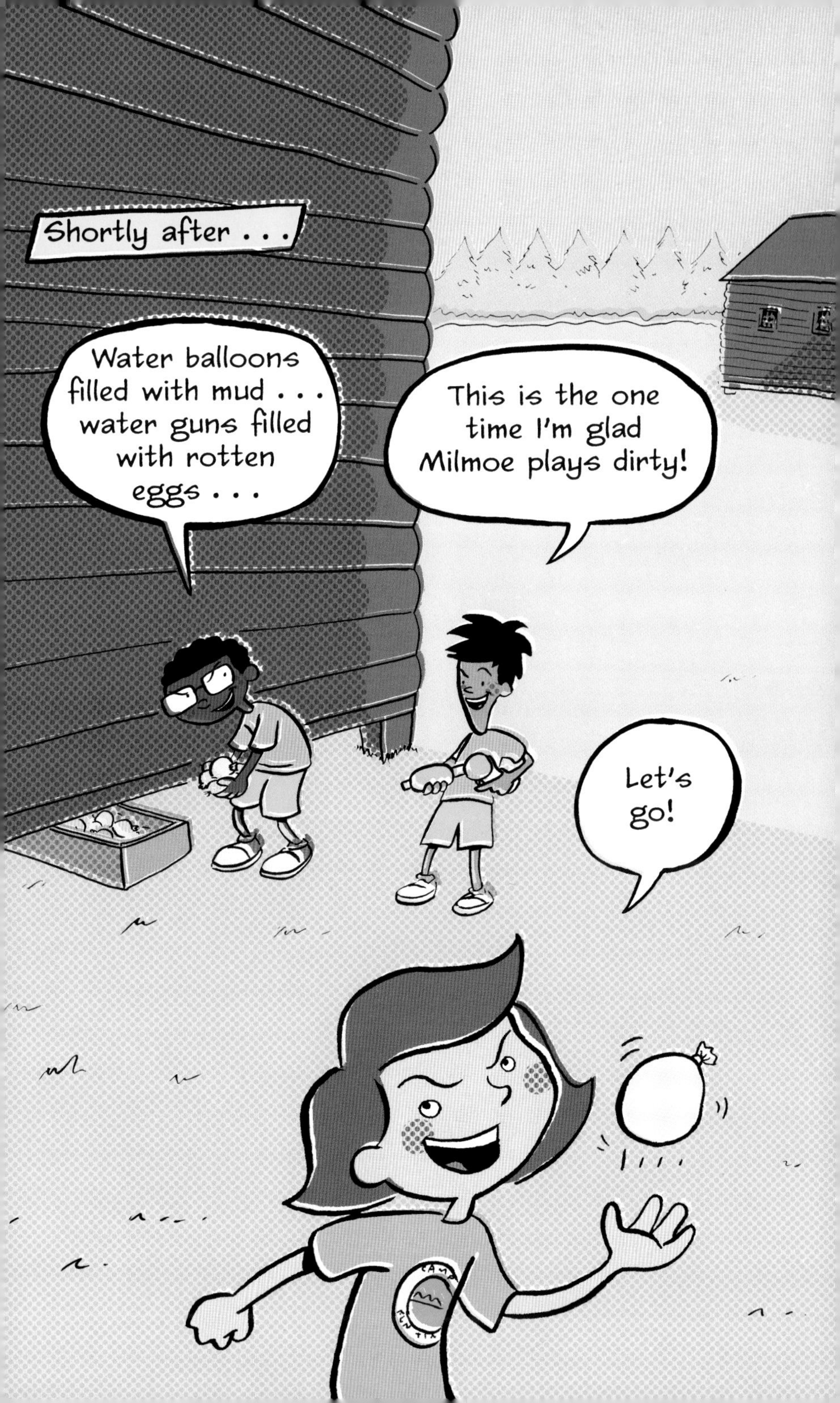
Shortly after . . .
Water balloons filled with mud . . . water guns filled with rotten eggs . . .
This is the one time I'm glad Milmoe plays dirty!
Let's go!

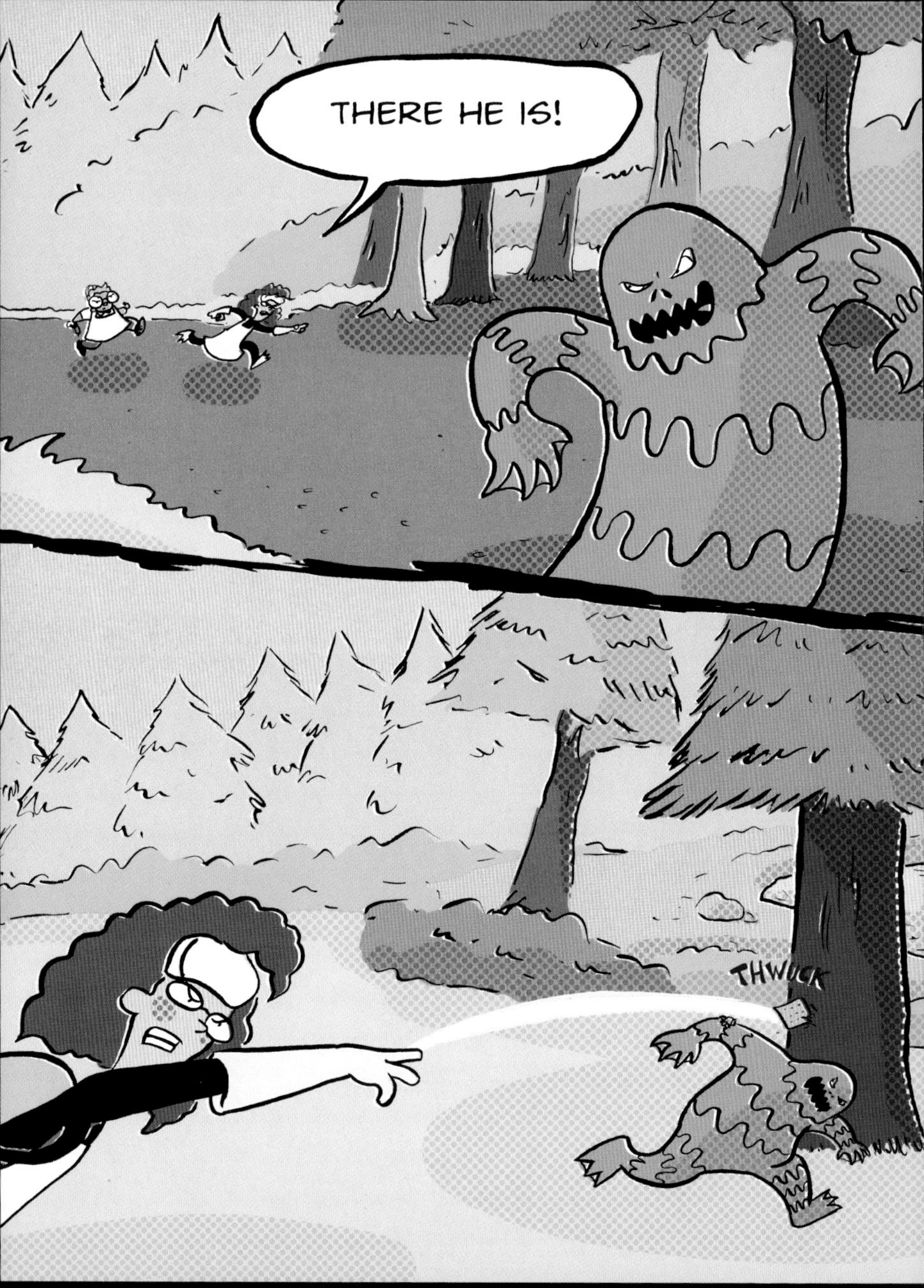
THERE HE IS!
THWUCK

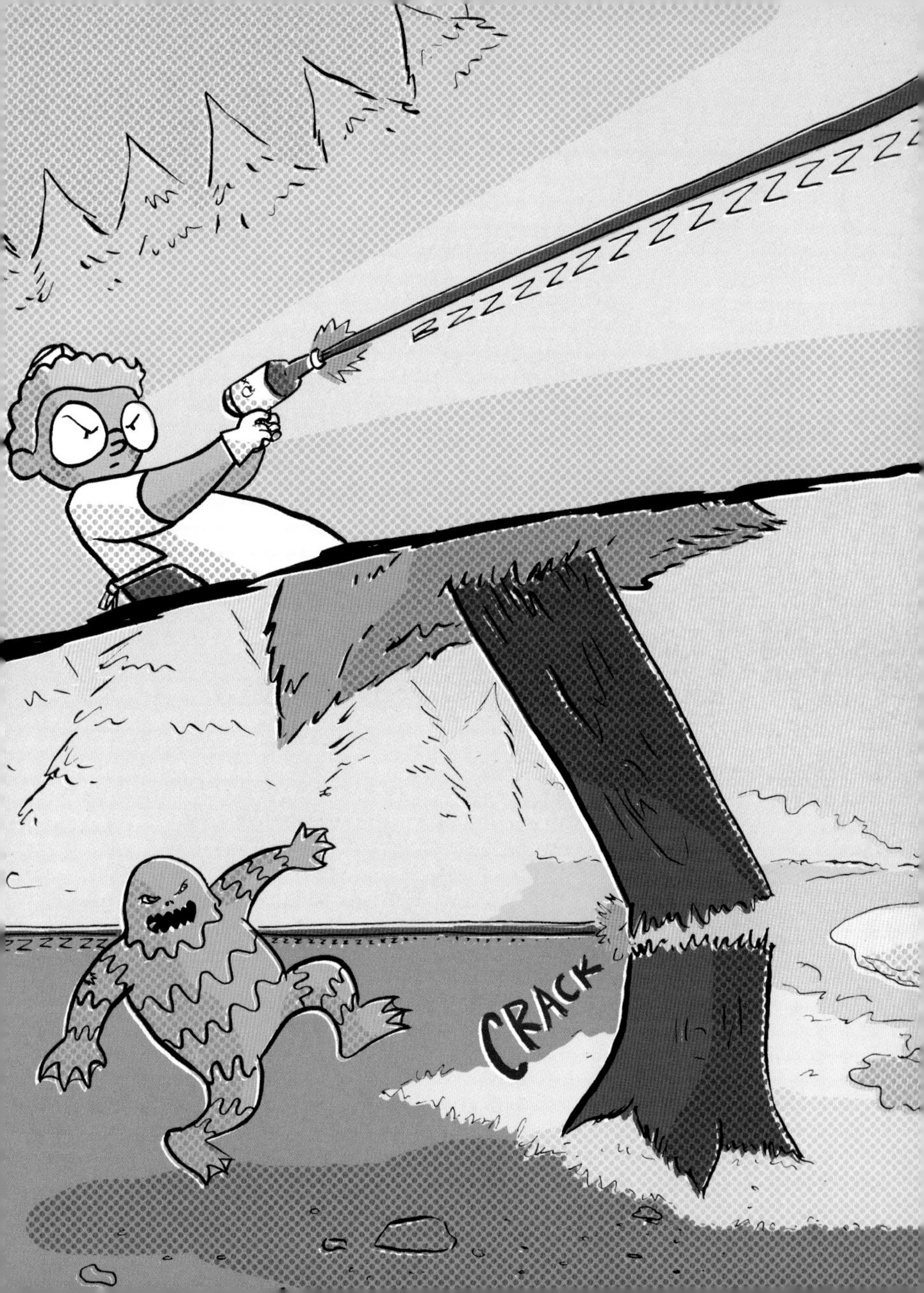
BZZZZZZZZZZZZZZZZZZ
CRACK

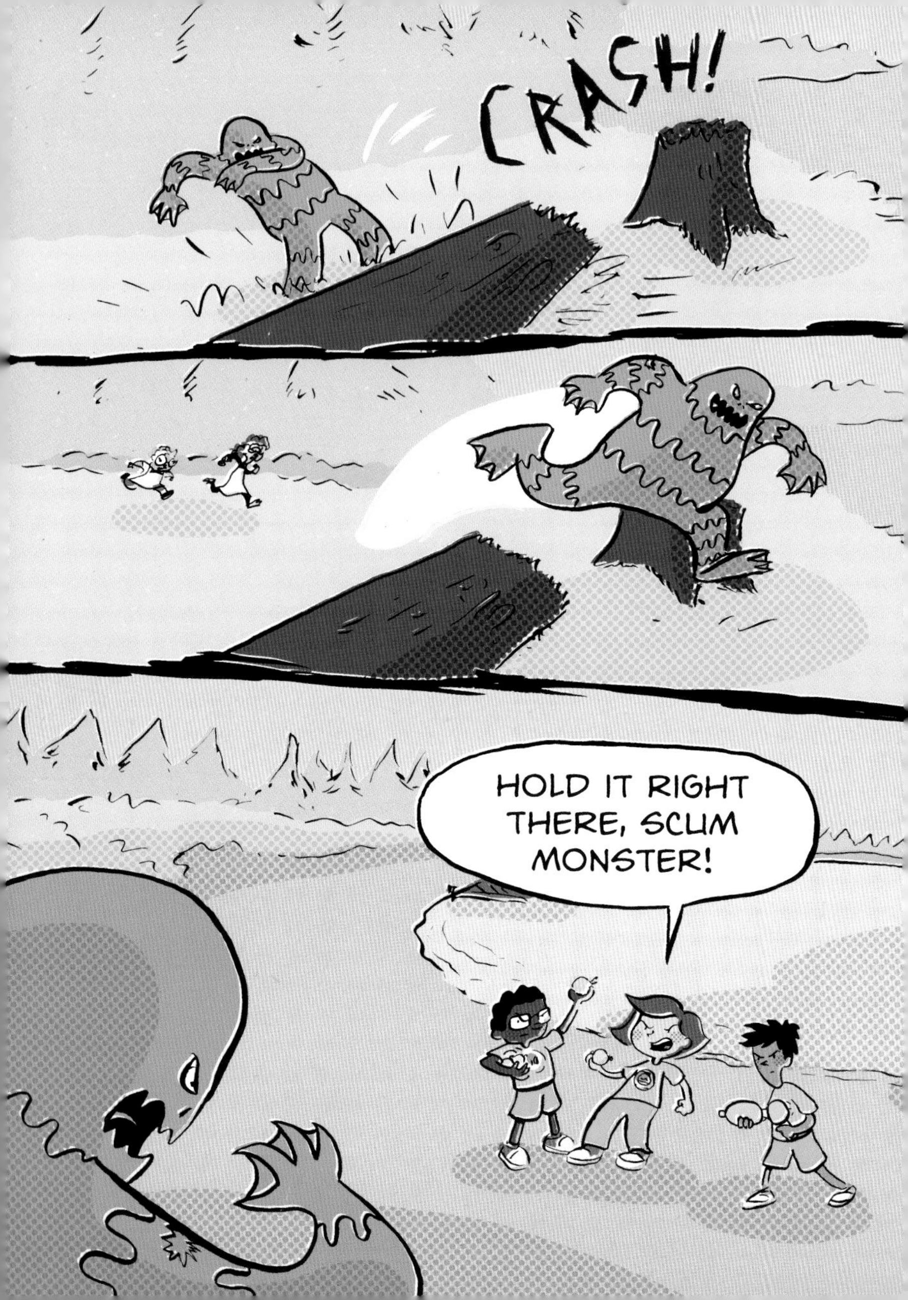
CRASH!
HOLD IT RIGHT THERE, SCUM MONSTER!

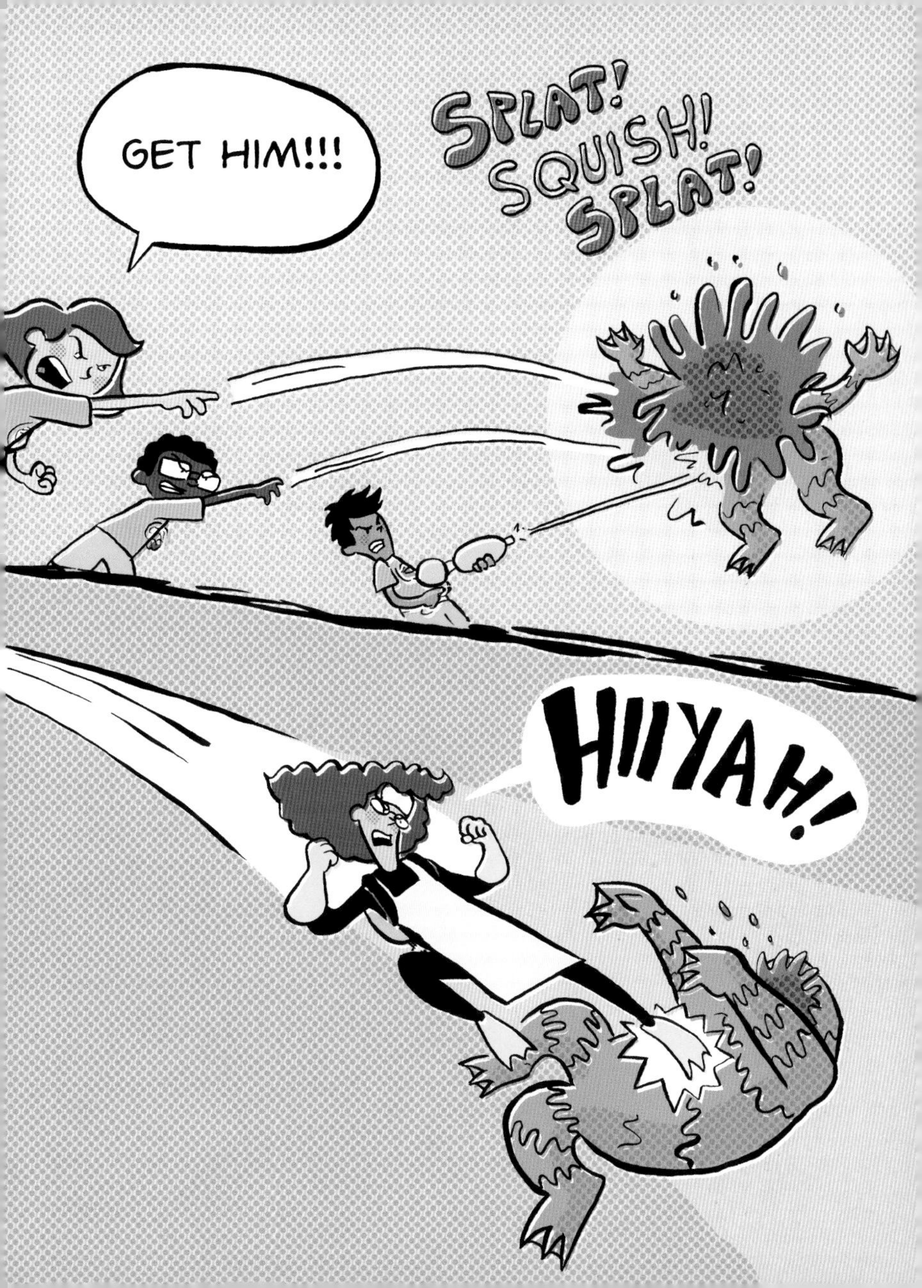
GET HIM!!!
SPLAT! SQUISH! SPLAT!
HIIYAH!

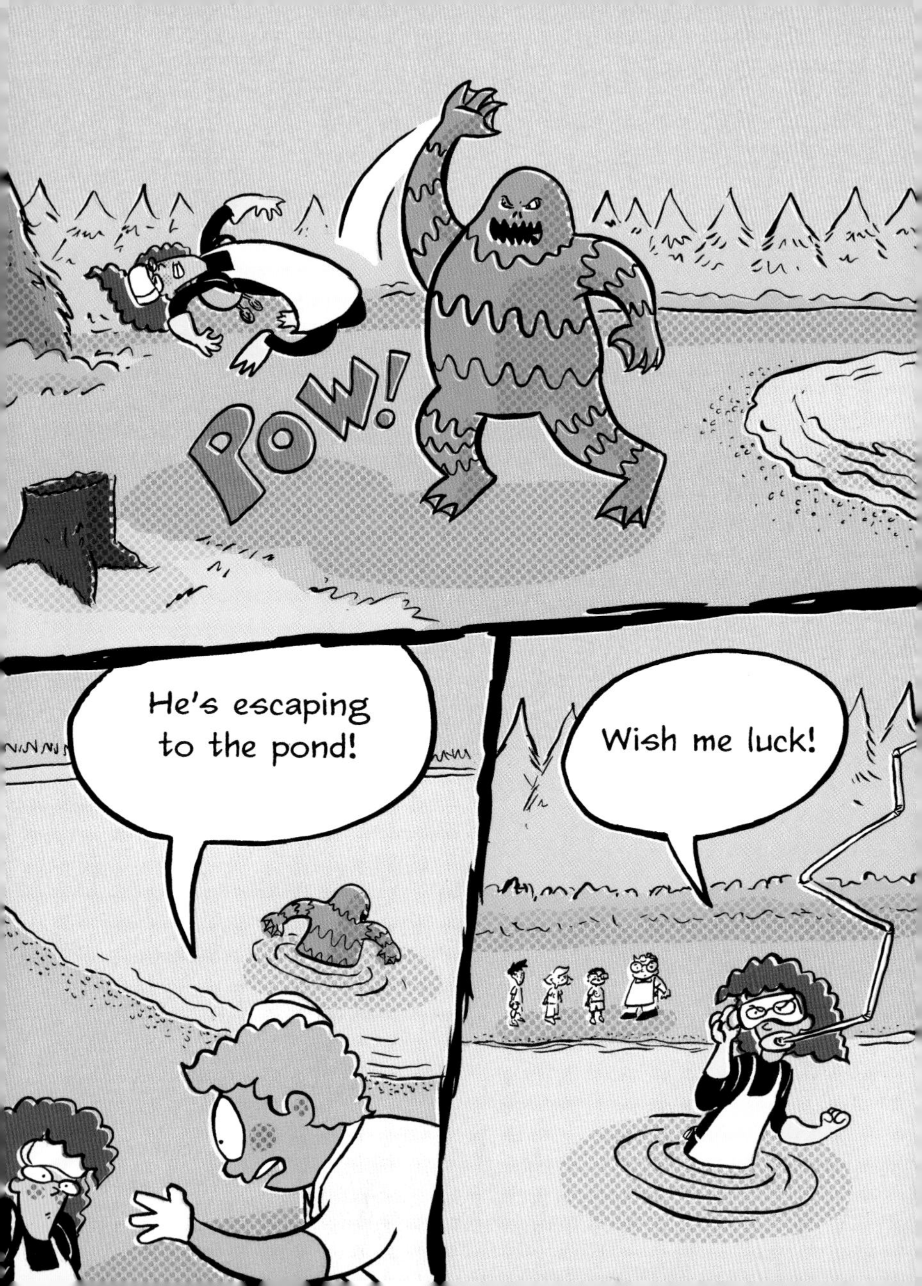
POW!
He's escaping to the pond!
Wish me luck!

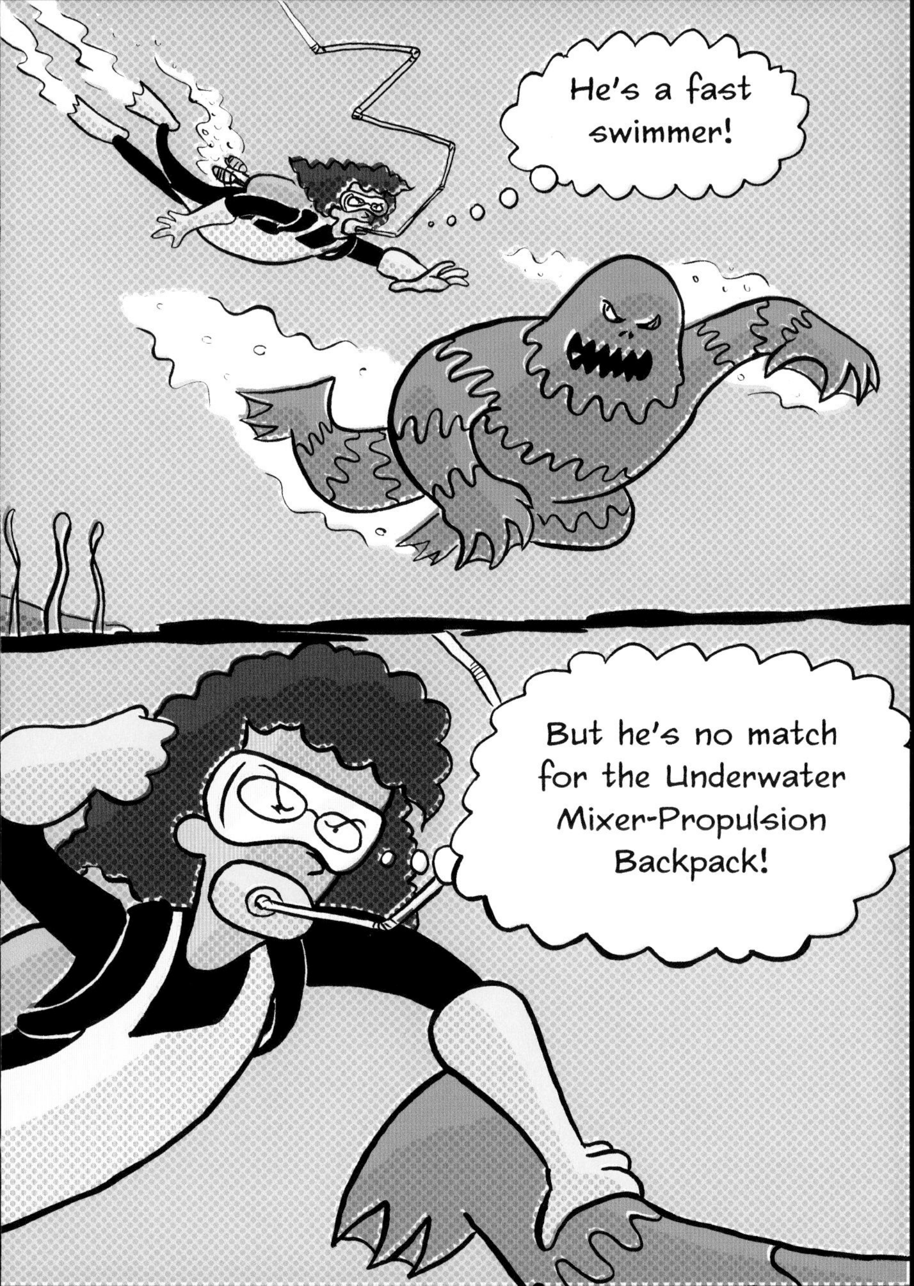
He's a fast swimmer!
But he's no match for the Underwater Mixer-Propulsion Backpack!

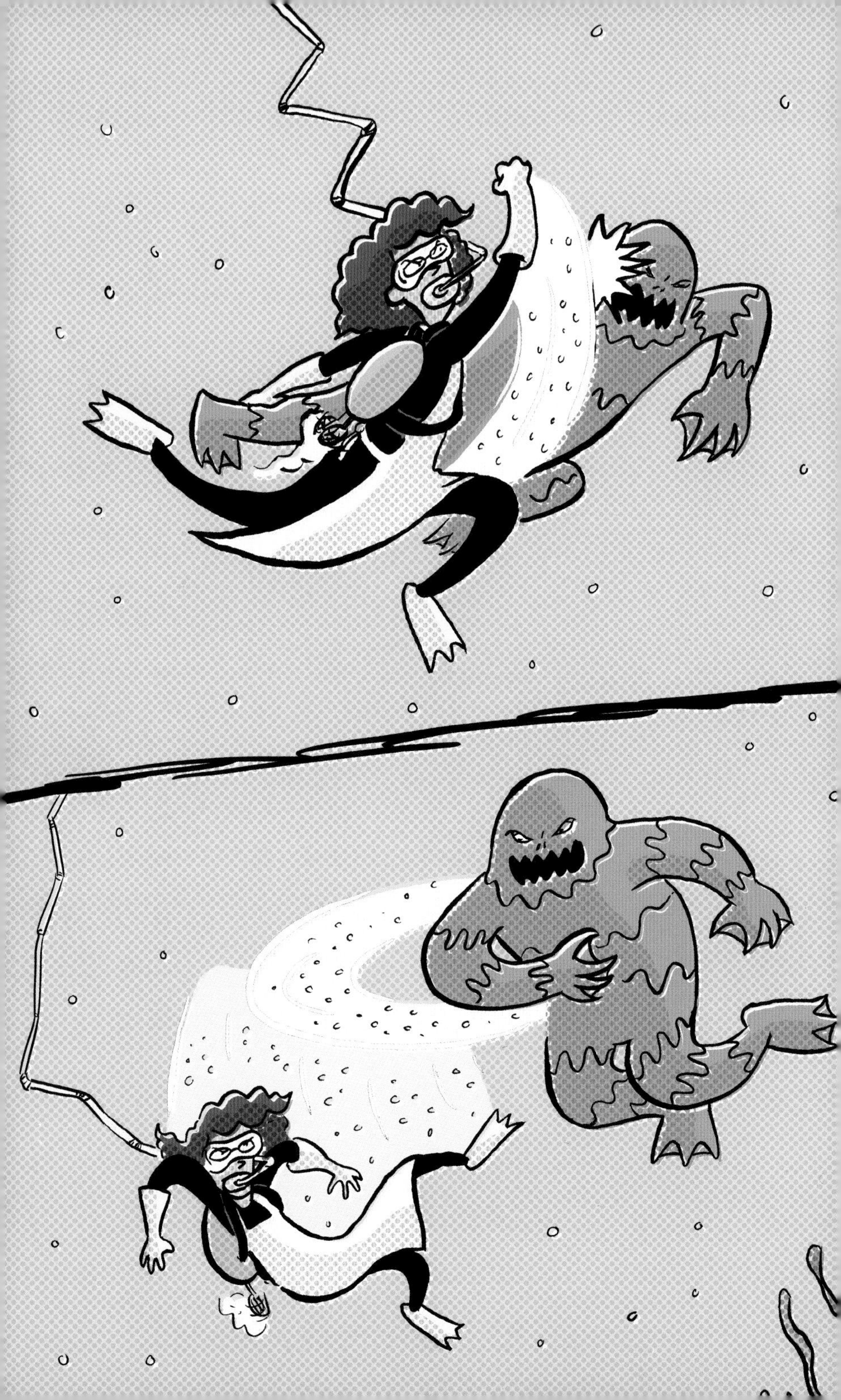

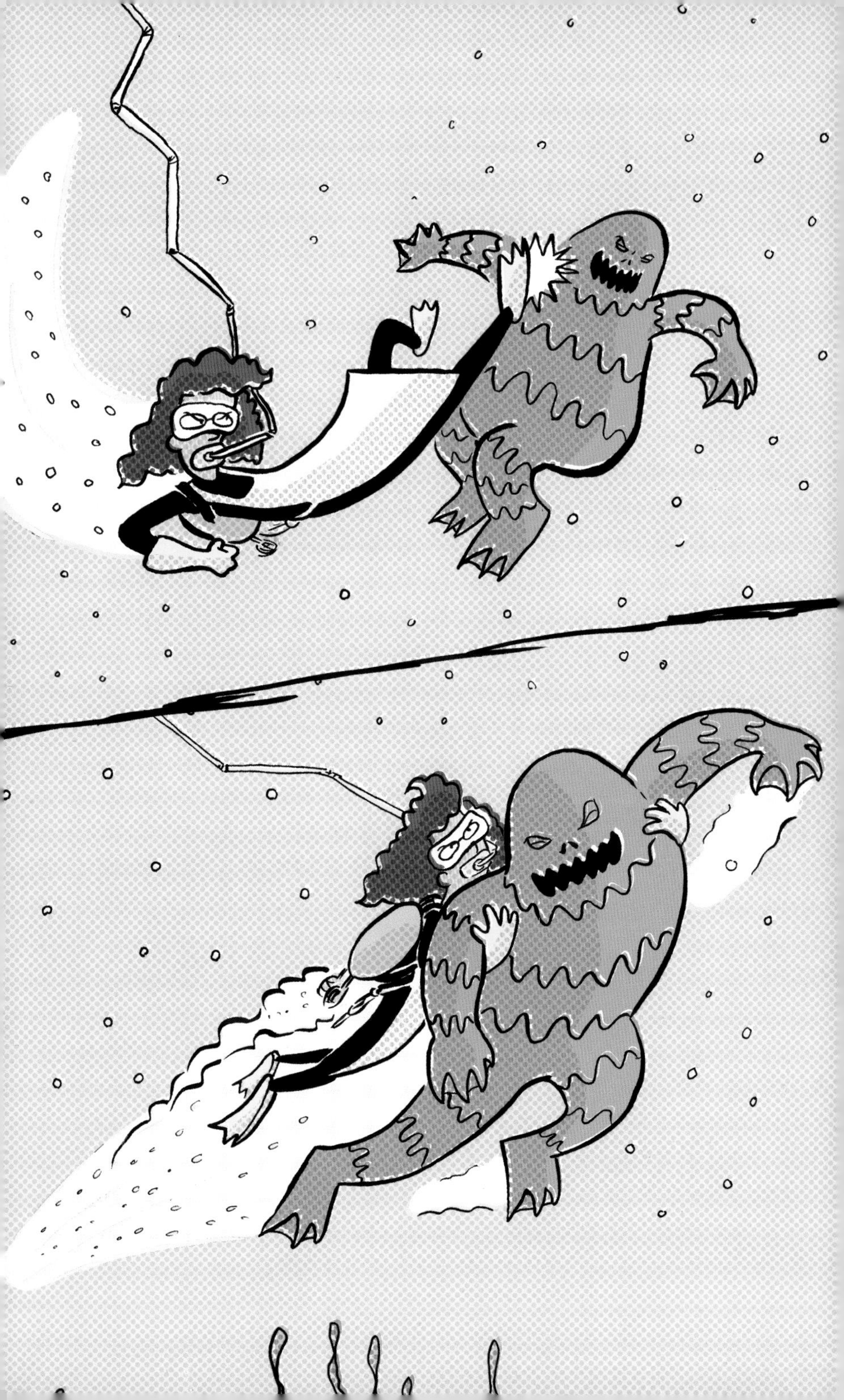

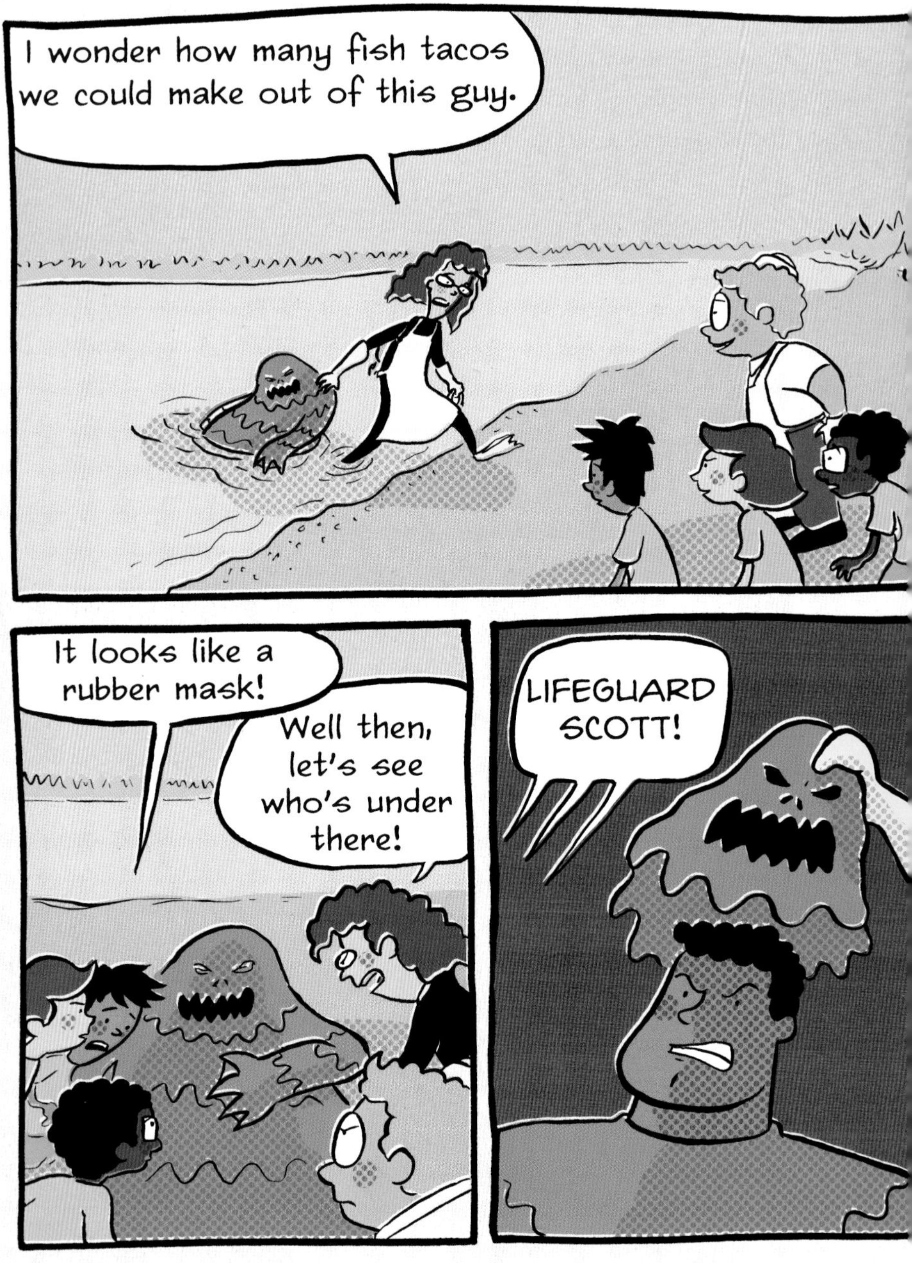
I wonder how many fish tacos we could make out of this guy.
It looks like a rubber mask!
Well then, let's see who's under there!
LIFEGUARD SCOTT!

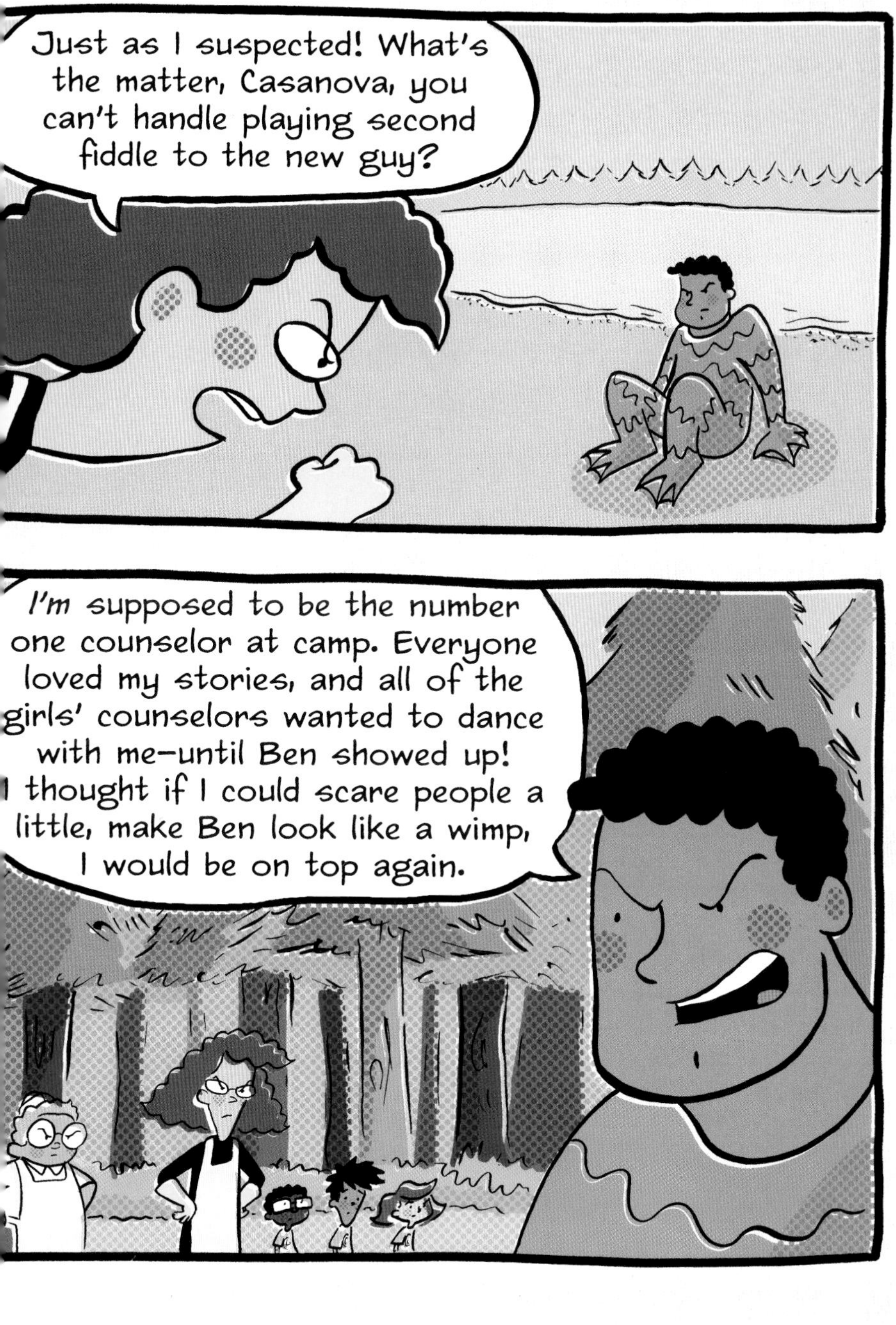
Just as I suspected! What's the matter, Casanova, you can't handle playing second fiddle to the new guy?
I'm supposed to be the number one counselor at camp. Everyone loved my stories, and all of the girls' counselors wanted to dance with me–until Ben showed up! I thought if I could scare people a little, make Ben look like a wimp, I would be on top again.

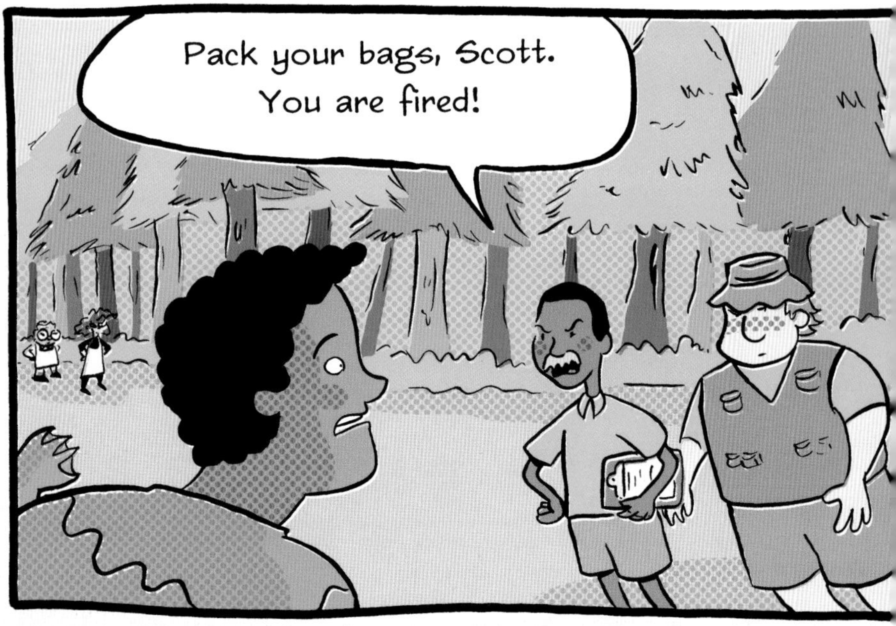
Pack your bags, Scott. You are fired!

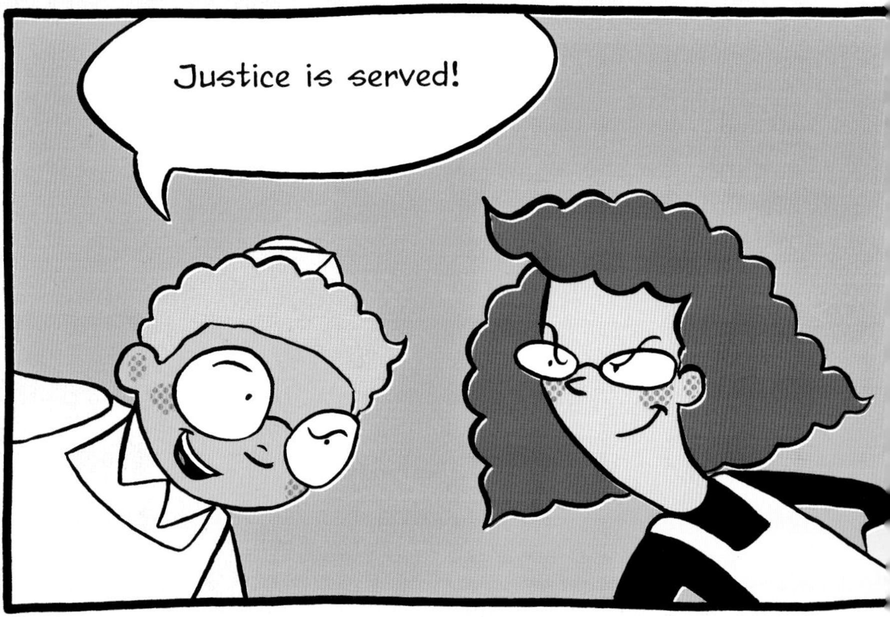
Justice is served!

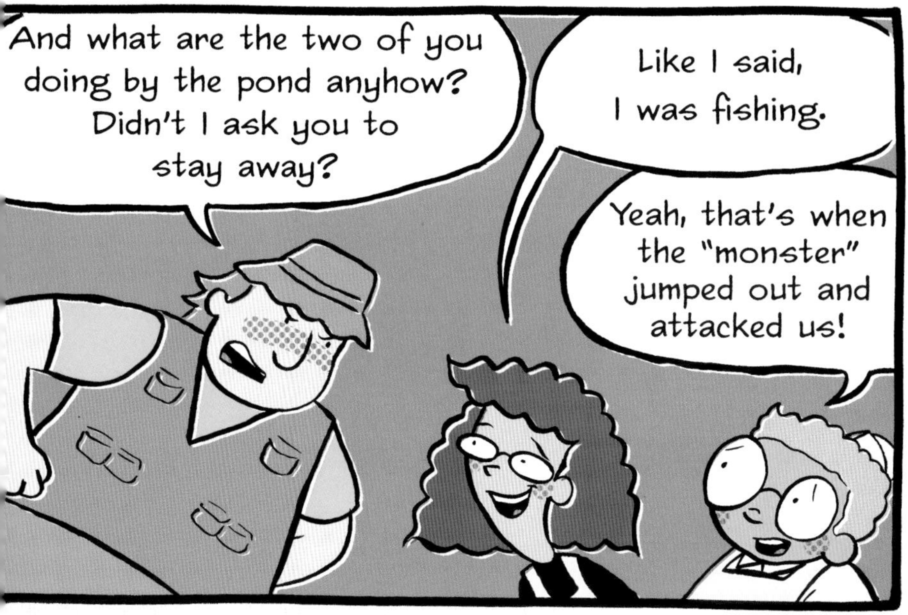
And what are the two of you doing by the pond anyhow? Didn't I ask you to stay away?
Like I said, I was fishing.
Yeah, that's when the "monster" jumped out and attacked us!

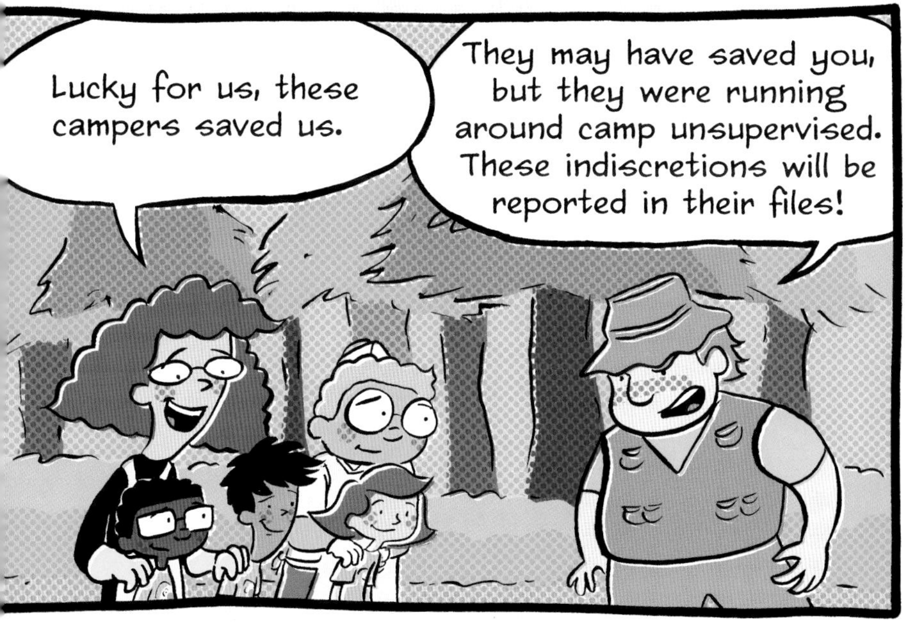
Lucky for us, these campers saved us.
They may have saved you, but they were running around camp unsupervised. These indiscretions will be reported in their files!

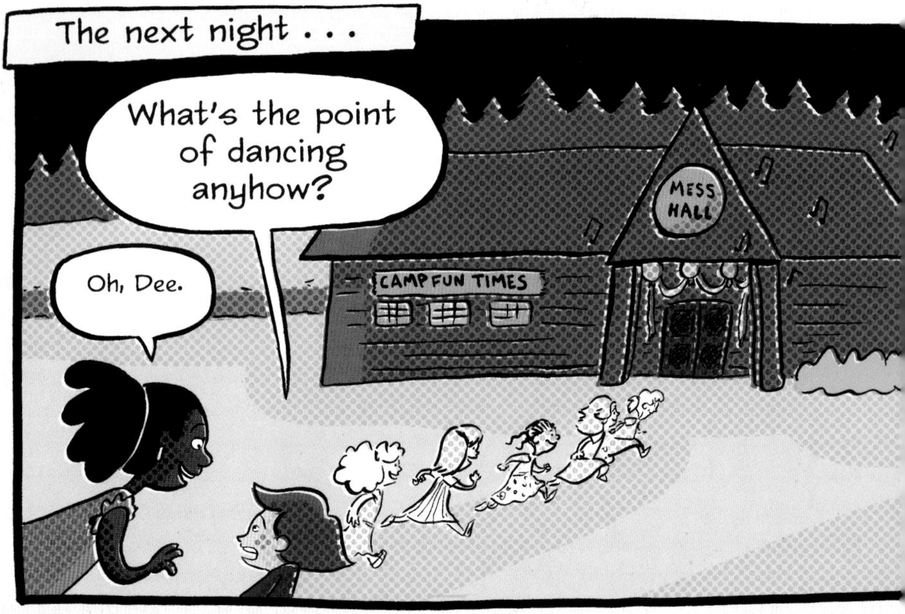
The next night . . .
What's the point of dancing anyhow?
Oh, Dee.
MESS HALL
CAMP FUN TIMES

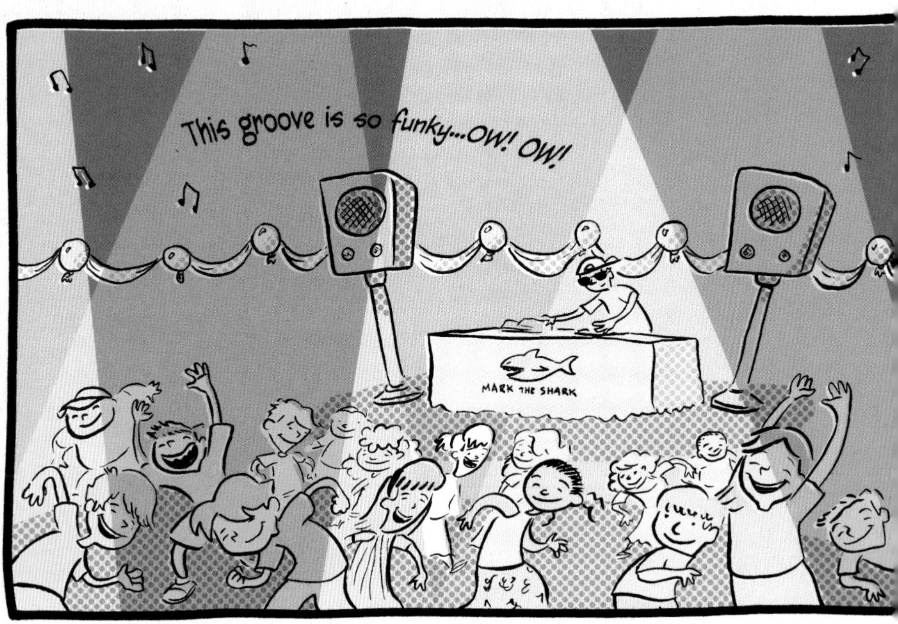
This groove is so funky...OW! OW!
MARK THE SHARK

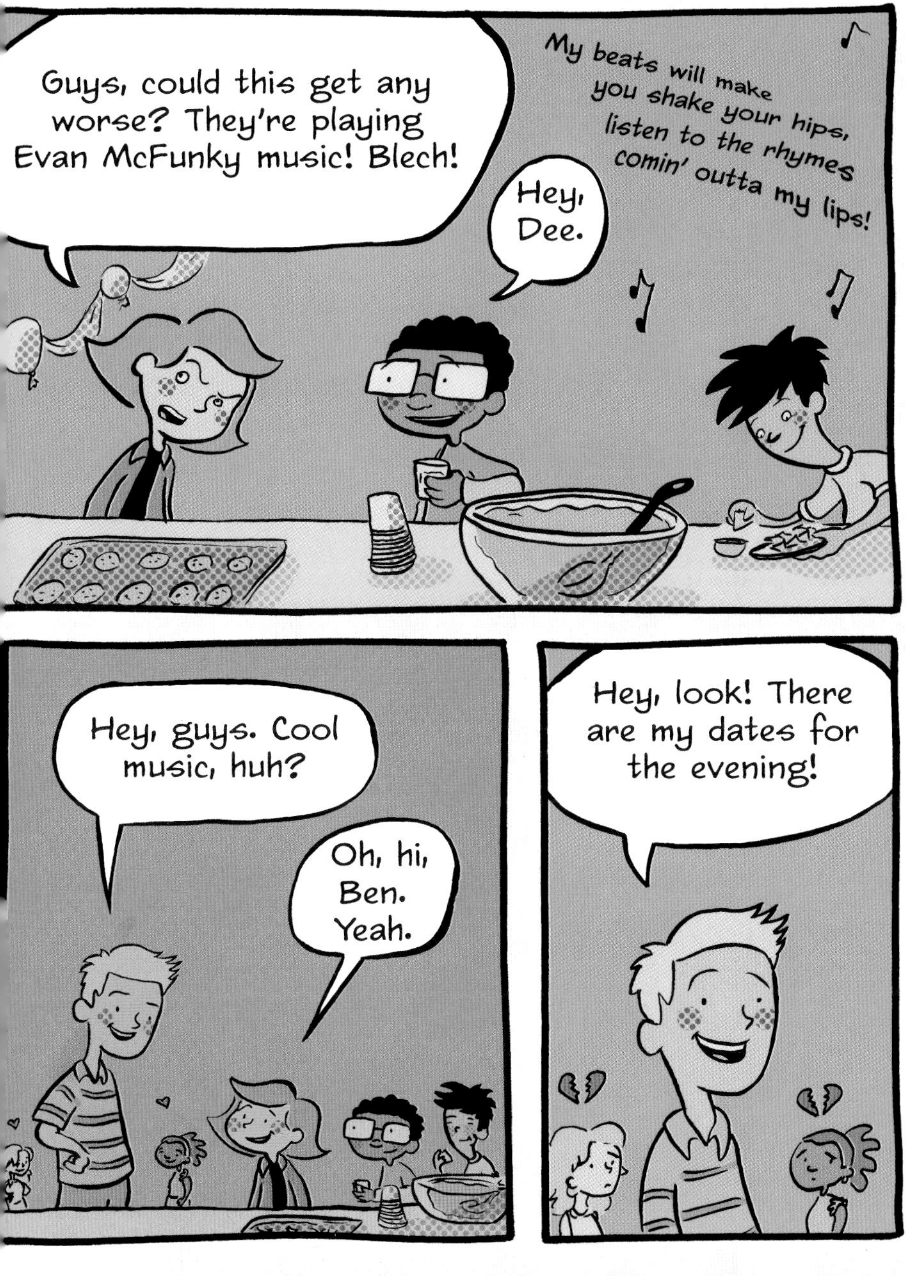
Guys, could this get any worse? They're playing Evan McFunky music! Blech!
Hey, Dee.
My beats will make you shake your hips, listen to the rhymes comin' outta my lips!
Hey, guys. Cool music, huh?
Oh, hi, Ben. Yeah.
Hey, look! There are my dates for the evening!

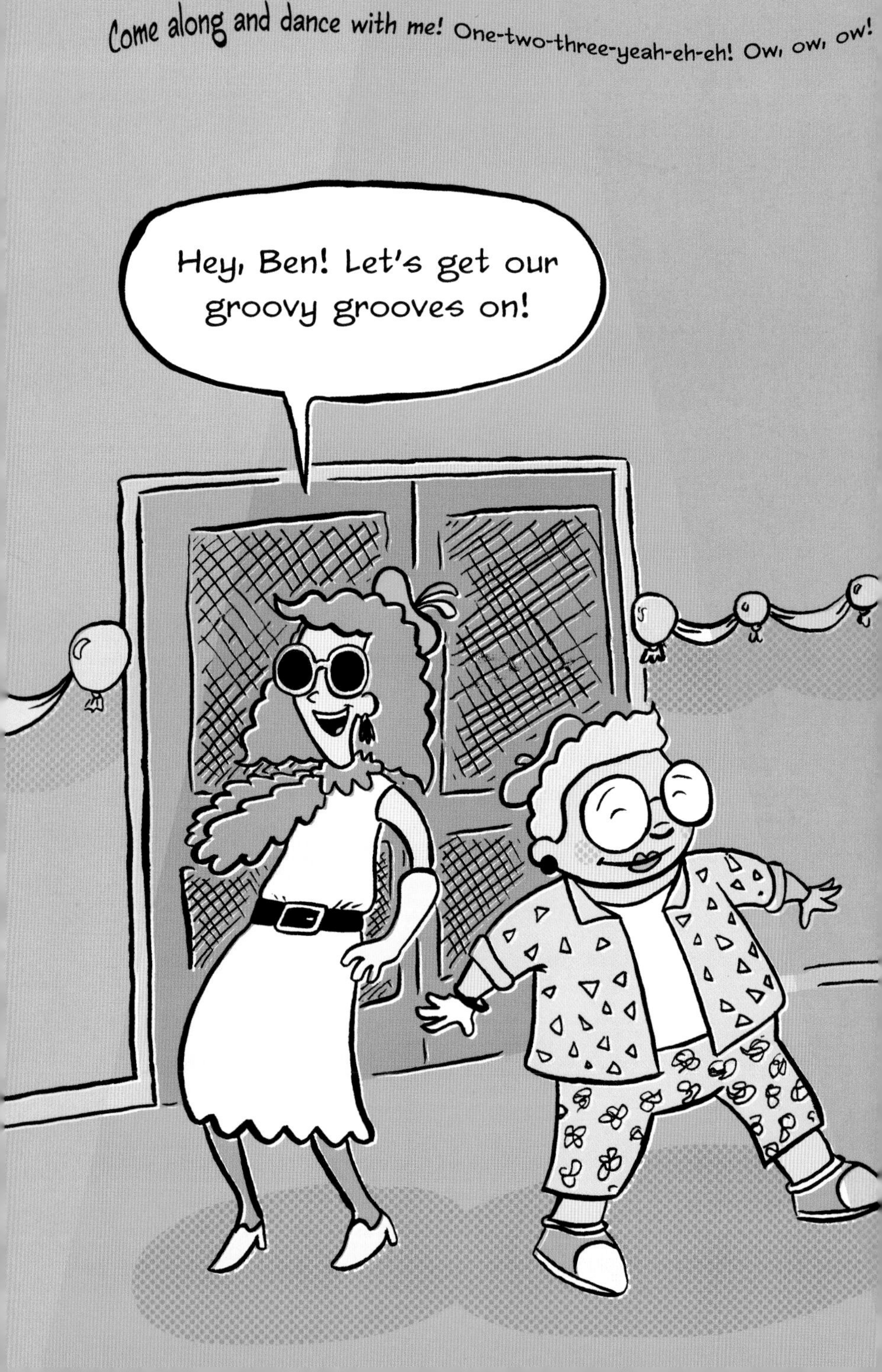
Come along and dance with me! One-two-three-yeah-eh-eh! Ow, ow, ow!
Hey, Ben! Let's get our groovy grooves on!

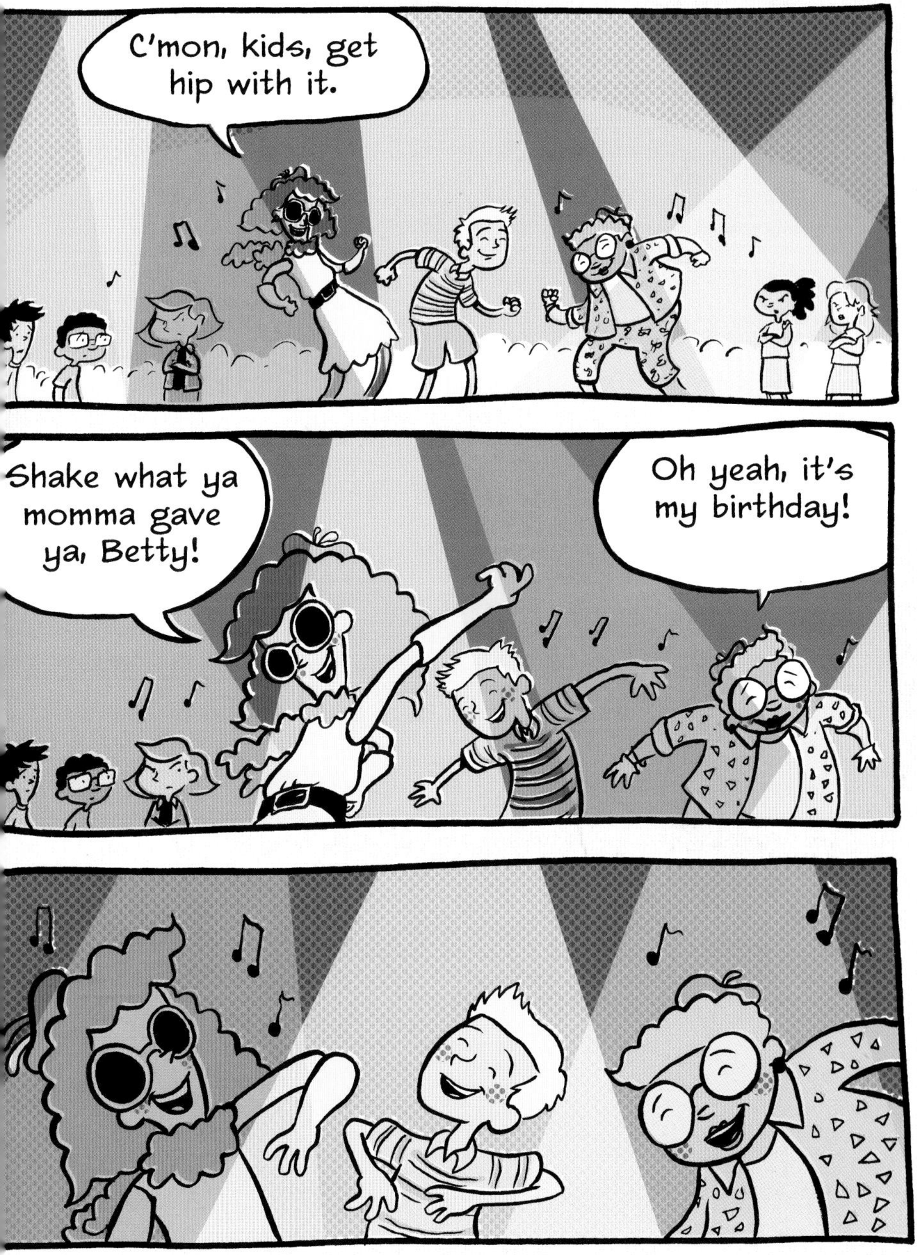
C'mon, kids, get hip with it.
Shake what ya momma gave ya, Betty!
Oh yeah, it's my birthday!

FOR SEVERAL LIFE-CHANGING SUMMERS, I WAS A COUNSELOR AT THE HOLE IN THE WALL GANG CAMP IN ASHFORD, CONNECTICUT.

It's most commonly known as the camp that was founded by the late actor Paul Newman to serve children with serious illnesses. It was during my years working at Hole in the Wall that I got my publishing career off the ground. I also, at that time, dreamed up a story about the spatula-wielding superhero you read about in this book. I would spend many hours of downtime with my campers, bouncing ideas off them. In fact, one of Lunch Lady's most popular gadgets was the brainchild of camper Galen. Well, Dr. Galen now . . .

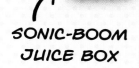

LUNCH TRAY
LAPTOP
SPORK
PHONE
SONIC-BOOM
JUICE BOX

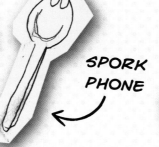

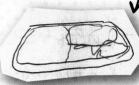

The group of friends that I made at camp always had my back and were there to celebrate with me as my first book went out into the world. One of my most steadfast supporters in both life and publishing has always been my pal Chris Milmoe. And if that name sounds familiar, yes, he is the namesake of the antagonist in these graphic novels. Chris (or, as he is known, "Milmoe") is nothing like the character. He is an athlete, though—and we always had fun playing off the trope of the jock and the artist. And here is another Easter egg for you. He and I worked together in cabin Green 15, which was the number on the jersey worn by the character. Another of my co-counselors, and for many years my housemate, Erich Birkby, became the affable PE teacher. Why the PE teacher? For one absurd session, he and I were tasked with running the sports and rec program.

When the time came to set a Lunch Lady book at a sleepaway camp, I went to town paying tribute to my camp family from those summer

MILMOE

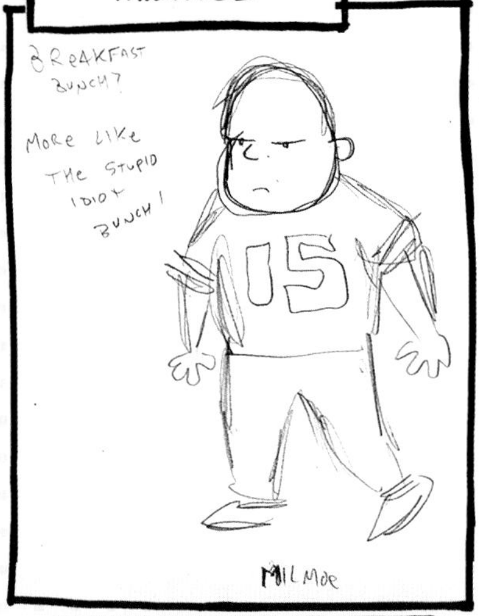
BREAKFAST BUNCH?
MORE LIKE THE STUPID IDIOT BUNCH!
15
MILMOE

COACH BIRKBY

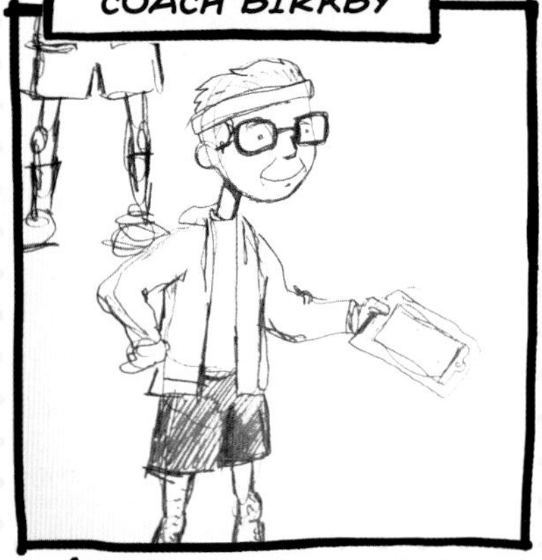

RAY MAGEE

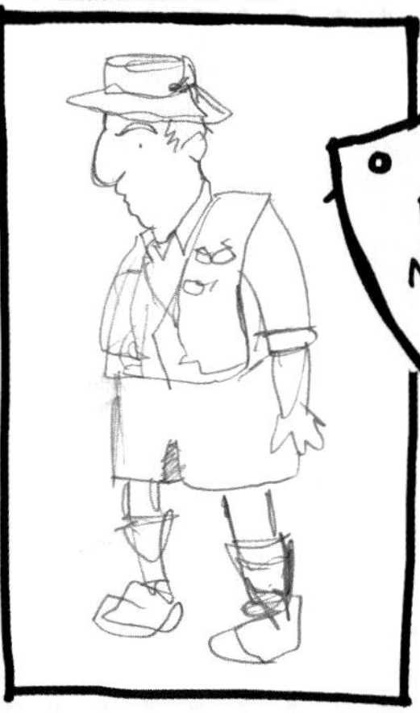

SWAMP MONSTER

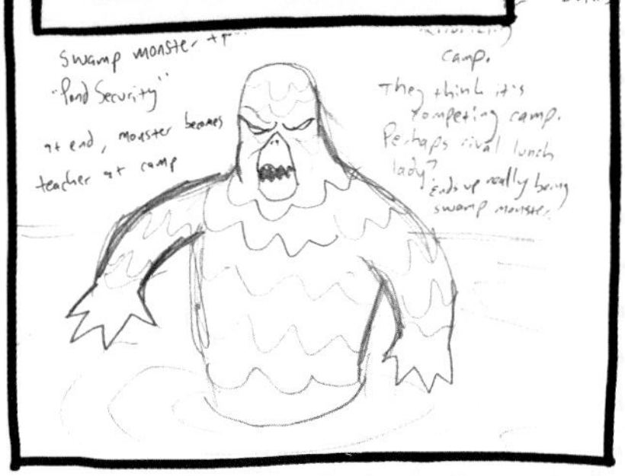
Swamp monster
"Pond Security"
at end, monster becomes teacher at camp
camp.
They think it's competing camp.
Perhaps rival lunch lady?
ends up really being swamp monster.

SAMPLE SKETCHES

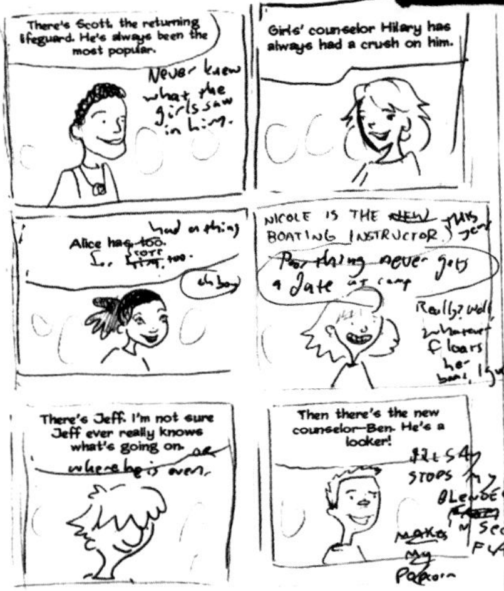
There's Scott, the returning lifeguard. He's always been the most popular.
Never knew what the girls saw in him.
Girls' counselor Hilary has always had a crush on him.
Alice had a thing for Scott too.
oh boy
NICOLE IS THE BOATING INSTRUCTOR this year
Poor thing never gets a date at camp
Really? Well, whatever floats her boat, I guess
There's Jeff. I'm not sure Jeff ever really knows what's going on.
Then there's the new counselor—Ben. He's a looker!
MAKES MY POPCORN

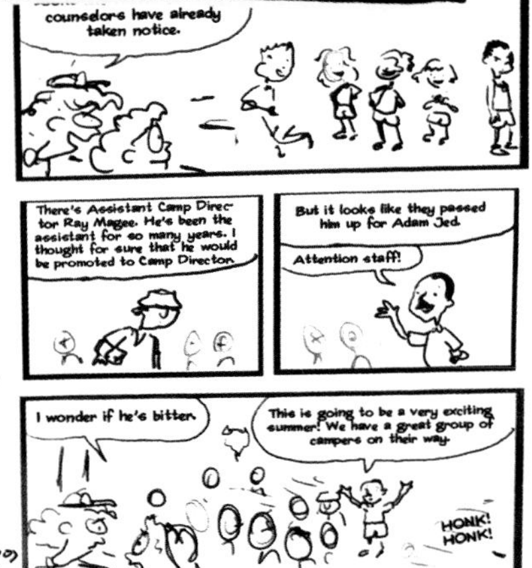
counselors have already taken notice.
There's Assistant Camp Director Ray Magee. He's been the assistant for so many years. I thought for sure that he would be promoted to Camp Director.
But it looks like they passed him up for Adam Jed.
Attention staff!
I wonder if he's bitter.
This is going to be a very exciting summer! We have a great group of campers on their way.
HONK!
HONK!

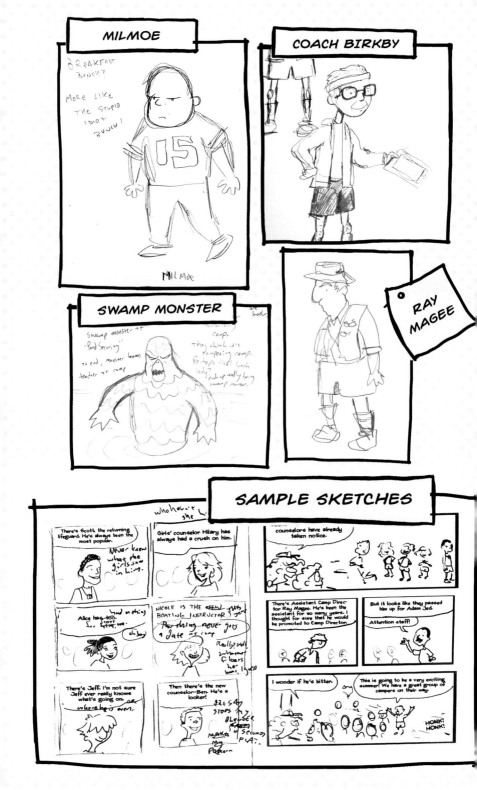

days. Ray Balboni and Kevin Magee, two of the "elder statesmen" of the camp, called themselves "Pond Security," an excuse to get out on the lake to fish. The character of Ray Magee is a tribute to them. Hilary, Nicole, and Alice became counselors for the girls' cabin, and for real, I completely changed their personalities. I swear . . . While most of my camp friends got nods in these books, another of my closest pals, John McNeil, was left out. To needle him, I gave his last name to the hallway monitor in *Lunch Lady and the Bake Sale Bandit.* Also, I should note that I always observed the dynamics between Charlotte and Anita, the camp's kitchen staff, whenever I picked up the trays of food for my campers' meals.

I will forever be grateful for camp, the experiences it gave me, and the friendships that I made there.

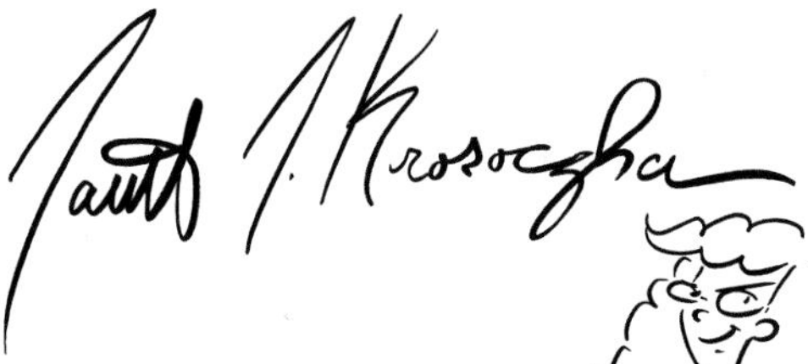

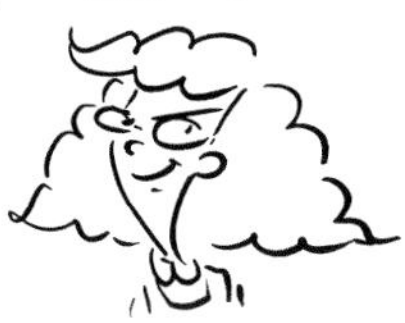

JARRETT J. KROSOCZKA is the *New York Times* bestselling author-illustrator behind dozens of books for young readers. These include the wildly popular Lunch Lady graphic novel series, select volumes of the Star Wars™: Jedi Academy series, the young adult memoir *Hey, Kiddo*, which was a National Book Award finalist, and picture-book favorites such as *Punk Farm*. Realizing that his books can inspire young readers beyond the page, Jarrett founded School Lunch Hero Day, a national campaign that celebrates school lunch staff. He lives in Western Massachusetts with his family . . . a crew that includes pugs Ralph and Frank and a French bulldog named Bella Carmella. Find out lots more about Jarrett and Lunch Lady—and check out some cool activities—at studiojjk.com.

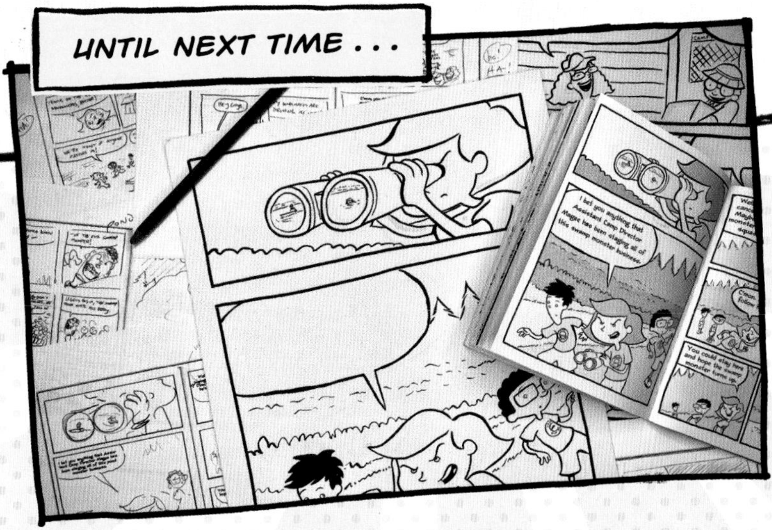
UNTIL NEXT TIME . . .
I bet you anything that Assistant Camp Director Maggie has been staging all of this swamp monster business.
You could stay here and hope the swamp monster turns up.